# Dare Ya!

## By

## Anthony Magyar & Jason Sibley

## All Rights Reserved ©

Published by:  Elevation Book Publishing
Atlanta, Georgia 30308
www.elevationbookpublishing.com

Magyar, A, 1975-
Sibley, J     1973-


Dare Ya!  by  Anthony Magyar & Jason Sibley
p.cm.
ISBN 978-1-943904-06-8 (hc)

BISAC FIC030000

# Part One: The Bad

# Prologue

## October 22, 2013

O n Friday afternoon, the Nebraska Cornhuskers football team traveled to play the Golden Gofers of Minnesota the next Saturday. At three hundred fifty miles northeast in Minneapolis, Minnesota, they were four days away. Members of the Husker Charter of Dare Ya stayed behind in Lincoln, Nebraska. Though they loved football, they couldn't worry about the next weekend. They had to focus on the upcoming dare. The Charter, in its first year, grew into a brotherhood stronger than any fraternity on campus, and its seventeen members were just as fanatic.

On the twenty-second of every month, the Dare Ya website sent all the charter members a dare, known simply as the Double Deuce Dare. This Friday in October was no different. At 2:20 PM, every member received an email containing the Double Deuce Dare. Three members actually skipped class to be in their dorm rooms when the dare came. They did so gladly.

When the email arrived, seventeen young men, all over campus, read it as one.

*Dare ya 2 find the nearest water tower. Climb it, and sit on its platform until 2 PM on Saturday afternoon. Be there by 4 PM today to ensure that it's a twenty-four hour sit-in.*

*Good luck!*

After everyone examined the dare, the text messages started.

> *I know just the spot. I'll send a map.*
>
> *On the way to grab snacks.*
>
> *I've got the beer.*
>
> *I'll get sodas, long day 2morrow.*
>
> *I have rope to haul it all up, meet u guys there.*
>
> *At least we'll b back 4 the game!* ☺

The Charter had only one Disciple, Clay Jenkins. Therefore, he was the Charter President. Clay arrived last to the structure at exactly 3:45. Some of the other members had performed a recognizance of the place an hour earlier. The water tower they chose was several miles out of town and away from prying eyes. Thirteen junior members sat at the top on the walkway awaiting the others. Two coolers and a number of backpacks, full of food, waited at the summit with them.

"Are we set, AJ?" Clay asked his second-in-command, Alan James.

"You know we're ready, Chief," AJ answered as he checked his watch. "We better head on up so we make it by four."

The last four college students climbed the hundred-foot ladder to a four-foot-wide platform that spanned the circumference of the tower. Clay stepped onto the platform last, and a subordinate handed him a beer. The two exchanged the charter handshake before Clay turned on the catwalk and took in the view. It was a mild afternoon, but the group knew it would get colder when night fell. For the start of the dare, at least, the weather was nice.

"Settle in, my brothers. It's going to be a long night," Clay told the group as he raised his can of beer.

Each man found a spot to sit and leaned against the massive, silver tower. They passed around beers, sodas, and snacks to celebrate the start of the month's dare. Several members played games or texted on cell phones. The night passed slowly.

The hour before dawn was the coldest sixty minutes of the night. The seventeen Dare Ya members, bundled in sleeping bags along with thick winter coats, clustered on the eastern side of the cold, steel monster anxiously awaiting the sun to break the horizon and deliver its balmy rays.

The huge solar disk poked its head up, and instantly, the college kids felt its heat. By the time it cleared the eastern boundary completely, they all stood with their heads held back, grinning, and soaking up the warmth. Clay said to the group, "Thank God. I was freaking cold up here, but that helps. I think I can make it now."

As Clay finished his sentence, AJ's head tilted further back and exploded. Blood and brain matter flew all over the tower and the members closest to him. His body bounced off the water tower's outer skin and rebounded toward the handrail. Neal Blanchard, the closest member to AJ, grabbed his friend by the waistband of his jeans just before he went over the railing. AJ's upper body dangled, pouring blood, as Neal held tight with both hands.

Over the screams, Neal yelled for help. He called, "I can't hold him! Grab his shoulders, God damn it!"

Another first year member, Ryan Cornish, leaned over the rail and grabbed AJ's limp body by the waist and by the back of his bloody shirt. As soon as Ryan's hand made contact with AJ's shirt collar, his own neck, where it met the shoulders, tore open and gushed blood. The second shot of the morning cracked in the still air as Ryan slumped over the balustrade and plummeted the hundred feet to the ground.

Neal released AJ's body as he watched Ryan fall. AJ followed Ryan on the express route to the earth. Clay drug Neal away from the banister and shoved him around the catwalk. He screamed at everyone, "We've got to get to the other side! Use the tower for cover!"

The members scattered around both sides. One more college student took a bullet in the back as he rounded the south side of the tower away from the ladder. He went down in a heap before he could round the curved structure to safety. The survivors huddled together on the western side, away from the sniper who had taken out three of their friends.

"What the hell is going on?" Neal asked Clay, as he wiped AJ's blood from his hands onto the tail of his jacket. "We have to get to the ladder and get down." Tears swelled in his eyes.

"We'd be in the line of fire," Clay answered as he touched Neal's right arm to calm him. "We hold tight until help..." The sentence hung unfinished as a red stain blossomed on the front of Clay's yellow Dare Ya sweatshirt. The shot that ended him echoed as Clay slid to a seated position and died without even reaching his hands to his wound.

More screams and more panic ensued. Students scrambled again in both directions around the tower. There was no reprieve. As one man rounded the north side, a bullet hit him in the guts. He fell over the edge and tumbled toward the Angel of Death, who waited for him on the ground.

The youth behind him made a try for the ladder. He started down and yelled to the others, "Come on, we have to get down!" Immediately, he caught a slug to his right hip, cartwheeled off the ladder, and fell, screaming in pain. The shriek did not last long.

The eleven remaining members lay down on the catwalk to give the shooters a smaller target, but additional projectiles found their mark, and the Grim Reaper harvested more souls.

Sobbing, Neal stood and mumbled to no one in particular. "I'm not waiting on a bullet." Then he threw himself over the rail. After his leap, silence ensued except for the sobbing from five survivors. Some hid behind dead comrades; others curled into fetal positions, reverting to blathering infants, but none dared move. No more shots were fired, and all five were found the same way when the authorities arrived thirty-seven minutes later. It was still hours from the 2 PM end of the Double Deuce Dare.

# Chapter 1

## June 14, 2008

"I'll be damned, is this how it's going to be the whole time I'm here?" Matthew Cassidy asked himself. Cass, as his friends called him, sat in a spotless dining hall in Parchman Penitentiary in the Mississippi Delta. Parchman, or "the Farm" as the staff and inmates knew it, was one of the most infamous prisons in the country. The penitentiary was located on the desolate flood plains in the northwestern corner of the poorest state in the union. It came to fame, decades ago, for its hard-working chain gangs and the lack of fences surrounding the outer perimeter. The chain gangs were long gone, but many parts of the Farm were still fenceless. Instead of the usual chain link fence, any would-be escapee faced five-pound mosquitoes and eight-foot-long cottonmouth snakes on their attempted break for freedom.

The biggest deterrent, however, was a special unit of guards known simply as K-9. They'd traded their signature horseback mounts of the sixties for huge four-wheel drive trucks in an attempt to modernize their appearance, but they would still hound any runner until he surrendered. Being found did not necessarily mean the escaped inmate would be seen again. There were rows of pecan trees on one corner of the property, and old cons said such absconders were buried there for their efforts to escape. It was also said, that there was one tree for every missing man, and there were hundreds of pecan trees on the penitentiary. No need for a judge and jury on the Farm. They had K-9.

Cass had only been in prison for eighteen days, but he'd already heard the stories more than once. He would not run—not because of the legends, but because he couldn't hurt his mother any more than he had by going to jail in the first place.

In his two and a half weeks of prison life, most days were filled with boredom, loud noises, and push-ups. He saw several fights and figured out quickly that everybody had some angle anytime they spoke to him. At six-foot-three and two-hundred-forty pounds of muscles, Cass made much too difficult a target for the usual intimidation tactics of his fellow cons.

The black inmates outnumbered their white counterparts almost six to one, so more often than not, the violence and thievery was aimed at the minority in the system. Cass had seen it several times already, and that day, it looked like he would see it again. He sat down to eat his lunch and noticed a small white man sitting at a table across the cafeteria with a larger, white prisoner standing over him. The standing man argued with four muscular black inmates. The athletic Caucasian looked familiar, but Cass could not be sure from where. He had been in a fugue state since he'd arrived on the Farm. In his opinion, four against two was good odds, especially in this place. The standing man looked as though he could hold his own. With any help from the little fellow, they would be able to, at the very least, hold out until the guards came to break up the altercation.

Cass decided to take his thoughts off the other inmates' plight. It was none of his business. He looked down at his old, worn food tray and noticed the runny mashed potatoes. The roll next to the potatoes looked edible, but it was probably two days old. Who was he kidding? It was three days old, at the least. The turnip greens, picked by inmate labor on the Farm, had a rock in them, and all their juices ran into the slot for the main course. Cass was not sure what the hell that slop was supposed to be.

Cass lost his appetite as he leered at the feast before him. He let his eyes leave the plate and return to the argument at the other end of the chow hall, which had intensified. He made up his mind that it was a good time to snap out of his funk. He stood, leaving his lunch untouched. He was not going to eat the garbage, so he figured he would go over and even the odds a little.

As Cass walked to the other table, the little guy passed him, leaving in a rush. The man never looked up from the floor as he went. Cass thought to himself, *Ain't that a bitch? I come to help and he bails.* The bigger convict was alone with his adversaries when Cass walked into the group. *Probably better, the pipsqueak would've been in the way, anyhow,* Cass thought.

To the assembly, he asked, "Anyone over here have some salt Ican borrow?" As he said it, he sized up the four inmates. No one answered his question. They had stopped talking, and they were now locked in a staring contest.

The four were, without a doubt, in one of the gangs that inundated Parchman. Their arms displayed prison tattoos with ink only slightly darker than the convicts themselves. The biggest and blackest ruffian was in front of the group. He was an even closer match to the ink on his arm. The leader was almost as large as Cass, and the three directly behind him were not much smaller. They were even more muscular than they had appeared to Cass from forty-feet away.

A couple of the back three looked toward Cass as they checked on the fifth member of their squad. He was distracting the dining hall guard that watched the inmates during feedings. His distraction would ensure a few uninterrupted minutes with their enemy. "Mind your business, white boy," Big and Black said to Cass without looking in his direction.

The front man had his left pants leg rolled up, like his friends, to signify their gang, but Cass had not been on the Farm long enough to know which organization it was. It didn't matter to him anyway. He didn't plan to get along with any of them. Gangs were just a gathering of weak, scared individuals, and Cass wanted nothing to do with such people. Cass noticed sweat beading up and running down Big and Black's shaved head. Cass told him, "Please don't call me that. And I'm trying to decide exactly what my business is at the moment."

"Big Freak will call you whatever the hell he wants. Trust me, Cracker. Your business ain't over here." This got a roar from his peanut gallery.

Cass grinned to himself as he thought, *Big Freak, huh? I wasn't too far off.* The big, white statue of a man beside Cass had not said a word or moved a muscle since Cass walked into the fray. Cass never took his eyes from Big Freak, but thought, *Great. I've come to help Quietusious, Lord of the Mutes.*

Then to Freak, he said audibly, "If you see a cracker, crumble it up, and put it in your water because after I break that block jaw of yours, that's all you'll be eating." Cass knew it sounded like something from a bad B-grade movie, but he was bored and not going back to the tray he left at his table. He may as well have fun with it. Any action was good action, Cass believed.

Big Freak turned to Cass for the first time, poked a long charcoal finger into his chest, and said, "You ain't gone do shit."

"Tell his cracker ass, Freak!" One of the back-up singers yelled.

*Those assholes in back can talk, but Muteman still can't make a peep,* Cass thought as he prepared to grab Freak's hand.

Before Cass could seize the hand, the Silent Statue took hold of it and twisted away from Cass. He did so lighting fast, turning Freak down and out of the way, toward the floor. As Freak went down, Cass' instincts kicked in, and he punched the closest back-up on the chin. There was a reason old boxers called this "the button." The guy went down in a heap. Cass kicked him in the face on his way down, to make sure he stayed there, out of the way.

The next gang banger stepped forward but glanced down at his friend. In that instant, Cass thought, *Why would you do that? He's not getting up, so he can't help you.* Then the standing opponent looked up in Cass' direction with his hands raised in front of him, ready for the fight. Cass threw a straight right into his sternum, between the guy's elbows. The punch knocked all the wind from his lungs. The enemy reflexively bent at the waist. Cass cupped the back of his head with both hands and yanked down. His knee shot up and met the man's nose. Sweat flew off his face as the crack of breaking cartilage echoed throughout the cafeteria.

The fourth and final would-be assailant never moved. Cass had seen in the coward's eyes that he wouldn't. Cass let number two fall to the floor beside his comrade. As he did that, Statue Boy drove his forearm down into Freak's elbow. This folded the big man's arm in the wrong direction, causing him to release an involuntary yelp as he grabbed for his newly disfigured extremity. Cass stomped the floor in the direction of the only uninjured opponent and said, "Boo." The man turned and melted into the growing crowd of spectators.

Cass then turned to his ally and said, "Way to go. Thanks for making me a liar. I told his big ass I'd break his jaw, not his arm."

The Soundless Sculpture then seized Freak's shirt collar in one hand, the back of his head in the other, and smashed him, teeth first, into the edge of the steel table. He shoved Freak to the floor, locked eyes with Cass, and said, "I don't know if that broke his jaw, but it didn't do it any good, that's for damn sure."

"Holy hell, he speaks," Cass said, looking at the three men on the ground.

Five guards, dressed all in black, ran toward the pair standing over their carnage. They blew whistles and yelled, "Get on the floor! Face first, now!"

Cass raised his hands and dropped down to his knees. He made sure to avoid the blood all over the once-spotless dining hall floor. When Cass and his new acquaintance lay down, the officers rushed over, put knees in their backs, and handcuffed them both.

They dragged the duo to their feet and pushed them toward the exit. As they banged his head into the doorframe, Cass thought, *That felt great, but I bet that roll over there wouldn't have been all that bad.*

\* \* \* \*

### 18 Days Prior

Working broke up the boredom of prison. Evan Masters was at work at the prison intake building. He worked for the officer-on-duty, responsible for processing new inmates onto the Farm. Evan had gone through the same intake process almost two years before when he'd first stepped foot on that cursed Delta soil.

He learned quickly, after his arrival, that most inmates no longer had to work during their incarceration. With the chain gangs gone and the actual farming jobs used as punishment, many of the modern convicts simply sat in their squad bay-type zones and tried to fend off the boredom. Evan decided that was not for him. He used his gift of gab to find something more productive to do—productive for *him*, that was.

That day, Evan was doing his regular paperwork when the intake sergeant walked into the office. Evan asked her, "What've we got today, boss?"

Sergeant Milner placed three files and a paper bag on the counter and said, "We just got three newbies today. It won't take long at all. I brought you some donuts, too."

Evan picked up the folders, started looking through them, and replied, "Thanks Serge; we'll get these guys processed in no time. What time will they be here from medical?" He bit into a chocolate donut as he flipped through the files to see if any of the new inmates could be useful to him in any obvious way. (He did this scan with records of every inmate new to Parchman.)

"They'll be here any minute," the sergeant told him.

The first dossier Evan looked through, in the stack, was that of a parole violator who had sold crack after his release. "Idiot," Evan mumbled. He moved to the next folder and looked for something more interesting. This young dumbass was a three-time loser who'd broken into a storage building. *I guess this genius likes this place,* Evan thought of the second inmate.

Evan used his file search to find new cons that he could use or 'help' in some way. His type of help consisted of protection for money, supplying practically anything a newcomer might need; or sometimes he helped newbies get a job or into a class, if the situation was right. All of these, he did for pay. He preferred cash. The first two inmates did not interest him. If someone had been to the Farm in the past, he either was affiliated with a gang or had someone looking after him already.

The third guy, however, Matthew Rogers Cassidy, was perfect. Cassidy was a first-time offender, prosecuted for assault on a police officer. *He probably hit a cop on a traffic stop while he was drunk,* Evan thought. The 'fresh fish,' as Hollywood movies called them, could be extorted and used easily enough.

Violence wasn't generally needed to make money. These guys just wanted to get along, do their time, and have no problems while in prison. More often than not, they did not mind losing a little money to make 'friends' around with whom they felt safe. A newbie would have heard of the things that happened on the Farm. So long as things did not turn physical, the unseasoned inmate was relieved. Evan decided he could be Mr. Cassidy's best friend if the funds were right. Cassidy went to the top of Evan's "useful" list.

This process of, going through the intake files, was precisely the reason Evan had paid the sergeant a hundred dollars for this job fifteen months previously. He no longer had to waste time feeling out the fresh fish or wading through all of their lies to see if they could be valuable. He received all the information straight from the prison record of the man in question, as soon as he stepped off the bus.

The three new men came into the steamy intake office as Evan finished the last bite of his second donut. He looked up and froze in the middle of sipping his coffee as a huge white guy walked in, followed by two common-looking black guys. The white man was almost as tall as Evan, but was massive.

"Y'all have a seat over there and head to that counter when your name is called," the sergeant said to the new guys as she pointed to some chairs by the far wall and then toward the partition where Evan was standing.

Evan said, "Matthew Cassidy." The big guy stood and walked his way. He was enormous. Evan himself was big, but the guy standing in front of the counter looked like a wrestler on television. His arms were riddled with veins and muscle striations that would be the envy of any Greek god.

*Well,* Evan thought to himself, *I guess I won't be making too much money extorting this giant, but maybe I'll think of something.* Evan wasn't intimidated by the size of Matthew Cassidy. He had never been afraid of any man, but in his line of work, Evan beat people with his mind. That left the physical stuff to less intelligent hustlers. There was always less trouble Evan's way—or so he thought.

# Chapter 2

June 14, 2008

### ----To the Hole----

The officers handcuffed Evan Masters and herded him to the hole with the Baby Hulk. A guard shoved Evan into the second cell down the segregation hallway and took off his handcuffs. The door slammed shut, and as he massaged his wrists, the shift lieutenant said, "You boys just got yourselves thirty days in my hole. Masters, I thought you knew better. Guess you're not as smart as I'd figured."

Another guard threw Cass into the next cell down the corridor as the lieutenant gave Evan his speech. While Cass looked around the small cell, he too rubbed his wrists where his own cuffs had been. With the paint peeling walls, there was not much to look at except a concrete bunk, a metal toilet with a sink attached, and a small barred window.

"What the hell was that all about?" Evan asked, none too nicely, through the cell wall as the officers left.

"You looked outnumbered, especially after the little guy bailed on you. I figured I'd come over and even it up a little," Cass said as he splashed water from the sink onto his face in an attempt to cool himself.

"Even what up, Blockhead? This isn't some damn prison movie where a white man surrounded by some thugs needs to be saved!"

"Hell man, from where I was sitting, Big Freak and his boys looked pretty pissed, and I can tell it's not a movie because you aren't thanking me profusely." Cass could sense the big blond in the next cell was angry, but he didn't care, really. He felt exhilarated from the fight and even had a little smirk on his face as he spoke.

Evan paced back and forth for a few minutes, trying to get his thoughts in order, and then asked, "Do you have any idea what you cost me by trying to play the hero?"

Cass furled his brow and answered with a question of his own. "Cost you? How the hell did I cost you anything?" He stepped away from the washbasin and toward the bars at the front of his cell. He dried his face with his shirttail as he went.

Evan bowed his head to the bars and lightly tapped his forehead a couple of times, attempting to calm himself. Yes, he was very irritated, but he'd learned long ago that there was usually a positive side to every situation. He just had to find the right angle. "First of all, my job," he said, but the anger was already lessening in his voice. "I can't keep that if I'm stuck in this hell hole with you for thirty days."

Cass said, "My bad, seriously, but I really did think I was helping."

"He thought he was helping," Evan chuckled and said more to himself than to Cass. Now he had a small smile on his face. "Just so you know, Big Freak wasn't against me. I've been selling MP3 players with him and actually turning a nice profit. That's definitely out the window now, thanks to your big ass."

"Let me get this straight, you were working with that Big Freak character? Then who the heck was the little white guy?"

"New guys, I swear." Evan exhaled loudly and said, "He bought an MP3 player from me a week ago but still hasn't given me all my money. The BDPs, that's Freak's gang, think Little Tupelo's a cash cow because he loses lots of money to them in poker. They were trying to convince me to ease up on him a little."

"They were trying to stop you? Jesus, I came to the rescue of an extorter," Cass said as he laughed at himself.

"Hell, Mother Teresa, look around. You're just getting in the system, but we're in prison. What does it matter whose money I take? This isn't summer camp, Hero. And just for the record, you in no way could've rescued me."

"Yeah, yeah, if you say so. Damn, it's hot in here." Cass slid down the bars and sat on the floor, making an effort to cool off a few degrees.

"You sort of get used to it. I'm going to find a cooler spot over by the window and get very still. Maybe that'll help." Evan moved across his cell but found no relief from the heat. He stretched out on the concrete, trying to doze off, but it was too hot to sleep.

The afternoon and evening hours passed at a snail's pace. When the sun fell over the western end of the prison's fields, the temperature in their cells finally dipped below eighty degrees. This felt like a cold front passing by in comparison to the high temperature of the afternoon. Cass got restless so he went to the middle of his cage and did push-ups to pass time.

Evan heard him stirring around and moved back to the bars, fanning himself with the t-shirt he had removed hours ago. He said to Cass, "Whatcha doing over there, Captain America? Saving any spiders from the flies they have in their webs?"

Cass finished his set of push-ups, rose to his knees, and said, "Ha, ha, very funny. I sincerely did think I was helping. Listen man, if we're going to be here for thirty days, we may as well get acquainted. My name's Matt Cass..."

"Matthew Rogers Cassidy, I know your name. I read your file when we processed you in. You're a walking western, aren't you, Trigger? I'm Evan Masters."

"Yeah, and you're a regular comedian. Everyone just calls me Cass," he said as he went down in the prone position and started another set of push-ups. "Are you the same Evan Masters that played quarterback at Mississippi State back in the nineties?"

"Yeah, that's me. Man, that seems like lifetimes ago. Who do you think'll win the SEC this year?"

"I'm not much of a sports fan, actually. My dad loves football, so he used to take me to all the home games at State. I remember him saying you had a hell of an arm and that you'd probably go pro." Cass finished his set of push-ups, letting out a loud exhalation.

He stood to get a drink of water from the metal sink as Evan said to him, "I played in the USFL, which was like the minor leagues, for one season, but it never took off, so I came home."

Cass stretched his shoulders, then went to a toe touch as he asked, "So when did you join the Air Force?"

Evan looked over at the cracked wall that separated their cells. The service was a part of his life that he seldom discussed, and so this behemoth surprised him. "What exactly makes you think I joined the Air Force?" he asked in a tone that showed a hint of defensiveness.

"Easy there, Jet Jockey, I saw the tattoo on your arm as they shoved us down the hallway. Combat Control, huh? That's a tough unit, even if it is the Air Force. Right behind the SEALS, some would say."

Now Evan was taken aback. The tattoo on his arm was indeed Combat Control's patch, but it was not something the average person would recognize, especially not at Parchman. "Impressive there, Trigger," he said with a quizzical grin that could be heard in his voice. "I've been locked up over two years, and no one's associated that tat with the Air Force, much less Combat Control. What makes you different? And I'll have you know, the SEALS are on our six, not the other way around."

Cass found this amusing, laughed, and said, "I did six years in the Marine Corps, Force Recon, which is the best of the best Special Forces in the world. So whether Combat Control is second or third, I'll let you Air Boys and the Squids fight that skirmish."

"The Marines. How'd I miss that in your file? No wonder you had no trouble with those BDPs in the chow hall. What did it take, like thirty, or forty-five seconds? I guess you didn't be all you could be today."

"That's the Army's motto, asshole, and I didn't see any need in seriously hurting those gentlemen," Cass answered sarcastically. "Plus, it was four on two. We clearly had the numbers advantage." They both laughed as a guard came down the hall with their belongings from the housing units.

"You boys sure are having a goodtime in my Segregation Unit," the night officer said as she kicked Evan's personal items into his cell. One of the inmates from the zone had no doubt packed the stuff while a guard watched. Evan had seen it hundreds of times—some acquaintance of the inmate in the hole took the blanket off his bed, spread it on the floor, piled everything his buddy owned in the middle, and then tied it all up with the corners of the blanket. When finished, it looked like a big hobo bundle, without the stick.

She looked at Evan, walked toward Cass' cell, and shouted back, "The three guys you two ran over in the dining hall won't be doing any laughing for a while. They look like they were riding scooters and got hit by a semi-truck." Then she looked to Cass as the tower guard electronically popped the lock on his door and said, "Damn, maybe they did get smacked by a semi after all.

"Masters," she added, "this guy's bigger than you."

"Yes ma'am, Mrs. Hicks. He's big as a house but about as dumb as one of the bricks." Evan knew the guard from his months of working around the compound. He knew almost everyone on the staff, and most of them knew him as well.

"Well, you must've let one of those bricks hit you in the head, Masters. I thought you had more sense than to be fighting," she said to him as she neared his cell door, heading back up the hall.

"Just a big misunderstanding, that's all. Maybe I can pull some strings and get out of here in no time flat," he said in an exaggerated Southern accent. Then he winked at her as she strolled past his cell door.

Officer Hicks' smile broadened as she stopped and said, "I wouldn't put nothing past you Mr. Masters, but for now, y'all get all the laughing out of your systems. Lights out in fifteen minutes." She turned and went back to the guard tower at the far end of the corridor.

"Aren't you a regular Casanova?" Cass asked as he untied his blanket and started putting his mat on the concrete bunk. "Do you really think you can get out of solitary sooner than thirty days?"

"You have a lot to learn about prison. Stick with me, Trigger, and I'll show you the ropes."

"It's Cass, and this prison thing can't be that hard to figure out, especially if a fly-boy ex-jock, like you, can do it. What the hell's so hard, anyway? It's just like the Corps in a lot of ways—yes sir and no sir to the officers, keep your head down, and the years just slide on by."

"It's nothing like the service," Evan told him. "First lesson, the officers don't outrank us here. Most of them, from a regular corrections officer all the way up to the warden, are barely above the poverty line. Nearly all of them are brain dead, either too dumb or scared to get a real job. If the price is right and they think it's safe, you can get just about anything you want."

"That may be so, but you didn't actually answer the question. Do you really think you can buy your way out of the hole?" Cass asked in a serious tone just as the lights went out.

"That's what we'll have to wait and see, tomorrow. Tonight, I'm going to get some sleep and take advantage of this peace and quiet. Those idiots on the zone can be loud as hell. Try not to let the mosquitoes carry you off in the middle of the night, Jarhead."

# Chapter 3

## June 18, 2008

Four days passed, and the guys fell into a routine. Morning was gym time. They did push-ups, prison squats, sit-ups, jumping jacks, and even bench dips on the sides their racks. They started each set at the same time and went rep for rep until one of them quit. They were both competitive, so some sets were long.

The days warmed quickly, so it did not take long to work up a sweat and fatigue their muscles. Evan had been doing a similar routine for several years; therefore, the first two days, he beat Cass on many of the sets. Cass had been lifting weights, and he found that body weight exercises were a very different workout. His muscular body adapted quickly, and in no-time, he beat Evan on every set.

"Damn, Trigger, it doesn't take you long to catch on to a routine, does it? " Evan asked Cass on their fifth day in the hole.

"You should've seen the way I fell into training on Parris Island. It all just came natural," Cass said during their lunch break.

"I bet they loved your big ass on the football field. Were you fast? What position did you play, linebacker?"

"I told you, I wasn't into sports. I never played any organized games except a year of little league. I was too busy studying and playing music."

"Okay, at least you were in a band. Damn, for a second there I was wondering if you might've gotten in the Corps on Clinton's 'Don't Ask, Don't Tell' program. No sports, studying all the time. What did you play: guitar or bass?"

"I can play both, but I wasn't in a rock band. My instrument of choice is the piano. I play classical music. I can also play the violin and French horn, and no, asshole, I'm not gay. As a matter of fact, all the chicks were with guys like me while you jocks were out there sweating and bumping into each other on the field."

"That's what all the nerds say, but there sure were a lot of hotties in the stands watching. How the hell does a classical musician that doesn't play sports wind up in the Marine Corps? Hell, not to mention, in one of the most elite Special Forces units in the whole world?"

"Now that, E, is a very long story, and Force Recon is not one of the *most* elite; it's far superior to all the rest."

"Well, my friend, we have all afternoon to sit in these sweat boxes. We have the time, and you have a very captive audience," Evan said.

"All right; you asked for it. The Life of Matthew Cassidy." He laughed as he said, "I was a music-loving semi-nerd from central Mississippi. I graduated first in my class, and decided I wanted to see something other than pine trees while I went to college. I was accepted to many schools, but I had my heart set on NYU. All the streets in small-town Mississippi are rolled up after ten every night, so I wanted to experience the city life. And what better city than New York? Everything you'd ever imagine is in one place. You ever been up there?"

"Nope, Andrews Air Force Base in Maryland is the farthest I've ever been up the east coast. It always seemed a little overcrowded on TV. No need adding me to all those people."

"Well I fell in love with the place: Broadway, Carnegie Hall and all the other stuff to see and do. I'd finally found a place where I fit in. I was in the Arts Department at NYU at the same time I was studying computer programming. I figured I still had to get a real job one day, and I knew I'd never be YoYo Ma."

"Who?" Evan asked.

"YoYo Ma. He's a classical musician, Jet Jockey. I'm a decent instrumentalist myself, but I'll never be good enough to make a living doing it. That was obvious, and since my second passion's always been computers, I actually majored in computer science. It was amazing, living in such a happening city, and I was having the time of my life. I never imagined when I was trapped in Mississippi that I could be so happy. "

"Why'd you leave all that behind? Did you graduate and join the Marines to pay off your student loans?"

"No, Fly Boy. Believe it or not, some Marines have brains. I went to school on full music and academic scholarships. My sophomore year at NYU was when September 11th happened, and everything in the world changed."

"You were actually there? Damn, man, that's insane," Evan said, amazed to meet someone who was in New York City on that dreadful day.

"Yeah, it really was crazy. When those towers came down, I completely lost it. I couldn't believe anyone hated us that much, but I found some hate of my own that day. I took a cab straight to the recruiting station and waited five hours to enlist. I don't really remember why I chose the

Marine Corps; I was just so damn pissed. Everything about those few weeks in September is a blur. All I know is, I woke up from my anger-induced stupor on Parris Island with a drill instructor in my face," Cass told him as he remembered that time in his life.

"Ouch, very bad wake up call," Evan said through the wall. "The recruiter probably saw your big ass coming a mile away and rushed out to make sure no other branch stole away the walking, breathing John Rambo."

"No, not at all. I was a gangly guy back then. Watching plays, learning all those instruments, and studying computers aren't conducive to building muscle mass."

"If that's true, then how the hell did you lose your neck to those shoulder muscles of yours?" Evan chuckled as he asked.

"It was the weirdest thing, but when I woke on the Island, I told myself that since I was there, I may as well make the best of the situation. I made every exercise, every drill maneuver, and everything a competition, and for the first time in my life, I really wanted to win. The muscles just started popping out everywhere. Hell, I never really knew I had muscles up to that point."

"You sure as hell have 'em now. Muscles on top of muscles," Evan said, laughing again.

"Are you hitting on me over there, Air Raid? You Air Force Bubbas have always been a little suspect to me," Cass said as he joined his new friend in laughing.

"Screw you. We stayed in the strip clubs in town while you grunts were *where*? Piled up in foxholes together, that's where."

"Chip and Dale's isn't something I'd be bragging about. Now, where was I?"

"On Parris Island, popping out muscles like a third world woman pops out babies," Evan said, in stitches at his own joke.

"Very funny," Cass said, but he did laugh harder. "It wasn't just the muscles; I devoured the Marine Corps history classes—so many boys making all those sacrifices for this country. I took all those heroic acts to heart. I was, and still am, proud to have followed in their footprints."

"If I had you on my couch to analyze what makes Matthew Cassidy tick, I'd say that is where our Dudley Do-Right was born."

"I'm no such thing. It just makes someone more mindful of the obligation to their country and the people around them—at least, it did for me. Anyway, enough about my patriotism. After all those classes, we went to the rifle range where I once again learned something about myself. I'm a natural with a rifle. It's like I can't miss no matter what the shot or the conditions. I couldn't comprehend how guys were having problems with the M16. On the day we qualified with our rifles, a Staff Sergeant called me into his office. He said I was just the type of hard charger he was looking for. He had my service record in front of him and wanted to know if I'd be interested in going on to Force Recon training."

Evan told him, "We have to actually graduate basic training first, in the Air Force. Then we can volunteer after we arrive at our duty station."

"Usually we do too, but on rare occasions, they see it in someone that's still in basic training. When they do, he's pushed into recon service as soon as possible. I was one of those Mr. Gung Ho types, to the letter."

"I see they aren't big on humility with you Jarheads, though, are they? Supply must've run out when you received your issue."

"It's not cocky if you can back it up, and so far, I've never had a problem backing it up."

"Okay. I can clearly see you loved the Corps, so why'd you get out?" Evan asked as their dinner trays were served. "And I hate asking this question, but how the hell did you end up in this Mississippi prison? Mr. Sophisticate himself, with all his big city ways."

"That's another story. We'll get to that when we finish eating. Plus, we have a rematch on the chess board, remember?"

Three days earlier, they'd drawn a chessboard on a piece of paper and fashioned all the pieces from other paper scraps so they each had a total chess set. Evan actually drew the pieces, but Cass' artistic side ended with music. He simply wrote each piece's name and color on a small square of paper. Making the game sets and playing chess helped pass their evenings.

"All right, but you've taken me from backwoods Mississippi to your Marine Corps training. Later, I want to hear how the hell the return trip went. Even though I've only heard half the story, I think you should write a book about your life," Evan said in a mocking tone.

"Not really my kind of thing, but if you don't hurry up and get us out of this hole, I may start one just to keep my mind busy."

"That hurt," Evan said as he took his tray from the trustee. "With all this mind-stimulating conversation we've been having, how can your brain feel inactive? Not to mention, you're the one who picked this week to introduce the penal system to your hand-to-hand skills, not me."

"Well, it's not my fault the warden's on vacation. You probably can't pull off getting us out of these boxes early, anyway," Cass said with a chuckle.

"Oh ye of little faith!  You better show some belief in me or I'll just leave you in here when I go. It'd be a lot cheaper; that's for sure."

"Just try leaving me here. When I do get back into population, you won't have to watch your back for the BDPs. I'll be coming for you myself." They both laughed and ate dinner, with more conversation.

# Chapter 4

## June 18, 2008

"Checkmate," Cass said through the wall as he swatted a mosquito biting his neck. "That's two for me and only one for you, my series."

"It's about time you won a series. What was I up to like eighty nights in a row?" Evan asked, growing more comfortable with ribbing his new friend.

"Three. Three nights are all we've been playing. I didn't expect you to be that good. Who'd ever think people in prison could give Bobby Fisher a run for his money?"

"Next to working out, chess is a convict's favorite way to pass time. I'll think of an excuse for my losing later tonight, but now back to your story. After training did you end up in Afghanistan or Iraq?"

"Straight to Bagdad. It was nerve-racking in many ways, at first. I'm sure you know this yourself, but it was exhilarating at the same time. Does that sound crazy?"

"Nope, not at all. I know exactly how you felt. I never could quite put it into words to anyone, either. Most people don't get it, and they always thought I was completely nuts. There were even some guys in Combat Control who couldn't relate," Evan said.

"The combat zone was more real than anything in my life. I was scared shitless, but man, was I alive. I never usually talk about this, but you were there, and this place is so damn therapeutic." Cass laughed again.

"I went to Afghanistan during the war, but I was in Saudi for a while before 9/11. How many weeks did it take you to see action?"

"Weeks? Hell, in a matter of *hours,* I was in it. They had a section on the southern tip of the city that needed clearing. They sent our Team to find a way in. We made it about three blocks north before the night erupted. Luckily, the ragheads were keyed up and blew the car bomb early. After that, small arms fire was everywhere. My team leader and I were caught in a doorway about forty yards from the rest of the team, and he was yelling orders to everyone. I was completely disoriented. There were rifle shots echoing off the walls, grenades exploding, and all the Team members yelling at the same time. Before I could even get my bearings, the whole thing stopped, and it was as quiet as a church. I hadn't even taken my rifle off 'safe'."

"Yeah, that first time in a firefight's hell on earth. I did manage to empty two magazines, but the first was almost straight up, and then I tried to compensate and blew all the rocks away five feet in front of me. It's crazy how fast some of those fights are. Then the very next one will drag on for hours," Evan said, relating with Cass.

"I finally pulled my thumb out of my ass and talked myself down. On the way back to camp, later that night, we were hit again. My first night in the field and two ambushes, but this time, after the initial scramble for cover, everything went into slow motion. It was like watching a movie. I could see people turning to fire, and I would be on them before they finished their turn."

"I had that same experience on the football field. They call it 'the game slowing down.' It was weird to me, though, when it got so slow in Afghanistan that I felt like I could see bullets flying through the air," Evan said. Then he asked, "Why did you decide not to re-enlist? Did you just get burned out or did you figure the war would end soon? That's one of the reasons I got out, myself. I figured Bush would end it quick, and I didn't want to be over here practicing for the next war. It didn't make a lot of sense to me, after all I'd seen."

"It wasn't that at all. I just got a little burnt out seeing all the stuff that went on over there. By the end, I was a Staff Sergeant and a Team Leader with a few new guys and a couple of corporals on my team. Everyone on my original crew was either out of the service, dead or had Teams of their own. One night my new Team and I left the safe zone for a supposedly-simple patrol. We were halfway down a block when some camel jockey popped off a few shots from our left flank. We returned fire and had the situation under control. Bagdad was a lot better by this time." Cass paused, remembering that day.

Evan said, to bring Cass back, "It seems like I heard that something like eighty percent of the city had calmed down and was what they called a 'green zone'."

"I wouldn't say eighty percent, but a lot of the city was clear of hostiles. This block was on a street right on the edge of that green zone. Three of us rushed the building and returned fire at the sniper. We took him out, and as we were returning to the group, two figures ran out of a building on the right side of the road, away from the initial shots. I had one of my senior corporals and a new guy over there covering us. The corporal had been on the Team for several months. Shefton was his name, but we called him Heat because he was such a hothead. He fired two quick rounds that dropped the lead shadow. I yelled, "Cease fire God damn-it! Nobody else fire a shot." Heat was already on the second target and took it down while I was yelling. He hollered 'Clear' like he never heard my order. We approached the shadows that he'd taken out, and it was two teenagers—a boy and a girl. They were probably just sneaking out for the night when they ran into us."

"Damn, man," Evan said. "You see shit like that all the time, especially in those freaking street fights, I bet. It's a little easier out in the middle of nowhere. All the players out there are in the game, on one side or the other."

"Of course I saw things like that in the past, but this was different. Heat was always quick on the trigger, but he never stepped on a command to do it. When I looked into his eyes, I knew he'd heard me scream and had disregarded it. I just knew it. When we returned to the apartment building where we were staying, I went to his room and told him as much. I told him to keep his trigger finger in check or I'd check his ass the next time. I wasn't going to put up with that bullshit on my team. We were there to help those people, not to kill their goddamn pre-teens."

"That'll start to eat at you, after seeing it enough. Did old Heat cool off any after you went and had your little talk?" Evan asked.

"Actually, he did, for a few weeks. He became a by-the-book, squared-away Marine. Then we went on a four-day mission to a small village that was a couple of hundred miles to the north. We had some heavy fighting for two days and then, luckily, it died down. We were crossing an empty lot, when a sniper started in on us. I dropped in a shallow ditch, and the rest of the Team scattered. All of us were all returning fire."

Evan interrupted.   "I hate those open spaces— especially when a sniper catches you out and about."

"But he couldn't shoot worth a damn or he would've taken out half the Team. He clipped a Lance Corporal in his bicep—straight through, no bone damage, thank goodness, and he hit me in the side of the helmet. It was at the perfect angle and deflected off. "

"In the helmet? Damn, you should've bought it with that one," Evan said with shock in his voice.

"Again, I was lucky, but it gave me a hell of a headache. That wasn't the worst of it, though. As we were returning fire in the direction of the sniper, I was hit twice from behind. One round nicked me in the ass, and the second hit me in the side. "

"Holy hell. I did five years and never got hit once. Did it hurt bad? How the hell did y'all let somebody get on your six?"

"Both hits were just grazes, really, so it burned more than anything. The cut on my ass hurt like hell, but nothing major. I turned to return fire, but all I saw was Heat changing magazines. A sergeant on the team called the cease fire and sent two guys to clear the sniper's nest. He was down."

"Shot in the ass, just like Forrest Gump." Evan roared with laughter. Then he stopped laughing and said, "Wait a minute, this Heat son of a bitch put two rounds in his Team leader? What did they do to his sorry ass, put him in Leavenworth for a couple of lifetimes?" He then started laughing again and said, "Even if he did just get you in the ass."

"I guess it is a little funny now, but it wasn't at the time. I wanted to bring down the hammer on him. Pat Tillman had just been killed, and it made me think how close I came to dying by friendly fire that wasn't so friendly. He told the commanding officer at the initial hearing that he was clearing a jam and that his weapon discharged by accident. They dropped the charges because no one on the Team had actually seen him shoot and they couldn't be sure if it was on purpose or not."

"What bullshit," Evan shouted adamantly. "They had to know that prick was gunning for you."

"Yeah the rest of the team came to my room, and we all went to the commanding officer's building together. We told him we weren't comfortable with Shefton on the Team. I went back some years with the major, so he said he'd see what he could do. They transferred Heat out three days later. He was sent over your way, to Afghanistan. "

"What happened to him after that?"

"Not sure, really. I made some calls to warn a few team leaders that he was on his way and that they should watch out for him. I'm not sure what happened with his dumb ass after that. Hopefully he walked into an IED and quit wasting my air."

"Did the Team improve after he left?"

"It did, but I couldn't get it out of my mind. I was coming up on re-enlistment, and for the first time in my military career, I had doubts. I wasn't afraid, but damn, I was pissed. My anger at that asshole stole my love and faith in my fellow Marines, and it consumed everything. It affected my performance. I'm a man of honor and integrity, and I always assumed that all my fellow Marines were, too. He took that from me. I hated him for it, and that hate was the reason I didn't reenlist. I didn't want it to get someone killed."

"I can feel for you on that one, too. You've got to have your head in it all the way or you'll get yourself killed. We all had jackasses over there to deal with, but that sucks. Why did you come back to our great magnolia state instead of going back to New York City?" Evan asked.

"That is another story, my friend. It's getting late. Reliving that stuff's pissed me off all over again and exhausted me at the same time. We'll get to that story tomorrow after the work-out. Then you have to tell me how you ended up in this place. I have been dying to ask, but some old guy on the zone told me it's not cool to ask such things."

"It's all right to ask, Trigger, and I may even give you my story."

"Allright, Fly Guy; I can't wait."

# Chapter 5

## June 19, 2008

The next morning Cass and Evan woke to a heavy rain that had moved into western Mississippi as they slept. Lightening flashed, and thunder echoed through their cells. The cool air that came with the storms provided a welcome relief to the heat.

"You awake over there, Fly Guy?" Cass asked as he stretched and dangled his legs over the side of his rack.

Evan spit toothpaste into the sink and said, "Yeah, I've been up for a while, listening to the rain. It may be a good day for a change. Of course, that does depend on no tornados blowing through here."

Cass chuckled as he got his own toothbrush out of his bag. "That would definitely put a dampener on the day."

They ate breakfast and went straight into their workout. The sweat that had come so easily the last few days took more work to attain in the cool, damp morning air. Before they finished their last set, a guard came to Evan's door. He told him that the warden was back from vacation and would see him after lunch.

When they were alone, Cass asked Evan, "How in the world do you go about offering money to these people? I mean, it is contraband, so all they'd have to do is confiscate it, right?"

"You're right about that, but if he takes the money by confiscation, then there won't be any for him in the future. Convicts talk, and we all know if an officer has or hasn't swayed in the past. Our good warden has been on the take for some time now. I can probably pull it off if I can convince him that our being in here is costing me money, and because of that, it's costing him money too."

"How is that? You can't tell me the warden is your hook-up in that little enterprise of yours."

"I wish, but no, not the warden. He does, however, get a little thrown his way to keep it all running smooth. He usually won't take anything outright from an inmate, but believe me, he's taking it just the same. I'll feel him out and make it work. He knows what I want before I even get there. Now all I'll have to do is hit the right price. I've got to make sure not to go so low that I insult him, but at the same time, I can't waste too much of my hard-earned money by going too high."

"Who knew the underworld could be so complicated?" Cass laughed. "If you're going to spend your money to get me out with you, what the hell's it going to cost me? I've got no cash, and I hate to make a deal with the devil for my soul."

"Oh, it's not your soul I'm after. I'm getting close to going home, so it wouldn't hurt to branch out a little and make my money faster. You can help with those branches."

"No drugs. I've never been too keen on drugs. I hate shit that makes people more stupid than they were born to be," Cass said stubbornly.

"We're on the same page, totally. I hate the drug trade as well, but we'll figure out some way for you to be useful. I've found that ideas just fall into my head if I don't force the issue too hard. Don't worry, Trigger. We're a team now. It's not every day you run into a fellow military guy in here, especially a bonafide goodie-goodie such as yourself. Just keep an open mind, remember who we're dealing with, and we'll go far." The cells lit up from a bolt of lightning, and thunder clapped louder than it had all morning. Evan looked out of his window before he continued. He said (over his shoulder as he eyed the storm), "The way I have it figured, I'll need ten grand when I get out of here for my startup money. I have a little over a third, of that with fourteen months left."

"Ten thousand dollars, damn. I never even dreamed that much money could be made in here," Cass said in awe.

"Not ten anymore; we're partners now, remember? It's more like seventeen grand from where I am now. You'll probably need a little nest egg when you leave yourself, so we'll do that branching out I mentioned and make eighteen our goal. I'm sure it'll cost a pretty penny to get us out of here and get some jobs. That's the only way we can move around and do the damn thing—as the natives would say." Evan laughed.

"I'm not sure we can really make that much money, but we can try. Count me in."

"All right. You just sold your brain to the devil. We don't trade in souls anymore." Evan roared with laughter at his own joke. "Now back to the story you were telling last night. As I recall, Forrest, you'd just been shot in the ass and decided not to reenlist."

"Well, it was actually eight months between the two, but close enough. When I cycled back to the States, I was stationed at Camp LeJeune, North Carolina. That's where I spent my last six months. I hadn't been home but four times in six years, so my mom and dad wanted to throw a big party for my discharge. That was last September. I figured, what could it hurt to come down here and see how my little hometown had changed? Boy, was that a bad idea."

"So you just got out last September? Damn, man. It didn't take you long to find your way into this hell hole, did it?"

"Not long at all, as it turned out," Cass told his new compadre.

# Chapter 6

## September 13, 2007

Matthew Cassidy stepped off the twin-turbo airplane onto the tarmac of the small airport in Jackson, Mississippi. It was a dreary, cool Wednesday in September. He pulled his collar up to block the wind as he walked through the glass doors into the reception area. It was his first day in six years as a civilian.

When he walked into the terminal, Cass stamped his feet and shook the drizzle from his jacket. He looked around the room at the smiling crowd awaiting their loved ones, and he saw his mother holding up a sign that read, "Welcome Home Matthew," in large, handwritten letters. He blushed slightly as his sister ran out of the crowd and hugged him. After she broke her embrace, his father shook his hand while he slapped Cass on the back.

"Welcome home son," his father said with a big smile.

"Thanks, Pop. It's good to see y'all," Cass said with a smile and the old Southern accent he thought he'd lost.

They drove the two hours north on winding, rural roads. Cass' family took turns filling him in on what had been happening in their lives, as well as those of extended family and friends. Cass sat back and enjoyed how comfortable it was to be around the people he had not seen nearly enough in the past six years. The recognizable landscape of his youth flashed outside the windows of his mother's SUV, and he smiled to himself as he remembered how boring this place was. He thought boredom might be exactly what he needed.

That night, the whole family, including aunts, uncles, and many cousins, met at the local catfish restaurant to welcome Cass home. His mom rented the back room, and they all ate catfish fillets, drank sweet tea, and laughed late into the evening. When they were paying the bill, several of the other patrons that Cass remembered from years ago came up to him and thanked him for his military service.

As with all small towns, word traveled fast. Someone at the restaurant told someone else they'd seen Cass, and the news spread like a wildfire. By the next day at lunch, his mom's phone started ringing and did not stop all afternoon. People he went to high school with called, and as soon as he hung up with one, someone from his parents' church called.

Some guys from his school days decided to throw a big party after the football game that Friday night. Tradition mandated it would be a bonfire at the sandpit out near the county line. Cass had hardly ever gone to such gatherings when he was a teenager, and he had never been very close to the guys throwing this one. When they called, they acted like they had all been best of friends, however. That is how the years affect people trapped in a small town. They remember the past slightly different than it really was. They think everyone was their friend.

Normally, Cass would have passed on such a sandpit get-together, but being with his family the previous night had him feeling nostalgic, so he agreed to go. On Friday night, he borrowed his dad's truck and headed to the sandpit.

The fire was roaring when Cass arrived. He backed in the borrowed Chevy so that its tailgate faced the fire. He got out, greeted everyone, found the beer cooler, and sat down on the dropped tailgate. The beer was ice cold, and the music was loud. This made Cass believe he might actually enjoy two nights of small town living. He listened to the group as they each took turns telling stories from a past he had all but forgotten.

Around eight, a carload of three women parked on the gravel road that passed by the entrance to the sandpit. The three of them walked into the ring of trucks and backed up to the blaze for its warmth. Cass thought they looked good even all bundled up against the cool night air. They were a few years younger than he was, but he could not recall their names. He recognized them school.

One of the girls, a cute little brunette, walked up to Cass and said, "Matt Cassidy, gone off to war and back home again a hero."

"I'm no hero," he said, loving the way she spoke as she grinned up at him.

She had a sparkle in her eyes that made Cass hotter than the fire ever could have. She pouted her lips and asked, "I bet you don't even remember me, do you?"

"I know your face, and who could forget those eyes, but it's been a long time since I've been home," Cass answered.

"I'm Ami, and I was a freshman when you were a senior. That's probably why you don't remember. Man, I had such a crush on you back then," she blushed as she told him.

The nine years Cass had been gone had been very good to Ami. She blossomed into a stunning country girl that any sorority at Ole Miss would've loved to have as a member. She had huge brown eyes, like a doe. Her sandy brown hair was curly and hung loose to her shoulders. She wore blue jeans and a heavy winter coat, but Cass thought she could not have looked cuter than she did standing beside the fire with her arms folded across her chest. Her high-pitched Southern drawl sent tingles up his spine. He decided that he had been away from such an accent for entirely too long.

She hopped up onto the tailgate of the truck, and they drank beer for several hours while catching up on the paths each of their lives had taken. Ami still lived at home with her father and drove the thirty miles to Starkville for classes at Mississippi State, the local college.

Cass was still taking pleasure in the small town atmosphere. Usually he was more of a wine-drinking type of guy (or perhaps a good dark microbrew), but tonight he wanted nothing but the Bud Light which he was sipping. While Cass and Ami reminisced, someone broke out a fifth of Jose Cuervo tequila. Ami loved the stuff and talked Cass into matching her shot for shot.

Before the two of them knew it, the crowd was thin, and Ami's two friends had left her to fend for herself. Cass suspected she'd sent them away when he went to the cooler for two longnecks, but he left it unsaid.

"You going to give me a ride to my place?" she asked. "It's all gravel roads and it's on the way to your parents' house. I can make a pot of coffee when we get to my house. That'll help you sober up for the rest of the ride."

"Now, that's probably a good idea. I'm not much of a tequila drinker, and it snuck up on me."

Ami giggled as she climbed behind the wheel of the truck. She said, "I'll drive. It's easier than trying to explain all the turns."

As they pulled out of the sandpit and onto the gravel road, Cass remembered something and asked, "Don't you live with your dad? He won't like me showing up at this hour."

"He's at his weekly poker game tonight. He'll be gone 'till daylight, at least," she said.

They took the snaking roads very slowly and chatted all the way to Ami's house. When she turned the truck into the driveway, Cass saw the house. It then struck him exactly who Ami was—or more accurately, who her father was. He was Sheriff Squires, a hard-nosed man who had been the sheriff for as long as Cass had been alive. He was known as much for the gigantic cowboy hat he wore as for the brutally physical tactics he employed with local criminals.

Cass had never been very conscious of the man in his youth because he never had any run-ins with law enforcement. The rest of his senior class, however, hated the sheriff. Ami noticed the recognition cross Cass' face and giggled again as she put her hand on his knee and said, "Even big bad Marines are scared of old Sheriff Shock Trooper." Everyone used that nickname for her father and his vicious ways—only when he was not around, of course. As she stopped the truck behind the patrol car in the drive, Cass looked from Ami's beautiful eyes to the car and then back again. He did not answer, so she continued, "I'm a grown woman, and my father has no say whatsoever in how I spend my time. I promise he won't be home for hours, so relax." With that, she opened her door, climbed out, and walked to the back door.

Cass just watched her walk up the sidewalk. She looked too good to let her out of his sight now, so he hopped out and jogged up to her. He caught her before she reached the door and stopped her by sliding his hands around her waist. He spun her around slowly and kissed her. She tilted her head back and wrapped her arms around his neck. That first kiss was amazing.

She backed away, grabbed his hand, and said, "Let's go get that pot of coffee going."

When they walked into the house through the kitchen door, Ami took her father's cowboy hat, which was hanging on a chair back along with his gun belt, and put it on. Cass slanted the hat backwards and kissed her again.

"It's only a little after one. You want another beer while we wait for the coffee?" Ami asked as Cass broke the kiss. She then turned and started the coffeemaker.

"Sure," Cass said as he looked around the kitchen. His attention drifted over the bar separating the small dining room and the living room. He saw a piano in the far corner of the den and asked, "Do you play?"

She turned, followed his gaze, and answered, "You bet your ass I play. I'm probably the best in three counties, too."

Ami went to the refrigerator, took out two beers, and led Cass into the living room. They took off their coats and threw them on the couch as Cass said, "You may be the best in three counties again when I leave, but for now, you'll have to settle for second best."

They sat together on the piano bench, and Cass played Beethoven's *Fur Elise*, which was a simple piece. Ami listened for a few seconds and then started playing along. She flawlessly transitioned the piece into a duet. Cass stopped and watched her hands glide over the keys as she changed to Bach's *Inventions No. 6,* a more complicated composition.

He pushed her hands off the keys and played exactly where she left off. Ami smiled, stood up, and walked to a lamp across the room. She switched it on and then turned out the overhead light. This gave the room a more comfortable feel. "You're pretty good," she said as she walked behind him and kissed the back of his neck.

"Good?" Cass asked as he shifted to a harder piece, Brahms' *Rhapsody in B Minor.* "I'd say much better than good."

She sat back down and played the same piece. Cass leaned back and gazed at the curves of her body while he took a drink of his beer. He told her, "Put your money where your mouth is, Mrs. Smarty Pants."

She stopped playing and locked eyes with him as she said, "What have you got in mind, mister?" and raised her eyebrows in a playful manner.

Cass smiled and stood as he finished his beer. He left the question hanging as he went into the kitchen. When he returned, he had two fresh beers, and he was wearing her father's gun belt. He strutted over to her, took the cowboy hat from her head, and put it on his head. He tucked his thumbs into the belt, leaned against the wall, and said, "Actually, we'll put more than money on it. We'll play it like a game of strip poker. I'll play a piece and then you replay it. We go back and forth until someone screws up. Any mess up will cost you one article of clothing."

She downed the rest of her first beer, took the fresh one he offered, and told him he had a bet. Then she added, "But why do you have on Daddy's gun belt and hat?"

Cass rested his right hand on the pistol and answered as he hung his head to the side, grinning. "I assume you're wearing underwear, and since I, myself, am not, these two items even it out."

She laughed and almost spit up her drink of beer. Cass bent down and kissed her soft lips. When they broke the kiss, Cass added, "Ladies first."

She turned out to be a formidable adversary, but Cass was a little better. She did have one advantage, and she used it to the fullest—that advantage was that she cheated. It was very distracting to have a beautiful woman kiss his neck and chest as he tried to play Mozart.

They battled back and forth for several rounds, and Cass was in the middle of her latest challenge when footsteps boomed into the living room. They were both preoccupied and did not hear the back door open and close. The cowboy boots that echoed through the room as they struck the hardwood floor, however, they did notice. Ami turned and froze, staring at the young man who stopped a few feet into the living room.

The contest was almost at a conclusion when the man interrupted. Cass was down to nothing except the gun belt and cowboy hat, while Ami still wore her pink lace panties and one sock. The intruder looked from one to the other and muttered, "What the hell?"

Cass looked at him as Ami stooped down, grabbing her shirt to cover her bare chest. She yelled, "What in god's name are you doing here? How dare you just walk into my house like this?"

The man asked "Who the hell is this son of a bitch?"

Cass answered for her as he stood and put the cowboy hat over his private area. He said, "Watch your mouth. Maybe you should just come back tomorrow, stud. You seem to've caught us at a bad time." Cass cut his eyes to Ami and said to her, "Who the hell is this clown?"

She stood looking shocked with her shirt held in front of her. The man stepped forward, grabbed her arm, and answered, "Who am I? I'm her goddamned fiancé; that's who I am!"

Ami shook when he touched her, snatched her arm away, and shouted, "Michael, you're my ex-fiancé, asshole! I told you to leave me the hell alone." She stormed to the other side of the room to put some distance between herself and the unwelcome guest.

Michael started toward where Amy had retreated, and Cass dropped the cowboy hat to free his hands, paying no attention to his own nudeness. Cass took hold of Michael's arm, much the same way he'd seized Ami. With that, Cass said, "It's time to go, Hotrod."

Michael spun and threw a slow, lame punch. Cass easily sidestepped it. His instincts and training kicked in, and he landed a perfect counterpunch to Michael's jaw. The blow was not all Cass had, but it was hard enough to knock Michael to the floor.

Ami gathered the rest of her clothes and redressed as she said, "I'm so sorry Matt. We've been broken up for a couple of months, but he just can't accept it."

Cass slid on his blue jeans and then put his arms around her. She was still shaking, and she started to cry as Michael stirred on the living room floor. He got to his feet, rubbing his jaw. Ami pulled away from Cass and screamed,

"Get the hell out of my house," as she pointed to the front door.

Michael snapped back, "To hell with the both of you, and you, Cassidy, you'll be sorry for this."

After Michael stormed out, Ami hugged Cass again and said, "I am so sorry. You better go, too. Michael will more than likely call Daddy and tell him about all this. He'll be home soon, I'm sure."

Cass finished dressing, kissed her goodnight, and left. He drove all the way to his parent's house before he realized he was still wearing the sheriff's gun belt. He thought about what to do with it but decided to return it the next morning. He was still a little drunk and did not feel like driving back to Ami's place.

Half an hour after Cass got home, the sheriff and two deputies knocked on the front door. Cass' father called him to the foyer where the sheriff told him, "Matthew Cassidy, you're under arrest."

"Arrest? What for, exactly?" Cass asked, dumbfounded.

'You're being charged with trespassing, and the young man you clocked is a deputy officer of this county—so, assault on a police officer as well." Then he raised his hand, holding the gun belt and pistol that Cass had left on his father's truck seat. "I guess we'll have to include burglary, too, just for good measure."

****

June 19, 2008

When Cass finished telling the story, Evan asked, "No way, man, those hillbilly assholes actually got away with that?"

"My lawyer told me the maximum sentence for all of those charges was twenty-five years. I was scared to death. Surely this was just some scare tactic and we could beat it at a trial. The prick told me if they spun it right, even without Ami's testimony, I'd get twenty years," Cass said with anger still in his voice. "He said these were serious charges, and whether or not they were true, I was screwed. The son of a bitch told me I should take a plea for five years, and with good behavior, I could be out in eighteen months. I didn't want to take a damn plea for such trumped-up charges, but what the hell could I do? They had enough bullshit evidence to actually get a conviction, and even if the odds were ten to one in my favor, was twenty years' worth risking? That's how I ended up here. I signed the damn plea deal like a dumbass."

"Damn, Trigger, they railroaded you pretty good, didn't they? That's how it's always been in our great state. If the powers that be see fit, then you have to go away for a while."

"You're right, but let's not talk about those powers any more. What they did to me is done and over with. I'll do this little time and then find a way to rub in their faces how well I do for myself in the years to come."

# Chapter 7

## June 19, 2008

The day passed slowly as the rain fell outside their windows. At 1:45, a guard came and took Evan to see the warden. As he walked into the office, the warden said to him, "Mr. Masters, clear a chair and have a seat. You wanted this meeting, so let's hear what you have to say."

Evan looked around the warden's office, which was in complete disarray. Stacks of paper covered every flat surface and officers' uniforms draped the backs of chairs. Evan couldn't see an inch of clear space on the desk, and clutter piled five or six inches high in most places. The warden did not appear disheveled enough to be the person responsible for such a disaster area, but his hair was a little long to be called well-kept, and his suit pants had the wrinkles of multiple wears. Evan looked from the messy room to the warden, then back to the chairs in front of the desk, and said, "I'll just stand, if that's all right with you, sir. I'd hate to disrupt the system you have in place."

"Don't be a smartass, Masters. It's not very becoming, and it sure as hell won't help your cause any. Now, what can I do for you today?"

Evan reverted to his military training on how to talk to a superior officer when he addressed the warden. He did not believe the warden was superior to him, but to make the man more amicable, he would play the game. He stood straighter, not quite at attention, but close, as he said, "Well sir, I've thought hard about this, and I've decided the best way to say it is the direct approach."

"Good idea. Okay then, let's have it," the warden said as he looked up at Evan.

"Sir, I want out of the hole, not just me actually, but the man in the cell next to me as well, Matthew Cassidy."

"Is that so? Masters, do you think it would look good on the administration of this facility if I just turned the two of you lose? There are rules as to how long you spend in the hole for fighting, and letting you two out over three weeks early would reflect on me badly. That doesn't even take into consideration the fact that, of the three men the two of you put in the infirmary, one is still there."

"I understand that warden, but it was just a very unfortunate misunderstanding that got out of hand. Neither Cassidy nor myself intended to hurt those gentlemen," Evan told him.

"Cut the horseshit, Masters. The way I heard it, you guys ate those boys' lunch. They never even had a chance. You say you've been thinking about this, so get to it. I don't have all day," the warden said as he pulled a cigarette from his desk drawer and lit it.

"Yes sir. The way I see it, we're both losing money here. If shit runs downhill, then the opposite must be true as well. Sugar rolls up hill. You are on top of that hill, sir, and I'd like nothing more than to start sending sugar your way again."

"I like your analogy, Mr. Masters, but there are plenty of less conspicuous ways for me to do my business. My guards will find a way to keep the gravy train rolling. If I let you and Cassidy out, it would be absolutely obvious y'all are working for my people."

Evan let it go that the warden had said working *for* his people and not with them. Once an officer of the law goes dirty or takes dirty money, he is no better than a common criminal. Evan believed this completely, but there was no need to knock the warden off his self-appointed high horse. He still wasn't used to doing so, but he let it go and said, "I understand that completely, sir. I know your officers are already making new contacts or doubling their efforts with old ones. That is nothing new, sir. You will receive that money either way. I want to cut out the middlemen for this transaction. Take all the hands but one out of the cookie jar, as it were."

"Exactly how big would this cookie jar be?" the warden asked as he leaned forward and flicked ashes from his cigarette.

"I was thinking five big cookies would be in that jar," Evan said. He so enjoyed the subterfuge of these types of negotiations.

"Five each," the warden leaned back again and said.

"A grand for three weeks in the hole? That's very steep, sir."

"Like I said, my integrity will be compromised for letting y'all out early. That integrity does not sell cheap." The warden grinned up at Evan.

"I'll go no more than five, total, and I have a plan to keep that supposed-integrity intact."

"I'm listening."

Evan cleared his throat and said, "We finish out today. Then, tomorrow, your officers hit five or six zones with a huge shakedown. Jam up enough dumbasses with contraband so that there won't be enough room in the hole to hold all of us. Your shift captain will be forced to let me and Cassidy go, since we've been locked down the longest. You would be totally out of it, sir."

"I'm impressed, Mr. Masters. I like that little plan. I'll expect my five cookies in no more than three days."

"Not a problem, sir. Would you prefer a Green Dot or good old-fashioned cash money?" Evan asked. A Green Dot is a prepaid credit card and is the favorite payment method in the prison system. Inmates simply keep up with a fifteen-number code that can be loaded on their card, which is kept out in the world by a girlfriend or family member. Therefore, there is no cash to be caught with, confiscated, or lost.

"I'm an old-fashioned guy. I think I'd rather have the cash. Now be gone, Mr. Masters, and forget this conversation ever took place."

"Not a problem sir. Good day to you." Evan turned and left the office. He was not thrilled about having just spent five hundred dollars, but it was almost erotic to have the power to get himself out of the hole in a place like this. Hell, the hole was actually nice in many ways. It was quiet, he did not have to deal with the lesser humans in population, and he did not have to go to work every day. The main problem with being in a cage all alone was the boredom. Yes, Trigger's stories were passing the time for now, but Evan missed the hustle. If he were out of the game for a whole month, he would quite possibly go insane.

He went back to his cell and gave Cass the rundown on what he had accomplished with the warden. The big guy was impressed that inmates could do such things in a prison situation.

# Chapter 8

## June 20, 2008

The next morning went just as Evan had laid it out to the warden the day prior. Six zones were shook down, two at a time, and the hole filled up quickly. By eleven, there were no empty cells for the new arrivals. The Shift Captain yelled, "Masters, Cassidy, pack up! Y'all are getting a blessing this morning."

The two packed their belongings and went to see the inmate that worked for the captain. He was the man in control of assigning the zone and rack when anyone was released from the hole. Luckily, Evan knew him, and for two packs of Newports, he put them on the same zone.

Cass and Evan walked into the zone, and since there is no air conditioning on the whole Farm, the heat hit them immediately. The smell of eighty inmates stacked in one place was a close second. The room was shaped like a big horseshoe, with the common area in the bend and the racks wrapping around the walls of the tips. The noise level in the zone could compete with the decibel levels of a Friday night football game. There were two televisions thirty feet apart and tuned to different channels, both of which were as loud as the speakers would go. When someone walked further than twenty-feet from one or the other, the television noise was lost to the background sounds.

To the right of the door entering the zone, in the bend of the horseshoe, was the toilet and sink area. There were eight sinks on the wall with the same metal mirrors above them as in the hole. In the zone, the toilets were separate from the sinks, but they were only separated from the next toilet in line by two feet. Nothing was between one toilet and the next. The little niche, in which the sinks and toilets were housed, was not separated from the zone by a partition or anything else. It was open to not only the zone but to the window that went to the hall, as well. The same was true for the shower area. Four showerheads were on each of three poles in another alcove. This was also open for everyone to see. Most inmates had adapted to this lack of privacy by dragging the big trash can in front of them to use the toilet, or showering while wearing their boxers.

The guys found their racks, which were metal bunk beds, and Evan said he should have the bottom bunk since he'd got them out of the hole. As they unpacked their things, Cass asked, "Now what? Hell, I think I'd have preferred to stay in the hole. At least it was quiet in there."

"Look at all these idiots, my friend. What's the old saying, 'A fool and his money are soon parted'? Well, I want to start some parting. I'm going to go see who's who in here. I'll be back." Evan walked away from the rack, leaving most of his belongings lying out on his mattress.

Cass put all of his things into the metal drawer that was under the bottom bunk. He made a cup of instant coffee and was standing by the microwave warming it when Evan walked up and said, "We only have three BDPs on the zone. They are back on the far rack to the left." Cass glanced at the BDPs without letting them see him looking.

"I guess you think it's a good idea to avoid them, huh?" Cass asked as he took his plastic coffee mug from the microwave.

"Quite the opposite, Trigger. I think we should go right over to them and make small talk. That way, they won't think we're bothered in the least by their presence. Why don't you head on back that way and ask them for a smoke?"

"A smoke? I don't smoke. What the hell, man? I'm not going to stir up a shit storm; we just got here," Cass told him, and he started walking toward their own racks.

"I dare ya," Evan shouted with his head tilted a little to the left, grinning.

"You dare me? What are we, like twelve? You go."

Evan walked beside his friend and said, "Look, in my world, a dare is some serious shit. If we're going to hang out and make a lot of money, I need it to be important in your world as well. This isn't even a hard dare; it's a stage three, tops."

"Stage three? I'm sure you'll explain that to me later. I can't believe I'm going back here just to screw with these guys—on a stage three dare, no less." Cass turned and walked toward the BDPs in the back of the zone.

"I said "tops." It's probably more like a two." Evan laughed and roared after Cass.

Cass walked slowly to the back of the room and came to a stop in front of the three BDPs. He stood over them as they each turned to see the enormous white guy in their midst. They all stood as recognition hit. Cass half smiled with his mouth, but his eyes told the three there was no humor in the conversation to come. Cass took a sip of his coffee and asked the closest one, "Do you happen to have a cigarette I can get?" It was a staring contest for a few seconds until he added, "I've been in the hole a few days and seem to have run out."

The BDP in front of Cass broke the stare, losing the contest, and told Cass, "I don't smoke." Then, to his friend behind him, "You got a spare smoke, Country?"

The one he called Country leaned over to the bed and picked up his pack of cigarettes. He handed it to Cass and quickly looked away. Cass shook a single cigarette out and asked, "Got a light?"

The same guy handed him a book of matches as he took the pack that Cass returned to him. Cass lit the cigarette, tossed the guy his matches, turned, and walked away. The three glanced back and forth at one another. As they sit back down, the first guy said to the group, "That big ass white boy be crazy as hell."

Cass walked back toward his rack, puffing on the cigarette like he actually wanted to be smoking it. He was trying not to inhale any of the smoke. When he got back, Evan was sitting on his rack and Cass asked, "So you weren't even going to be close in case those assholes decided to refuse me this smoke or maybe be a little braver and try to avenge what I did to their brothers?"

"Those guys weren't going to do shit. I knew it just from seeing them. It worked out exactly like I thought it would. They were shocked you walked up to them and asked for a square, and they couldn't give it to you fast enough. I see you got them to give you a light as well. Dare complete, Trigger. Now put that damn thing out before you choke us to death."

Cass walked back to the front of the zone, found an ashtray, and snubbed out the rest of the cigarette. He came back to Evan and said, "Okay, man. Now out with it. What the hell is up with you and these dares? I didn't come to Parchman Farm to play kiddy games. Let's hear it."

"It's been a part of me since I was little. I guess you could say it's what my dad used to make me tougher. Everything to that old man was a game. He was a football coach, and he even found a way to make his dares a part of training his players. He dared them in the weight room and at practices. Stage One Dares were for the weakest. They were what we all called 'cheerleader shit'."

"What?" Cass asked as he sat down on Evan's rack next to his comrade. "I don't follow you at all."

"It was like this," Evan tried again to explain. "There are five degrees of dares. One is the easiest; five is the hardest. Dad would set a goal for each level. Based on a player's past performance, he would then dare each one to reach a certain level in an allotted time. If the player did that, he had completed his dare and was given a sticker for his helmet."

"I guess I follow you. It sounds like a good motivating tool, but why do would you still do it?"

"That example was just for the football field. He took it to the next level, at home. Almost everything was a dare to him. I remember once when I was maybe ten or eleven, he came out in the driveway where my cousin and I were jumping a ramp on our bikes. We built it out of some bricks and an old piece of plywood. My dad went into the garage and came out with some jack stands he used on the car, and he propped the board on those, making it more than twice as high as the one we'd made. He then dared us to jump the new ramp. My cousin said no way, it was too high, but not me. Being my father's son, I backed up and got a good run at it." Evan stopped the story and lost himself to the memory while he stared at the floor.

Cass asked, "Did you make the jump?"

"Hell, no. I took off like a rocket, came down like a stone, and broke my damn wrist."

"Ouch." Cass laughed.

"Hurt like hell, and my Mom was pissed. She wanted to know why the hell Dad would have me jumping like Evil Knievel when I was so young. He told her that I had to learn that I wasn't ready for some dares. That's why there are levels put into the system. He told her this while we rode to the hospital, but the whole time he was talking, he was looking in the rearview mirror at me. Then he stopped talking to Mom and said to me directly, 'Only you know when you're ready for the next level. Don't let anyone else hold you back or push you too hard.'"

"Sounds like good advice, I guess. I would say that's a hell of a way to teach it, though."

Evan chuckled and said, "He told me once that you learn a lot from failure. The main lesson was that it sucks to fail. Avoid it at all costs."

"That's always been exactly how I've looked at failure, myself. I like his way of thinking. Did he keep dares like that going all through high school?"

"All my life he kept at it. Through college, it was one thing or another every time we talked."

"Does he still do it these days?" Cass asked.

"Na, he died a while back," Evan told him with a hint of emotion in his voice.

"Man, I'm sorry. I should think before I talk."

"It's okay. I've dealt with it. He lived a hell of a good life and taught me a lot about how to live mine. As a matter of fact, the last dare he ever gave me was one of the best."

"Oh yeah, and what was that?"

Evan rubbed the tattoo on his arm and said, "The USFL was falling apart, so my football career was about over. I knew I'd never play in the NFL, so I came home. I rented a house and started looking for a job. Dad came over one night to have a beer and told me, in his deep voice, 'Son, it's time to pull your head out of your ass. Get your life on track.' Then he dared me to join the Air Force. We finished those beers, and two days later I joined."

"And the rest is history?"

"And the rest is history, Trigger. For better or worse, that was one of the best dares the old man ever gave me—and the one I appreciate the most."

It was getting late, and even though the noise levels had not died down much, the two decided to go to bed. It would be a busy day the next day, especially for Evan. He had to get them jobs or the plan would fall apart before it even got started.

# Chapter 9

## June 21, 2008

The next morning the sun shone on the fields, and the birds sang their songs—the song birds, of course, not the jailbirds. Evan showered, dressed, and left the zone for work. He had found, over the years, that the easiest way to move around in prison was to act like it is what you were supposed to be doing. Most, if not all, of the officers guarding the housing units were low-level and usually just starting on the job. If an inmate simply told them he had to be at work, the officers would open the door to the zone and let him go, typically without another question.

Many inmates could not figure this out. They wasted time trying to sweet talk or beg the officers. Evan determined that if he acted like he was working for someone important, the younger guards would treat him like he was important as well. That morning was no exception. He was allowed to leave the zone and went to the administration building as though nothing had happened the previous week.

When he walked into the intake office, the sergeant behind the desk looked up, smiling, and said, "Mr. Masters, I was wondering when you'd make an appearance. You have a nice vacation?"

"Yes, ma'am. It was actually peaceful. You haven't gone and replaced me, have you?"

"Na, we ain't been too busy. I figured you'd find a way out of there early." She stood and said, "I believed holding such a spot would be rewarded." The sergeant grabbed her coffee mug and headed for the door. Before she walked out, she turned and added, "I got to go see the nurse, and I'll be back in a minute."

"Okay, I'll wait here," Evan said as she left. As soon as she let the door close behind her, he went to her desk and sat in her chair. The seat was still warm. He pulled the big file drawer out as far as it would go. He then reached his hand all the way to the bottom, back of the drawer, and pulled out an envelope—one of several he kept stashed around the facility.

When he'd started his hustling, one such hiding place was accidently discovered by an officer. That mistake cost him almost two hundred dollars. He never kept all of his money in one place again after that. This spot, however, was his largest by far. The sergeant knew he hid money in the office, but she'd never bothered looking for it. Evan was good to her, buying them both lunch or paying to have her hair and nails done, so she never snooped.

He flipped open the envelope and pulled out a hundred and two twenties. He placed this money into the folder the sergeant had left on the desk when she went to the nurse's office. He secured the money there using a paperclip from the center desk drawer. Looking in the envelope at the rest of his money, he found five hundreds for the warden, along with eight more twenties. That would be plenty to get Cass a job, so there was no need to raid another stash.

He folded the five hundreds inside three pieces of paper, wrote "thanks" on the top sheet, and put it all into a new envelope. Then he licked it, sealed it, and wrote "Warden Cobin" across the front. Lastly, he tightly folded the rest of the money and put it into a small pocket he had sewn into the crotch of his boxer shorts for exactly this sort of transporting.

The sergeant came back after Evan finished rearranging his money. She opened the folder, saw the cash, and smiled. After she unclipped the cash, she folded it so it fit nicely into the shirt pocket of her uniform. "Nice to have you back, Mr. Masters," she said. "Lunch is on me today. What about a plate lunch from the Piggly Wiggly?"

"Sounds good to me, Serge," he told her as he picked up the warden's money and handed it to her. "Will you take this to Warden Cobin sometime today, please? I saw some things broken in the hole, so I made him a list. I doubt he'll do anything with the stuff, but I may as well report it. Think he'll fix these problems?"

"Thick as this damn list is, I doubt it," she winked at him and said.

He told her he had lost some of his clothes when the other inmates packed his things for him. He said he needed to go to the issue officer's building to get them replaced. She called the issue officer and told him Evan was on his way to his workplace. Evan was very happy to have his boss back. He could use her to clear the path for him to move around more easily.

Evan did not really need new clothes, but he had been thinking of a job for Cass. The issue officers' clerk position would be perfect. The issue clerk was the inmate responsible for passing out new clothes and bed linen to all the inmates on the Farm. If Cass was the clerk, he could see inmates from all over the compound every day. What better way to move goods? The issue office also had two computers, one for the officer to do all of his reports, and the other for his inmate clerk to keep up with the clothing inventory. This would work nicely for Cass to transfer music to the MP3 players that Evan loved to sell.

In this instance, it was not the issue officer Evan would have to persuade. It would be his present inmate clerk, an old con that everyone called Casino. Evan had worked with him in the past, and they had actually made some good money together. Evan heard Casino's time was getting short and that he was scheduled for release in six or seven weeks. That was good for Evan's plans for Cass. All he had to do was convince Casino that his friend would be a good replacement. If they worked out such a deal for Casino to hire Cass, then it would be up to Casino to take care of his sergeant.

When Evan walked into the office, the smell of new clothes was overpowering. The issue officer excused himself, leaving Casino to handle his business. That was the way things worked on the Farm, bosses let the money be made so they could receive their cut, but they did not want to be present when the deals were being fashioned. That way, if anything ever went wrong, they could deny any knowledge of such acts and not be lying.

Evan sat down across from Casino at his desk and told him that he had a perfect understudy for him. Casino knew Evan was a businessman. Therefore, he listened intently as Evan made his pitch. They settled on a hundred dollars and ten percent of any profits Cass had a hand in until Casino went home. Evan pulled out his hidden money and gave Casino five of the twenties before he replaced the rest. Casino gave him a pair of pants and two T-shirts in a plastic bag to make the visit look official. He then told

Evan that he would bring Cass in later that day to start his new job.

Evan returned to his own job and felt good to be active again. He was back on the grind, and he loved it.

That evening, Cass could not believe how quickly Evan had, not only gotten his own job back, but procured him one as well.

The weeks passed into months, as time always does. Days dragged as they went, but when looking back, they seem to have flown. Casino went home and left the issue position to Cass. The sergeant liked Cass, so the transition went smoothly.

Evan branched out, finding more officers willing to buy ten-dollar pre-paid cell phones, bottles of vodka and gin, MP3 players, or even simple things like toothpaste and deodorant. All of these items were then sold at huge mark-ups around the Farm. The cell phones sold for one hundred to one-hundred fifty dollars; the gallon bottles of liquor costing fifteen dollars were broken down and poured into twenty-ounce Sprite bottles and sold for twenty-five dollars each; a twenty dollar MP3 player would sell for eighty; and the two-dollar toothpaste or deodorant would go for as much as ten dollars. The officer expected the purchase price back plus half of the profit, but it was still a very lucrative venture for Evan and Cass.

They had eight officers on the payroll and actually made most of their money on the hygiene and liquor trade. The high-end items were more profitable but were more dangerous and harder to sell on a regular basis. In the weeks after Casino left, they made excellent money and were well on the way to meeting their goal of eighteen thousand dollars.

# Chapter 10

## September 2008

One day, while Cass was at work, the recreation officer came into the office and put up a flier for an upcoming talent show. The show was something the recreation department did every six months for the inmates. It gave the contestants and the audience a chance to blow off some steam and have some fun. There was a lot of talent wasted behind those walls. The talent show was their time to show off, but when Cass saw the flier, it gave him a crazy idea. That night, he took the flier back to the zone and showed it to Evan.

Evan said, "I've seen too many of those shows over the years. I'll probably just skip this one."

"I beg to differ, sir," Cass told him with a mischievous smile. "You'll be there with bells on."

"What the hell are you talking about? You got a scam to make us some money?"

"Nope. I dare you to sing that 'I'm Too Sexy' song with your shirt off and perform a dance number with it. I'd say that's a good four-star dare, wouldn't you agree?" Cass laughed at the expression that crossed Evan's face as he realized he was stuck.

"Damn, why didn't I think of that?" Evan asked, disappointed with himself.

"I'm getting the hang of these dares, my friend. You're in trouble now." Cass fell back on his rack, laughing as he thought of how silly Evan would look performing in the talent show.

Evan reluctantly signed up for the show but refused to attend the practice sessions. He memorized the words of the song and practiced his routine at work when no one was around. He saw no reason to start the embarrassment earlier than the actual show itself. The date of the show rolled around quickly, and Evan was slotted to take the stage last, thanks to Cass bribing the rec clerk. Cass figured that last was the best, that way everyone would leave laughing, with the sight of Evan's antics fresh in their minds.

His turn came, and Evan stepped into the floodlight in the middle of the stage. Cass pushed play on the cassette recorder, and the music exploded through the gym. Evan ripped his shirt off like a wrestler from the eighties and went into his dance routine. As he did, the inmates in the audience leapt to their feet as one. The off-key words came from Evan's mouth to a multitude of whoops, dog barks, and yells. They never left their feet and actually got louder as Evan sang, "I'm so sexy it hurts," and gyrated like a drunken Elvis on steroids.

The performance ended, and Evan left the stage without so much as a bow. He walked to Cass, snatched his extra shirt from the hands of his comrade, and said, "One for you, buddy, but as they say, payback's a bitch." Evan turned on his heel as Cass laughed and joined the cat calls still pouring forth from the spectators.

The song and dance number was the talk of the entire Farm for months. It seemed like every officer on every shift had watched the recording of the act. Each of them had some comment to make every time they saw Evan. For months, he heard comments like, "You *are* too sexy, Hey, Sexy, and show us those abs."

****

December 2008

One Saturday, several months, after the ribbing died down, Cass and Evan were on the yard walking laps, trying to keep warm. The yard was a huge square that was almost a quarter of a mile around. The gymnasium was in one corner of the enclosure. Double fencing (whih was topped with razor wire that served the purpose of preventing escape and looked menacing while doing its job) surrounded all of this. Everywhere the two looked, inmates gathered in knots with friends or fellow gang members. Each knot contained guys talking business with prisoners who lived on different zones. Yard call was the best time for non-workers to handle business, and there was plenty of it going on that day despite the cold wind blowing across the Mississippi Delta.

Evan and Cass walked the perimeter of the yard, staying as far from the groups of other prisoners as they could. They discussed their enterprise and decided they were a little ahead of schedule to reach their goal, but determined that they should still step it up, just to be safe. Cass had a new officer he was feeling out, and he wanted to bring her into the fold. He ran her name by Evan when they rounded a secluded corner close to the gym. Not often did they have a chance to get on the yard. They were at work most days, and a weekend recreation call was rare. They took advantage of it and enjoyed the chance to strategize in the fresh air.

Cass told Evan, as they made a loop, "My damn stomach still isn't right after that stupid-ass dare you made me do, and that was two freaking days ago."

"It serves you right after that talent show bullshit. At least yours isn't on video for the staff to enjoy over and over." Evan laughed.

****

The previous Tuesday night, most of the zone, including Evan and Cass sat in front of the television watching "Cool Hand Luke," a 1970's movie about life in a prison. A light went on in Evan's head. He had an idea for not only paying his friend back for the talent show dare, but also to make a lot of money doing so. He dared Cass to challenge the biggest guy in the zone, a gluttonous heavyweight named Luther, to a slight variation of Luke's original bet. The wager would be that Cass and Luther would have twenty minutes, and the person who ate the most hard-boiled eggs in that time would win. Cass not only had to challenge Lu to the eating contest, but he had to beat him in the contest as well.

Cass shot back, "Are you crazy? I can't keep up with that big bastard when it comes to eating. What happens if I don't win in such a dare?"

"Now you're thinking like a freaking loser," Evan responded. "We'll make it very advantageous for you to win. I'll take all bets against you for two days."

"All bets?" Cass asked, and looked at him with a dumbfounded expression on his face. "Hell, everyone on Parchman will bet with Luther. That'll get expensive."

"Well, Trigger, you better win—then it becomes very profitable, not pricey. I told you that payback would be a bitch." Evan laughed.

Cass went to Lu and told him about the challenge. Cass figured Thursday could be the night of the competition, and of course, Lu accepted the challenge. Anytime he could eat a lot of food for free, he was all for it. Everyone on the zone, at one time or another, had stopped to watch him make some of the meals for which he was famous. He would eat alone, and a lot. He bought anything he could from the kitchen and mixed it with items purchased from the canteen, such as Ramon noodles and potato chips. He never spent his own money on these items because he made holiday or birthday cards and sold them for food. It was a profitable job because he was good at making such cards; therefore, he could eat to excess.

Evan immediately started telling everyone around the compound about the bet. He talked to one of his contacts in the kitchen and lined up a hundred and twenty boiled eggs. These he would have smuggled into the zone on Thursday night. It blew his mind how many people chose to bet on Luther. Even the officers wanted to get in on the 'free money' they said Evan and Cass were giving away. That was the consensus everywhere Evan went. For two days, he took so many bets, he had to borrow a notebook from work to keep up with them all. When it was said and done, as the competition was set to start, Evan had taken bets for fourteen cartons of cigarettes and nine hundred and fifty dollars. They were both amazed. Evan also had it set up for a couple of guards on his payroll to bring fifteen extra Sprite bottles full of gin. He would have the liquor sold, thus adding to the profit of the evening.

Evan gave some old convicts on the zone two packs of smokes to peel the eggs, and they placed them in big bowls on a table in the front of the zone. They finished pealing at eight, and the contest was ready to begin. Luther came down the aisle from his rack, bouncing like a veteran boxer ready to take the ring. His entourage was patting him on the back and giving him encouragement as he sat at the table opposite Cass.

Evan counted down and started the timer as he said, "Get ready, set, go! Twenty minutes, boys. Eat up!"

Luther took off like a man possessed. He crammed eggs into his mouth two at a time. He had eaten eight before Cass ate three. It was looking like a true tortoise and the hare kind of race as Cass took one egg at a time and chewed it thoroughly before swallowing. His whole process looked like slow motion taking place across the table from Lu. The big man grabbed an egg, stuffed it in his mouth to his back teeth, for more chewing power, and then repeated on the other side of his mouth with the second egg.

Evan yelled, "Come on, Trigger! Hell, he'll be through sixty before the time's up! Eat, damn it!"

Cass did not change his technique or even acknowledge that Evan spoke. He may have even slowed a little, taking two bites to finish each egg. When Lu reached thirty eggs, Cass was only on ten, with seven minutes gone from the clock. That was when Lu started to falter. He turned a peculiar shade of green as the thirty eggs tried to come back up.

Lu picked up a cup of water, took a sip, and then poured some in his hand to rub on his forehead and the back of his neck. He did not look well at all. He picked up an egg, held it in front of his mouth, and exhaled loudly.

"Take a break, Lu. He's damn near twenty back. Rest," yelled one of the guys betting on Luther.

Cass paid no attention to the slightly-green behemoth across from him. He simply grabbed, chewed, and swallowed; grabbed, chewed, and swallowed. At the fifteen-minute mark, Cass hit thirty, and Lu had actually found the inner strength to consume five more. It was neck and neck going into the home stretch. Then, with Evan standing at the head of the table yelling encouragement to Cass, Lu turned his head and projectile vomited egg pieces everywhere. He sprayed yellow yoke juices all over his corner men, causing them to jump backward and out of the line of fire. The smell was horrible, almost unimaginable. Evan laughed, looked at Cass, and said, "Six more eggs and we win. Fat Bastard's done!"

Cass took his thousand-yard stare to a new level—one in which no visual cues, sounds, or even smells could penetrate the room in his mind where he had locked his inner self. He ate thirty-seven, thirty-eight, and counting. Evan yelled, "That's it, Trigger! We won!" The big Marine could not hear him and finished three more eggs before Evan finally shook him out of his eating trance.

As soon as he returned to the smells and sounds of the zone, Cass almost lost the eggs in his own stomach. He told Evan to get him a wet rag as he stretched out on the floor beside the table, in pain, and waited.

"Hot damn, Trigger! You beat his big ass! Here you go, big guy. You'll be okay. Just relax and be cool," Evan told the bloated version of his friend as he handed him the damp cloth. Evan then collected cigarettes and cash from the betters on their zone.

Friday morning at breakfast, in the dining hall, Cass suffered through a cup of coffee when Evan returned from gathering their winnings from the kitchen staff. He sat down at the table with his tray, slid it toward Cass, and asked, "Want some eggs, Trigger? You earned 'em." He roared with laughter as he ate a biscuit off the tray.

"If I didn't feel like Jabba the Hut, I'd knock the hell out of you. Get those damn eggs away from me before I find the strength to hurt you somehow."

# Chapter 11

The next Saturday, making laps on the yard, Cass finally began to feel like himself again. As they continued to talk business, he said to Evan, "Hold that thought, E. I'm going to run a couple of laps to shake off the last little bit of a hangover from those eggs."

Before Evan could respond, Cass took off like a shot. He made two laps and passed Evan once. Each step was like dropping a piece of lead tied around his waist. When he stopped running, he felt like a new man. He looked and saw Evan as he walked into the gymnasium about a hundred yards ahead. Cass said to himself aloud, "Now what the hell is he doing? Probably collecting more money off that stupid-ass dare."

The gym, during yard call, was the hangout for the Dixie Aryans. They were a tough prison gang of rednecks who had found some connection to Adolf Hitler to go with their James Earl Ray infatuation. Those guys controlled the maintenance department, giving them more knives than a Japanese Ginsu party. No one made the mistake of going into their lair, the gymnasium, unless they had business or it was pouring rain. When the weather was bad, the officers saw to it that the gym was open to all. Today the sun was high in the sky, so Evan was obviously handling business in there. Cass trotted to the entrance door, peered inside, and saw five DAs, standing in front of his buddy.

Cass walked in and said, "You boys aren't too upset about the eggs, are you? I barely got by ol' Big Lu. Man, that dude can eat."

"They didn't make any bets, Trigger," Evan told his partner without looking back. "They asked us in here to have a little meeting."

"That's correct," a big, tattooed convict said as he and two other DAs walked onto the basketball court. They came from the main office in the back of the gym to join their five fellow organization members. "It seems you two have managed to piss off some very powerful folks, Trigger."

Cass pointed his thumb to Evan and said, "He barely gets away with that "Trigger" bullshit, and I like him. Your Jefferson Davis ass can't get away with it." Then, as he stopped beside Evan, he whispered softly enough that only Evan could hear, "I dare ya to get us out of this one with no trouble."

"I don't know if I can manage that one. Watch the steel these rednecks tote," Evan answered in the same hushed tone without moving his lips. As he did, he turned his body slightly, readying himself for the battle.

Each of the Aryan's drew a shank from the waistband of the state pants they wore, and a couple of guys actually pulled out two knives. Their weapon of choice was a piece of chain-link fence which they had straightened and, sharpened like a pencil. Then they wrapped old fabric around the dull end to make a handle. These were easy to conceal but very good for stabbing, much like an ice pick. A few DAs had a more conventional-looking knife that could slash as well as stab. Those were by far the more dangerous of the two weapons.

In a feisty, sarcastic tone, Cass asked them, "Where is that sense of Nazi integrity I've heard so much about?

Eight armed men against the two of us is a little much, wouldn't you say?"

"We heard what y'all did to those BDPs a few months back, and the money on your heads is so good, we ain't taking no chances," the big spokesman for the group told Cass.

"I hope you boys received your payment up front, or you may never get it," Evan told the group just as he punched the nearest DA in the throat, sending him to the floor gasping for breath. Then Evan shoved the guy on his right side in the chest as hard as he could, sending him into the path of the three from the office as they came running into the fray.

Cass hit the far left guy in the solar plexus, instantly knocking out all his wind. He dropped his pig sticker as Cass grabbed him by the shirt and slung him into the other two in the original semicircle. Cass kicked Evan's first victim in the face, bursting his nose and mouth into a spray of blood. Then he turned quickly and did the same to the man he had punched.

Evan followed the one he'd shoved into the three new-comer's, kicking and punching his way through the group. They slashed and stabbed at him, but he was too fast. Evan swung, connected, and moved away from the pack. He moved in a big loop to his left, connecting with hard punches as they slashed at and missed the moving target.

Cass rolled across the floor, scooped up one of the ice pick fence pieces, and stuck it into the side of the knee of one of two guys who were not chasing Evan. The tangled DA let out a roar, reached for his leg, and went down in a heap. He tripped the last two warriors whom Cass was battling as he flopped in pain. Cass snapped back to his feet and smashed his boot heel into the face of his third assailant. The guy's face erupted in blood as he fell backward, and the back of his head cracked on the hardwood floor. This knocked him out instantly.

Evan had three DAs left thrusting at him in a comic half-circle as he bobbed and weaved. He held them at bay with powerful punch-kick combinations that were lightning fast. Cass ran behind the big leader of the Nazi attack squad and put him in a chokehold. He squeezed with his huge bicep until the redneck stopped resisting. When Cass let go, the tattooed guy slid down his body to the floor and went into convulsions from the lack of oxygen.

One of Evan's two remaining assailants turned to Cass as the other knifed at Evan. Evan stepped around the thrust, placing his leg behind those of the enemy. He then reached up, grabbed the guy by the throat, and pushed backward. This caused the foe to trip, which made Evan's choke slam very fluid. The man's head bounced off the court like so many basketballs of the past. Evan hit him with an unyielding straight right, plunging the DA into instant darkness.

Evan stood and turned to Cass, who had stepped in-between Evan and his last opponent. The adversary whom Cass had left in a tangled heap stood and made his way to Cass. He was almost twenty-feet away and closing when Evan whistled loudly and yelled, "Hey, Trigger, get back to your own party! This one's mine."

"He's hell-bent on stabbing me. We'd better just switch," Cass said, and chuckled, breathing hard. Then, to the huffing DA, he said, "I guess you're my dance partner now, big boy. Is that okay?"

"Fuck you," the man barked through clenched teeth.

"They don't seem to mind either way, E," Cass ignored the foe and said to his friend.

Evan spun as his new adversary came toward him. In his spin, he jumped and kicked the man in the temple. The guy was out before Evan had landed from his kick. Evan looked back in Cass' direction, rolled his neck in a slow stretching circle, and asked, "What's taking you so long over there, Devil Dog?"

Cass kicked the guy on the outside of the knee, elbow-smashed him in the face, and grabbed his knife-wielding wrist in one fluid motion. Then Cass finished him with a head butt across the bridge of the nose. More blood flowed as the last Dixie Aryan hit the floor.

"That was fun, but let's get the hell out of here," Cass said as he surveyed the carnage spread across the gym floor.

"Hold on," Evan said as he walked to the redneck that Cass stabbed in the knee. The guy whimpered, holding his leg, as Evan squatted beside him, putting his knee on the man's chest. Evan grabbed his thigh and the ice pick handle, squeezing the first and twisting the latter, as he said over his shoulder, "Stop squirming, asshole. Now, who sent your little gang after us?"

The defeated man moaned loudly and said, "I swear I don't know. Come on, man; it was just business. The call came down from way higher than any of us, though. Shit, man; get me some help! That hurts like hell!"

"Last chance," Evan told him as he let go of the thigh and positioned his hand over the handle of the weapon sticking from the knee. The two locked eyes so that the DA could see that Evan meant to drive it deeper.

"Okay. Okay, I'll find out! That's on everything I love," the guy said in a rushed panic. "I'll know who ordered it in less than a week. Just don't, please."

"He doesn't know shit and never will. Let's go," Cass said. "No more time in the hole for the dynamic duo."

"You're right," Evan said as he released the shank's handle. Before he stood, he said to the man on the floor, "This was fun, but if we ever have a problem with you fascist pricks again, you'll all take a dirt nap. Today was just sparring practice; next time, it'll be a fight to the death." Then Evan slammed his left hand into the man's face and stopped his sniveling immediately.

The victors casually left the gym by the side entrance and resumed walking laps. Officers would find the destruction when yard call ended, or perhaps one of the beaten men would wake early and rouse the rest. Neither way mattered to Evan or Cass. They now had only one thing to talk about, and Cass started it by asking, "What the hell was that all about? Surely those Dixie Dumbasses weren't working with the BDPs."

"Not their style. I've never heard of them working with black gangs before. Hell, with all the irons we have in the fire, it could be anybody. I'm sure half of the imprisoned world hates us for making all this money."

"We'll just have to be a little more careful. I'm sure a hit by a squad of DAs isn't cheap. We haven't cut into anyone else's profits that deep, have we?" Cass asked as they turned another corner on their current lap.

"I wouldn't think so. It definitely got my heart rate up, but I hate the fact we don't even know where the hit came from. We'll keep our ears open and see if we can figure it out, but we may never know who sent those boys," Evan said.

As the yard call ended and they were headed into the building, Evan looked back in time to see guards running into the gymnasium. He nudged Cass in the ribs, motioned his head back, and said, "We're getting close to our goal, and I've only got eight months left, so we can't slow down now. We'll just have to watch our backs."

Cass laughed and answered, "If that's the best this place has, we should be fine. You just keep your ass out of secluded places and don't take candy from strangers." They both laughed harder and turned back toward their building.

# Chapter 12

The next day, Warden Cobin paced in his office. He waited for the phone on his desk to ring. All that he could think about was how the hell he would explain his failure. *Not actually my failure,* he thought. *It was those worthless Dixie Aryans.*

As he turned from the door back toward his desk, the phone finally rang. The warden leapt over the scattered piles of paperwork and clothes. He plopped down in his chair and looked at the light on the phone that indicated his private extension ringing. He took a deep breathe to calm his nerves, picked up the receiver, and said, "Warden Cobin."

"Are you expecting someone other than me?"

"Mr. Felsner, no, I've been waiting on your call."

The mysterious Mr. Felsner had contacted the warden several weeks prior with a very lucrative business proposition. As the warden thought back to the previous conversation, Mr. Felsner said, "I assume everything went according to the plan you presented me before." It was not a question.

"As to that," the warden answered, "we had a small problem."

"A problem, you say? I seem to recall your guarantee that the plan would work perfectly."

"It should've worked perfectly. I sent eight armed men, all known for violence, to take care of your problem, but..."

"There is always a 'but'," Mr. Felsner interrupted. He then let the silence grow before he added, "You're about to tell me the target took out eight armed, vicious convicts? Not believable."

"He has another man that he's been associating with. I don't care for either one of them too much, so I authorized the DAs to take them both out."

"So what you're telling me, Cobin, is you authorized these villains of yours to add another objective for my money?" Mr. Felsner asked in a very unhappy tone.

"I, um, thought..."

"That is unacceptable," Mr. Felsner again interrupted. "I expect my deposit to be returned, and for your carelessness, I assume you'll do what I originally asked, free of charge."

The warden sat quietly for several seconds and then said, "Let's be reasonable." The deposit Mr. Felsner referred to was being spent as the two men spoke. The warden's wife was having their home remodeled, and she loved to live beyond her means. All of this flashed through the warden's mind as he contemplated what to say next. Mr. Felsner, which had to be a false name, did not seem to be the type to negotiate. "Okay, Mr. Felsner, I'll get your money back to you, but this ain't some prison scene in a movie. After what those two did to the Dixie Aryans, you don't have enough cash to get anyone, and I mean anyone, on my Farm to try again."

Mr. Felsner let his own silence grow before he finally answered, "You've no idea what I have at my disposal, Warden Cobin."

"If that's so, I recommend you wait 'till your man is out of this place and on the street. Then you can put a couple of large-caliber rounds into him."

"You may be right. I should have known better than to have used incompetent help. I think I'll add his friend to my hate-list just for good measure, but I'll handle them another way."

"I did all I could. I didn't know I was up against the goddamn Special Forces," the warden said.

"Enough excuses, warden. I'll expect my money soon. Just send it back the way you received it."

"I understand, I'll wire it there ASAP."

Mr. Felsner hung up without another word. The warden held the telephone receiver to his ear for a moment and then returned it to the cradle. He stared at a pencil on his desk without really seeing it and asked himself, "How did I get myself mixed up with this shit?"

He decided to get the deposit back to Mr. Felsner quickly, no matter what headache it would cause at home. Being tied in with such dangerous people was not something the warden relished, so he would send the money back and be done with it.

****

A couple of weeks later, as Evan was going through some folders for new guys coming to the Farm, the mail officer came in. He talked to Evan's boss, but did so loudly enough to be heard throughout the room. He asked, "Lolita, did you hear the news?"

"Naw, Jeff, I've been busy this morning. What is it?" the sergeant asked him.

"Yesterday evening, after work, the warden was plowing up a food plot out at his hunting camp and fell off the tractor."

"My word, is he hurt bad?"

"Hurt?" Jeff said. "Hell, he got caught up under the disk, and it ground him up like hamburger meat. They just found him this morning."

"Oh my god," the sergeant said as she raised her hand to her mouth.

"His wife was outta town, so nobody even noticed him gone 'till this morning. The damn coyotes even ate some of him."

"How awful. He was such a good man."

Evan stopped listening at that and thought, *Everybody's a good man when they're dead. What kind of an idiot falls off a tractor? Our dear warden was just that kind of idiot, I guess.* He chuckled under his breath as he turned to a file cabinet.

# Chapter 13

## February 15, 2009

Eight months had passed since that day in the cafeteria when Cass and Evan first met. In many ways, those two-hundred-fifty or so days flew by for both of them. Looking back, they thought that the months had gone by in a blink, but each week had days or hours that drug on and on. In that way, time in prison is crazy; months fly, and days crawl.

A Sunday afternoon in February was full of those hours that go by at a snail's pace—so slow, in fact, that Evan thought he could feel his hair growing as he lay on his rack. He dropped the book he was half-heartedly reading onto his chest and said to the bottom of the bunk above him, "Come on, Trigger. Shit, entertain me. I dare ya!"

Cass was on the top rack playing solitaire with a deck of cards so old that they looked like they were around when Parchman farm was built in 1901. He stopped his game, leaned over the edge of the rack, looked down at Evan, and said, "How, exactly, am I supposed to do that? Take a nap or read some more of your book or something."

"This book sucks ass. I should've known better than trying to read this dragons and magic bullshit. I'm going to take a piss. While I'm gone think of something for Christ's sake," Evan said as he got up, turned, and walked toward the restroom area.

Cass gathered all of the cards together, pulled a rubber band around them, and put the deck under the head end of his mat. He was not going to win the game anyway. There was no need to drag it out. He swung his feet over the side of the bed and jumped to the floor in his stocking feet. After he put on his shoes, he leaned over and reached into his locker to gather the stuff to make a cup of coffee.

He scooped two spoons of instant coffee into his mug, then stood and went to the sink for water. As he filled the cup, Evan walked up to wash his hands. Evan looked at Cass sideways in the mirror and asked, "Coffee, seriously? It's a little hot, wouldn't you say?" Parchman was weird like that. It is hot on the zone twelve months a year, no matter how cold the weather outside was.

Evan walked away, drying his hands on his pants as he went, without giving Cass a chance to answer. Cass just shrugged as he casually walked to the microwave. There was no one using it, so he put his coffee mug in and set the timer for three minutes. As it was counting down, Cass read about the child lock above the reset button. The lock was activated by holding the button for three seconds. This was written in small letters that were hardly noticeable when using the machine. He grinned to himself with an idea as he took the hot cup out and headed to his rack.

By the time he got back to the bunk, his grin had grown into a full, toothy smile. Evan looked up at his friend and asked, "What the hell's so funny?"

Cass took Evan's coffee cup from the floor and poured half of his coffee into it. He handed it to Evan before he sat down and said, "Watch this. I locked the child safety on the microwave. These dumbasses should take our minds off of our boredom."

Evan took a sip of coffee and then asked, "Locked the what? That damn door doesn't have a lock on it, Trigger. I told you it was too hot for coffee. You've gone and fried your brain, my friend." He laughed and drank another sip.

"Not the door, moron. If it's so damn hot, why are you sipping so fast?" He turned to his own coffee mug before he added, "Just watch, and you'll see your fellow nitwits give us a show."

"Whatever you say, but who's dumber, them for being born stupid, or us for watching them?" Evan asked, which made Cass laugh again.

It did not take long before the first person walked to the microwave to heat up some Ramen noodles. The old man put his bowl of water and noodles in, closed the door, and pressed the numbers to set the timer. Nothing happened. He opened the door, closed it, and tried the number pad once again, to no avail.

Cass and Evan watched the old con repeat this same pattern three times before a young, thugged-out inmate walked up with a cup of water to heat. The two pranksters were too far away to hear the conversation at the front of the zone. They got up and went to the television area so they would be able to hear what was being said.

As they neared, they heard the young outlaw ask the old man, "What the hell'd you do, Old School? None of the damn buttons work." Evan and Cass held back laughter as they continued to listen.

The old man replied, "I ain't did shit. This ain't my fault. I just put my noodles in there. It never even come on."

A crowd grew around the microwave as the old man spoke. A guy that had tattoos covering his entire body walked up. Cass nudged Evan and said, "Here comes Tat; now it gets good." He almost lost it and laughed aloud.

Tat was a thirty-four-year-old man who had been locked up since he was twenty-one. To hear him tell it, he could do anything, and he knew almost everything despite the fact that he had lived on the Farm for thirteen long years. His mind had taken him in all directions through movies he had watched and books he had read. He had listened to himself tell the same stories so many times that he now believed them to be true.

He was actually handy to have around if something small needed fixing. He could repair a broken set of headphones or tune a Walkman radio. He did these jobs as he told about all the many speaker systems he had put into the twenty cars he'd owned before he came to prison.

As he walked into the circle of convicts, he put his hands on both sides of the white box that had initiated this group. He told everyone, "The magnetron's got too hot. Y'all can't heat gallons of water in this thing. It's only a thousand watts."

The old man who had put the small bowl in said, "I don't know nothing about watts, but I just put my one little bowl in there, Tat. And wasn't nobody up here 'fore me."

"Somebody was up here. It's hot in this zone, but not this hot," Tat told the crowd as he squatted and unplugged the cord connecting the microwave to the wall outlet. He stood and added, "We'll leave it unplugged for ten minutes. That should be enough time for it to cool back down."

Evan held his side as he tried to suppress the laugh that was escaping from the corners of his mouth. He whispered to Cass, "The magnetron got too hot. What the hell's he talking about?"

Cass laughed and pointed to the television as though that was the source of the hilarious thing causing his outburst. He told Evan, "Hold it together, man. I'm not through yet."

Everyone waited the entire ten minutes, and no one left the circle. Tat counted the ten minutes down to the second on his wristwatch. As he squatted to re-plug the machine, Cass walked up to the microwave and felt the sides like he was checking to see if it had cooled. It beeped when Tat plugged it in, and Cass pushed and held the reset button unlocking the safety while everyone was watching Tat. Cass asked, "So, Tat, you got this thing working or what?"

Tat opened the door, closed it, and pressed the quick cook button. The microwave beeped and started heating the old man's bowl. Everyone in the circle cheered. Life on a zone at Parchman Farm was just a little better with a working microwave. Having that one running again was reason for applause.

Cass and Evan walked back to their racks as everyone patted Tat on the back and thanked him for his expertise. They were both laughing like two hyenas on the African plains as Tat explained the inner workings of the microwave and how he grew up fixing just such problems.

Over the next couple of hours, as their laughs slowed, Tat repeatedly went into the details of how he saved the day to anyone who would listen on the zone. Evan laughed and said to his friend, "Thanks, Trigger. I needed that."

"Hold that thought," Cass told Evan as he stood and walked to the front of the zone. No one was at the microwave, so he was alone to set the safety lock once more. He knew this would get the whole thing started again.

Sure enough, within five minutes, there was someone yelling for Tat to come save the day. He came and told everyone listening that they were tearing up the microwave.

Cass went through the same ritual of unlocking the safety as Tat was plugging in the microwave. For a second time, no one around him noticed as he pressed the button and made a clean getaway. Evan sat back on his rack laughing as Cass walked up beside him. He took a breath between laughs and said, "You're too much, Big Guy, too damn much."

# Chapter 14

## April 9, 2009

"I can't believe you've got less than five months left in this hell-hole," Cass said to Evan as they sat down for lunch at a metal table in the cafeteria.

"Eighteen-weeks, six days, and a wake up, but who's counting?" Evan looked around to see who was within hearing distance, lowered his voice anyway, and added, "I have some kick-ass news regarding the time you have left, partner."

"Right at ninety days after you leave, I'll hit the street, as they say."

"About that, do you remember Officer Jamison? You know, the guy who works in the education department?"

"I know of him, yeah. Why?" Cass asked with a quizzical look on his face.

"You remember I, well, *we*, loaned him twelve hundred dollars a few months back for a down payment on a car or something like that. Anyway, he came to pay it back the other day, and I just let him give me a grand and keep the two hundred plus the interest," Evan told Cass.

Cass traded the quizzical look for one of displeasure as he said to his friend, "Your business prowess never ceases to amaze me. I know we're already over our twenty-grand goal, but come on man. What could that guy possibly do for us in the future?"

"Not what he can do for us in the future, Trigger, but what he's already done for us. You, my friend, are officially a GED graduate as of last week. Congratulations, I am so proud of you."

"You gave that son of a bitch seven hundred dollars for me to get a GED. Seriously? I have a high school diploma, jackass."

Evan sighed and said, "Yeah but it's from Ackerman High School, so it may not really count." He had to put his Spork down and sip his water because he was laughing so hard at his own joke. After laughing alone for a few moments, he included, "Come on, man, that was funny," before he lost it again.

"Whatever, but I'm not following your logic here. Can you stop cracking yourself up long enough to fill me in, or what?"

"Think about it, my big, simple-minded Jarhead friend. What comes with earning a GED in prison?" Evan asked. Then, before Cass could answer, he continued, "Three months of good time off your sentence, that's what. Good old Officer Jamison worked it all out. We'll be leaving on the exact same day."

Cass leaned in and said to Evan, "Bullshit. The State of Mississippi isn't going to give a guy who is less than thirty hours away from his college degree a GED, much less the ninety days of good time that goes with it."

"Oh I think they will. Hell, I know they will, because they already have. Get your boss to look up your release date this afternoon. It's there. Trust me, Trigger, eighteen weeks, six days, and a wake up. Then, it's over, my brother."

Cass reclined back on his seat, looking at his friend in admiration. Evan was always a jokester, but Cass could see nothing but seriousness on his face now. He was telling Cass the truth. "Hot damn, E. You're a freaking genius. Only nineteen weeks and we're out of here? Hot damn!"

Cass said, a little louder than he intended to. Then, back to his normal tone, he added, "What are you going to do when you leave?"

"Like I've told you before, I can't see myself working for someone else. Why don't we take our twenty plus and start a business together or something, like we talked about? We make one hell of a team."

"I agree, but we've been through this. What kind of an enterprise would we get into?" Cass asked.

For the past several months, the two friends had discussed many ventures they could pursue. Evan decided he was finished with working hard and wanted to find a way to become the millionaire he thought was his destiny.

Evan had read books from the library about all types of startup businesses. He thought he could make money opening a dry cleaner franchise, an oil change place, or maybe a bar and grill. His latest idea was to buy foreclosed homes and fix them up to resell at a profit. Cass had read several books on flipping houses, himself, and had truly liked the idea.

Evan was certain they could make flipping homes profitable. They could possibly become rich doing it, but it would take a lot of work, especially in the beginning. A lot of effort was not what Evan had in mind. The State of Mississippi had taken five years of his life on this God-forsaken Farm, and the way Evan saw it, that time was owed to him, by the universe or whoever was in charge, with nothing less than the millions of dollars he deserved.

He said as much to Cass as they were leaving the dining hall. "Surely, we can put our minds to the task and come up with a million-dollar idea, preferably one with little to no work."

"You'd think two minds like ours could do that," Cass responded. Then he added, "But Trigger is a bad enough nickname, so please don't start calling me Shirley."

"Hardy har har," Evan said without a smile. "That joke never gets old. Let's make it official. I dare the both of us to come up with two new ideas each by the time we get off work tomorrow. That's two, million-dollar-ideas each."

They both went back to work that afternoon, and when the day was complete, it was back to the zone. They both agreed not to discuss the ideas that they came up with until the following night.

The next morning was extremely slow at the state issue office. The sergeant was so bored, in fact, that he left Cass alone and went to find something to do. Cass paced the floor, trying desperately to think of his million-dollar idea. He focused on computers, since those were his favorite things besides musical instruments. Then, like a bolt of lightning from the sky, the idea hit him.

Cass was almost giddy with excitement that night as he sat down with Evan to eat. They made a chili and Ramen noodle meal because that evening was chicken and dumplings night in the dining hall. When Cass first arrived on the Farm, he'd heard they were serving chicken and dumplings, and his image was that of a good meal. He had loved dumplings since he was a child. The picture he had in his mind turned out to be way off base. After that first meal of dumplings, he decided it would be better to call it bones, gristle, and biscuit dough. It was, easily, the worst meal served by the kitchen staff.

For that reason, the chili and noodles meal had been a ritual for the past several months. Any night dumplings were served, they cooked some kind of a meal with stuff they bought from the canteen. They sat down to eat, and Evan asked, "So, you been thinking or what? I have some so-so ideas. How 'bout you?"

"Oh yeah, Fly Guy, I've got the idea of all ideas. You are welcome to tell me your garbage, but we can just skip that, and I'll tell you mine." Cass could hardly chew his crackers and chili because of the smile he flashed in Evan's direction.

"You're so certain that my ideas are trash, so let's hear your idea, big boy."

"All ideas are junk compared to this one. Here it is. Let's take your crazy-ass infatuation with dares, pair it with my computer skills, and build a website—something where we dare our clients to do stunts, which they can film and put on the site." Cass beamed, but Evan just stared at his friend and chewed slowly. The grin slid from Cass's face and he shrugged. "What?"

"That sounds good. Hell, they could even dare *us* to do stuff. We could film each other doing some wild-ass stunts." Evan slowly dipped another cracker in his chili and chomped on it for a second. He swallowed and took a drink of water. "But how in the shit is doing crazy stuff on the internet going to make us money?" He shook his head and looked around the room at the idiot prisoners doing idiot stuff.

"Seriously, Fly Guy?" Cass asked as his smile slowly came back to his face. "You think all those assholes online do that shit for fun? You think Yang or Dang or whatever his name was invented Yahoo for kicks?" Cass laughed and looked at Evan.

"What? Who the fuck is Yang Dang?"

"One of the founders of Yahoo. I'm sure you've heard of it." Cass raised his eyebrows and shrugged. When Evan did not respond, he continued, "You think Mark Zuckerberg created Facebook to talk to his buddies across the country?"

"No, but now that you mention it, how the hell *do* they make money? Facebook and Yahoo are free." Evan raised his eyebrows mockingly at Cass.

"Come on man; you're screwing with me, right? Those sites are covered with ads—ads for companies that actually sell shit—or ads for credit cards where they want people to sign up." Cass continued to explain that free websites bombarded their users with hundreds of advertisements per visit to the site. The free sites charge advertisers like billboard space.

"So we charge companies for ads?" Evan responded, "I like it."

"Well, the website has to be popular—you know, get a lot of hits before companies will want to advertise on it, but yeah, a good website could make us a decent living—especially if we can get a nice little following. This is the age of the internet, my friend."

"A decent living wasn't the freaking dare, Trigger."

"I was being conservative, E. Hell, it could make us filthy rich if it caught on."

Evan looked at Cass and finally smiled with him. "I guess you're right. I've heard about people getting famous just by uploading videos to you-boob, or whatever it's called."

"YouTube," Cass replied with a laugh. "That's why we've got to make a kick-ass website—to get a shitload of people to go to it."

"What should we call it?" Evan asked, taking a bite of his dinner. He looked down and chewed as he stared at the floor in thought.

"That's simple. We call it Dare Ya. Simple but memorable, wouldn't you say?"

Evan agreed and said, "Dare Ya. I love that name. It's catchy as hell."

Evan wasn't sure Cass could actually build a website that could generate so much buzz. He had no idea how a thing like that was done, but Cass assured him that with a little studying and some trial and error, he could build the Dare Ya website.

# Chapter 15

## April 10, 2009

The next day at work, Cass used his boss' computer to search the internet for books related to website design. He found seven books that he thought could be useful and gave the list to his boss. He also furnished the sergeant with two hundred dollars cash with which to buy the books. The sergeant assured Cass that he would go to Memphis the following day and find the books. His wife had been begging him to go shopping anyway, and he could use this as an excuse.

On Monday, the sergeant made good on his promise and delivered all of the requested books except for one. He told Cass that it was unavailable, but the girl at the bookstore helped him purchase it online, and the book would be sent sometime within the next ten working days.

Cass took a highlighter from his desk drawer, along with the first book, and went to work. He spent every spare minute of his days studying internet codes. He devoured the information as though it was a well-cooked steak.

Evan was amazed by how much time Cass actually spent learning about websites. Evan, himself, had always coasted through school. The courses were so easy to him back then that he never needed such all-encompassing study. Listening in class and doing the required homework always seemed sufficient to Evan. He'd never had a subject or career path that drew him in, so he never cared to learn more than was necessary in order to pass a class. In that regard, he was in awe of his friend.

In the first week, Cass learned enough to build a rudimentary webpage. He did so using his computer in the state issue office. Actually, he created three such pages, each with a simple link to the next. On the first page, he put 'Matthew and Evan's First Website' as a title. Under that, he put a picture of a cartoon casket with a vampire bat flying out of it.

When he called Evan over from the intake office to see his handy work, Evan said, "What the hell's with the bat? And I hate the purple background. That won't be Dare Ya's color scheme. I guarantee you that."

"I just used the coolest picture I found without looking too hard. How the hell do you not like purple? That's always been my favorite color."

"It would be, Trigger. Did you have a purple boa to match your purple pumps? You're a good old Clintonesque Marine."

"Piss on you," Cass told Evan. Then he showed Evan how, by clicking on the casket picture, the user was linked from the homepage to the next page he had built.

This one had a bright yellow background with "Dare Ya" across the top in bubbled green letters. Below the header, Cass put a table with his own name, Evan's name, and names of several other fictitious people. He called this group the Dare Ya Board of Supervisors. The table listed each person's time with the company and their upcoming dares left to complete.

Cass' name was blue to denote it as a link. When the user clicked on the colored name, he was taken to the third webpage Cass had built. It contained nothing but a full-screen picture of him with a huge smile. As soon as Evan saw that, he said, "Cute, but where were your purple boa and pumps when you took that picture, Big Guy?"

"Again, piss on you, E."

In fact, Evan was quite impressed with the progress his friend had made. There was a lot of work to be done, but with four months left in prison, they were right on track. While Cass continued studying computer codes, Evan closed up all of their other business fronts. He had his sergeant open a savings account in his name. He bought Green Dot numbers and loaded them on his pre-paid credit card. Then, each time the card balance became too high, he deposited the money into his savings account.

**\*\*\*\***

## July 5, 2009

The balance of the account had grown to $22,982, which was well over their goal of $18,000. Cass also kept two Green Dot cards, one for each of them. He loaded each card with eight hundred dollars. He stashed the physical credit cards until the day they left. That way, when they left Parchman, they could purchase clothes, food, or whatever they needed before they made it to a bank.

Evan was still an old-fashioned guy at heart, sort of like the warden had been. Therefore, he also had a couple hundred in cash for each of them to have in their pockets when they walked out from behind these walls. He knew the pre-paid Visas were just as good as cash, but there was nothing in the world like good old American greenbacks, to make a man feel free.

Cass was still researching codes every day, and Evan continued to shut down every aspect of their once-thriving businesses. He did all the preparing for their release in just four months. The tedium that came with waiting for their glorious day was all that remained. It would come, Evan knew, but it would take a long time to get there. The few days he had left would seem longer than the entire three years he had spent on the Farm up to that point.

The two friends woke on the morning of their release with smiles and butterflies. Each man had been in this structured, zoo-like environment for so long that the fast-paced, free world seemed a little unnerving. Neither of them understood or would ever admit it to anyone else, but somehow their time on the Farm had brainwashed them into being apprehensive about being free. Apprehensive or not, both were very ready to watch Mississippi State Penitentiary grow smaller in the rearview mirror.

They changed into old blue jeans and t-shirts, which had been donated to Parchman for prisoners being released by a church near the prison. The transportation officer took them to the bus station for their trip out of the Mississippi Delta. Across the street from the station, there was a local clothing store and a convenient store. Walking into the stores was unsettling for reasons neither of them could put into words.

When they walked out of the convenience store wearing the new clothes they'd bought and sipping Cokes, their anxiety and nervousness were gone. Evan puffed on a celebratory, gas-station cigar as he slapped Cass on the back and said, "We made it, Trigger. By God, I never thought this day would come, but it's finally here." He put the cigar in his teeth and smiled a huge smile. He talked through clinched teeth around the cigar as he added, "Yesterday was the last day of my life I want to spend miserable. Every day from here on out will be nothing but good times."

Cass sipped his Coke and responded, "I like the way you think. Now let's go catch that bus and get the hell out of here."

# Part Two: The good

# Chapter 16

Nine months passed, and the day finally came to officially launch the Dare Ya website. They had left the bus station in the Delta, each going to their hometowns, but neither felt at home in the particular town of his youth. They both felt just as confined in small-town Mississippi as they had on the penal farm. Each decided quickly that leaving the state was the only option.

In the same week they were released, they loaded all of their belongings, which were not much, into a Chevy Tahoe. Cass had bought the truck cheap from his uncle the week he was released. After talking at length, they decided to move to Dallas for a fresh beginning. Evan had some family out there, and a cousin of his agreed to let them stay with her for a few weeks—at least until they could find a property to flip.

The two looked for and found just such a house that was in foreclosure, and they bought it for ten thousand dollars. They put in a little work by cleaning and repainting it, and then they sold it. Each agreed he did not want to invest all of their time and money into the first flip house. Even so, it took a few months and almost drained their cash reserves, but after their repairs, the home sold quickly for over fifty thousand dollars. After that, they found a slightly better house and did the same thing. They worked long hours, seven days a week, doing things such as, scrubbing bathrooms, tearing out and painting walls, and putting down new flooring. At night, while Evan finished whatever project they had worked on that day, Cass worked on Dare Ya.

After they sold the first house, Cass researched and bought the domain name www.dareya.net. He then started building the social network they had envisioned months before. It was an arduous task, but he worked late into most evenings to make it a reality. If a work day was slow, or if it was something Evan could do alone, Cass would work long hours during the day, on Dare Ya, as well. As long as the house didn't fall too far behind schedule, he devoted all of his time to the site. They could not lose sight of the fact that the houses were still their primary income, but Dare Ya was an investment in the future.

One day, months before the Dare Ya launch, Evan was at Lowe's picking up a sink for the second house. While he was loading it into his shopping cart, his cell phone beeped with a text message. It was from Cass.

*Got it built. Need a kick-ass dare 2 B the first posted.*

Evan smiled to himself as he replied *−Dare ya 2 bungee jump NUDE!* Then he went down another isle to see what other useful items he could find.

When he got back to the house, he walked up the front steps carrying the sink. Cass met him at the front door and said, "Payback will be a bitch, Flyboy, but I've got it all set up. We have to be at the bungee location at ten in the morning for the jump."

"Damn, man; that was quick, but we don't have a camcorder," Evan responded as he sat the sink down and began unpacking some cabinet handles. He added, "You like these for the kitchen?"

"Yeah, they'll do. I thought we were going to just use the old ones to save a little money?"

"These were on sale, and they'll look better. So, what about not having a camcorder?" Evan asked his friend.

"I've got all that lined up; trust me. Now let's get the sink in, because we still have to take the old windows out of the master bedroom this afternoon. That way we stay on schedule."

They finished all of their planned work for the day, and Cass went to bed early for the first night in a long time. He was anxious about the next day, so he figured he better get a little extra rest. He had never bungee jumped before, and the next day he was going to be doing it nude—and on camera. "Sorry Mama," he said aloud to himself as he fell asleep.

The next morning, Cass awoke at daylight and went down the hall to the living room where Evan slept. They were staying in the flip house while they worked on it, thus saving money on rent. He kicked Evan's cot and said, "Come on, Flyboy, we've got a lot to do today."

****

Evan rubbed the sleep from his eyes as he threw back his covers, sat up, and put his feet on the floor. He grabbed a pizza box that was on the floor. He opened it and took out a half-eaten piece of pizza crust. As he chewed on the rubbery, cold dough, he said to Cass, "Well, Trigger, at least we don't have to worry about your wardrobe."

The two left the house early that morning. There would be no construction work done, but they still had plenty to do, and it was strictly Dare Ya related. Cass had found a rental business downtown and reserved two digital video cameras for the day. The rental place even gave them a quick tutorial on their operation. He decided that the dare should be filmed from two angles. He could splice the videos together to make it look professional.

Evan was still hungry even after eating the day-old pizza crust for breakfast. After they left the rental store, he said to Cass, "Pull in somewhere, I need a biscuit."

Cass stopped at a gas station with a deli area that served breakfast. He told Evan, "Grab me a sausage and cheese biscuit. I'll go get some bottles of water for later. It's going to get hot."

Evan called back as he headed to the warming lamps to grab the biscuits, "Get me chocolate milk, but you better skip that, Trigger. You're going to be on one hell of a roller coaster ride. Don't want you to puke." He laughed at Cass as he turned and walked away.

Cass ignored the jab and went to get the drinks. They put the bottles of water on ice in a cooler they had brought from the house. Cass drove to the dare spot while each ate his biscuit. Neither man talked. For Evan, it was too early to come up with many witty retorts, while Cass was getting his mind ready for the bungee jump in his near future.

Cass pulled the SUV into the clearing of a stand of trees about ten miles north of Dallas. Evan looked around through all of the windows and asked, "What the hell, Jarhead? There isn't a bridge out here for miles. You going to do this jump out of an oak tree or what?"

"Be patient, Flyboy," Cass turned and told his friend. Then he pointed back south, causing Evan to turn in his seat look out the back window. Cass added, "There it is."

****

That was two months before the launching of Dare Ya, and the coworkers had been extremely busy since the bungee jump dare. They had finished the second house and were well on the way to completing their third. Cass edited the video of the first dare and uploaded it onto the

Dare Ya website. Each man worked independently and together and made lists of dares to be posted on the site. They broke the site into Degrees, and each Degree of Dare Ya had ten initial dares posted from their ideas. Those ten dares would give visitors to Dare Ya some initial challenges to film and upload. Then future guests could watch those videos and try to outdo what they saw.

Since Cass and Evan had come up with the initial dares and put them on the site, they did not want any liability if someone hurt themselves by taking a dare. For this reason, they met with a lawyer. The duo had an attorney friend, Brian. He had been their attorney on the house closings. Brian told them that he could help them write an airtight disclaimer that would protect them from any responsibility if someone injured him/herself. When visitors checked the site, before they could become a member of the Dare Ya Nation, they had to read and agree to Brian's disclaimer with an e-signature. Then, and only then, could a visitor apply to Dare Ya and become a full-fledged member.

Eventually, if enough people visited Dare Ya and became members, they could form small groups called Charters. They could instant message other individuals or their whole group to dare each other to post videos on their Charter's page. On the launch day, however, Dare Ya only had two members: Dare Ya Deity, which was Evan, and Dare Ya Designer, Cass' screen name.

Cass wrote an email containing the Dare Ya link, and he sent it to all the people in his and Evan's lives. It invited them to visit and join the Dare Ya site and asked them to share the web address. The week before, Cass also bought some ads on other sites on the web to announce the launch and to get Dare Ya's name out to the public.

Evan was sitting in a plastic lawn chair beside his friend. Cass was behind the computer on a worktable set up in the flip-house living room. Cass typed a few keystrokes and pressed "enter." He then closed the document full of code on the screen and said to Evan, "Well bro, that's it. Dare Ya dot net is now an active website. It's officially open to the public."

Evan took out a big cigar from his shirt pocket and lit it. Cass fanned the smoke, used Internet Explorer to open his email, and sent the invitation. Next, he went to the top of the screen to the URL bar and typed the domain name, www.dareya.net for the first time. When building the site, he had included a visitor counter at the bottom of the homepage, and it now read "one." Evan looked from the screen to his companion and then back to the screen. He took the cigar from his mouth and asked, "That's it? Shouldn't something be happening?"

"It         will;        just        be        patient."

Evan stood, went to the kitchen, and took two beers from

the refrigerator. As he opened one and passed the other, Cass said, "Well I guess I can play the only video we have. I'll never get tired of that." Cass laughed alone as Evan sat and rechecked the counter.

"I'm already bored with it," Evan told Cass. He opened his mouth to say something else, but he never got the chance. The counter turned over to two. "Holy shit. We have our first guest," Evan said loudly before he puffed on the cigar around a massive smile.

Cass waited as the new visitor filled out the forms and became the first visiting member of Dare Ya. Then the member name showed on the right side of the home page, which denoted that another member was on the site with Dare Ya Designer. Evan saw his member name, Beauliscious, and said, "We should've known Beau would be our first member. Good old Beau." Evan pushed Cass aside and typed a Direct Dialog to his old friend from Mississippi.

*Welcome to Dare Ya Beau! Check out Cass' crazy ass, and yes, I mean that literally. Ha Ha.*

Beau DD'ed back saying, *I will. Cool-looking site. BRB going to check out the vid.*

As the two comrades waited for Beau to watch the video and browse the site, the counter rolled over twice more. Then, while Cass pointed it out, the white numbers rolled over again. Beau DD'ed them back as each stared, wanting to see it click again. *Sick guys! There's no way Cass did that. I'm going to find me a dare and post myself doing it!*

Evan replied immediately. *No shit, he scared the hell out of me. Don't find anything too crazy, bud. Be careful.* Then he turned to Cass and said, "I hope he don't try a four- or five-star. He's hard-headed, though."

"You can't baby him all his life. He's able to take care of himself."

"I know that, but I can't be responsible for him getting hurt again."

# Chapter 17

Cass was still sitting at the computer chatting with new Dare Ya members as Evan returned from the front door. He carried the Chinese food they'd ordered. Holding up two bags, he said, "I have the sesame chicken. You want a beer?"

"Na, I'm good. Look here. We just hit forty members." He stood, grabbed his bag full of food, and added, "Chat it up for a while. I'm starving."

"Has anyone uploaded a dare yet?" Evan asked as he sat down. He unpacked his own supper and started eating as he checked out all the people who had joined Dare Ya. He recognized two of his cousins, a classmate from high school, and some old Air Force friends . "Here's the first video post, Trigger, our first uploaded dare—on your guys. Dare Ya Devil Dog's his name. I like that one."

Cass put down his chopsticks and walked to the computer. A young Marine was on the screen in a still picture that denoted a video ready for viewing. "That's Hackman; we called him "Hack" over in Bagdad. He's a total nut, so this should be good."

Evan pushed Hackman's still frame, and the film began. Hack was standing in front of the camera holding a fifth of tequila in one hand and a funnel with a short hose attached to the end in the other. He crimped the end of the hose and poured the whole bottle of liquor into the funnel. "He's going for a three-star," Evan said as Hack put his mouth over the end of the hose, uncrimped it, and let the entire 750 ml flow down his throat in a matter of seconds.

The man on the monitor shook his head vigorously from side to side as he dropped the cone-shaped tool and slapped himself in the face with both hands. "Whoa! Hell yeah," Hack shouted into the camera. He reached for the keyboard to shut off the video, but as he did, he coughed, covered his mouth with his free hand, and puked through his fingers. Straight tequila ran down his arm as he choked the rest of the Mexican liquor back down his throat. He pressed stop on the camera, and the video ended.

"Damn, he almost made it," Cass said. He typed a DD to Hack as he added, "What do you think? Should we give him the points?"

"I say yes; he kept most of it down."

"Our first disagreement—you say yes, and I say no. Points or no points? How do we break the tie?"

"I didn't think it would be a problem—especially not on the first damn dare. Let me think," Evan said as he walked to the kitchen for a fresh beer.

The points in question were awarded to members for completing a dare. Each degree dare, one through five, gave a point per degree. For example, a third-degree dare awarded three points. When a member reached two-hundred and forty-five points, he became a Dare Ya Disciple. Disciples were the only members eligible to watch the videos of other Disciples doing or attempting the 'So Dumb a Marine Wouldn't Try It' Dares. Those were the most demented stunts on the site, but only disciples were allowed to read, watch, try, or add to the list of those dares.

Evan came back to the living room and sat down. He said to Cass, as he checked the counter in the corner of the computer screen, "I say if they make a good faith effort and the video is entertaining, award the points. We want Disciples, don't we?"

"Of course we do, but we want them to earn it."

"Right, but we don't want to discourage people from trying. If the video is clever enough, give 'em the points. Remember, Trigger, this is about getting the viewers to come to Dare Ya. Without the hits, we won't be able to sell ads. No ads, no money. Besides, it's about entertainment, my friend."

"I guess you're right. Okay. I'll concede this one to you, but the next decision is mine. I'll give Hack the points."

Cass leaned over the keyboard and awarded the points. When he finished, Evan took control of the keyboard and sent Hack an open forum message, which, unlike a DD, would be seen by all members. The message read, *Congrats! You are our first member to earn pts. Now can you be the first to become a Disciple?*

Hack had logged off earlier, probably to clean up his mess from the tequila. He would receive the message when he logged back on to Dare Ya. Cass yawned as the counter turned to forty-three. It had been an exciting and exhausting day. Their dream had finally come to fruition. Dare Ya was off the ground and running. Cass stood and said, "I'm going to rack down for a few hours. I think we did pretty good for our first afternoon."

Evan stopped a chat conversation that he was having with a member and said, "Hell yeah, we did, and we're on our way to the big time."

The next morning Cass woke up and rubbed the sleep from his eyes. When they'd moved into the third flip house, he had not bothered to set up his bed. The work would be finished, and he hoped they would move out very soon; therefore, he saw no need in the extra effort. His mattress lay on the floor with the head and footboards propped against a wall in one of the smaller bedrooms.

Cass rolled over and took his Fossil watch up from his pile of clothes. It was almost ten in the morning.

How he had managed to sleep so late, he did not know. He was always up with the dawn. Dare Ya's kick-off must have worn him out more than he thought, the night before. He pulled on his Levi's, slipped his feet into the imitation Croc's at the bottom of the pile, and went into the adjoining bathroom to brush his teeth. As he rinsed his mouth, the cell phone in his front pocket rang. It was his mother. He had dreaded this call from the moment he and Evan had filmed the bungee dare. He walked out of the bathroom, pressed "talk" and said, "Morning Sunshine, how are you today?"

"Well, Matthew, I was fine until I got an email from your sister and went to that Dare Em what-you-call-it and saw my son like I haven't seen him since he was in diapers," his mother scolded.

He stopped himself from correcting her about the site name. There was no need in adding to the fire. To his mother, he said, "Come on Mom; it wasn't that bad. We put that blur thingy over most of me."

He shrugged on a clean T-shirt as she said, "Blur or not, it was obvious. Take that pornography off of the internet before someone like the preacher from the church sees it."

Cass smelled coffee from down the hall, so he went into the kitchen and poured himself a cup. Evan was sitting at the desk typing, just as Cass had left him the night before. "It's not pornography, Mother. No one will see it; trust me. It's just a two-minute video on our little website."

"Well, your father thought it was funny—especially your friend's reaction, but I saw no humor in it what-so-ever. If anyone in my Sunday school class sees it, you ain't too big for me to cut a switch."

Cass laughed, but his mother did not follow his lead. Sensing her anger, he told her, "Okay, okay, Mom, I'll try to block it from all of central Mississippi. That should keep anybody in town from seeing it. I've got to go, but I'll call later. Tell Pop that I'll call y'all tonight. I love you, Mom."

"Okay, Matthew, but block it from the whole state, okay? Your Aunt Jean lives up in Southaven, and I'd hate for her to see it. Call us later, but not too late. You know we go to bed early in this house. I'm mad, but I still love you, son." She hung up and Cass wondered if she actually believed he could block a website from an entire state. Cass decided that she probably did believe he could perform that function.

Once again, he said aloud to himself, "Sorry, Mama." He walked in the living room, sipping from his coffee mug. To Evan, he said, "Damn, I slept like a log. What time did you crash out?"

"I haven't been to bed yet." Evan looked away from the computer monitor and rubbed his eyes. He stretched his arms above his head and yawned before he added, "You'd be surprised how many people are up all night playing on the net. We're up to over a hundred members, and some crazies actually posted videos. A couple of them are funny as hell."

Cass sat down in the lawn chair, watched the posted dare videos, and agreed that a few of them were hilarious. Then he checked the dare email. The night owl members had sent several new ideas. The procedure for new dares was set up where members could email ideas for dares to a special account. Members could include a recommendation in the email for the degree they believed each dare should be. The founders considered the advice but assigned a degree based on their own thoughts. Evan moved aside so Cass could designate each a degree and post each to its proper degree page. The founders discussed each new idea, and they posted videos before they gave a degree or awarded points.

Cass went through the steps of assigning degrees and awarding points slowly, to teach Evan how to do it. The process would eventually become time-consuming as more and more members submitted videos and dare ideas. In the future, they would have to divide time running the site. When Cass built Dare Ya, he made this step simple, so it would not take long to do either task. Evan learned the process quickly and was able to follow the steps by the second try. Cass wrote the procedure down, step by step, on a piece of paper that he taped to the side of the computer monitor. "Just in case you forget something, Flyboy."

"I've got it now. It ain't that hard," Evan said. He yawned loudly before he continued, "I'm going to catch a few zzz's; then, this afternoon, we have to get that sprinkler system dug. If we don't return the Ditch Witch by nine tomorrow morning, we've got to pay for an extra day."

"Damn. I forgot all about the Ditch Witch. Dare Ya will have to run itself for a day. We've still got to pay the bills," Cass said.

# Chapter 18

Unlike Cass, Evan saw no need to buy a conventional bed. The way he saw it, he and Cass would be moving around for a while working on flip houses, and a bed would just add to the things he had to pack and lug with him each time. When the two guys first moved to Dallas, Evan went to an Army surplus store where he found a good deal on a used, folding military cot. It easily collapsed and fit into a small bag that he could carry over one shoulder.

Evan was used to a small sleeping area from his time in prison, and his makeshift bed was actually more comfortable than the rack he had at Parchman. He crawled into the faded green cot that morning to get some much-needed sleep. The nap would not be what he desired because as soon as his eyes closed, his dreaming mind took him back to the most horrible day of his life.

****

Saturday August 20, 2005

Evan stepped between two cars on the lot and asked the couple looking at the used Ford, "She's a beaut, ain't she? Would you like to take it for a spin?" He reached out and shook hands with the man in front of him.

"We're just looking right now, thanks."

"Allright, I'll be in the showroom if y'all have any questions." Evan smiled as he handed the guy his card. "Just wave if you decide on a test drive."

He looked up at the big clock on the wall as he walked into the dealership—almost noon. It was entirely too hot to be trying to sell cars, he thought. He turned around, looked out the window, and saw the couple get into their old car and drive away from the parking lot.

As they left, Evan watched an aged Chevy pick-up pull into an empty spot in front of the building. The driver's side door opened, and a tall, skinny man jumped out wearing blue jeans, a white T-shirt, and the same Mississippi State baseball cap he always wore. He saw Evan through the display window and waved.

Evan met him at the entrance door, pulled it open, and felt the searing air rush in as the frosty air blew out. The man entered and asked, "What's up, bro? Selling any cars?"

"Hell no; it's too damn hot. I bet its one-ten out there on that asphalt."

"Well, let's blow this joint and go have a few beers. That'll cool us off; I guarantee it."

"Give me a minute," Evan told his friend. Then, to a man sitting behind a desk on the other end of the room, he said, "Hey, Winston, I'm going to take the jeep we just got in and call it a day. That be okay, boss?"

"Yeah," the shop manager said. "That's fine. Don't you and Beau get in too much trouble out there."

Evan went to the key case hanging on the wall and took the keys for a black '05 Jeep Wrangler that the dealership had taken as a trade-in earlier in the week. He walked past Beau and nodded to the side door as he headed that way. He said, "Let's get the hell out of here before Winston changes his mind."

James Beauchamp and Evan had grown up half a mile apart in the rural southwestern corner of Mississippi. Since the second grade, the two had been inseparable. Any time someone in town saw one of them, they would ask where the other was, and usually, he was not far away. Once Evan returned from the Air Force and started selling cars, the two fell back into the familiar pattern. They even started dating twins a few months after Evan moved home.

"I called Mandy and told her we were on the way," Beau told Evan as they jumped into the front seats of the topless jeep.

"You were that confident I'd bail on work?"

"Not a doubt in my mind, bud. Pull up by my truck, and I'll grab the cooler."

Evan did just that. Beau retrieved the cooler from the bed of his truck and heaved it into the backseat of the jeep. "Get in, I don't want to see this place anymore 'till Monday," Evan said as he reached into the blue icebox and brought out two longnecks. He handed one to Beau as he climbed back into the passenger's seat.

They picked up Mandy and Sandy, the twins, and headed out of town. Both women wore matching cutoff denim shorts and an American flag bikini top. Beau climbed into the back seat with Mandy, leaving Sandy the seat up front. Beau had to move the cooler to the cargo space behind the rear seat, but it was still within easy reach. Sandy leaned over the center console and held Evan's arm as he shifted gears and left their driveway.

"Let's see if we can find some mud," Mandy yelled from the backseat over the rushing air as the jeep sped down the road.

"Yeah, head out to Spring's Bottom. We can rip it up on the sand bars," Beau leaned forward and told his friend.

"Bet! Now hand me another beer, would you?"

Beau reached into the icy water and brought out two fresh beers, which he passed to the front seat. Then he took out two more. He handed Mandy one, twisted the top from the other, and took a long, satisfying drink.

The group came upon a dirt road and turned left. They all bounced in their seats as they made their way to the creek at the end of the old trail. "Put on your seatbelts," Sandy told the other three.

All of them clicked their seatbelts before the jeep burst out of the trees onto one of the many sandbars on Spring's Bottom creek banks. The ruts in the dirt lane and the creek made the seatbelts necessary. The locals who came to this spot to blow off some steam used the waterway as a road to go from one sandbar to the next. Evan had driven through the water hundreds of times, himself.

The jeep left the sand and entered the foot-deep creek. The rear tires shot sprays of water and loose gravel into the air as the two couples laughed and held on tightly, enjoying the bumpy ride. Beau took a gulp of his beer, making sure not to spill a drop, before he howled into the summer sky. Everyone was having a blast in the August afternoon.

The partiers drank beer and rode from shoal to shoal through the creek, laughing and drinking for an hour. Then they stopped on a large sandbar next to a deep pool and swam the afternoon away. At five o'clock, Sandy and Evan were lying on the sand enjoying the sun. Sandy said, "Let's head back to town and get something to eat! I'm hungry."

Her sister walked out of the water, twisting water from her ponytail. Mandy joined the conversation, saying, "Me too. We'll get something to eat, take a shower, and figure out what to do later tonight." Everyone agreed it was an excellent idea. They all dried off and climbed back into the jeep. Evan did a three-point turn in the creek bed and goosed the jeep, heading out the same way they came. He had not thought about it before, but now that the girls mentioned food, he felt famished.

As they sped down the creek, Mandy thrust her arms into the air and yelled, "I love this jeep!"

As she said this, Beau unbuckled his seatbelt in the backseat and stood, holding onto the jeep's roll bar. He held on with one hand and twisted his hat in the air with the other. "Come on, man; kick it in gear. We're not only hungry; we just ran out of beer, too."

Evan gave the jeep some more gas, and the water sprays behind the tires climbed higher. The turn for the logging road came up on their right side sooner than Evan anticipated, and all the beer and sunshine slowed his reflexes. He spun the steering wheel to make the turn, but the jeep's outside tires fell into a rut as soon as it made the curve. The vehicle was going so fast, it tilted up on two wheels and rolled onto its side.

The empty cooler flew out, the sisters shrieked, and Evan held tight to the steering wheel as the jeep tipped. Beau, who was still standing, wrapped his arms tighter around the roll bar and braced himself for the wreck. His grip weakened, ever so slightly, and he slipped in the wet backseat as the jeep came down on the driver's side door. Beau fell to the side of the bar, and the jeep landed on top of his left arm. He screamed as loud as Evan had ever heard anyone scream.

****

Evan sat straight up, back in his cot, with sweat pouring off him. The screams of his past woke him as if it were actually happening. He took his shirt from the floor and wiped the perspiration from his brow. As he stared at the wall, hundreds of miles from Spring's Bottom creek, he remembered the wait after Sandy called for help on her cell phone. He'd kept Beau's head above water until the EMTs arrived. They pulled his friend from the stream. A deputy sheriff arrested Evan for reckless driving and DUI. At the same time, they loaded his life-long friend into a nearby ambulance.

Evan thought back to how he'd felt when a guard came to him in the county jail and told him that Beau had been rushed to the hospital and immediately sent into surgery. "He'll survive, but they had to take off his arm," the old man told Evan. All he could do was slide down the bars and sit on the floor with his face in his hands.

He could still hear Beau telling the judge that the accident was as much his own fault as that of his friend. The adjudicator must not have been listening because he sent Evan to prison for maiming his best friend.

Evan fell back on the cot and thought how that sentence had turned out to be nothing compared to the nightmare he'd suffered through since the wreck, every time he closed his eyes. Beau had made it clear that he never blamed Evan for the loss of his arm, but every day since it happened, Evan held himself responsible.

Evan was snapped back to reality by the sound of the ditch digging and equipment rumbling from the front yard. He felt as though he had not slept a wink, but there was work to be done. He shook off the after-effects of the nightmare and pulled on his work boots. When he stood up, his stomach growled loudly. He went to the kitchen and made two ham and cheese sandwiches. With them, a bag of potato chips, and two Gatorades, Evan strolled through the house and out the front door.

Cass turned and saw his friend standing on the porch eating a sandwich. He shut off the ditch digger and walked to the shade of the front stoop. "That wasn't much of a nap. Go back to bed. I've got this for a few more hours," Cass said as he took a Gatorade and the bag of potato chips.

"I'm up now. We may as well get this done," Evan said before he scoffed down the second sandwich and reached into the bag of chips once again.

The two men worked all afternoon and into the night digging trenches, laying sprinkler pipes, and covering them with dirt. Both were exhausted by the time the job was completed. It had been a long, hard afternoon in the sun. Evan was especially tired, given that he'd had no sleep the night before, and his short, restless siesta had done him no good.

They took turns showering to wash away the grime of the day, and then they retired to the back porch with a delivery pizza and a few beers. Evan took a slice from his half of the pizza—pepperoni and mushrooms, and wondered how Cass could eat the Supreme. Evan hated black olives and bell peppers, so they always ordered the pizza with two different halves. He chewed a few bites, then took a pull from his longneck before he asked, "How you think our baby's doing? You think it's got two hundred hits yet?"

"I don't know. I hope so, but I'm too tired to log on and have ten people DD me. You check if you want, but I'm going to sit here and, relax a while, and then I'm going to bed."

Evan popped his neck from the tension of the day as he said, "You're probably right. If I get on there, I'll be chatting for hours. We'll just check it in the morning."

They sat on the back porch listening to the crickets and other night sounds while they drank a couple more beers. Cass rolled his head in a circle to stretch his shoulders and noticed Evan dozing in his lawn chair, still holding an empty bottle. Cass stood and kicked Evan's chair leg, causing him to startle awake. When Evan looked up, Cass said, "As my dad used to tell me, 'Call the dogs and piss on the fire. This hunt's over.'"

# Chapter 19

The next morning, Evan woke with the sunrise. He got off his cot, went to the kitchen, and started the coffee maker. While he waited on the machine to brew, he logged on to Dare Ya to see how many hits they'd received the previous day. He promised himself he would not stay on long enough to be involved with any chats.

Cass had set up Dare Ya as the homepage. Anytime either man went on the internet, Dare Ya's login page popped up immediately. He signed in using his member name and password, scrolled down to the counter, and froze. He stood staring at the screen and then yelled down the hall, "Cass! Get your ass in here!" After he received no answer, he turned, trotted down the hall, and beat on Cass' bedroom door. "Come on, Trigger; you've gotta see this!"

Cass snatched the door open as he buttoned his blue jeans and glared at his friend. He sharply asked, "What the hell is it? It's the crack of dawn, if you haven't noticed."

"Just come in here and look at this," Evan responded. He went back to the living room with Cass on his heels.

Cass was saying, "Damn it, E, this better be…" He left the sentence unfinished as he looked down and saw the counter roll to 2548 members. He sat down, and with a few keystrokes, he saw 218 videos posted. He awaited the viewing and scoring. 487 emails with new dares had to be assigned a degree. There were numerous DDs sent to the founders commenting on the first dare and giving praises for the site. Cass raised his eyebrows and slowly shook his head back and forth, as he said, "Damn, E; this could get out of hand fast. How the hell can we watch that many videos?"

"Screw the videos for now. When can we start selling ads? And how does that work? Do we contact companies? Or do they contact us?"

"Slow down, man. We're getting visitors fast, but we need a hundred-thousand hits before we can even get to that step. The way it's looking, though, we'll get there, but we've got to maintain the site to keep generating hits," Cass said, wiping sleep from his eyes.

"Yeah, well, see why I got your big ass up so early?" Evan asked with a know-it-all grin. "Go get yourself together while I check some emails and get a couple of the dares to their pages. I'm not sure what's on the construction calendar for the house today, but we've got to load the ditch digger on the trailer and take it back for sure. Then it's Dare Ya all day long, looks like."

Cass went to get ready for the day as Evan took over in front of the keyboard. They both thought to themselves, at opposite ends of the house, that Dare Ya was growing faster than either had anticipated.

****

Over the next week, they took turns viewing, rating, and chatting on the site. While one was at the computer constantly typing, the other worked to keep up with the remodeling of the house. The flip work was taking a back seat to trying to catch up on all the internet posts, but there was no keeping up, no matter how hard they tried. The hits grew exponentially as each member revisited the site daily. Membership soared as the craziness of the videos spread throughout cyberspace.

Ten days after Dare Ya launched, Evan came across a strange email. The sender claimed to be an internet agent/publicist, who left her phone number. Evan called Cass, who had gone to the hardware store to pick up some paint. He told Cass about the email, and they decided Evan should investigate the agent, Melinda Brooks, and the Weinsenstein Institute, the agency for which she worked.

Evan researched the agent and her firm on the internet. By the time Cass returned with the paint, Evan had established both to be reputable and located in New York City. He filled Cass in on his findings, and they decided to call to see exactly what Mrs. Brooks had to say. Before they made the call, Evan asked, "What the hell do we need a publicist for? We didn't write a book, Trigger."

"Seriously?" Cass responded. "It's publicist, not publisher. As in publicity—they get their clients' names out to the public."

Cass laughed at his companion as they went into the kitchen. Evan poured two glasses of sweet tea while Cass dialed the number from Mrs. Brooks' email. He put the phone on speaker as it rang through to New York.

"Mrs. Brooks' office, how may I direct your call?" a sexy-voiced secretary asked as Evan handed Cass his sweating glass of tea.

"Yes, this is Matthew Cassidy. Mrs. Brooks emailed me and my business partner and wanted us to call her."

"Mr. Cassidy, yes, she has been expecting your call. Hold one minute, please."

The two friends exchanged a look across the kitchen, and Evan shrugged his shoulders as they listened to elevator music and waited. The music stopped, and they were greeted by an even sexier voice that had a low gravelly tone to it. Cass was hypnotized by the voice instantly as the woman on the other end of the line said, "Mr. Cassidy, I am so pleased you called. How are you today?"

Evan threw a dish towel at Cass to break the spell. Cass blinked and said, "I'm doing fine, Mrs. Brooks. You said in the email that you wanted to speak with me and my associate?"

"Please, call me Melinda. I would like to discuss the website you built, Dare Ya dot net. Are you representing Mr. Masters, as well?"

Evan said, "We're on speaker-phone, Melinda, so both sides are being represented." He stymied a small laugh at himself for trying to sound so proper.

Melinda did not act as if she'd noticed the laugh as she continued, "Wonderful. I can say this once, and nothing will be lost in a retelling." She proceeded to explain how her agency represented start-up websites. They did so by marketing the new site with other sites for which they worked, and by placing ads on new sites for their older customers. If by chance the site went viral, she, as an internet agent, would be a liaison between the clients and the television and print media that commonly wanted the latest hot topic to appear to their audience.

Melinda sounded like she was reading from a script and the two listened without interrupting. She continued to explain how her firm could help make Dare Ya many times more profitable than they could do alone. When she finished with the prewritten presentation, she asked if they had any questions.

"Well," Cass responded, "what exactly do you mean by more profitable? I've already looked into advertising on the site, and television or, as you say, print people can contact us directly, can't they? Why should we pay you guys?"

"Very good questions, Mr. Cassidy," she said.

She had already learned their voices. *Impressive,* Cass thought, and then he said, "Please just call me Cass, my dad was Mr. Cassidy."

Evan added, "And I'm E, Melinda. Let's not be too formal."

"Very well; Cass and E, it is. The WI has been doing this a long time, and we represent many websites. We have more advertisers than both of you could possibly have time to talk to, and those television people do not always contact us. We get the client's name and, when possible, represent their faces to such clients. I do not wish to discuss all the projected profits or plans to gain those profits over the phone. My firm will gladly fly the two of you to New York City for a face-to-face meeting."

Evan asked, "Y'all will fly us to New York? For free?"

Melinda held back a laugh, but they could hear the smile in her voice as she said, "Yes, E, we will take care of all expenses. I can arrange for a flight the day after tomorrow. How does three days in the city sound? We can have our meeting on the second day just in case it carries over to the third morning. Have either of you been here before?"

Cass answered for them, "Yes I have, but my friend hasn't. I would like to be clear, Melinda. By accepting this trip, we are in no way agreeing to any offer."

"I understand completely, Cass. Just come and listen to what we have to say. There is no obligation, but I assure you both, that you will like what you hear."

She proceeded to tell them about the travel arrangements, and they ended the phone call. Cass took a swallow of tea before he asked Evan, "What do you think?"

"It's completely nuts, but we'll go see what they have to say." Evan went back to the living room to work on the videos, leaving Cass alone with his thoughts.

****

The Dare Ya two-some worked long hours on the computer, trying to put a dent in all of the posts and emails. It seemed like it was two steps back for every step forward. The trip to New York City would not help the battle in any way. The night before they left, Evan decided to borrow two laptops from some friends so they could both attack the mountain that was piling higher. They did that for the entire four-hour flight to the Big Apple until the pilot asked for all electronic devices to be turned off for the approach. Cass closed the laptop he was using, stretched in his seat, turned to Evan, and said, "Damn it boy, I haven't even made a dent. We'll need some help soon."

"Did people start working for free?" Evan asked. "Our cash is all tied up in the house. I've done all the research on the ads, so I think we should start putting them on the website. We're over ten thousand hits already."

"Maybe, we'll just have to buckle down and get that damn house on the market."

Both mentally went through what was left to finish the third house, as they rode the landing out in silence. When they deplaned, they saw a man holding a sign that read, 'Cassidy and Masters.'

They followed the driver out to a black Lincoln Town Car, and he packed their personal belongings into the trunk. They rode from the airport through Manhattan and stopped in front of the Trump International Hotel on Central Park Avenue. Cass said, "Shit, man, they're sparing no expense. These rooms are over a grand a night."

"Fifteen hundred dollars, at the least, for a suite," the driver informed Cass as he passed their luggage to a bellman.

"A night?" Evan asked with an unbelieving look on his face. "We could finish the house with our two nights here."

They thanked the driver, and Cass tried to give him a twenty-dollar bill as a tip. The driver refused by telling him, "No thank you, sir, Mr. Weinsenstein takes care of us so we don't have to rely on tips. He prefers we don't take them, but, thank you just the same. Enjoy your stay in the city."

They went to the front desk to check in, and as they were waiting in line, Evan said, "I want the bed by the window, Trigger. You've seen New York before. I want to soak it in." This turned out to be a pointless statement because when they got to the clerk and gave their names, she handed them two card keys. Each man had his own room.

Cass twirled his pass card around in his hand as he said, "Almost three grand a night for two nights. This is some big-time stuff we're walking into—quite unprepared, I might add."

"I'm beginning to feel the same way. We're here now, so let's just see how it shakes out."

"Like we have a choice. What are you supposed to be, a philosopher, all of a sudden?" Cass rolled his eyes and headed to the elevators. He was aggravated at himself for being so ill-prepared for the meeting tomorrow.

They separated after agreeing to meet in the lobby two hours later. Cass decided they may as well have a night on the town. It was too late to prepare by then, anyway. He got to his room and looked at the laptop. He decided not to work for a while, kicked off his shoes, and stretched out on the plush, king-size bed. He was dozing when the bedside phone rang. He answered with a groggy, "Hello."

"Mr. Cassidy, this is the hotel message service. You have a message from a Mrs. Brooks saying you should be in the lobby in an hour for dinner. 'Dress casually', she said."

Cass said, "Thank you," but the messenger had already hung up on the other end. He sat on the edge of the bed while he dialed Evan's room, and when he answered, Cass said, "Did you just get a message?"

"Yep, I was just about to get in the shower."

"Casual doesn't mean jeans and an Abercrombie T-shirt, Fly Guy," Cass told Evan before he returned the receiver to its cradle.

# Chapter 20

Each man showered and dressed before they met in the lobby at the rendezvous time Melinda had given them. The driver from earlier in the day entered through the front door behind a stunning redhead. She covered the distance across the vestibule in long, easy strides. Her knee-high skirt revealed just enough perfectly toned and tanned legs to leave every man in the lobby wanting to see more. She flashed a perfectly white smile as she walked in front of Evan and Cass, saying "Melinda Brooks; it's great to meet the two of you" as she presented her hand to Evan and then to Cass.

When she shook hands and locked eyes with Cass, he understood immediately why green was the color of envy. Her eyes were such a shade of green that every woman envied her for having them and, at the same time, all men envied the one that captured the girl behind those eyes.

Evan elbowed Cass in the ribs and said, "Good to meet you too, Melinda. I'm Evan Masters, and this big mute is Matthew Cassidy."

Her smile grew wider as she nodded. They turned to the entrance door and made their way through the leering crowd. The two muscular men crammed into the Lincoln's backseat while Melinda slid into the front. She turned and said over the headrest of her seat, "No business tonight, guys. We'll have dinner, and I have tickets to 'Spider Man' on Broadway; the New York Philharmonic is having a concert, or Mr. Weinsenstein has box seats for us to go to a Yankee's game. They all start in a couple of hours. That gives us plenty of time for dinner, and to decide what to do."

The two exchanged a look in the back seat that showed each man's shock at their treatment. They rode the seventeen blocks to The Lambs Club, a swanky, high-class restaurant off Broadway. Cass and Melinda took turns pointing out the sights of Manhattan. They had dinner, and Melinda didn't mention Dare Ya. She seemed very interested in every other aspect of their lives, especially the houses they remodeled. She told them that she loved to watch those fix-it shows on television. "It would be so much fun to actually do such a thing," she told Evan as dessert was brought to the table.

"It's a lot more work than fun, but it can be enjoyable at times, I guess—especially when the escrow's closed," Evan said, and winked. He asked a waiter for an after dinner cigar and then added to Melinda, "What time is the first pitch? We should probably head on to the stadium."

"Whoa, Evan. I'm sure the lady doesn't want to watch a silly baseball game." He looked to Melinda as he asked, "Would you prefer the show or the concert?"

"Actually, Cass," she said, looking into her raspberry fondue, "I have to side with E on this one. The Red Sox are in town, so I think it's going to be a great game."

Evan slapped the table and said, "Hot damn, Trigger. I like this gal." He clipped the end of his cigar and lit it with a smile.

"I'm clearly outnumbered, so I guess the ballgame it is," Cass said without a smile.

They left the restaurant, and the driver took them to Yankee Stadium, where he pulled in front of the VIP gate. He hustled around the car and opened the door for Melinda. Evan, Cass, and Melinda took an elevator to the box with seats reserved for the Weinsenstein Institute.

Evan looked around the room and saw the buffet and full bar and said, "Hell, we could've saved money and ate supper here." Then he caught sight of the lush green field on which the players were going through their warm-ups. "That's the only green I've seen in my life that could compete with your eyes, Melinda, and it's really not even close."

Cass laughed at his friend's one-liner as he walked toward the bar. The others followed, and they ordered drinks and went to their seats just as the National Anthem began. They were treated to a great game, indeed. Cass even got into it a little bit, and though he had lived in New York, he cheered for the Red Sox, just to be different. Cass' team was victorious, so he talked trash to Evan all the way back to the hotel.

As they exited the car and stood on the curb, they both thanked Melinda for a great night. It was nice to get their minds off Dare Ya for at least one evening. She told them, "It was my pleasure, guys. I had fun, too. Marty will be here with the car at eight in the morning. That way, we can finally get down to business."

They all said goodnight, Melinda got back into the Lincoln, and both men watched the car pull out into traffic. Cass said, "Cool your jets, Fly Guy. If we strike a deal with her agency, we have to keep it strictly professional."

"Then I vote we don't sign with them. We don't need some big city publicist at Dare Ya. I, on the other hand, could find some personal use for just such a thing."

Cass pushed his friend out of the way and walked inside. Evan followed, and they rode up to their rooms. Neither could shake the first impression Melinda Brooks had made on them. Cass thought she might be good for Dare Ya. He had to keep Evan away from her, though.

****

The next morning it was raining, and the low clouds covered the tops of Manhattan skyscrapers. Even with the bad weather, Evan was still impressed by the landscape and hustle of the city. It took almost an hour to traverse the ten blocks to the offices of the Weinsenstein Institute. They could have walked it in a quarter of the time, and Evan said as much in the elevator going up to the WI's offices. Then he added, "These big city guys like to waste money just for show, don't they?"

Cass chuckled and responded, "If by some miracle Dare Ya catches on, I'll remember you said that."

"*When*, Trigger, *when* Dare Ya catches on; not if," Evan told Cass as they stepped off the elevator. They both chuckled as they walked to the receptionist's desk.

Melinda rounded a corner into the lobby, causing all laughter to stop. Neither of them could believe it, but she looked even better in her pantsuit with high heels and a frilly tie than she had the night before. As one, under their breath, they whispered, "Damn." She was stunning.

"Good morning, boys," she said, pretending she had not heard them. This time, instead of handshakes, both received a small hug of welcome. "Follow me. Mr. Weinsenstein is excited to meet you guys."

They followed her down a hall like two lost puppies. Both enjoyed the view as she led them. They turned into a huge corner office and were greeted by a small Jewish man with a gigantic smile. It took no time after the introductions to know that Mr. Weinsenstein's smile was nothing compared to his personality. He was a whale of a man, with a giant mind trapped inside his five-foot-four-inch frame.

"Gentlemen, come in; sit," Mr. Weinsenstein boomed as he motioned to three chairs in front of his desk. He walked around, sat behind the huge mahogany desk, and opened a box of Cuban cigars. "Please have a cigar."

Cass declined. Evan, however, took the offering, slid it under his nose, inhaling loudly, and said, "Now this is a good cigar. Thank you, sir."

"Please call me Sully. I find it easier to work without the formalities. I take it Melinda showed you boys a fun evening in our fair city."

Cass spoke as he turned to look at Melinda again, "She did, sir." Then he turned back to the desk. "Sorry Sully, old habits die hard. It was a lovely evening, and thank you for the rooms at the Trump International as well. You really shouldn't have, sir, Sully."

"I've not yet received a knighthood, Matthew, but I like the sound of that. Perhaps one day. Don't mention the accommodations; nothing but the best for potential clients, boys. Speaking of which, let's get to business."

Melinda excused herself as Sully explained exactly how the Weinsenstein Institute went about finding potential advertisers for websites. Also, with the paid announcements, the WI scrolled one client's domain ads on all of its other client's sites many times every day. All of the WI's clientele sites were linked through these ads. He told them the names of several of his high-profile sites and explained how they could be used to funnel web surfers to Dare Ya. He explained to them that advertisers paid not only for hits to a site, but for the duration of time a user spent on a site as well.

Melinda came back into the office and handed each man a colorful green binder. Evan looked from the binder to her eyes and smiled as he winked. She grinned and said, "Guys, Sully has explained loosely how the WI can help Dare Ya grow. Now, let me go into more detail. We have done the fundamental research on Dare Ya, and from that, we made some predictions. Dare Ya has the potential to garner multiple hits from its members daily, and it can also keep them there an average of thirteen minutes longer than the time spent on any other random site."

"That's good, right?" Evan interrupted as he studied the charts in the binder, smiling.

"Quite," Sully answered, nodding the affirmative. "Proceed, Melinda."

Melinda cleared her throat and started again. "Right. As I was saying, our researchers believe the Dare Ya membership will continue to grow; becoming very large very fast. We estimate a membership of just over a million worldwide by this time next year."

She paused and let this sink in. It hit Cass first, and he said, "Did you say a million members? How accurate are these calculations?"

"Yes, Cass: a million. The math is sound, but they were run assuming you guys sign with the WI. Turn the page, please. Now, this graph shows the numbers if you guys decide to run Dare Ya alone. You'll notice the figure in one year is less than a quarter of the previous total."

"How is that?" Evan asked. "We can get Dare Ya out there pretty good. Look at what we've done in a month."

Sully held up a hand before Melinda could respond, and he explained, "Exactly, Evan. You boys have done a remarkable job, and that is precisely the reason the two of you are here now, experiencing the royal treatment. I have over a thousand client sites, gentlemen. Let's let them work for you."

Cass asked, cutting directly to the point. "What kind of deal does your institute make, Sully?"

"Ah yes, that's the important part, isn't it? The bottom line. I'll take it from here, Melinda," Sully said, and stood.

Melinda took the seat next to Cass as she replied, "Yes, sir."

"Okay boys, here it is. I, or rather we, at the WI, believe that Dare Ya can grow into one of if not the biggest sites that we represent. With your brilliant idea and our team behind it, we can make a lot of money." He paced to a window overlooking Manhattan and gazed out for a dramatic pause.

Evan could not take it any longer and asked, "We understand that, Sully, but what kind of a split are we talking, here?"

"We take twenty percent after any expenses Dare Ya incurs, of course. In those expenses, the two of you can include a base salary for yourselves." Sully walked back to his desk, opened the center drawer, and removed two plain white envelopes. One read "Cassidy" on the front, the other "Masters." He tapped the envelopes on his knuckles as he added, "My friends; look again at the numbers: eighty percent of one million members is still greater than one-hundred percent of two-hundred thousand. This could be very lucrative, and I am prepared to offer you boys a signing bonus, if you will." Sully handed one envelope to Cass and the other to Evan. "Go ahead, have a look."

The two exchanged glances before they opened their respective envelopes and pulled out the cashier's checks inside. The friends both froze. When he shook off his astonishment, Cass leaned over and snatched Evan's check from him to see if the figure on it was the same. It was.

Sully smiled broadly and said, "Consider this an interest-free loan, of sorts. The checks are yours. Of course, that hinges on the stipulation that you sign with the WI. Then we keep all profits from Dare Ya until it is repaid. After such time, only twenty percent of the profits are ours from then forward. The other eighty is for the two of you."

Cass asked, "Profits *after* a salary are taken out for each of us?"

"That's correct," Sully responded as he once again sat behind his desk. "A reasonable salary, of course. We can negotiate the numbers in time."

Evan yanked his check back from Cass, looked at it once more, and asked, "What if Dare Ya never makes that much profit?"

"Then my company made a poor investment choice, and heads here will roll. The loss, however, would be ours. The bonuses will forever be yours. Remember, Evan, we keep all profits prior to repayment, so we would never lose all of our investment."

Cass shook himself free of Sully's trance and asked, "Have you ever taken a loss, Sully?"

"No, Matthew, we never have. I possess an exceptional research team, and they find winners to invest in. With us, Dare Ya will be a winner as well."

Evan did not say another word as he clutched his check, stood, and walked to the window. Cass looked down and then quickly up into Melinda's deep, green eyes. From the window, Evan asked without turning, "Is this some kind of a joke? Are we on Candid Camera or something?" He laughed dryly and added, "That has to be it, right, Cass?"

"I assure you both, there are no hidden cameras. My offer is legitimate. Here is a copy of the contracts. Carry them to the Trump Hotel and have your attorney look them over," Sully said as he sat a stack of papers on the corner of his desk. Then he added, "Your plane leaves at three tomorrow afternoon. I'd love to have a deal by then, but if you must, take everything with you to Dallas and decide there. Take everything but the checks, that is." Sully laughed, walked around the desk, and slid the check from Cass' fingers. "These are yours only *after* a deal has been signed." Evan turned and reluctantly handed Sully his check.

Melinda stood and ushered the stunned duo to the door. Sully walked over, shook their hands, and thanked them for coming. "Take your time with this decision. I understand it's an enormous one. I know you boys are smart. Let the WI work for you."

They left the office and walked back up the hall to the receptionist's area. This time even Melinda's stride could not distract their minds from their racing thoughts. Each could not stop thinking about the checks and what all of that money could do. Melinda took a card from her pocket and said, "This is my cell number. Call me with any questions, or if you make a decision."

Cass took the card and put it into his breast pocket. They thanked Melinda, but no hugs were exchanged on the way out of the office. The pair rode the elevator down, and the WI's driver escorted them to the car. The return trip to the hotel was made in complete silence. When they arrived at the hotel lobby, they sat in a pair of wingback chairs. Evan said, without looking over at Cass, "Okay, Trigger, I'll say it. Holy Shit! Did you see all those zeros?"

Cass ignored the question and asked one of his own. "Do you know what Dare Ya would have to make just so Weinsentein could break even? And after it does, what we'd make?"

"I don't do math, Jarhead. But did you see all the damn zeros or what?"

"Yeah, I did. It looks like your "when" is now, my friend. We need to talk to a lawyer, bad."

"I need a beer. I'm going to go get us a six-pack. You get on the lawyer thing, and I'll be back to your room in a little bit," Evan said as he stood and walked across the reception area.

Cass put his head in his hands and sat like that for several seconds. The Trump International Hotel in New York City was a long way from Parchman Penitentiary in the Mississippi Delta. He let the entire day sink in before he went upstairs to make a phone call. He called their attorney in Dallas, Brian Tully. Brian had been a friend and fishing buddy of Evan's, but Cass had grown to trust him completely.

# Chapter 21

Cass called and explained the situation to Brian. He also told the lawyer that they needed him to look over the contract.

"Sure thing, Cass; just fax me a copy," Brian told him. "Contracts can be tricky documents. I'll have a look and tell you what I think." Cass had a lot of faith in Brian. He was unlike any other attorney that Cass had ever known—an honest man.

Cass went back down to the lobby and asked to use the fax machine. He sent the contract to Brian and went back to his room to lie down and think. Evan was sitting outside the door drinking a beer when he got there. Cass looked down and said, "I see you're still no good at doing math. In case you didn't know it, a six-pack has only six beers. Twelve is twice as many as six." He opened the room door, and Evan followed him in.

"I know that much math, Trigger, but shit; there are too many people out there. I'd hate to run out of beer and have to go back to that freaking store." Evan handed Cass one of the bottles and then put the rest of the beer into the room's refrigerator.

"I faxed a copy to Brian; he's going to look it over and get back to us," Cass said, and then drained half of the Corona in one, long swallow. "Is this real, E?"

"Tastes like a real Corona to me, and with what it costs up here, it damn well better be." He took another bottle and walked to the bathroom. He yelled back into the room as he urinated with the door open, "I have a little more reality for you, Trigger, but all those zeros I'm still not sure about!" He came back into the room and told Cass, "Brian may be calling in a few hours, so there's no need in us discussing it until we hear from him. We'd just have to go through the same discussion when we know what he says. Want to go get some lunch?"

"I don't think so. I'm going to lay here and think on this. Maybe I'll go over the contract myself. Just leave me a couple of those beers."

Evan left four beers in the fridge and took the rest to his room. He decided he would just order room service instead of trying to fight the masses outside. The afternoon passed slowly for them both. Cass was in his room going over the contract, and Evan actually dozed off. He was still sleeping when his phone rang. He answered it, a little groggy from the beers and the nap. He grunted, "Yeah."

"E, it's me, Melinda. It sounds like I woke you. Were you napping?"

"I was just resting my eyes. What's up?"

Melinda laughed and asked, "I thought you guys might like some company for dinner. Would you like to get something to eat?"

"Dinner up here is supper, right?" Evan asked, and laughed as he sat up. "I'm kidding, of course; and we'd love your company. Tonight it's on us, though. Is there a good Thai place around here?"

"I know just the place. I'll be there to pick you guys up at seven," she told him, and then hung up the phone.

Evan checked his watch—3:30 pm. Then he texted Cass. *We have a date w/ hottie. B ready at 7.*

****

That evening, they got ready, and Cass went to Evan's room at ten minutes to six. He told Evan that Brian had called, before he left his room, but said the contract was over his head and not the sort of thing he was used to reading. It looked sound, but he could not swear by it. Brian said that his father had a friend that used to work for oil companies and that this kind of thing was right up his alley. "The old man's going to read over the contract tonight, and he'll give me his opinion as a favor. I should hear something first thing in the morning," Brian told Cass.

Both of the men thought back to the checks they'd had in their hands hours earlier. Evan plopped down on his bed and asked Cass, "If they are offering us a million dollars apiece up front, how big is this thing going to get, Trigger?"

"That's exactly what's kept me distracted all afternoon while I tried to read that contract." Cass sat in a chair by the big window overlooking Central Park. "I don't think we even dreamed this big, Fly Guy."

They were thinking of where Dare Ya could take them in the future. Each considered how those checks would change his life. Whatever came after that day seemed unreal, but it became clearer through the haze of daydreams.

"Oh yeah," Cass began as Evan turned on the television and flipped channels, "Who's the hottie? Melinda?"

"You assume that in a city of eight million people I can't get us a date?" Evan asked. Cass just gave him a look, and Evan added, "Yeah, it's Melinda, but I could've gotten us some other chicks if I'd set my mind to it. I was just a little distracted by that damn check."

As it neared seven, they headed down to the lobby to meet Melinda. She was coming through the front door as they exited the elevator. Evan whispered to Cass, without moving his lips, "My God, man. Blue jeans and a T-shirt, and she looks like a super-model."

She greeted them with a hug and told them that the restaurant was only a few blocks away, so they could walk. They mingled with the foot traffic and made small talk as they went to the restaurant. They were seated and placed their orders before Melinda said, "Last night I was working, and we didn't discuss Dare Ya. Tonight I'm here on my own accord, and that's exactly what I want to talk about."

Evan felt the need to impress her and replied, "We have our attorneys in Dallas looking over the contract as we speak. We should hear back from them before lunch tomorrow."

"That's excellent, but I want to make sure you both understand that I'm not here on Sully's, or the WI's, behalf. I like you guys and wanted to give you my personal thoughts on a few things."

Evan leaned back in his chair and sipped his drink, grinning at Melinda. Cass laughed and said, "Easy, Fly Guy, I don't think she meant like that." Then, to Melinda he added, "Thoughts on things such as what? But now that you mention it, we could use all the input we can get."

"No, you guys did a great job on Dare Ya. It's the best idea to ever come through the WI. I just have one small suggestion to help take it to an even higher level."

Evan leaned forward with on his elbows on the table and said, "We're all ears."

She told them, "Add a set of dares to challenge people, morally. For instance, have some dares that get members to do charitable work or to help the community around them. With a feel-good side like that, it gives Dare Ya an extra dimension, which becomes a publicists' dream."

"No, that's a good one. I love it," Cass said, and set his drink down. "We'll discuss how to set it up, and I'll work on it ASAP."

The food arrived, and Melinda waited for the waiter to leave. When he did, she said, "Now the next thing is just my belief, not the WI talking."

"I believe you said that already, Mel. This is a dinner amongst friends. Relax," Evan told their new acquaintance.

"Okay, I'll just say it. I think you should take Sully's offer. Maybe you should suggest that he only gets eighteen percent, so you sound like you're dealing, but take the proposition. Then use all the money he's giving you and get a building for Dare Ya and hire a staff. You guys cannot do this at home anymore. It's already too big for that, and it'll only get worse—or better, depending on how you look at it."

"Yeah, that's the understatement of the century," Evan said as he cut a piece of his New York strip steak.

"Bigger than you can imagine, especially with me and Sully on the team. Take the money and build Dare Ya with a good group of people."

"Isn't this like insider trading or something?" Evan sat down his fork and asked. They all laughed with him.

The rest of dinner was spent getting to know one another, and little else was mentioned about Dare Ya. They did not have to say it aloud, but they could feel it from each other's vibe. They would wait to hear from Brian, but before they left New York City, they would sign the contract. On the plane ride home, they would be millionaires.

# Chapter 22

Brian called early the next morning. "Take the offer," Brian said. "You can't lose. The two million dollars is exactly what it appears to be: an advance on suspected future earnings." Brian sounded amazed that he was speaking of such figures, but it also sounded natural, coming from him. He added, "The only thing is, the old man's never seen only one party take all of the risk; especially not the lender."

"Kind of crazy, huh?" Cass asked.

"I'd say, but it's valid; that much I can tell you, for sure."

"Thanks, B; we'll see you tomorrow."

Cass hung up the phone and immediately called Melinda to tell her they had a deal. She told him she would call Sully with the news and set up the contract talk and signing. At eight, they walked into the WI as regular guys with one Tahoe and an under-construction house between the two of them. At ten thirty, they walked out of the building filthy rich. Evan managed to sound professional when he asked for the eighteen percent instead of Sully's offered twenty percent share. Sully put up a weak argument but caved without much protest. Either way, if Dare Ya took off as expected, he would make huge amounts of money.

The WI's attorneys, in the meeting, told Sully they could change the contract and have it ready for him the next morning. Sully exploded, saying, "These young men have a plane to catch this afternoon at three o'clock. They have an empire to build, and now is a crucial time in its building. Have those papers ready and signed before that damn plane leaves. Is that understood?"

****

The lawyers met Cass and Evan at the airport, where the pair signed the contract and received their checks. Melinda was with them and stayed to see her new friends off. She said, "Remember the things we talked about doing next. Set up the charity side of Dare Ya, find a building, and hire a staff."

"Got ya, we'll be on it as soon as we get home," Evan told her as they hugged, and he kissed her cheek.

Cass finished Evan's thought as he pushed him aside and took his place in Melinda's embrace. "Thank you for everything. When will we hear from you again?"

"You guys will be doing your parts, and I'll be doing mine. I'll be in touch soon. Have a great flight." With that, she turned to leave. Then she glanced over her shoulder, catching them watching her walk away, grinned, and added, "You can look at the checks now." She winked and blended into the crowd.

Neither man did as she told them until Melinda was totally out of sight. "Which one do you like better?" Evan asked as he slid his check out of the envelope. He looked down for the first time and added, "They both make my insides feel funny."

Cass closed his envelope and slid it into his front pocket. He picked up his carry-on bag and said, "You've never been more right. Let's catch this plane and get home. We've got lots of stuff to figure out."

The flight was long and uneventful. That night, they were on the back porch, sipping Miller Lites and staring at the checks. They had tons of work to do on Dare Ya, but once again, they agreed that they'd spend the night talking about the near future and planning how to proceed. The next day would bring back work.

Evan spoke first, asking, "Okay, Trigger, what's the plan?"

"We're going to have to find a building and start hiring a staff. I know a guy I can call. He would be a great second in command in the tech department."

"Where do you want to find this building, Big Guy? In Dallas?" Evan asked with a sideways glance.

"It's as good a place as any, I guess," Cass told him as he opened a bag of pretzels. "Why? What do you have in mind?"

"I've been thinking; and if any place is as good as any other, why don't we make it Vegas? I'm bored to tears here. There are just so many cowboys and western themes I can take in my night life."

"Vegas does have a better night life. I bet we could get some kick-ass dares going out there. I'm good with that." They toasted beer bottles, and Cass added, "You could go out there and find us a place. I'll deal with things here for a few days."

"We'll go see B in the morning and get some accounts set up, and then I'd better head on out there. The sooner the better, I'd say," Evan said with a grin.

"Just find a good building and keep the partying to a minimum until you do."

Evan laughed and said, "I'm hurt."

"You will be if you screw this up. I'll get this house sold while you're gone. I think we can make a small profit, even with all the work left to do."

"Did you forget that we're millionaires now, Trigger?" Evan asked. "Give this place away. Who cares? Just get that tech guy and about five or six more people lined up. Dare Ya needs help."

"I like that. The first Disciple can have it."

"What? Did you drink too much? I was making a joke," Evan scolded his friend. "This place is worth a hundred and fifty grand, easy. The first Disciple is too simple to get that much. Hell, we're not Bill Gates yet, Trigger,"

"We'll think of something while we get everything else going. Maybe we can give it away for charity on one of the dares on that side of the site."

"Hold that thought," Evan said, trying to change the subject and make Cass forget about giving the house away. "I need a beer, and I've got to piss."

****

Cass sat for a moment and decided to call his parents with the news of their newfound riches. He pulled his phone from his pocket, dialed the number, and waited as it rang. His mother answered on the second ring, saying, "Hello."

"Hey, Mom. How are y'all doing?"

"Matthew, did you forget to block that little video of yours down here or what? Tina at the post office said she saw it yesterday."

"Uh, yeah about that, Mom, I can't really do that. Sorry, but I have some fantastic news that'll make you forget all about Tina seeing it," Cass tried to explain.

His mother, however, cut him off before he could tell her the news. She yelled, "Then take it off, now! I will not be the laughing stock of this town again. It was bad enough when you pissed off the sheriff and went to prison. Don't make me suffer through the humiliation one more time, son."

"Mom, slow down and listen, will you?" Cass proceeded to tell her the story of the last week, right up to the two-million dollar checks.

Cass' mother was speechless as Evan returned to the porch and handed Cass his beer. Cass mouthed "Mom" and pointed to the phone.

Evan leaned over and yelled, "Hey, Mrs. Cassidy." Then, to Cass, he asked, "Did you tell her the news?"

Cass nodded yes. He said into the phone to his mother, "Mom, are you still there? Where's Pop?"

"You're serious this time, aren't you, Matthew?" she asked, sounding a little more upset. "You told me last time that no one would see that God-awful video."

"Yes, mother, this time it's true. I swear. Now we want everyone to see it. Give me a few months and I'll buy you and Pop a new house anywhere you want. Then everyone in that town can kiss our asses." Cass had had a bad taste in his mouth for the hypocrites in his hometown ever since they'd stood by and allowed him to be railroaded. The sheriff was even reelected.

"Watch your language, young man. We don't need a new house, Matthew. We just want you to be happy."

"Well Mom," Cass said. "I am very happy; trust me. I love you, and tell Pop I love him too."

"We love you too. Come see us soon."

"I will, Mom." Cass hung up the phone. Then, to Evan, he added, "We're the talk of the post office."

"At least it's not because of some wanted poster."

# Chapter 23

The next morning, Cass and Evan left the house early. They decided the night before to get Evan to the airport before Cass went to see Brian. On the way, Evan asked, "So where do you want your apartment? On the strip?"

Cass answered, "Just find us a building for Dare Ya: about twenty offices with a big enough space for all the computer equipment, like we talked about. I'll find myself a place to live or I'll sleep in my office for a while. Maybe I should be the one going to Vegas; this may be too much for you."

"I'll handle it; don't worry your pretty little head over it, Trigger," Evan said. He glanced toward Cass in the driver's seat and added, "On second thought, it isn't that little."

"Just follow the plans and look for exactly what we talked about."

They arrived at the departures drop off lane in front of the terminal. Evan opened the SUV's door and stepped out. "I got this one, Trigger, but neither of us will ever sleep in a damn office. We're rich!" he yelled as he slammed the door.

Cass shook his head and pulled out into traffic. He had a lot to do. The main thing was to get the two checks put into accounts so that he and Evan would have access to their money as soon as possible. Evan would need a way to pay a deposit and rent for a building when he found one.

**\*\*\*\***

The man who once called himself Mr. Felsner was waiting for the phone to ring. Unlike the nervous anticipation he'd instilled into the warden over six months before, he was completely at ease.

He'd followed his adversaries' every move since Warden Cobin botched his previous plan for revenge. The man, going by the code name Director, had formulated a simple but flawless plan to end his wait. During all of his watching, the Director learned everything about the friend of his enemy, and he grew to loathe him just as much. His scheme would be the end for Matthew Cassidy and Evan Masters.

The disposable cell phone on his desk finally rang. He pushed the button to answer the call. "Go."

The man on the other end of the phone said, "It's Jenkins. Their truck just left the house. We'll be all set up when they come back."

Jenkins was one of his own. No local yokel would screw up this attempt. He handpicked Jenkins and another man to travel to Dallas and carry out the mission. The way he saw it, the two men in his group were far more capable than every Dixie Aryan on that piss-ant prison farm in Backwoods, Mississippi. He had told them as much when the man left seeking their targets.

"Excellent; while they're gone and you're waiting, go in and trash the house."

The subordinate asked, "If you say so, Boss, but shouldn't we just lay low and wait, the way we planned?"

"I must've gotten confused somewhere along the line. Is this a democracy, all of a sudden?" the Director asked. Before his man in Dallas could answer, he continued, "Hell no, it's not! I want everything those two care about to fall apart, just the way it was done to me. Is that understood?"

Jenkins knew better than to contradict the Director more than once. He wondered how trashing the house would affect two dead men, but he let the thought pass unspoken. Instead, he said, "Understood boss; we'll handle that and be in place for the rest of the plan."

The Director said, "See that you are." He hung up the phone and returned it to his desk. Time for more waiting.

****

Cass met with Brian, who agreed to handle the checks and set up everything. Cass offered him the position over at the legal department at Dare Ya. Cass asked him to move to Las Vegas and over-see everything, especially at the beginning.

Brian answered Cass by saying, "For something like that, I'd need two or three other lawyers just to get started."

"I'll leave that to you. E is already out there, and it'd probably be good if you joined him. I want you to be there when this thing takes off."

Brian agreed and told Cass he would leave for Vegas as soon as he could. The team had increased to three, with a few more to be added to the legal division soon. Cass went by the realtor's office and told her to put the house on the market as is. The Dare Ya team would have to come up with another way to support the charity side of the operation. Then, on the way back to the house, he phoned his tech friend Al Hollister and set up an early supper to meet that afternoon. Hopefully Al would have some recommendations for other technical employees who would want to come to Dare Ya.

Cass turned into the neighborhood. It was in a subdivision far enough from Dallas to be considered rural.

Most people worked in the city, so they were gone at that time of the afternoon.

Cass pulled up to a stop sign on one of the deserted corners and came to a stop. He glanced in the rearview mirror and saw an old Toyota pick-up truck in the distance. He figured it was merely someone's lawn crew. Then he took his right foot from the brake and slowly accelerated through the intersection. As he was turning right, the Toyota behind him ran into the rear of his Tahoe. It was not an earth-shattering crash, but Cass could tell that there would be damage.

He continued through the crossroads and pulled to the right side of the street. "Damn," he said to the dashboard as he opened the door and climbed from the SUV.

The guy driving the Toyota pulled over behind him, and as he jumped from his truck, he said, "I'm so sorry. I just looked down for a second." He rounded the driver's side door and made his way toward the hood.

Cass walked in between the two trucks and looked down at the damage. "It's just busted a taillight and dented the bumper a little. Nothing major."

"I've got my insurance card right here in my wallet," the guy said as he reached around to his back pocket.

Instead of a wallet, he came around with a semi-automatic pistol and leveled it at Cass's chest. Cass slowly raised his hands and said, "Hell, man, I said it ain't that bad, but it's about to get a whole lot worse for one of us."

As Cass calculated a way to turn the tables on the man in front of him, he heard the distinct sound of a revolver cocking just behind his left ear. The second man said,

"That's very true. Sorry to say, but it'll be you who has the worst end, mister."

Cass knew from his training that the best time to make an escape was in the first few moments immediately following capture. The kidnappers were on a small high because they perceived they'd won, and they assumed that the prisoner was dejected about being caught. This caused their guard to naturally go down ever so slightly, at the beginning of the abduction.

The man from the Toyota, in front of Cass, lowered his weapon, glanced around the neighborhood, and said, "Where's your friend?"

The question took Cass by surprise because he'd assumed that he was in a random carjacking. He did not let his curiosity show. Instead, he decided he would trade his opportunity for escape to see if he could get a little information as to why they were asking about Evan. Cass said, "Friend? I don't really have any friends. I'm more of a loner, actually. You must have me confused with someone else."

The man behind him punched Cass in the ribs. Cass barely flinched as he slightly lowered his elbows and half turned to gain a glimpse of the guy behind him. The assailant said, "Cut the shit, tough guy," and hit Cass across the ear with the barrel of his handgun.

Cass spun his head with the blow and then turned back again before saying, "Easy, man. What did E do? Sleep with one of your wives or something?"

The man that caused the wreck looked over Cass's shoulder at his partner. He had his pistol hanging loosely by his side as he said, "We'll get the other one when he comes back to the house." Then he made eye contact with

Cass and added, "Get in the truck, asshole." He nodded toward the Toyota beside him.

Cass took a slight step backward so he had both of his potential captures in his sight. The man with the revolver aimed at Cass's head looked to his partner, as if asking what he should do. When he looked away, Cass saw his best chance to make his move. The first rule of a hostage situation: make your escape attempt early, followed closely by rule number two: never go anywhere with the captors.

Cass leaned to the right and toward the weapon in his face. The barrel was over his shoulder when the bad guy pulled the trigger. Cass used the fact that his hands were raised to grab the aggressor's wrists, and he twisted hard—very hard. The man let out a small yelp as his wrist broke, and the pistol fell from his grasp.

Cass then pulled the injured man to his body, using the man's broken appendage to lead the way. Cass wrapped his free arm around the guy's neck and squeezed tightly as the weapon finally made contact with the ground. Cass spun the man so that they were both facing the Toyota driver. Cass used the assailant's body as a shield.

The driver finally reacted, raised his own pistol, and fired twice. The first round shattered the back glass of the Tahoe, and the second caught Cass's human shield in the ribs just below his heart. He instantly went limp in Cass' arms. Cass controlled the man's fall and went down with him, making sure to keep the man in front in case the other guy decided to fire again. The gunshot victim and Cass went down in between the two trucks, and Cass snatched the revolver from the asphalt and rolled to the curb. He landed in the grass on his knees and raised the weapon to return fire.

The driver stood behind the hood of his truck and shot at the spot where he'd last seen Cass. The pistol in Cass's hand was cocked, so he took aim and shot the man once just under his arm, and again in the side of his face. Cass had not been trained to fire warning shots at an enemy who was trying to kill him.

He stayed in the ready position with the pistol leading the way as he went around the rear of the Toyota. Cass made his way around to the man he'd shot, and kicked the semiautomatic away from the guy's unmoving hand. Cass squatted and checked the man for a pulse. His jaw was barely attached to his head, but Cass figured it was better to be safe than sorry.

He found no pulse; the man was dead. There was no time for remorse. In a kill or be killed situation, Cass had always done what needed doing. This was no exception. He stood and slowly went toward the hood of the truck where the other would-be kidnapper had gone down. Again, Cass crouched and felt for a pulse. There was a slight heartbeat.

Cass pulled his cell phone from his pocket and dialed 911. He placed the pistol on the ground and started performing basic first aid as he told the dispatcher he needed an ambulance and the police. He gave her his location. He did not care if the man lived or died, but Cass thought the only way to get some answers would be to save the prick's life. Almost as soon as he hung up with the dispatcher, a police cruiser turned through the intersection and two cops jumped out.

The officers drew their service weapons and ordered Cass to stand and put his hands behind his head. He did so as he said, "While one of you sorts all this out, the other one better tend to that guy, or he may not make it." Cass pointed to the ground between the two trucks with his elbow as he stepped up onto the curb once more.

The police officer who had been driving re-holstered his weapon and began first aid. His partner went to Cass and put handcuffs on the big man's wrists. The cop searched Cass and put him in the back seat of his squad car. Cass tried to explain that he was the victim, but the officer was not listening. He leaned in through the rear door and said, "We'll get this all sorted out; but for now, you're on the sidelines."

Cass hated the way law enforcement talked, but he waited anyway. The ambulance arrived, and two more patrol cars came with it. The paramedics took over the emergency treatment, loaded the guy on a gurney, and put him in the back of the ambulance. As they sped away, the two officers returned to their cruiser. The one in the passenger's seat twisted back and said to Cass, "We've got to take you to the station and let a detective talk this over. One man's dead and the other's knocking on the door: this is some serious shit here."

"Those pricks tried to carjack me or something. I'm the damn victim here."

"That may be so, but a detective will have to figure out exactly what happened. Now just sit tight."

Cass rode the rest of the way without another word. He saw no need in trying to explain himself to the two security guards with guns. He would wait for a detective to hear his story. When the three men arrived at the police station, the cops escorted Cass to some kind of interrogation room and handcuffed him to a metal chair which had been bolted to the floor. "The detective will be in here in a little bit. I'll try to bring you a Coke or something in a minute."

Cass assumed he was being lied to, and it turned out that he was exactly right. After four hours in the same chair, a man in a wrinkled suit finally came through the door. Cass said, "I've got to piss."

"All right, Mr. Cassidy, we'll get to that. It seems to be your lucky day."

"How the hell is that?" Cass asked. "Two jackasses attacked me, and I get arrested. What's so lucky about that?"

The detective leaned over and unlocked the handcuffs on Cass's wrists. Cass rubbed his arms and looked up, waiting for the cop to answer his questions. The man said, "Well, there just happened to be a house across the street from all of the action this afternoon, and in that house, an old lady was watching her soap opera. She heard the fender-bender and looked out the window." The cop paused, but Cass did not respond. Cass waited for the detective to continue. "She says those thugs were attempting to rob you, just like you told my officers."

"Isn't that good to hear; because I have no doubt that without her statement y'all would've found some way to pin this on me," Cass said bitterly.

"Mr. Cassidy," the officer interrupted. "We would've gotten to the truth one way or the other. Now, do you have any clue as to why those men may have targeted you?"

"They wanted my wallet and the Tahoe. That's all they told me." Cass still had a problem trusting law enforcement personnel, so he left out the part about the thieves asking about Evan. "Did the second one make it?"

"He's in the ICU, but the ER doc says he'll probably pull through."

"Well, he can be thankful that his friend shot him and not me. Now when the hell can I get out of this place?"

"I'll have someone in traffic take you to the impound yard to pick up your vehicle."

Cass rode with the patrol officer and retrieved the Tahoe from the impound lot. He looked at the shattered back glass, but decided to wait until the following day to have it fixed. He wanted nothing more than to get home, have a beer, and call Evan so they could try to figure out what the hell happened.

When Cass walked through the small foyer, he stepped on sheetrock chunks. He continued through the house and took in the destruction of every room. Mirrors were shattered, doors had holes in them, sinks were smashed, and almost every appliance had been beaten to a useless heap. The refrigerator door was torn from its hinges, so Cass reached straight in, grabbed an overturned Bud Light, and moved the remaining four beers to the freezer. "At least the beer's still good," he mumbled.

He walked onto the back porch, plopped down into a lawn chair, and dialed Evan's cell number. Evan answered on the second ring, saying, "Damn, Trigger, I just got here. Give me some slack, would you?"

"I hear ya, but your blowing off work isn't why I'm calling. We have a situation here that I don't understand at all."

Evan could tell the seriousness of the circumstances by the tone of his friend's voice. He used the same tone when he asked, "What's up, Big Guy? It can't be that bad."

Cass told Evan about the attempted carjacking and how he'd killed one of the men. He said he would try to get to hospital the next day to see if the other guy was awake. Maybe he could shed some light on it.

Evan asked, "So why don't you think it was just two random dumbasses who messed with the wrong Devildog?"

"They wanted to know where you were, and they had trashed the house before they ambushed me," Cass said, and took a swig of his beer.

"What did the cops say about the house?" Evan asked.

Cass thought about the question and answered, "I didn't even call them back. What are they going to do anyway? Push some papers? I mean, they've got enough to nail the guy that's in the hospital without adding vandalism."

"True. Plus, I wouldn't want to talk to a bunch of pigs, either. It's your call, Trigger," Evan said, trying to lighten the mood.

"I'm going to clean up a little. I'll call you tomorrow. Keep your head down and your eyes open."

"You too," Evan said. "And calm down, Jarhead. I'm telling you, it was just random. I mean, come on, man: who could hate us?" He laughed as he hung the phone.

Cass tried to remember exactly what the two kidnappers had said. *Perhaps it had been just a chance act of violence*, Cass thought. They could have known about Evan from being in the house.

****

As Cass sat on his patio contemplating the actions of the day, a pretty nurse walked down the hall of the ICU. She stepped at the sentry posted outside the door of room twenty-one. "Can I get you anything?" she asked as the man made a lame attempt to glance at her chest without being caught.

"A cup of coffee would be wonderful. Thank you."

"Let me check on the patient and I'll run down and get you a cup," she said as she slipped through the door.

As soon as the mechanism clicked behind her, she pulled a syringe from her front pocket. She walked to the side of the bed and injected the clear liquid into the unconscious man's IV port. The nurse put the cap back on the needle and returned the rig back to her pocket.

When she walked back out into the hall, she said to the guard, "He's still asleep, but everything looks fine. I'll run down and get that cup of coffee for you. I'll be right back." She turned and strolled down the hall toward the nurse's station and the elevators.

She rode the elevator down to the lobby and exited through the front entrance of the hospital. The nurse walked to a waiting car and climbed inside. The man behind the wheel handed her a cell phone. "It's done, Director," she said as she pulled the wig from her head and fluffed her hair.

"It better be, Constance; you know my tolerance level for failure is very low."

"It is, sir. Don't think about it again," she said as the car she pulled into traffic.

At the same time, the man in room twenty-one convulsed violently and flat lined. The guard at the door sat in the hall as nurses and doctors rushed into the room with a crash cart. While they all tried desperately to save their patient, the young officer walked into the room. He looked around at the medical staff, searching for the cute brunette who was supposed to bring him a cup of coffee. She was not in the room, and he would never receive the coffee she promised.

# Chapter 24

## A Month Later

Evan found a nice building of the outskirts of Las Vegas. It had eighteen offices and a huge space on the lower floor: exactly what they needed for the computer servers. Brian and Al moved to the desert and were still in the process of hiring new staff members. Al worked with Cass and Evan for long hours to get Dare Ya caught up. They added two more tech guys the first day because they saw that keeping up would be a massive job.

Cass built the Dare Ya Charity pages while the others graded the dares and videos that had piled up. It was a lot of work for everyone, but they fell into a routine. Dare Ya was still growing. One day, as Evan worked on the videos, the phone on his desk rang. He had yet to hire a secretary, so he answered it, saying, "Hello, Evan Masters, how may I help you?"

"Evan, its Melinda," she said from her office in New York. "I see you boys are catching up. I know it's a busy time, but can you and Cass get away for a few days?"

"I'm not sure. What's up, Mel? You and Sully want to take us on vacation?"

"Not quite. I've got a few interviews lined up. The morning news and talk shows, a conversation on MTV, and then I have Conan O'Brian lined up for the afternoon slot. I need you guys here before five in the morning."

"I thought Conan was out in California someplace."

"He's doing a special three-day gig in New York City, and I booked you guys on the closing night. This is a big deal, trust me."

"I'm texting Cass to get him over to my office now. I'll fill him in, and we'll catch a flight tonight," he told her as he took out his cell phone.

"I'll meet you at the airport; just text me the itinerary."

"We'll just catch a cab. It's already after two here; so what's that - like four something over there? There's no telling when we'll get there."

Melinda said, "That's okay. I'm a night owl, so send me the flight number and arrival time, and I'll see you guys then."

"Okay, see you tonight. Then you and Sully can fly back out here with us and see the new Dare Ya Headquarters."

"I'll tell him about the invitation. You guys have a good flight," she said as she hung up the phone.

Cass walked into Evan's office about the time his friend hung up the phone, and Evan filled him in on the interviews. Evan then called Cass's secretary and told her to book the flights. Cass called Al and put him in charge of everything while they were away.

****

Melinda was waiting for them when their plane touched down in New York only fifteen minutes behind schedule. She took them to their hotel—not the Trump International on this trip; but nice, just the same. It was late, so the three had a few drinks in the lounge.

After the waitress brought everyone their drinks and Evan a cigar, Melinda said, "I talked to Brian the other day. He told me the charity side was up and running. I checked it out, and it's nice."

Cass took a drink and responded, "Thanks; we think it'll be a huge success. You came up with a winner on that one."

The three had been nurturing their friendship over the phone for the last five weeks. Any-time one of the founders had an idea or wanted to add a new employee to the Dare Ya team, he called and told Melinda about it. After the first few times, she told them that it was not necessary and that the company was their baby. Melinda explained to them that they should run it the way they saw fit.

Cass and Evan both knew they had the power to do as they pleased with Dare Ya, but any excuse to call Melinda was welcomed. She was very insightful and glad to give suggestions about changes they were making. She visited the site numerous times every day.

"I just put a small piece in an already-brilliant puzzle." Melinda pushed Cass' shoulder, almost causing him to spill his bourbon and Coke. "But I'm not going to puff your heads up any bigger than they already are. Do you both still like Vegas?"

"I do," Evan answered. "Cass, not so much. The damn headquarters could be on the moon and he wouldn't care. He hardly even leaves the office. I mean, I'm single-handedly spreading Dare Ya's name all over the city."

"That's right," Cass told Melinda. "One bleached blond at a time. I wouldn't be surprised if four out of five of those girls could even *spell* Dare Ya."

"That hurt, Trigger," Evan said. Then he puffed his cigar and added, to Melinda, "If he'd get out on the town and saw the girls he's referring to in the surf shorts I gave them, with Dare Ya across the backsides, then he'd appreciate all the PR work I've done."

They all laughed aloud, and Melinda said, "I'm sure we would, E. Your service is commendable."

For a few minutes, they sat in comfortable silence watching the bar's patrons mingle. Then Evan said, with a completely straight face, "By the way, Mel, I brought you a pair of those shorts, just in case you wanted to do a little extra advertising."

Cass almost chocked on his Maker's Mark, but Melinda just chuckled. She patted Evan on the back of his forearm and said, "I think I'll pass this time, but if we're ever on a hundred-foot yacht drinking daiquiris, I'm your girl."

The three friends and coworkers had a few more drinks and talked about the early morning that was approaching quickly. They agreed that since the next day would be their first time in front of television cameras, they should call it a night earlier than usual.

****

The following morning at five AM, Evan and Cass were nervous before their first interview with a national news show. The interviewer asked broad questions and focused on Dare Ya's charity pages, which Cass had gone live with, two weeks previously. The addition of the charity side was a hit and a feel-good story for the news media.

All day it was practically the same. Though some interviews focused on funny videos posted and others on the fast growth of the site, all of them wanted to know about the two friends who had started such a successful website. By the fifth interview, they were on autopilot. Melinda was with them every step of the way, giving encouragement and nudging interviewers to ask questions that would be good for publicity. When they took a break and were having lunch, she asked, "So do you have a dare planned for Conan?"

Evan answered, "We're way ahead of you on that one. We came up with a good idea on the plane. I figure we'll take him by surprise and just spring it on him after the interview."

"What is it?" she asked.

"You'll have to wait and see," Cass said with a mischievous smile.

"We wouldn't want you to give anything away," he winked and added. Evan excused himself. They had a little over an hour until their next interview, and he had some things to set up before Conan's show later in the afternoon.

# Chapter 25

At the Conan O'Brian Show, they were waiting just off stage with Melinda when the broadcast started and Conan went through his opening monologue. Then he introduced the founders of Dare Ya, and they walked onto stage to the cheers of the audience. Each man shook hands with the host and sat in the guest chairs.

Conan cut right to it and said, "Okay, let's look at the video that kicked off all of the national hype."

The crowd cheered again, and the video started. Cass, Evan, and Conan watched on a monitor positioned on Conan's desk. It showed Cass climbing into a hot air balloon basket with a platform extending from one side. Evan was on the ground, filming. The balloon pilot was also filming from inside the basket, giving two angles of the same shot.

Cass and the pilot started their ascent as Cass followed the man's instructions on how to put the bungee cord onto his feet. Before he began putting on the rope, the camera cut to a third view that showed both Evan on the ground filming and Cass rising into the air. This new camera angle was from somewhere off in the distance.

The video cut back to Evan's point of view as the balloon kept rising. Evan said, "That's high enough. Come on, Trigger—jump." The dirigible did not stop its climb. Evan zoomed in tighter on the balloon's platform as Cass shuffled out of the basket.

Cut to the pilot's video. Cass was on the edge, stripped down to nothing but a backpack. He raised his arms above his head, counted backward from five, and jumped. The recording went back to Evan's shot and showed Cass falling to earth as the huge rubber band started to arrest the big man's decent. Evan said, "Too high, Jarhead. This won't be right." As he finished the last sentence, the cord went taut; but instead of rebounding his comrade up, like Evan expected, it snapped at Cass's ankles.

Cut to the camera filming Evan's reaction. Evan screamed, "No!" While he drew out the scream, he dropped his rented camera and ran toward the place where it looked like Cass would land. Then, from the pilot's camera, the audience watched Cass freefall for a few seconds before a parachute exploded out of the pack at the last instant. Cass yelled, "Whoa! What a rush!"

The camera filming Evan caught the look of sheer terror slide from his face as disbelief took its place. It panned to catch the final thirty feet of Cass's slow, nude fall. He landed close to where Evan stood, slack jawed, and Cass was still yelling about how much fun the jump was.

The video ended, the lights on Conan's stage went back up, and Conan said, "Matthew, tell us about what we just watched."

"Well," Cass said, "we had Dare Ya ready to go, and needed our first dare. E came up with the idea of me bungee jumping nude, and he dared me, so I had to do it."

"But he didn't know about the cord snapping, did he?" Conan asked.

"I figured I'd get a little instant payback for him making me jump nude," Cass answered, laughing with the crowd. "I had a friend of ours get another camera, hide in the tree line, and film E's reaction."

Evan shook his head, looked from the crowd to Conan, and said, "It happened so fast that I didn't have time to think, but when that chute opened, it hit me that I'd been set up."

"Well, the response and that look on your face made the video, that's for sure," Conan said, laughing. Then, to the crowd he added, "If not for that, it would've just been a big naked guy jumping from a balloon. Right, guys?" This made the studio audience boom with laughter.

"Yeah, I get that a lot," Evan responded over the hooting.

"I've actually filled out a membership to Dare Ya, myself," Conan said after the laughter died down. "There are plenty of other crazy videos to watch that go along with the one we've seen. I could watch that stuff for hours."

"That's true, Conan, but we don't want you to just watch the recordings of other peoples' dares," Evan told the host. "We want you and your audience to be active participants."

Cass finished his friend's thought. "That's right. Take a dare, and film it."

Evan started again, "As a matter of...."

Conan cut him off midsentence. "I think I'll do that, Evan. As a matter of fact, I want to propose a dare to you."

The crowd roared as a curtain rolled back and a side stage slid forward. On it, there was a ten-foot ladder and a small blue swimming pool filled with a bright red substance. At the near side of the stage, was a Chinese changing screen. Cass and Evan exchanged a look of confusion as they stood and walked in the direction of the props.

Conan stood with them, and as they walked to the side stage, he said, "Matt we've all seen you in your birthday suit, and as much as some of my female viewers would love to see it again, I've got a little something set up for Evan tonight."

The crowd howled as Conan pointed to the screen and added, "I dare you, Evan, to go change into your costume and belly flop from that ladder down into the pool of Jell-O."

Evan shook his head in dejection and walked to the veil. Cass said to Conan, as his friend left, "I knew I liked you for some reason," which made the spectators laugh even louder.

"Wait until you see his outfit," Conan said chuckling.

A few moments after disappearing behind the shroud, Evan emerged wearing nothing but a furry, zebra-print G-string. Every muscle in his body was flexed as he tried to smile at the crowd. He climbed the steps, but before he jumped, he yelled down, "Now I don't feel so bad about my dare for you, Red." With that, he leapt from the top of the ladder and plummeted into the Jell-O, belly first.

The smack made a loud pop, knocked the wind from Evan's lungs, and splattered Jell-O over the first two rows in the audience. Evan stood trying to catch his breath as he took a towel from a stage hand who had walked out to help him get to his feet. He wiped his face and chest before he wrapped the towel around his waist to hide the skimpy underwear. His whole body was bright red—not from the dye, but from the impact.

Cass said, "I'll give you an eight, Fly Guy. Your landing was a little off."

Evan rubbed his chest to soothe the stinging as he said, "Piss on you, Cass." He looked at Conan and added, "Now I've got one for you, Red."

Conan was laughing, but instantly stopped when he saw the smirk grow on Evan's face. He told Evan, "That wasn't my idea. Your publicist suggested it."

Evan looked backstage and said, "Good one Mel. I'll get you later." Then he turned back to Conan, pointed to a cute Asian woman rising from her seat in the front row, and said, "This, Mr. O'Brian, is Yang, and she is considered an expert in her field."

Evan paused for affect. Conan saw that he was not going to continue, so he responded, "I hate to ask, but what exactly is that field?

Yang left her spot in the audience and came to Conan's side. Evan said, "She is a tattoo artist and piercer. I dare you, Conan, to pierce your nipples—right here, right now."

The crowd roared so loudly that Cass thought someone must be adding noise electronically, but the audience and crew members were responsible for the sound. Conan asked, "Are you serious? We'd better take a break while I think this one over." The television audience was taken to commercials while Conan looked from Yang to Cass to Evan. "Come on guys, I can't do that," he said.

"It no hurt bad," Yang said, "and grow closed no time."

"I cannot believe I'm agreeing to this," he said. He shook hands with Evan and put his head down, looking at the floor. The same stagehand that had brought Evan his towel brought out a high stool and a small table.

As the director counted down and the cameras began rolling, Conan sat and removed his shirt. Yang placed a bag of piercing instruments on the table, pulled out a pair of latex gloves, and withdrew some fresh needles from her bag. She removed them from their plastic wrappers, sat them down, and rubbed Conan's left nipple with an alcohol swab. He jumped a little and said, "That's cold, Yang."

She put a piece of cork against Conan's nipple and said, "Be very still, Mr. O'Brian."

He closed his eyes and flinched as she rammed the needle through. He let out a small cry when she removed the needle and wiped the puncture with another alcohol pad. Yang then pulled a hoop ring through the hole and said, "You can take that out if you no like." Everyone in the room cheered as he stroked his chest and looked at the shiny new piece of jewelry.

"Man, that sucked," Conan said. "But at least it's over. What Degree was that?"

"The dare was to pierce your *nipples*. That's plural, Red. One more to go," Cass told him, like he was the referee. "When you're done, we'll say it's a Third Degree Dare; but just barely."

"You guys are too much," Conan said. "Let's get this over with. Go ahead, Yang, before I change my mind."

She went through the exact same process on Conan's right nipple. This got the same reaction from him as well as his audience. Conan closed the show sitting on the stool, without a shirt, between Evan, wrapped in the towel, with Cass, the only one still fully dressed. "Let's thank the founders of Dare Ya, Matt Cassidy and Evan Masters, for being here tonight. It has been very memorable, but I doubt you'll ever see them here on this stage again. It's just too damn painful." With that, the crowd erupted in yells and laughs as the lights faded.

When the crowds were gone and several autographs were signed, Conan joined Cass and Evan in their dressing room. "Kick-ass show, guys," Conan told them while he gingerly massaged his nipples through his shirt. "Matt, we owe you a good dare. You both'll have to come back soon. I have a feeling this is going to be one of my highest-rated shows."

"Call me Cass, O'Brian. We'd be glad to come back, and if you're ever out in Vegas, look us up."

Conan said, "Now that sounds like a wild night. I'm in."

The three exchange private cell phone numbers and said their good-byes. Melinda met them in the hall, where she had been on her phone. "That was Sully. Research says the numbers are off the charts. Brilliant show."

Evan responded, "I don't feel so brilliant. My damn stomach and chest are still burning. Let's go get a drink."

"I agree," Melinda said. "Let's go celebrate a great day. It turned out better than I could've imagined."

The two friends took their cell phones from their pockets to turn the ringers back on as they left the studio and went out to a waiting car. Both phones showed multiple missed calls. Evan said, "Looks like we're pretty popular tonight. I'm just leaving mine off."

"Me too," Cass said. "I've had enough of the celebrity lifestyle for one day."

# Chapter 26

Cass, Evan, and Melinda went to dinner and had much more than one drink. They left the restaurant and went to a dance club to continue their festivities. At three-thirty in the morning, Evan and Cass stumbled through the lobby of their hotel, where Melinda and her driver had dropped them off. Evan had picked up a blonde bombshell in the club, and she was leading him to the elevators. The receptionist called out to Cass before he could join them. Evan's hand disappeared under the drunken bimbo's shirt as the night clerk yelled, "Mr. Cassidy, Mr. Cassidy!"

"There you go, Trigger. She's actually pretty hot. Grrrr," Evan said as he and his lady friend let the elevator doors close. The last thing Cass heard from the elevator was their giggling.

He turned to the front desk, staggered to it, propped his elbows upon it, and said to the clerk, "That's me, darling. What exactly can I do for you?"

"Umm, yes, sir." She blushed as the big man smiled at her. "You have eight messages from a Mr. Hollister. The last one came less than five minutes ago."

She handed Cass a stack of messages, and each was marked urgent. Cass pulled one from the middle of the stack and closed one eye to read it. It said *—Cass, call the office as soon as you get this. Very weird stuff here!-*

Cass straightened up, lost some of his alcohol-induced buzz, and headed for his room. He turned, smiled at the clerk, and said, "Thank you very much, sweetheart. Have a good night."

She said, "You do the same, Mr. Cassidy." Then she watched him stumble across the lobby.

On the way up to his room, Cass read the rest of the messages from Al. Every one of them said roughly the same thing—that Al was at Dare Ya Headquarters and wanted a call immediately. Cass wondered why on earth Al was working so late. They had hired a couple of tech guys to go over emails and videos at night so the main staff could work normal hours.

Cass walked into his room, took off his shirt, collapsed on the bed, and speed dialed Dare Ya. On the second ring Al answered. "This better be you, Boss."

"It is. What's up, my nerdy friend?" Cass asked as he kicked off his shoes.

"Big problems here, Chief. A couple of hours after you and Evan were on Conan, the damn site crashed."

"Damn, we had that many hits?" Cass interrupted, sitting up in the bed. The room had started to spin. "Did you get it back up and running?"

"That's exactly what I figured it was, too: that we'd been overloaded by new members. I rushed in at the first call and went to work. I've got the site going again, but that's not the weird part."

"Come on, bud, it's four in the morning, and if you can't tell; I've had a little too much to drink. Spell it out for me, will you?" Cass asked, becoming a little frustrated.

"It's like we're under attack or something. Every time I fix one thing, something new goes wrong. Some guy who, calls himself The Director keeps hitting from different ISP's all over the world."

Assailing a computer system through different regions of the country or the world was a common practice for hackers. It helped such people avoid being located by the people who were looking for them. The practice made locating a hacker virtually impossible.

"Probably some nut who didn't like the show," Cass said. "Keep fending him off. Our plane leaves at nine this morning, and we'll be there by lunch. Hang in there, Big Al."

"Will do, Boss, but this guy's good."

"You're good, too. Just do what you can, and we'll boost security when I get back."

"Thanks. Make sure you sleep some of that off before you get home."

"Will do. Good job, Al. I knew you'd be a hell of an asset to Dare Ya," Cass said into his pillow as he lay back down and dozed off.

"That's the booze talking," Al said, but he could tell that his boss never heard him. Al hung up and went back to work.

****

At the same time Cass was dozing, the Director walked into a windowless room in a building on the back side of his compound. Constance stood over three young men at computer terminals. The Director stepped beside the shorthaired vixen and asked, "How's everything going?"

"We had them offline for a time, but they're back up now. I doubt we'll actually crash the site, but they know we're here."

"I would much rather destroy it completely," the Director told her.

Constance stroked the charm necklace around her neck and replied, "We understand that, sir, but their security is very good. We'll be like a hornet stinging an elephant."

"Walk with me, my dear." The Director turned and left the room, and his associate followed closely behind. They left the building and strolled through the crisp night air.

Before her boss could speak, Constance said, "Sir, if we could use our best people, I know we'd take down the site."

The Director kept walking, looking up at the starry sky. Finally, he responded, "There's not a doubt in my mind, but I don't want to involve our own people yet. We'll let those three novices inside pester the site for a while just to let Cassidy and Masters know that nothing is safe."

"Yes sir, but afterwards, what should we do with the computer geeks?"

"You need not ask, Constance. They have no ties to us, so let's ensure they never form any."

"Understood, Director. I'll handle it. There's no chance of exposure with those nerds. Even the security men didn't see them enter the compound."

"Excellent. Now make sure no one sees them leave. Actually, make sure no one sees them again, period."

"Not a problem," Constance said.

****

After what seemed like five minutes of sleep, the bedside phone rang with Cass's wake up call. He got out of bed, took a shower, dressed, and then packed his few belongings into his suitcase. He left his room and went to get Evan out of bed.

Cass banged on Evan's room door for a while before the blonde from the night before finally swung it inward. She was wearing a hotel robe that barely contained her large bust line. Cass squeezed past her without a word and went to the bed where Evan was still passed out. Evan was lying sideways across the bed, face down, wearing only one sock. Cass lifted the mattress and let it drop, bouncing Evan into the air. "Get up, E. We've got a plane to catch."

"It's not the last freaking plane ever going to Las Vegas, is it?" Evan asked into the comforter without moving.

"He promised we'd go shopping today," the bimbo said as she closed the door, "and I want to show him off to some of my friends at a party tonight."

"There'll be no shopping and definitely no partying tonight, sexy," Cass told her. "He'll have to take a rain check."

She put a pouty look on her face and started to speak. Cass never gave her the opportunity to do so because he said to Evan, "Come on, damn it. Al says we've got problems at Dare Ya; major problems."

At the mention of their website, Evan rolled over, rubbing his eyes. He exposed himself to the room, causing Cass to turn away quickly and curse aloud. After Evan rose and dressed, he kissed the blonde on his way out of the room and promised to call her as soon as he made it to Vegas.

When he and Cass were going through the lobby, Evan asked, "You didn't happen to get that chick's name, did you?"

"Nope, but does it really matter? You'll find one just like her by tomorrow."

"You're probably right. I just hate forgetting their names. It makes me feel dirty." To that, Cass had no reply; he could only smile and twist his head from side to side.

They barely made the flight and slept all the way back to the desert. Even with their sunglasses, the glare of the sand was murderous on their eyes. Cass had to drive the entire way from the airport to the office with one eye closed.

At Dare Ya Headquarters, Al greeted them in the lobby. He looked as exhausted as Evan and Cass felt. Both Evan and Al said "You look rough," at the same time.

Al kept speaking. "It's been a hell of a morning. This guy won't quit."

"He's still at it?" Cass asked as he made a beeline for the coffee pot in the receptionist's area.

Al followed behind him and answered, "He had us offline for thirty-seven minutes a few hours ago. Chad and I somehow wrestled control back from the asshole."

"All right, Al, take a breather. We had a nap on the plane, so let me see what I can figure out."

Cass drank coffee and battled The Director all afternoon. He would build a firewall, and his adversary would find a way around it. He wrote code to encrypt important data, and it was broken into in less than twenty minutes. Evan walked into Cass's office around four and said, "Listen, Trigger, I'm going to the apartment to crash. Al's asleep on the couch in his office, and he said to wake him up when you need a break."

"All right. I'll get him up in a little while. This son of a bitch is good, E, but I'm better. I'll have Dare Ya so freaking secure that the CIA'll be jealous, when I'm through."

"You do that, but let Al help. He's good too; don't forget: we only hire the best," Evan said, and then left the office, leaving Cass alone with his work.

Cass wrote code for over an hour until Al woke from his nap and walked into the office with two cups of fresh coffee. Al told him, "Here you go, Boss," and then asked, "How long have I been out? You made any progress yet?"

Cass took the coffee, leaned back in his chair, and said, "Thanks, Al. You weren't out that long. You needed the sleep, and I've kept this prick out. I'll have to bury the firewalls a little deeper, but I think we beat the bastard for now."

"You should've woken me earlier."

"Ah, I like a good challenge. Now you should be rested enough to take the next shift."

Cass proceeded to explain what security measures he had taken. He gave Al instructions on what he wanted done next and told him to keep an eye out for The Director. "I doubt he'll be back; he probably moved on to greener pastures and easier targets, but we'll keep a watch out for a while, just in case."

"Got ya Chief, I'm on it. Now go get some sleep; you look like hell," Al told Cass as he left his boss' office.

# Chapter 27

The Conan Show was very successful for Dare Ya, and prosperous for Sully's WI as well. In the ten weeks after the show, Dare Ya became so popular that Sully made his loan money back. Therefore, Cass and Evan were seeing their share of the profits. He told Melinda to get them more publicity, but she had already been working on it.

The Dare Ya Headquarters was a-buzz twenty-four hours a day. All of the offices were full, and some had to be occupied by multiple employees. Evan spent his days sending DD's to members and encouraging them to make the Disciple level. At least once a week, he and Cass traveled all over the country to attend "Dare Ya Bashes."

A Bash was simply a group of members getting together in a party atmosphere. Some Bashes showed videos from several of the Chapters present, while others actually filmed dares with the gala as a backdrop. Disciples presided over the festivities because they held all of the rank in the local Chapters. The founders never knew what to expect at a Bash, except fun.

Melinda lined up a get-together in Bel-Air for a group of celebrities at an after party for a movie premier. This one was called a Dare Ya Charity Bash, and it would help raise money for the new charity Evan and Cass had started called the Dare Ya Foundation. The party was set up at the leading actor's mansion and was scheduled to begin as soon as the movie was over.

Evan and Cass had to be at the airport to catch a private jet that one of the entertainers had sent for them. They were becoming recognizable figures themselves, with all the public appearances they had made in the past several months. Walking to the private gate, they were noticed by numerous people waiting on their own planes. They told Evan and Cass that they were members and loved the website. Fans received a handshake and picture with the founders, if they had their camera phones ready.

After the flight, they were dressed and on the red carpet greeting or being greeted by all kinds of famous people. The pair wore two of the nicest tuxedos in the group. Evan wore a tailored Brioni, just like the ones James Bond had made famous, and Cass decided on a Burberry that was more of a classical style. They walked past a group of reporters, and as the cameras flashed, one of the interviewers yelled, "Evan, Cass; where are your dates tonight?"

Cass ignored the question and spoke to one of the stars on the red carpet. Evan stopped and answered, "Would you take sand to the beach, hotshot? This room's going to be full of the hottest chicks on the planet, and since we're here stag, it's like a buffet to the two of us."

Evan turned away from the press corps and saw Cass entering the theater with two dazzling members of a rock band. They were dressed in very short skirts and wore tall go-go boots. They were all legs and gorgeous. Evan turned back to the reporter, winked, and asked, "See what I mean?"

The movie was a bore, so Evan and Cass spent most of the second half in the concession area with the two musicians. They were huge fans of Dare Ya. They had come to the premier because their latest single was on the sound-track. Cass was flirting with the dark-haired Trea while Evan talked to the blonde named Michelle.

When the movie finally concluded, everyone left the theater and headed for the after party. Evan and Cass arrived to the picture in one limo while Trea and Michelle had arrived in another. The seating arrangements were altered on the way to the after party, however. Cass rode in the ladies' limo with Trea, and Michelle got in with Evan.

The Bash was set up on the grounds of a huge manor. Tables were lined up, and a stage constructed on the back lawn. When the two couples at last entered through the main house, the estate was already abuzz. There was a band playing on the stage, and stars from every aspect of the entertainment community mingled.

Cass gave Trea a small kiss beside the stage just before he and Evan climbed the stairs. The music faded as Cass stepped to the microphone and spoke to the crowd. "We would like to thank everyone for coming to our first ever Dare Ya Charity Bash."

The crowd of celebrates gave a small round of applause. Then Evan pushed his way to the microphone and said, "I've been here five whole minutes and no one's offered me a single drink. Is that how y'all do it out here in Hollywood?"

The crowd cheered louder, and someone yelled to the stage, "Here's a beer, Evan; dare you to slam it!"

"Too easy, Nick," Evan said as he caught a flying bottle from an A-list actor. He opened it and drained the Sam Adam's Lager in one long swallow. "Not my favorite brand, but it's a start." He threw the empty bottle back to the star.

Cass squatted and took a beer from a passing waiter. He stood and added, "I see most of you read the invitation and have changed. Penguin suits and ten-thousand-dollar evening gowns won't quite cut it for a Dare Ya Bash, charity or not." He took off his tie and stuffed it into his front pocket. He took a drink and continued, "Most of our Bashes are about the dares and all are a very good time, but this one has the purpose of raising money for our new Dare Ya Foundation." The crowd clapped as Cass looked out at all of the renowned people. He shook his head, amazed that they even knew who he was. He pointed and said further, "If you'll direct your attention to the far end of the tree line, you'll see a couple of tarps hanging there. Travis, if you'll do the honors, go ahead and drop the curtains please." Cass's assistant at the other end of the lawn did as directed. He pulled a cord, and the three canvases fell to the ground, revealing a big, brown mechanical bull surrounded by thick cushions. Cass drew everyone's attention back to the stage when he said, "Here's the deal, people. We dare each of you to ride our bull for eight complete seconds. Guys, you'll be on a level twelve of fifteen, and the ladies will try it on level nine."

Evan leaned in again and said to a semi-stunned crowd, "If you fail to complete the ride, you have to make the ten thousand dollar check out to the Dare Ya Foundation." The pack of stars came alive with nervous laughter and murmurs throughout.

The eighty-five guests all protested the dare weakly as Cass and Evan lead them to Travis and the bull he operated. Evan gave him a wink and a nod as they shook hands. Then the first celeb walked across the padding to mount the bull. Evan had hired Travis to work the controls and instructed him not to let anyone stay on the entire eight seconds. He had told him, "Cheating is acceptable. It's for a good cause." Travis had no qualms with that because he loved to watch riders fly from his bull.

And fly, they did. Most were gone before four seconds ran from the big clock on Travis's control table. Everyone laughed as another would-be rodeo rider was dismounted in a heap. Only on three occasions did Travis actually have to turn the difficulty level higher than was agreed upon to throw the urban cowboy at the last instant.

The checks piled high, and in a little under two hours, Evan and Cass had raised $850,000 for their new foundation. Four celebs skipped the bull entirely and wrote a check without attempting a ride, and they received boos and jeers for their lack of effort. When all the willing guests had tried and failed, they all turned on the hosts. They yelled, "Your turn!" Then, "Can either of you two make it?" Someone else yelled, "Let's see you guys try!"

Evan looked at his friend and said, "You first, Trigger." Then, as Cass was taking his mount, he added to Travis, "Crank her wide open. Give his big ass a real ride." The crowd exploded as the bull started gyrating and the clock ticked down from eight. Cass made it down to three and a half seconds before his hand slipped and he was tossed high into the air. He landed hard on the back of his head. "*Ouch*," Evan said to himself.

Cass stood and shook off the pain from his horrendous dismount. He left the mat and said, "Your turn, Fly Guy. I almost had it." He pulled his wallet out from his hip pocket and wrote his check to the foundation. To the crowd, he added, "I can't let you guys make donations and me not."

They all shouted approval as he slammed the check on top of the stack.

Evan climbed on the back of the mechanical beast, grabbed a strong hold with his right hand, and locked his knees into the brute's flanks. He had not told Cass, but for a few weeks he had been going to a bar off the Vegas Strip to practice his bull riding.

The bull bucked, the clocked started, and the crowd roared. Evan tightened his grip and locked his knees rigid. The robotic monster spun and bounced as it tried to free itself of Evan's weight. The crowd was in a frenzy as the clock hit zero and the buzzer sounded. The bull slumped down in defeat and stopped moving. Evan stood on its back, raised his hands to the crowd's ovation, and did a back flip from the creature's haunches.

He strutted to the controller's table. Cass stood there shaking his head, not believing that his friend had just outdone everyone on the bull ride. Evan slapped Cass on the shoulder, pulled out his wallet, and proceeded to write a check of his own. He said to everyone in hearing range, "I can't be the only asshole not making a donation."

Michelle walked up, rubbing her hip where she had landed from her own fall from the beast. Evan leaned over and massaged the tender spot for her. She looked up into his eyes and he said, "I'm sure we can find somewhere around here where I can take your mind off of that hip. Maybe I can even give you a few pointers for your next ride." They kissed and disappeared in search of just such a spot.

****

Evan and Michelle returned to the party some time later and started making their way through the crowd. "Great ride, Evan," the lead actor from the movie premier told him as they passed.

They found Cass and Trea at the bar talking to some other guests. Evan asked Cass, "What's up, Trigger? What have we missed?"

Cass looked at the two, saw how Michelle's hair was a mess, and said with a smile, "Looks like nothing at all. I've held it down, but let's go thank everybody and wind this thing down."

They made their way to the stage and once again climbed the stairs. The group quieted as the two men stepped into the spotlight. Cass began, "We just want to thank everyone for your support tonight. Your donations will be greatly appreciated at the Dare Ya Foundation, and I hope like hell everyone had fun in the process."

The throng of stars cheered, and Evan did his usual lean in and was about to add to his friend's speech, but he was cut off by a familiar voice echoing through the PA system. The mystery voice said, "Not so fast, boys. The fun is just beginning."

Everyone in the crowd, including Evan and Cass, exchanged looks of wonder, trying to put a face to the voice. Then they turned to the opposite end of the stage to see Conan O'Brian walking from behind the stage curtain with a playful grin. The Hollywood royalty in the audience clapped and yelled as Conan added, "I believe I owe you two a little dare; especially you, Cassidy." With that, he raised his shirt to reveal a silver hoop dangling from each nipple. "Remember these?"

"Put those away; O'Brian, but I see you decided to keep the hardware," Cass laughed.

"Yeah, I did," Conan responded as he lowered his shirt and pointed at Cass. "But this isn't about me, Cassidy. It's about you."

Cass looked around the crowd and said, "What have you got in mind? This is a charity event, so it'll have to be worth my while."

"Oh, it will be," Conan said. He looked to the crowd and addressed them, adding, "A couple of weeks after these two made their famous, or rather infamous, appearance on my show, we had a little less recognizable gentleman on from Texas. Holt Colson was his name, and he's actually a fascinating fellow."

"Okay, O'Brian I know you love the spotlight; but get on with it already," Evan said, causing the crowd to cheer again. "What's the dare, Red?"

"I had sore nipples for a month. I will not be rushed." Conan smiled broadly.

The side of the patio met the driveway at one corner of the house. A big bearded man in a cowboy hat pushed a clear Plexiglas box, resembling a coffin, onto the back porch. Two more men followed, pulling wagons stacked with black boxes that had air holes in them. "Ah, hell," Cass said, turning to Evan. "This doesn't look good at all."

O'Brian answered, even though Cass had not asked a question. "No it doesn't, Matthew. Mr. Colson is a real life rattlesnake wrangler." The crowd let out a gasp, and the people in the front started backing away as they realized what was in the boxes. Conan continued, "He's brought twenty-five of his prize darlings here with him tonight.

Cassidy, I dare you to lay in the snake pit. Mr. Colson will put one snake at a time into the box with you, and for every snake that goes in the crate, I'll donate two grand to your foundation."

The audience burst into cheers. Cass leaned to the microphone and said, "As the famous Indiana Jones once said, 'Snakes, I hate snakes.' But it's for the foundation, so I'm game." He went down the steps of the stage.

"You've got this, Trigger," Evan said into the mic as Cass shook hands with Mr. Colson. "If one happens to bite you, just don't jump too much, or the rest will follow." He laughed at his own joke, covered the mic, and whispered to Conan, "How did you know he hated snakes?" Conan just grinned and shrugged his shoulders.

"I hate this crap," Cass said as he lowered himself into the rectangular container and glanced out at the pale faces looking back at him. He gave them a weary smile as Colson put a divider in place around his neck. "This should at least keep any of my snakes away from your face," Mr. Colson told him.

Colson and each of his assistants grabbed a snake hook from beside the cages and started lifting out snakes. They put the hook under each one's head and took it by the tail. The men then walked slowly to Cass in the box and gradually lowered the serpents in one by one. Some slithered over Cass' legs and body, while others simply coiled up on him and made the distinctive rattling sound that they were famous for in all of those old Western movies.

It took almost fifteen minutes, but the wranglers loaded all twenty-five reptiles into the chamber with Cass. His heart was still pounding in his chest and his body tingled even as the last snake became his bedmate. Despite the stress of the situation, he did not move a muscle. Conan said, as the last viper was lowered in, "Go ahead, Mr. Colson; get those things out of there before my big friend has a stroke."

"Get that checkbook of yours out, Red," Evan said. "You owe us fifty big ones."

Conan laughed and did as he was told. As the handlers removed snakes, he gave Evan a check for fifty thousand dollars. When all of the snakes were removed, Cass stood on rubber knees, and his whole body shook violently. He managed a bow to the accolades and thanked Colson for getting him out alive. Then he walked to the nearest waiter and grabbed two beers. He slammed the first and sipped the second as he walked to the stage to join Evan and Conan. As he passed Trea, he leaned down and gave her a hard kiss on the mouth while he grabbed her backside.

He said to her, "Thank god I'm alive," and smiled. To Conan he said, "Damn it O'Brian, you got me this time. I'll have a dare for you that'll be out of this world, the next time we see each other." Cass reached out and bumped fists with the late night host.

# Chapter 28

Six months after the first Charity Bash, Dare Ya was at the pinnacle of online entertainment. The two founders agreed that the old headquarters building was becoming too crowded. Cass thought they could just find a bigger property on the outskirts of Las Vegas and buy the existing structure. Evan disagreed. He thought Dare Ya should construct a place that perfectly suited their needs.

Evan went so far as to find an empty lot and hired an architectural firm to design the ideal building to house Dare Ya as it continued to grow. It took several conversations, but when Evan showed him the finished plans, Cass was sold on the idea. They hired a construction company and began building the six story edifice, sparing no expense. The exterior walls would all be mirrored glass from the sidewalks to the roof.

They had a full gym installed on the top floor between their two offices. Any employee would be permitted to come upstairs and use the workout facility, and most days, after they moved into the new building, the majority of the workers spent half an hour working up a sweat. Evan and Cass had the Charity Foundation situated on its own floor and put in a huge cafeteria that ordered food based on what the employees requested.

It took almost a year to complete the construction, but when all of the Dare Ya associates moved in, the two owners knew they had made the right decision. The place felt like home.

One afternoon, a couple of days after everyone moved in, Evan and Cass went into the conference room to address the staff. The building had a state of the art intercom system that included a video display on small screens in every cubicle and flat screen televisions placed on many walls throughout the building. The conference room had an area with a camera mounted so that a video announcement could be made over the entire system or it could go only to certain areas of the building. That day, Evan and Cass wanted to talk to the complete staff.

They started the camera, and their faces appeared on each display. Cass started. "Attention, all. This is a video memo from your Commanders in Chief, and we have some things to say. First, welcome to the new Dare Ya Inc. Headquarters. We hope we can make the work environment feel nothing at all like work."

Evan interjected, "Let's never use that word again. From now on, "Work" is a curse word here and will be frowned upon. We come here to make lots of money and escape the bad parts of our lives."

Cass picked up again, "What we're here to discuss today is the fact that we need a dare to christen our new abode. We first thought we'd dare the whole staff to do something, but you are all such busy little minions that we didn't want to disrupt your labors." They both grinned at the camera to show the good-natured intent of the conversation.

Evan persisted, "We decided to let you all send *us* a dare to complete. The department heads will then vote on the two best, and Cass and I'll do them soon afterwards." He broadened his smirk and added, "Because unlike you underlings, we up here in the penthouse offices get bored as hell and need things to fill our days."

"So post your dare ideas on the newly-designed community page," Cass said. "Make them good, and we'll pick the coolest two. Now, everybody have a great day and make us some money."

The two supervisors logged off the video memo camera and Cass said, "This has gotten enormous, Fly Guy. How the hell are we going to do all of our PR stuff and run the office at the same time?"

"Al's been doing a good job taking care of things every time we've left, so far," Evan answered.

"True, he's good over the tech stuff, but what about all the other bits and pieces? We leave Brian over legal and Rebecca over the Foundation department and all that, but we need an overall office manager that any of those department heads can go to. That way all decisions can go through them and they don't have to track us down every time."

Evan responded, "I like it, Trigger. We put someone in charge and we can get to spending more money and having way more fun."

"I was thinking of getting out there with the Disciples and promoting Dare Ya, but I guess that's the same thing as having fun. You got any ideas on who we can promote?" Cass asked.

"That's easy; we steal Mel away from Sully," Evan said matter-of-factly.

"You said that as if it's no big deal," Cass replied. "Sully's made us a lot of money. He may not appreciate us going behind his back too much."

"Come on, Jarhead, he makes money off us, too, remember? I think we can convince him to see that it'll be more profitable with Mel out here and us out with the masses doing that "PR stuff" as you called it," Evan smiled again and said.

"I love it, and we might actually be able to sell him on it. We're going to New York next week to do the Jeter dare, so we can meet with Sully then and convince him this is a good idea."

"Sully first, then Mel: good idea, Trigger. I'm going to hit the gym. I hope our staff doesn't come up with something too crazy," Evan told his friend as he stood to leave the conference room.

"I'm sure they will."

****

In the City that Never Sleeps, Evan and Cass attended the meeting with Sully. He was not very open to the idea of losing Melinda, at first. However, Evan convinced him it would be advantageous to everyone if she went to work at Dare Ya headquarters.

Sully told them that if they could convince Melinda to move to the desert, he would not stand in the way. He would put some other agent in charge of the Dare Ya account. "The team will keep on keeping on," Sully told them as the meeting broke up.

Cass texted her an invitation to lunch the following day. They took the private car to the hotel, and she replied immediately. Her response said that she would be busy at lunch, but they could all go out for a nightcap in a few hours.

At the lounge, where they met, they all ordered drinks and discussed how Evan had done on the Derrick Jeter dare earlier that day. A few months prior, Jeter had sent a challenge for Evan, Mr. Athlete of the Dare Ya squad, to take batting practice against the Yankee's ace pitcher, C.C. Sabathia. The team had pooled together a hundred grand to donate to the Foundation. They gave Evan ten outs against their defense, and every hit he got on, C.C. would add ten thousand dollars. A home run would be worth twenty-five thousand extra.

At the bar, Melinda said to Evan as the drinks arrived, "I can't believe you actually hit C.C. five times."

"With one home run; don't forget that," Evan said, poking his chest out.

"One sixty five for the Dare Ya Foundation is a good afternoon," Cass added, "but Melinda, we're here to talk about something more important than fundraising and baseball."

"Is that so?" she asked with an inquisitive look on her face.

Evan puffed on his cigar and said, "We want you, Mel."

Her curious look changed to a mischievous grin when she responded, saying, "Hmm, now doesn't that sound tantalizing? But I'm afraid I don't do that sort of thing. It is alluring; but sorry guys."

Cass actually blushed as what Melinda referred to became obvious to him. Evan boomed with laughter and said, "My big, and now red, friend made rules against such fraternization or you wouldn't be able to resist my charms."

Cass interrupted before Evan could go on and said, "At Dare Ya, Mel. We mean, we want you at Dare Ya."

"I'm no less confused," she said as the quizzical look returned to her face.

"Let me start over," Cass said. He took a drink of his Maker's Mark whiskey before he continued. He took his time and then said, "We want you to come run Dare Ya. We have a hundred different events lined up and can't be at the headquarters very much. We need someone to run the day-to-day stuff, and we want that someone to be you."

"Sully would kill me for even having this talk," Melinda said to Cass.

"We did the right thing for once, darling," Evan said, making her look his way. "We talked to Sully earlier this afternoon like we were asking your dad for your hand in marriage."

"He understands how good you'd be in Vegas," Cass finished his friend's thought, "and how we'd all benefit from you out there instead of here in the city."

"You guys are serious, aren't you?"

"Very much so," Cass said. "Come to Vegas and make us better."

She did not hesitate before she took each man's hand in one of hers and said, "I'll do it."

"Hot damn!" Evan exclaimed. "We need another drink to celebrate." They ordered several more drinks and celebrated the new covenant.

****

The department heads were inundated with proposed dares for the two founders to perform. Employees dared suggested they live on the roof of the new building for six months or sail around the world on a thirty-nine-foot catamaran. The supervisors liked most of the thoughts and could make an argument for many of them, but they could not have the main representatives tied up doing a single dare for months at a time.

One dare stood out, and all of the managers unanimously agreed it would be perfect. They discussed and came up with a plan to announce the dare to Evan and Cass, along with how to accomplish the challenge. The plan was to have a Dare Ya Headquarters Grand Opening employee picnic. The department heads, along with the new Operations Director Melinda, arranged everything and left the founders out of every stage of the planning. Carnival rides were set up for the families, and local bands performed on two stages that constructed on either side of the building. In the first floor reception area, tables were arranged for employees to have a cool place to eat.

When the barbeque was at its height, Melinda went up on the stage at the rear of the building and gathered all of the supervisors with her. She called all employees from inside and around front while Cass and Evan climbed the steps and leaned against the railing of the stage.

Melinda then addressed the crowd, saying, "On behalf of the department heads and the owners of our great organization, I would like to thank everyone for coming out today. Is everyone having fun?" The crowd answered with a cheer as Evan and Cass waved.

Melinda continued, "The new headquarters building is amazing, and it's going to be wonderful working here, but we all work for a company named Dare Ya, so what would a party be like without a good challenge?"

The gathering applauded as a man walked onto the stage with a video camera and panned it over their heads. The proprietors of Dare Ya lost their smiles as the guy turned the camera on them. "And what good would such a dare be," Melinda asked looking at her employers, "if we didn't post it on the site?"

She winked at Evan and Cass before she added, "We're streaming live, by the way, and Al assures me that there are thousands of fans watching." To this, Al nodded from the stage. Evan looked to Cass and shrugged his shoulders. She turned again to the group of staffers and kept speaking, "When you all moved here to this new HQ building, I was told that Cass and E asked for everyone to come up with some dares, and boy, did you." She pulled the microphone from the stand and walked around the stage as she talked. "I read a lot of really good ideas, but your supervisors narrowed it down to one dare for both of them to do." Melinda patted the nearest manager on the back. "It's a damn good one, too. If you guys would please direct your attention to the big screens," she said as she pointed to the large video screens on either side of the stage.

On the screen, a picture of Evan's office appeared. The furniture had been rearranged, and what looked like a massage table had been placed in the center of the room. Behind that table, sitting at Evan's desk with her feet propped on its corner, was a gorgeous brunette covered with tattoos. She was a tattoo artist who had climbed to fame through a reality show on which she starred.

The woman took her feet down and leaned her elbows on the desk as the camera in the office zoomed in on her face. In her well-known, gravelly voice, she said, "Evan and Cass, we wanted to do this on the stage down there, but it's a little windy, and I hate the sand." Cass looked down at his feet and shook his head. The woman continued, "If you two would be so kind as to come up here, we'll get this dare started."

The employees shouted encouragement as their bosses walked from the stage and went into the building. They skulked into the chamber and onto the camera shot there. "Okay, guys," the tattoo artist said as she stood and walked towards her equipment. "Who's first?"

The two exchanged glances and Evan answered back, "I guess I'll go ahead and get it over with."

"Then take your shirt off and lie on your back, please." She smiled and pulled on a pair of latex gloves.

Evan did as instructed as, six stories below, the crowd cheered so loud it could be heard in the penthouse. He asked, "What exactly are we doing here?"

"That, I am not supposed to tell you. You'll just have to trust your "minions", as I've been told you referred to them. Cass, if you would, please wait in the hall or in your office so you'll be surprised when it's your turn." She had told the camera operator to be sure that the artwork was not displayed. She wanted it to be a surprise to everyone when the time was right.

Cass left without saying a word as Evan mounted the table and lay down. The tattooist grabbed her gun and went to work. Evan made a face as the needles pierced his skin but refused to squirm or make a sound to show his pain.

She finished with him and instructed Evan to put on his shirt. Then she went to the hall and told Cass to return to the room. She followed the same process on Cass as the employees downstairs continued with their celebration at the barbeque. When she completed her work, the cameraman again zoomed in on her face, taking the owners out of the shot. She removed her gloves as she said, "Well, you guys asked for a dare, and you got it." She looked from the lens off-screen and added, "Let's go join the party, boys."

The three left the office, and a few minutes later, they emerged from the back door of the building. The assembly of employees clapped and roared as they made their way to the stage. Evan stepped to the microphone first and addressed the people. "They wouldn't give me a name, but whoever's idea this was, be ready. I will find you, and this means war." He laughed at his own joke as Melinda shooed him aside.

She responded to the threat. "You two asked for it." Then, to the audience, "Have no fear, people, the darer's name is top secret, and he or she, is perfectly safe." Evan attempted to terrorize the masses with his stare, but ended up laughing and shrugging his shoulders. Cass just smiled and once again shook his head. Melinda continued. "Let's thank our tattoo artist for Evan and Cass' new ink." She stepped from the mic, clapping as the spectators joined her.

The woman curtsied and stepped to center stage. She said, "It's been an honor. I love you guys' site and was more than happy to come out here today." She glanced back at the two owners and asked, "But exactly where do I send my bill? House calls aren't cheap, you know." The men smiled, and they both pointed towards Melinda. She shook her head and started to speak, but the tattooed woman beside her beat her to it, saying, "I'm kidding. I was ecstatic when Mel called. No one could've kept me away. Now, you two take those shirts off and let everyone see the ink."

The founders removed their shirts and showed the audience their fresh tattoos. Each man had matching work with the word 'Dare' on the front of his right shoulder and 'Ya!' on his left. Behind the word 'Dare' the artist had placed a psychedelic computer monitor with the company's logo on the screen.

Their employees cheered as Evan and Cass both flexed and showed off their artwork. The tattooist asked, "So, what do you guys think?"

Cass stepped to the mic, flexed his right bicep, and answered, "We love them. Now y'all get back to the party and enjoy yourselves the rest of the day. I have some catching up to do. Somebody find me a beer."

# Chapter 29

Melinda had a huge office on the fifth floor that they had remodeled in anticipation of hiring an office manager. It was every bit as nice as the ones on the sixth floor that they called their own.

Melinda found a nice house in a very pleasant neighborhood and settled into a routine at the office. Evan thought they should do something to show her their appreciation. He told his secretary to find out which bank Melinda had the house financed through, and he sent a cashier's check to pay off her mortgage. He told Cass it was a signing bonus.

"Then why did you pay for it with your own money and not DYI funds?" Cass asked. He was hurt because he had not been asked to put in half the payment.

"Six of one, half a dozen of the other," Evan said. "What's the difference? Half of DYI funds are mine, so who cares what name's on the check?"

"Okay, Fly Guy; if you say so, but remember the rule," Cass admonished his friend. "Don't try any funny stuff with Mel. Keep it in your pants and strictly professional."

"I've got you, Trigger. She's a unicorn—off limits, only fantasy," Evan said. Then he held up three fingers and added, "Scouts honor."

"Were you ever a Boy Scout?"

"Nope," Evan answered, laughing.

"I didn't think so. I've got my eye on you, Casanova."

****

The following months were extremely busy at Dare Ya. Melinda took over and ran the office. She made Dare Ya better with her effort. Evan and Cass made numerous appearances at Bashes and charity events. They practically lived out of their suitcases.

They rarely made it back to Vegas. When they did make it home, Evan used his time to enjoy the nightlife of the city he loved. He chased, and usually caught, every beautiful woman that crossed his path. He became well known as one of the biggest playboys in town, even with the fact that he was seldom in the city.

Cass, on the other hand, enjoyed going to the office and working on his days back. He worked closely with Al and Melinda and loved the progress of the company. He bounced ideas off them that had come to him in some lonely airport or hotel while he was away. He and Melinda became very close. Electricity grew between them, but they tried to ignore it and kept the relationship strictly professional.

Then, one day, the unthinkable happened. Cass and Melinda were in her office going over a new ad campaign that Sully's new publicist had faxed to them that morning. Mel was sitting in her desk chair and Cass was standing next to her looking at the photos. They both reached for the same picture at the same time and their hands brushed. The electrical current they had been fighting went instantly into a full spark, and that spark ignited into a flame.

They locked stares and held each other's gaze for what seemed like an eternity. Then Cass leaned down and kissed her. It was a kiss for the ages, like something in a classic love movie. That one touch of the lips fanned their flame into an inextinguishable level.

Cass ran the tips of his fingers down her cheek as they pulled back from each other. They gazed as they held the embrace, and he said, "We can't do this."

She shook her head from side to side, trying to break the spell. She stood, walked across the office to the bar, and put ice into a tumbler. She said, without looking back at Cass, "You're right. Damn it. I hate to say it, but you're right. You want a drink?"

"Yes, a whiskey, straight up. How are we going to play this?" Cass asked as he walked up behind her. He leaned down, took in the scent of her shampoo, and wanted so badly to take her into his arms.

She turned with a drink in both hands and handed Cass his glass. They again locked eyes, but she turned and walked away. She spoke again, not looking at him, "We're not. This never happened. Remember the rule you made with E? He told me that it goes for you, too." She gulped down her drink in one swallow and placed the glass on the corner of her desk.

"He'd lose it if he found out. That's for sure, and you know how he is; we'd never hear the end of his crap," Cass said. He waited for her to turn and face him. When she did not, he added, "It's almost worth his bullshit though, Mel."

"Stop it, Cass. We've got to think of Dare Ya in all of this. No two pieces can be bigger than the whole."

"Damn, were you a philosophy major or something? Okay, okay. You're right. Hell, we start our two-week European tour in three days. Maybe the time apart'll help us cool our jets a little."

They each had another drink and swore to forget the day had ever happened. Cass told her to figure out the ad campaign herself because he could not think about it. Cass decided that it would be better if he stayed away from headquarters until the trip. He would come up with an excuse to tell Evan, but as little as his friend came to work, he doubted Evan would notice.

****

He didn't. The two left for Europe, and neither went to Dare Ya even once beforehand. In the two weeks overseas, they made appearances at Bashes all throughout Europe. The members were a little less reserved on that side of the pond, so it was a lot of fun for them both. The only problem was that, as the trip wound down, Cass found himself thinking of Melinda more and more. How would he be able to go to the office on their days in Vegas, he wondered.

"E, we need to talk," Cass told his companion on the flight home.

"What's up, Trigger? You think you've got the German clap?" Evan asked, and slapped his friend on the shoulder.

"No, Fly Guy. It's a little more serious than that. This Dare Ya stuff's what we dreamed of, right?"

"I'd say so. Where are you going with this shit?" Evan asked.

"I say it's plenty big enough to sustain itself. Why should we keep living in hotels?"

"Because it kicks ass and we're living the dream," Evan told Cass, and looked at him like he was crazy.

After a few moments of silence, Cass said, "Well I think we should ease off all the Bashes and just travel to the big stuff."

"And do what?"

"Exactly. We can do anything we want. I'm thinking of finding a penthouse in New York and moving there full time."

"Are you serious? You want to split up the Dare Ya Duo?"

"Hell, this thing can run itself. We've got Mel at the office, so we can just meet wherever the next big charity bash is. What's the difference? We take different flights to get to the same place, half the time, anyway," Cass said as he looked away from Evan and out of the cabin window.

"Good point," Evan said, "and if we didn't travel so much, I could spend more time with some of the local gals I've grown so fond of." He elbowed Cass in the ribs and chuckled.

"Yeah, and I want to put a show together and get it on Broadway."

"Trigger, that's the least straight crap I've ever heard. I won't say "gay" because it's not politically correct these days, but don't ever say that again."

"Whatever.  Just because I don't bed three different chicks a day doesn't make me gay."

"Well, maybe not, but it makes me wonder." Evan laughed without Cass. Then he added, "Come on man; that was funny."

"If you say so.  It's kind of a bummer, though. A great chapter in our lives is ending."

"My ass, Trigger.  When you're as rich as we are, chapters don't ever end. We can rewrite the whole damn book, and with the technology today, we're only a text apart."

"Not to mention I can finally get out of that hedonistic desert city. You always did love that place more than I did. It got old to me way faster than I thought it would," Cass said. Then he thought to himself, *and I can get a couple of thousand miles away from Melinda.*

****

The next day Evan and Cass went to Dare Ya's headquarter building to tell Melinda and everyone else that they intended to take a semiretirement. As soon as they burst into Mel's office, Cass could tell he had made the right decision. The sexual tension that he had left weeks ago was so thick, it was like walking into a fog.

He could not believe that Evan did not feel it, but as soon as he spoke, it was obvious he could not. Evan exclaimed, "Great news Mel; we've decided to retire!"

"Retire? You guys don't do anything now but jet set around to a bunch of parties," she replied, not looking in Cass's direction.

"Even that gets old after a while, Doll," Evan said as he walked to her bar and made himself a drink.

She looked from Evan to Cass for the first time since the two had walked in and asked," So, what's the plan then, boys? Keep partying, just closer to home?"

"Actually," Cass started telling her, "I'm going to move to New York and sponsor a Broadway show."

"Not straight, Trigger—we had this talk," Evan said, not noticing the look Melinda gave Cass. Still oblivious to the fire in the room, he added, "I will still be here though, Mel."

"So you're staying and Cass is going to the other side of the country? What the heck brought this on?" She asked, never taking her eyes away from Cass and trying (but not succeeding) to sound nonchalant.

He answered, returning her glare, "I just figured it's time to switch gears. You know, start enjoying some of our successes. Plus, it's so damn hot out here."

"I know what you mean, but I've grown to like it out here," Mel said, breaking their stare and looking at some papers on her desk without seeing them.

"The big Jarhead is leaving Vegas to us, Mel. We'll just have to make do." Evan interrupted their private conversation. He waited for her to look his way. When she finally did, he gave her a wink.

She returned the wink with a lame smile and then to Cass she said, "So when are you headed east?" "Sully has me lined up with his real estate agent in the morning. He says she's got the perfect place for me." Cass turned and made himself a whiskey on the rocks.

"What's the rush? Tomorrow is kind of fast, don't you think?"

Evan answered as Cass took a swallow, "Sully told him this is a hot-ass place he's going to be shown, but his broker can't hold it for long. So our boy has to fly out this afternoon."

"Yeah," Cass said before he slammed the rest of his drink. "I have a flight leaving at three."

"I see," was all Melinda could say as she slumped like a deflated balloon.

"The world's a small place nowa-days," Cass said in a lame attempt to smooth things over. "I can fly out here and y'all can come to the city anytime."

The effort did not work. The sexual tension seemed to have evaporated and was replaced with total frustration on Melinda's side of the room. Cass left her office feeling horrible, but he had to act happy around the rest of the employees. He went through DYI and told everyone his plans. He shook hands, hugged friends, and told everyone how good a job they were all doing.

In the early afternoon, Evan found him on the Foundation's floor saying some last-minute goodbyes. Evan nodded to a few of the workers but said to Cass, "Trigger, you've got a plane to catch. We'd better get going."

The old friends left Dare Ya, and Cass watched it grow smaller in the SUV's side mirror. The leaving seemed so final, but it had to be done. They arrived at the airport and went to the departure gate with no conversation, with each man lost in his own thoughts. At the gate, Cass stuck his hand out for a shake and said to Evan, "Well brother, this is it."

Evan ignored the hand and hugged his friend hard. He slapped Cass on the back and said, "I'll have us something cool as hell lined up before you know it. Good luck on your show thingy. It's not straight, but good luck anyway."

Cass picked up the carry-on bag he had dropped when Evan hugged him and said, "Thanks, I guess. Take care of everybody and DYI for me, bud."

The public announcement system announced at the gate, "First class boarding for flight 577 direct to New York City. Last call for first class boarding."

"That's me," Cass said. "Be easy, Fly Guy."

"You too, Trigger. We've done good; now let's enjoy it."

With that, Cass turned to the loading tube, and Evan turned to leave the airport. It had been a long time since the two were not planning or working on one project or another, going all the way back to their time on the Farm in the Mississippi Delta. Life would be different for each of them, but it was time to move on.

# Part Three: The Ugly

# Chapter 30

October 22, Around Midnight

Constance smoked a cigarette while she waited in the dark. After hours of careful surveillance, the site was chosen with a singular purpose. A lot was riding on her success, as her boss had made abundantly clear. This event was arranged with an explicit goal in mind. Certain people needed to take notice, and their perfect worlds needed to be rattled. Now that the job was before her, it was as if she were standing on a cliff, looking down. All she had to do was jump.

Midnight arrived, and she needed to start the slow journey to get into position if she was going to be ready in time. Her training kicked in, and all thoughts of mortality and consequences were gone. Only the assignment remained.

Constance looked over at the man in the passenger seat next to her. He was lost in his own thoughts. "It's time," she told him.

Without even looking in her direction, he opened his door on the SUV and stepped out into the cold Nebraska night air. He opened the back door without a sound, retrieved his duffle bag, and quietly closed it; again with no word. Constance had no doubt that he would do his part because his hate was even greater than her greed. She started the truck, drove to her own position, and squashed the cigarette butt into the ashtray. She zipped her coat and grabbed her gear. It was now or never.

Into the night she belly-crawled slowly, inching her way to the location she had earlier discovered. She didn't want to chance even the smallest encounter with a person or spot-light. An hour before dawn, her nest was prepared and her things set into place. At the edge of the woods, she had a clear view and ample room to operate. The optics were up, and she did a dry run as she had been taught years ago. Lying there, she brought her watch up to her face to see the time—almost ready.

Constance let her mind wander to the man with whom she partnered. A frisson ran down her spine at the thought as the handheld walkie-talkie propped beside her head clicked twice. That was the agreed upon code for "in-place and ready." She took her hand from the stock of her rifle and keyed the radio mic twice to belay her readiness in return. No more communication was needed until the mission was complete and they were headed to the rendezvous point.

She put the small radio into the pocket of her bag and took a deep breath of the wintry night air. The dawn light was just breaking behind her. She could feel the cold night air slowing, giving way to the warmth of the morning sun.

That day would be like any other road game day in the town of Lincoln. The streets would be deserted, shops closed, and those not choosing to travel would be at home preparing the steaks or barbeque for the grill. The only person to record that day's events would be Constance, lying on her belly at the edge of the woods with the small camcorder already in position a couple of feet to her left.

The alarm clock on her watch flashed its light, letting her know the time had come. She reached over and touched the field grade camcorder. The record button was red, and with a flick of her finger, she started a video recording of the event.

Constance was lying comfortably in the shooter's nest she had constructed. A tarp was spread on the ground so no fiber transfer would occur and it could catch all of her spent brass, of which there would be a lot. Simply roll up the tarp, stuff it into her large backpack, grab her rifle and camcorder, and leave. She knew she had no time to police loose shell casings in the morning light.

With the smoke trail of her breath going into the morning over her head, she flipped up the sight covers on the Remington .308. Her eye adjusted to the magnified view in time to catch the students on the tower rousing from their night positions to greet the sunrise. She waited until she found the leader of the Husker Charter and settled the crosshairs on his center mass.

Just as she squeezed the killing device, the boy right next to the target leaned back, stretching out a yawn. She wanted to put down the leader with the first shot, but their mission was to terminate as many members of the Dare Ya Charter as possible before the local authorities arrived. She swung the muzzle to the yawning boy and fired. Shot after shot rang out in the stillness of the Nebraska plain. She did her best to cut off their escape.

As the students ran for cover, she lost sight of all the remaining targets behind the water tower, but that did not worry her; they would be back in her reticle in no time. Then she heard the first shot echo from her collaborator a hundred and eighty degrees on the other side of the big metal structure; a classic crossfire ambush with no escape.

The terrified students came back around toward her side of the gray dome and she fired, bolted, and fired once again. Her wristwatch alarm went off; this time with an audible beep-beep, to let her know playtime was over. It was time to move. After all the earsplitting shots, an abrupt silence suddenly enveloped the Nebraska field. Even at three hundred yards, Constance thought she could hear the whimpering and sobs of the few surviving students.

She rolled her tarp, stuffed it into the pack, and hurried to the SUV just as she had planned. Then she turned the key, started the Chevy Tahoe, and drove down the gravel, retracing her path from earlier in the morning. At the predetermined position, she once again keyed her radio mic and her partner dashed from a ditch to the back door. He stowed his gear in with hers and then climbed into the passenger seat.

She put the big truck into gear again and started down the dirt lane. As she accelerated away, she looked to her right at the man beside her. He was blowing into his balled-up hands to warm them from the October cold. Neither of them said a word.

After an hour of driving a serpentine route further into the Nebraska nowhere, they parked next to two old, unremarkable automobiles that had been left for their escape. Each transferred their equipment to one of the cars. Constance went to the trunk of her vehicle and found a full five-gallon gas container. She went back, doused the inside and the exterior of the Tahoe, and stepped back. Her partner stepped beside her, popped a road flare, and tossed it into the open driver's door. The gasoline exploded in a thunderous whoosh.

He turned back and grabbed the handle of his car door as Constance asked his back, "You know where to head to next don't you? The next step is just as important as this one was."

The nod of his head was almost imperceptible as he opened the door. Then he slumped behind the wheel and slammed the door again behind him. Constance said, "I'll take that as a yes," to his taillights as he sped away.

When she was in her own car and on the move once again, she fished her phone from her jacket pocket and held down the preset number. After the third ring, it was answered. "It's done. I'm leaving Nebraska now," she said.

"Good, Good. How many did you all get?"

"Eleven or twelve," Constance answered. "Plus, one of them jumped at the end."

"Jumped? Why would anybody jump from that high up?" the caller asked; then began to chuckle. "That's insane."

"If you were a kid and somebody was putting bullets into your buddies," she said, a little annoyed, "you might just do the same."

"How did our man do?"

"He went through the motions like a god-damned robot, but we got it done," she answered. "Are you sure we can trust him? I mean, he's pretty much completely consumed by his hate."

"Not your concern, my dear," the Director replied. "He is but a tool I am using to accomplish my own loathing-fueled objectives."

"I'm not sure the son of a bitch is even stable."

Constance stopped at a stop sign at a small town crossroad. The sun was overhead and the day had warmed considerably. She reached over and turned off the heater as her boss responded, "If he proves to be too unbalanced to utilize, we can find a way to use that to our advantage, as well." She switched the phone to the other ear as he continued. "Especially after the next phase of the plan."

"What do I know? This is your show." She chuckled. "I'm the only one doing this for a reason that makes any sense—money."

The Director laughed softly in return. Then he said, "Yes, money is important, but at times people must be held accountable for their actions."

"Just keep the cash flowing, and their reckoning will follow all you want."

"You did very well, Constance, as usual. Head to your next objective, and I'll be in touch," the Director said, and then clicked off the line.

She lit another Marlboro Red and cracked the window. Out of habit, she looked in the review mirror to see if she was being followed. She had passed only one car on the roads that day. "Thank you, Husker Nation," she said to herself aloud.

# Chapter 31

## The Phone Call

It's funny how a phone call can change a life forever. Like a marker on the highway signaling you to turn, a phone call can mark the point in someone's life where it leaves its intended path. Some are good, (the "I love you" calls) and some are bad, like the announcement of a death. Matthew Cassidy was sitting on the balcony of his million-dollar upper Manhattan apartment watching the sun go up over the Manhattan high-rises to the east. Other than night in the city he loved, with a bottle of vintage '68 Merlot, this was his favorite time of the day. He had just run back from the gym and was enjoying a smoothie and a Power Bar. He sat beside the quasi-fireplace with a wealthy man's smile. He was living a dream. Hell, it was better than he could ever have dreamed.

Cass knew there was only one thing missing from his life. He had moved to the city a few months ago to get his mind off Melinda and gain perspective on his future.

When the telephone rang, Cass almost didn't hear it. As though he could sense the negativity of the call, a feeling of gloom washed over him. When he attempted to place his smoothie on the edge of the table, it failed to find the surface and ruined his outdoor rug along with his New Balance running shoes. Cass took a deep breath and tried to convince himself that some of the techno-savvy Dare Ya Disciples had managed to get his private number.

Cass picked up the receiver and uncharacteristically asked, "What is it? This had better be important, or..."

Before he could continue, he was cut off by the sound of sobbing. From the tone of the crying on the other end, he could tell it was Melinda. She was on the verge of hyperventilating and couldn't speak, so Cass made an effort to calm her.

Melinda finally composed herself enough to speak, and the entire horrifying narrative rushed out in what seemed like one sentence. He asked, "Have you called E, yet?"

"No, you came to my mind first."

He wanted to take her in his arms and shield her from the misery, but he was halfway across the country, and they had agreed it could not be that way. No comforting words would help, so his old training kicked in and he went directly into processing the situation.

"I'm on my way to the airport now. I'll call him on the way, and we'll get this figured out." The words sounded hollow and far away, but he had to reassure her.

"I'll keep digging." He could hear the strain in her voice. She continued, "I'll be at the office when you get out here."

"Okay, I'll swing by and pick up Evan and we'll see you at Dare Ya." Cass clicked off and leaned on the balcony railing, looking at the phone in his hand. One damn phone call and life would never be the same.

****

Cass shook himself from the bad thoughts and almost mechanically rushed to pack a few things for the trip. Twelve innocent people murdered. More importantly, someone had used Dare Ya to kill those young people. All of the Disciples had become like extended family to him, and nobody hurt his family. Right then, he decided to find out who was behind the cold-blooded murders and make them pay.

In the private car taking him to the airport, he decided it was time to call Evan, tell him the story, and see how they could handle the situation. Cass took out his cell and hit the number for Evan. He waited, hoping Evan was semi-coherent and not watching some bimbo slide down a polished pole. He never knew when Evan's night life would bleed over into the next morning.

Evan picked up on the third ring. "Hi ho, it's Trigger," he said laughing.

"Cut it out, E," Cass returned. "I need to talk to you."

"Easy, Bro, I was just about to call you anyway," Evan said. "I've got one to top that last dare of yours." Cass was just about to say something when Evan continued, "Sent the G5 to you. It should be landing now. Tag: you're it." Cass tried furiously to talk, but the last thing he heard Evan say before his friend hung up was, "See ya in a few, Jarhead."

Cass slid his phone into his jacket pocket and rode to the airport, thinking. When the driver pulled next to Dare Ya's luxurious jet, Cass climbed out and trotted up the stairs, barely nodding at the pilot.

He settled into his seat, unzipped his laptop case, and set the computer on a work station that had been custom built into the cabin. He began a very intensive and illegal search through back channels to see what more he could find.

The G5 was loaded with every amenity needed to travel in style and comfort. After thirty minutes of searching, his phone beeped with a text message. He leaned over to the seat next to him and retrieved the smart-phone. He looked at the message and instantly knew it was from Evan.

*Trigger, check out your e-mail attachments while you ride. Peace.*

Cass minimized his searching and brought his e-mail to life. Inside the e-mail, Evan had attached a file that described the dare he was planning. This magic trick involved one of the coolest prestidigitators alive. "Wow," he said aloud, forgetting the trouble in Nebraska. "This dare's going to be big."

A picture attached showed a death tank filled with water. The e-mail explained that Cassidy would be put in the tank, shackled with four sets of locks, and expected to escape, Harry Houdini style. Magic Man had exactly forty-eight hours to teach Matthew how to cheat a watery death.

He had to admit that this was one awesome dare. As he subconsciously gave the dare a 5-star rating in his head, he thought back to the problem at hand, trying to figure out what he could do about the murders.

On the tarmac in Las Vegas, walking down the stairs of the plane, Cass, knowing Evan, expected to see a red carpet or at least his friend and a few scantily-clad women in tow; but instead, he saw a sight that made him laugh aloud despite the heavy load on his heart. A pink stretch limo pulled up and let out one of the most horrific horn blasts he had ever heard. At that moment, Cass knew he would never get Evan to help him find the people accountable for the killings.

The traffic was surprisingly light from the Las Vegas airport. Cass figured he would have had more time to think, but when the limo pulled into the Palms Hotel, he got out and went to the elevators. He watched the excited gamblers in the lobby and then punched the number for Evan's suite, taking the long ride up. Evan had always been a smooth talker and had somehow managed a permanent suite in the hottest place in Vegas. When the bell chimed and the elevator doors opened, Cass blew all the air out of his lungs and stepped into the hall. He walked directly to the door, knocked twice, and waited. A beautiful big-breasted blonde swung the door inward. Cass smiled, shook his head, and then walked into his friend's home. Evan was on the phone smoking a cigar, and waved for Cass to come in. After a few minutes, Evan hung up and asked, "What took you so long, Jarhead?"

Cass pulled out his wallet, gave the bimbo a hundred, and told her to hit the slots downstairs. She looked over at Evan; he shrugged and gave her a slight nod. She put the money in her tiny purse and left without a word.

Cass walked over to the bank of windows that stretched from the floor to ceiling. Overlooking the modern day concrete paradise, Cass already felt tired. He turned to face Evan and said, "E, I think we've got a problem on our hands."

"Say, Trigger," Evan replied, "don't tell me you have cold feet before I even explain this dare to you."

"No, no it's not that; but something serious has come up," Cass said. He watched a drunken couple down on the street stumble out of another casino and head off into the night. "We need to talk about something Melinda told me earlier today."

Evan eyed him with a mocking expression. "She's not pregnant, is she?" Evan asked, and laughed. He walked beside Cass and slapped him on the back, continuing to laugh. "Come on man, you Army boys are all the same. Get a good woman knocked up then want to bail."

Out of habit, Cass deadpanned. "Jarhead - I mean Marine - you prick." Cass even gave Evan a small smile. He had missed the banter with his old friend. The moment passed, and the smile faded as he said, "E, seriously, some people were murdered, and I think the perps used a dare to do it."

"Perps?" Evan asked. "What are you, some kind of cop, now? You know I can't stand when people talk like that."

Evan turned from the window and walked over to the refrigerator He pulled out a Miller Lite, popped the top, and took a long swig. Cass walked into the kitchen and set on one the vintage bar stools.

"Listen to me, Evan; people were murdered doing one of our dares. They were doing a group dare - you know the Double Duce Dare on the 22nd. Anyway, Melinda has the footage over at the office. We need to get over there and look at that video. Maybe we can at least find something useful for the cops," Cass finished.

He was glad he got it out before Evan could dismiss it totally. He could tell by the look on Evan's face that he was not sold on the idea. "Whoa, Trigger." Evan held up his hand. "I know your name is Hopalong Cassidy, but give me a break here, will ya?"

"Evan, we need to take a look," Cass pleaded. "These were our people that got killed, bro."

Evan shook his head, exasperated, and said, "Let's do this magic dare, give it a week or so, and see where everything stands. How about that? Maybe the cops'll have gotten lucky and nailed the 'perps,' as you call them." He made quotation marks with his fingers. "Then everybody can go back to their merry lives."

Cass exploded. "Go back to their merry lives? You've got to be kidding me, Evan!"

Evan set his beer down and leaned on the kitchen counter with his hip. He tried to calm his partner down by saying, "Let's just let the cops find out what's going on, Cass. If nothing pans out, then we'll get involved. It *is* their job, remember?"

Cassidy got up and started to pace around the massive suite, finally turning back to Evan. He said, "I'm going over to Dare Ya to find out what I can. If you don't want to come, I'll go by myself."

As he got the words out, a knock came at the door. Evan left his friend and went to answer it. He opened the door, and a short dumpy man stepped through the threshold. The man wore a rumpled pair of kakis with a Hawaiian shirt and penny loafers, no socks. He looked from Evan to Cass and back again before he said, "Hope I'm not interrupting anything."

"Cass, you remember Rob Moffett?" Evan asked, and then he patted the man's shoulder. He turned to Rob and said, "Why don't you give us a few minutes, Robbie? Go get a drink or something, and I'll call you in a little bit."

"Not a problem, Masters," Rob said. "Cass, it was good to see you again." Cass gave him the slightest of head nods and Rob turned and left the suite.

When the door closed and the Dare Ya partners were alone once again, Cass asked Evan, "You still hang out with that dirty cop?"

"Come on, Trigger, why's he gotta be a dirty cop?"

"What sort of normal civil servant can afford to hang out in the places you do?" Cass shrugged his shoulders and asked.

"Maybe he does a hell of a good job with his budget, how should I know." Evan shrugged back and took a drink. "I think he told me once that his family had money."

"I guess the choices of friends in the high-end stripper click are limited," Cass said, letting his frustration bleed through his tone.

"Whatever, man.  He's all right. Remember last year when that cokehead stole my Vet? Rob had it found and back to me the next day." Evan gave Cass a look as if to say, 'see, he is good.'

Cass started to the door, and with his back to Evan, replied, "The Vet has On-Star. We could've found the damn thing in ten minutes with the freaking GPS."

Evan snorted as Cass made it to the door. He grabbed the knob, and Evan called behind him: "What about the dare I set up?"

"Do it yourself."

When Cass slammed closed the door to the suite, he walked to the bank of elevators and leaned his forehead against the wall. It felt terrible to walk away from his friend and a dare, but at some point, they had to start investigating these murders. Evan was never going to skip a dare, especially one that big. Cass wanted his partner with him, but he wasn't going to change Evan's mind, so he decided not to think about it anymore and to just do what had to be done.

Still in the suite, Evan started doing some pacing of his own. Cass had never acted like that before. Evan knew his comrade had an extremely high moral standard, but this was a little over the top. This was about business, and big dares equaled big money. Their names, which both men had fought hard to bring up out of the gutter, were at stake. Evan had already set it up with the magician's people when Cass boarded the plane. Evan snipped the end of a cigar, poured a little Kentucky bourbon into his glass, and sat down to worry.

Somebody had to do the dare. This was Vegas; the show must go on. Only a fool would pass up this act, and the Dare Ya founders were no fools. If it were anybody else, Evan would not be even thinking about it. That made him more upset. Dare Ya was what he had to think about. Evan broke out his phone, hit the number he had saved for the Magic Man, and waited. Once he picked up, Evan said, "We've got a slight change in plans, Hot Shot. I'm your Huckleberry now."

****

Cass had forgone the stretch limo and taken a cab to DY headquarters. Once he finally got to the building, he walked to the lobby and spoke to a few people before he took the elevator to Melinda's office. He found her sitting behind her desk. Her classic beauty took him aback all over again. Her full, always-moist lips were missing their trademark smile that Cass loved so much. She flipped her dark red hair out of her face as he cleared his throat to announce his presence.

Melinda looked over the computer screen, locked her envy-green eyes on Cass, and mouthed a smile that tickled the corners of her mouth. She dropped both hands into her lap and said, "Hey, Trigger."

"Not you too," Cass replied, and slumped into the chair across from her.

She let out a dry chuckle devoid of all of its usual pizzazz, stood up, and went around the desk. She leaned down and gave him a small peck on the cheek. "You want a drink?"

"Yeah, a Beam and water would be good." He took out his smart-phone and started going over the notes that he had made on the plane ride. "Any more news on your end about Nebraska?"

She handed him his drink and went back to her seat with one of her own. After she sat down again, she answered, "Not really, no, but I've got the location where the video originated from. It's probably a false trail, but we can start there."

"I found out the authorities have a burned-out SUV about thirty miles south of Lincoln," Cass told her. He took a swig of his drink and then continued, "It was out in the middle of nowhere. They're not actually saying it's connected, but I'll bet it is."

"Okay, Matthew, we'll dig on that and see what turns up," she finally answered. "But it's not much to go on."

"It's almost so little that we'll have to wait and hope the bastard makes some kind of contact with us," he said, looking at a shelf behind her desk at a picture of himself and Evan on either side of Melinda. "We just have to keep searching the net, but I think he'll want to brag about it pretty soon."

"You're probably right. I'm going to get on the video and see what else I can learn." She turned back to the computer and started typing again. Then she stopped and turned her green eyes back to Cass. "Where's Evan?"

Cass shook his head and said, "He doesn't think it's our place to be investigating." He rubbed a hand up and down his thigh, obviously upset with his old pal. "Even had some dumbass dare lined up for me to do."

"Yeah, he sent me the specs," she said, and moved a few pieces of paper around on her desk. She held one up and added, "Since we're in a holding pattern for now, are you going to go play David Copperfield?"

"Hell, no, I told him to do it himself." He stood and placed the empty drink glass on the corner of her desk. "I'm going to Al's office and see what he's got."

"Okay," she said, "but don't be too hard on E; it's just his way."

Cass grunted his frustration as he turned and left Melinda's office.

# Chapter 32

Evan woke the next morning—(well, what he called morning, a little after noon). He forced a workout, took a long, hot shower, and then shaved. Choosing a black tailored Brooks Brothers suit with a black shirt and black leather Cole-Haan shoes, he dressed. Then he grabbed a quick bite to eat and headed out to have some fun.

Evan always enjoyed the preparation leading up to an awesome dare. All aspects of an event had to be just so because all of the Dare Ya nation would be watching. When the founders did a dare - any dare -they all watched. Therefore, it had to be perfect.

This dare was not going to be just good; it was going to make history for him and his friend, even if Cass was not there to go along with it. The Magic Man who proposed the dare was one of the biggest names, not just in Vegas, but in anything to do with magic. His name, associated with Dare Ya, could only help propel the company higher. Since he was covering for his friend, Evan would be up one on Cass—a big one.

Evan walked down to the indoor garage, surveyed his cars, and selected the Maserati. Damn, he loved that car. On the drive over to the venue Evan tried to clear his mind, but found his thoughts drifting back to what Cass had told him. Twelve dead and no answers. What could be the reason behind such a heinous attack? Evan once again pushed the thoughts from his mind as he pulled into the parking lot and tossed the keys to the valet.

A welcome committee of magical assistants was waiting for him. They led him into the dressing room, made him pull off his suit, and put him in diving gear. Evan had worn the rubber suits on many occasions during his life, but he still hated the tight feel of them. The team said he was ready except for the last stage, which the magician would handle. He walked over to the tank where the Magic Man was waiting with a smile. "Want a drink?" he asked as he dropped a curtain around a ten-foot-tall cylinder full of water.

Evan recoiled and said, "Hell no. I hate water. Why you think I chose the sky instead? A stiff shot would be good, but I'd better keep my mind clear. We'll save that for after our practice session. Let's just get this over with, Merlin."

"Merlin, huh," Magic Man chuckled, and said: "You mess this up and even the real Merlin couldn't bring you back."

The magician took Evan through the process of the trick without the water first, and they went over it repeatedly. As he had said, there was no room for error. Evan found a new perspective on how great the man was at his craft.

Evan went through several test runs, some without water and others with just a few of the locks. The magician performed the whole act once, himself, just to show Evan exactly how it was done. After hours of practice, Evan was drying his hair with a hotel towel and thinking how good being prepared felt. He was sure the next night would be a hell of a show.

In his dressing room, he tied his shoes, stood up, and flipped his suit coat over his shoulder. He checked his phone for any word from Cass. Nothing. As he walked out of the room looking down at his cell phone, he almost ran into his magical mentor. "Whoa there, big guy," he said to Evan. "You did pretty good for your first day." He stuck out his hand, smiling.

Evan slid the phone into his pocket, grabbed the offered hand, and shook it, smiling back, but his eyes were on the assistant to the magician's right. "I've gained a whole new respect for your commitment. I see it's not all card tricks and fuzzy rabbits."

"No, it isn't." He slapped Evan on his shoulder and laughed. "Be here early tomorrow so we can run through everything a few more times."

"Yeah, yeah, I got it, Merlin." Evan winked at the beautiful blonde aide. "But early for me is five minutes after the show starts."

The girl blushed and looked to her boss, who told Evan, "It looks easy when I do it, but that's from hundreds of times of going through it to get the details down pat. Don't take this too lightly, Masters. Sure it's a show, but it wouldn't be a good one if it weren't right on the edge of dangerous."

"Aren't you Mr. Drama?" Evan asked. "I'll be here, and we'll knock this thing out of the park." He pulled the cell phone from his front pocket again and began typing a text. He called over his shoulder, "You'll see. Evan Masters was made for the stage!"

Going out to the parking lot and waiting on the valet, he sent a text to Cass.

*Any news, big guy? Still got a magic wand for ya!*

As he climbed into the sleek sports car, the phone in his hand chirped. He looked down, expecting a text from Cass, but instead, it was from his old friend Beau.

*Good one! But you better believe the next one's on me.* ☺

Evan figured Beau had talked to someone at Dare Ya and heard about the Magic Man dare and wanted one of his own. Evan smiled to himself because Beau was always trying to do the normal stuff that Evan took for granted. He hated being left out of anything. Cass had told Evan a hundred times that he could not watch over his childhood buddy their entire lives, but following the accident, even after all the years, he still felt responsible somehow. He hated to treat Beau like a cripple; however, he just refused to give him too tough a dare and put him in harm's way again. Evan figured it was simply best to avoid it all together.

*If you say so, JB. U still flyin out here for our birthday thing?*

Evan drove through the city he loved and, as he often did, he thought about how far he had come since those hot summer days on the penal farm. He hoped Cass didn't let himself get wrapped up too tight about what some nut job had done to a few college kids. Yes, it sucked, but crazies do what crazies do. This was their time to live out their dreams.

As he was sitting at a red light, his phone chirped once more in his lap. This one was from Cass.

*Not yet. We need you, Fly Boy. Come on by HQ.*

Evan was shaking his head in frustration when a car horn brought him back to reality. The light had changed to green, so he gunned the turbo-charged engine and headed for his hotel. In the parking garage, he replied to Cass's text.

*Not today. I'm exhausted and gotta get my bourbon levels back up to be ready for the MM dare tomorrow.*

Evan refused to be drawn into Cass's fanatical detective work. In the elevator, a chirp again—Beau.

*Wouldn't miss it for the world. See you next month. Later, Bro.*

Evan loved Beau like a brother, so he decided he and Cass would have to put their heads together and come up with a good dare for him. They had a big bash scheduled for the following month because Evan's birthday was coming around. That would be as good a time as any to let Beau have some fun.

Evan Masters walked into his suite and went straight to the bar. As he poured his drink, he thought preparing for the Birthday Bash was an excellent way to get Cass to quit thinking about those damn murders, as well. It would do them good to plan a bunch of cool dares for the big party.

****

The next morning, close to lunch, Cass was in his old office with Al scouring the internet. Melinda came through the door, saying, "Another dead end. The shooting video just appeared on the site and tracks back to Dare Ya itself, some freaking how." Cass looked up and noticed she had pulled her curly hair back into a ponytail. His hands froze over the keys as she walked in front of his desk toward the window. She continued, as she looked outside: "Have you guys found anything?"

Al stood by Cass and he looked from Mel to Cass, expecting the big man to answer. When Cass just stood rooted in place for a few seconds, Al elbowed him in the ribs. That snapped Cass back to reality, breaking the spell Melinda had placed over him. He looked at Al and then said, "Uh, no; nothing at all new."

With Mel's back turned, Al raised his eyebrows as if to ask Cass what he should do. Cass either didn't see the gesture or didn't understand it because he looked once more at Melinda. He was actually watching two Melinda's:—one real and the other a reflection in the glass. In the mirror image, he could see the tension on her face, and he wanted to take her in his arms.

Al cleared his throat and said, "I think I'm going to run downstairs and get something to eat; you guys want anything?"

Both answered "No thank you," at the same time. Neither looked in Al's direction. When he left the room, Melinda continued to look out onto the city, and Cass watched her for a few seconds. He decided he could not stand to see so much pain on her face. He stood to go around the desk.

He took a step in her direction, and as he did, her cell phone beeped. She dug it from her back pocket and pulled up a text. The moment had passed, so Cass stopped and asked, "What's up?"

Without a word, she came around his desk, nudged him out of the way with her hip, and began typing. He glanced over her shoulder at the monitor and saw she was going to the discussion board on the Dare Ya homepage. She typed some more and then stopped, looking at the screen.

"I think we've got something," she said. "He just put a post on the site."

****

That afternoon, Evan was back with the Magic Man. They were going over the routine for what seemed to him like the hundredth time. He was sitting just off stage, letting the weight of the locks and chains slip from his muscle memory, when his phone on the seat beside him rang. The caller ID said it was Dare Ya Headquarters. He pushed the talk button and said, "Talk to me."

"E, where are you?" Cass asked. "I've been calling you for an hour."

"Easy, Trigger," Evan responded. "I'm with Merlin going over *your* dare."

"Yeah, whatever. Look, Mel's assistant found a post on the site a little while ago. It said the Nebraska shooting was for our enjoyment, and that no dare is safe."

Evan looked around the arena at all the faces of the people getting the arena ready for the night's dare. There were camera operators, cleaning people, and many others in the stands milling around. "What the hell's that supposed to mean? For our enjoyment?"

"Whoever it is, intended it's for you and me. Meaning it wasn't just some random shooting whose victims happened to be Disciples. The Carter members were targeted on purpose."

As Cass told him this, Evan stood and paced around the stage. "Hang on a sec, Cass; let me think." He made a couple of circuits around the water tank and then spoke again. "It's probably from some opportunistic prick that's yanking our chain. Some geek that doesn't even know which end of a rifle to point downrange."

"I don't know, man," Cass replied after some thought of his own. "To me, it adds up. You just watch your ass out there while we try and figure out what the hell's going on."

"Awwww." Evan stopped walking and tried to put some humor back into his voice. "Is the big Devil Dog worried about little ol' me?" Then, more seriously, he added, "I'm good on my end, but if you let this shit twist screws in your head, you'll be seeing boogiemen everywhere."

"Listen to me, E." Cass took a deep breath and blew it out, trying to take the edge out of his tone. "I've got the feeling this isn't over and this prick is just warming up, so keep your freaking head down."

"Sure thing," Evan said with a dry chuckle. "That should be easy enough to do. What with me being in front of all the folks at the show tonight. Come on, man..."

"Postpone it," Cass cut him off. "Put it off for a month or two, and then I'll do the damn dare myself."

"*Now* you want to do the right thing. I've already put my name on this check Cass." Evan walked back to his chair, picked up his towel, and threw it over his shoulder. "I've gotta go get ready; the show goes as scheduled. You know how it is." He hung up the phone and headed to his dressing room determined not to let Cass's worries get into his head.

A couple of hours later, as everything was finally in place and ready to start filming, the crowd started coming in and taking their seats. A new level of anxiety overcame Evan, though he tried to quell it. He looked through a crack in the curtain and saw the faces in the room, and suspicion raced up and down his body. If somebody was trying to hurt him or Cass, doing this Dare would not be smart. Now Evan was pissed at Cass for putting doubt in his mind.

The Magic Man walked up and put a hand on Evan's shoulder. Evan startled but regained quickly and said, "Be sure that somebody is standing close by with an extra set of keys, my friend."

"No extra set of keys tonight," The magic man grinned and answered. "What would be the point of the show if you could just have somebody *let* you out? You and only you can free yourself."

"What the hell are you talking about? If I die in there, I will come back and haunt your ass till the day you die." Evan looked over to see if the man was serious and then he added, "You'd better get that sledgehammer on standby ASAP."

"Calm your nerves, Evan. You'll be just fine. Remember the steps that I taught you and we'll be drinking Jack Daniels' Single Barrel before you dry off."

"Do you remember meeting my friend Cass at the party last New Year's?" Evan asked intensely.

"Cass?" he asked.

"You know, the Marine I Introduced to you?" Evan asked. "The guy who was trained to kill people; the big guy?"

"All right, Evan." He smiled like the performer he was and slapped Evan's shoulder again. "I'll get a sledgehammer to bust you out right before you flat-line."

When everything was in place and the audience had taken their seats, the curtain lifted. The Magic Man introduced Evan, who ran onto the stage with his arms raised, pumping them up and down. The enormous roar of those in attendance completely wiped away any lingering thoughts Evan may have had about what Cass had told him earlier. He was right where he loved being: in the center of attention.

Evan took the mic from the magician and shook his hand. Then he turned to the crowd, waited for the applause to die down, and said, "On behalf of Dare Ya, I'd like to thank y'all for coming out tonight, and to all those on the website watching, thanks for logging on! We love doing these celebrity dares, so if there are any brave, famous people out there, log on to Dare Ya and give us something cool." He paused and surveyed the spectators again. "We'll certainly have a payback dare for Merlin, here," he continued. The conjurer pointed to himself, mouthed the word 'Me,' and grinned. "That's how it works, Houdini; we'll do a dare that any celebrity sends us for charity, but we get a revenge dare."

At that, the audience again erupted as the Magic Man hung his head and shook it back and forth. Evan held up his hand and quieted the room once more. "But y'all didn't come out here tonight to hear me yap on and on. Let's get to the dare!" He tossed the microphone back to the magician and walked to a group of assistants who waited at center stage.

****

Late that same night, Evan wrapped himself tighter in his terrycloth robe after his second hot shower since returning to his suite. It felt as if he would never be warm again. *The cheap bastard could have at least brought the water up to room temperature*, Evan thought.

He sat down on the couch overlooking the strip with a mug of hot chocolate, an alcoholic additive. When he had gone to the center of the big stage, the aids went to work. They locked a chain around his waist and handcuffed his wrists to the chain. Then one of the lovely ladies put an old pair of shackles on his wrists over the more modern pair of manacles.

The audience had quieted, and all eyes watched the Dare Ya founder being hog tied by chains. The Magic Man spoke into the mic, explaining, "Now on top of the two sets of wrist restraints, an eighteen-foot chain will be wrapped around Evan's upper body. This will secure his arms to his sides and make the removal of the cuffs all the more difficult."

As Evan spun in a slow circle and the massive chain wound around his torso, a digital clock as big as a picnic table lowered from the rafters and hung on the opposite side of the stage from the magician. It showed three minutes in big red numbers, and the Magic Man pointed at it as he continued to speak. "The average human can go three minutes without air." Evan could barely make out his words over the thunk-thunk-thunk of his heart slamming in his chest. "Evan, here, is in pretty good shape, but he does love his cigars."

The crowd gave a nervous chuckle as the assistants helped ease Evan to the ground. A cable descended, with leather straps and more locks dangling from the end. The Magician continued, "These will be the next to last locks on his body. Mr. Masters will have to navigate them to escape a watery death."

Evan heard that loud and clear; he snapped his head around to glare at the man and said, "Real encouraging there, Merlin."

"Just telling it like it is, E." Again, the crowd laughed. The leather strips were secured around his ankles and the locks were secured. As Evan was hoisted up, the blonde assistant that he had winked at the day before gave him a quick kiss on the lips and wished him luck. She then put a clamp over his nostrils to keep the water out of his nose.

Merlin continued. "I think the hardest part of the trick is being inverted upside down in the water. The weight of the chains pulls down and makes the escape all the more difficult." The cable hoisted Evan up higher and over the rim of the tank. He took several deep breaths before his head was lowered into the water. He plunged deep into the freezing water, and it almost made him release the air in his lungs. He thrashed around for a few seconds and then a curtain fell around the tank. As the magician had told him the day before, "Can't let the audience see the "magic" happen." The clock started its countdown.

The timepiece was ticking down toward two and a half minutes as another aid climbed a ladder fitted atop on the tank. She reached through a hole in the lid and clamped yet another padlock shut. As she was climbing down, the magician said, "In some ways, that one's the hardest, because every part of his body will be screaming for air by that time." He continued to narrate to the awestruck crowd, and the timer kept approaching zero.

Inside the water container, Evan pulled a hidden key from his swimming trunks and went to work on the locks. They had all been keyed the same, but it was still a hard task to unlock them all. Several times he almost dropped the key, which would have been disastrous.

When seventy-five seconds remained, the audience continued to watch as the cable from which Evan hung jerked back and forth. It looked like a fishing line with a huge catch on its hook. Then the line abruptly went slack. Only thirty seconds left on the clock as water splashed from the fop of the tank. Everyone could see Evan's fingers come through the hole in the lid working franticly at that lock.

"Now he's in real pain; his chest is on fire which almost forces him to suck in a breath."

The clock reached ten and the crowd started to chant the countdown, "Nine...Eight...Seven...", until the clock hit zero. The intensity of the splattering of water increased and then suddenly ceased.

The magician found himself holding his breath along with the entire audience. Thoughts quickly ran through his mind. *Should I go save him? Is he still conscience? Come on Masters, shit.*

More time passed with no movement from the tank. The Magic Man took two steps forward and motioned for an aid to get the sledgehammer. When he looked back toward center stage, the top shot up and Evan burst from the water with his arms held high. He slumped to the side of the tank gulping huge mouthfuls of air. Pushing his wet hair from his forehead, he smiled a tired smile at the crowd. They erupted in applause.

The magician climbed the ladder, grabbed Evan's wrist, and raised it back into the air. The viewers clapped and cheered louder. "You're a natural, Masters. I was so worried that I was just about to come and get you," he said under his breath as both men chuckled.

Back in his living room, Evan shook his head, still unable to believe he had done such a dare. "Cass, you owe me one," he said to his hot cocoa just before he drained the cup. He went to the kitchen, clicking off the lights as he went. The coffee cup rattled around in the sink as he turned toward the hall to go and lie down for the night.

The knock on the door came just as he crossed the threshold into his bedroom. He went back through the suite and looked at the microwave clock. 2:30 am. He half grinned, hoping it was the little blonde assistant from the show earlier that night.

# Chapter 33

Evan opened the door to the hall, but instead of the petite magic aide, Cass stood before him. Cass had the look of a haggard man. His face was slack with no expression, and his shoulders slumped. Evan propped his hand on top of the door to block the entrance to the apartment. "Damn, Trigger, you look like I feel. What the hell are you doing up and awake this side of midnight?"

"We need to talk, Evan," Cass said without making eye contact with his partner. He pushed past Evan and entered the foyer of the suite.

"By all means, come on in," Evan said, dripping sarcasm. He made no attempt to close the door as he continued. "Come on man, it's late. I don't want to hear 'bout perps, investigations, or cops tonight. Try me about noonish tomorrow."

"I've got some terrible news, E," Cass said. He raised his head and finally made eye contact with Evan.

Evan saw the bloodshot eyes. *Had he been crying?* His friend's eyes gave Evan a look of utter sadness. Evan ignored the look and said, "What, that you're a lousy friend? Yeah, I figured that out when I was hanging upside down in a thousand gallons of water a few hours ago."

"Seriously, Evan," Cass tried again. "Let's go sit down and talk."

[Evan finally closed the door, but went no deeper into his apartment. He crossed his arms over his chest. "Spill it, Gomer. I said I'm too tired to play games."

Cass held eye contact and ran his hand through his hair as he tried to figure out what to say. "It's Beau, man."

His eyes glistened as he continued. "I'm sorry, but he's dead."

"*What*?" Evan dropped his hands by his sides and flexed the muscles in his forearms. "I just fucking talked to him yesterday. You must be mistaken!"

"They put video on the site that showed..."

"Oh, I see," Evan erupted. "You want me to help you so bad, you make shit up! You fucking prick." Evan rushed past Cass into the suite. Cass reached out to his friend and put his trembling hand on Evan's shoulder.

Evan slipped to the side, grabbed Cass's hand, and spun a wide circle around the bigger man. Cass's right wrist buckled and in one swift motion, Evan pinned the arm behind Cass's back, swept his plant leg, and shoved him onto a small table in the entranceway.

"Fuck you, Cassidy," Evan yelled as he leaned into his friend's ear. "Do you think that telling me that my friend is dead will make me help you?"

Cass stomped Evan's instep, pushed off the wall with his left hand, and broke Evan's grip. Then, full of his own frustrations from the past few days, Cass rushed Evan, gripping him around the waist. He lifted Evan into the air and tackled him into the living room.

The two men crashed onto the couch and toppled it over backwards. Punches landed as the friends rolled throughout the room. An end table overturned, sending a lamp crashing to the floor. Stools under the bar toppled. Like two giant grizzlies locked in a death match, they grunted and thrashed. One would land a blow and then the other would return the favor.

They were both so lost in the mêlée and aggravation that neither heard the front door open, nor saw Melinda come into the room. That was, until she grabbed the bucket of melted ice off the bar and dumped it on the gladiators. "Cut that shit out," she said as she threw the empty bucket to the floor. Evan and Cass reeled apart because of the blast of cold water and looked up at Melinda. She wiped away a tear. "This isn't helping us in any way."

Cass scooted backward and sat with his back to the wall. He dabbed a small trickle of blood from his lip and wiped it on his jeans. Evan stayed seated on the floor and leaned on the end of the overturned sofa. He straightened the robe he was wearing and locked eyes with Cass. "There's a mistake somewhere," Evan spat. "I just freaking talked to Beau yesterday."

"They sent a video of Beau doing some kind of dare, or something," Cass said with the sadness returning to his voice. "I'm sorry, man."

"What did he say yesterday, Evan?" Melinda asked.

"What dare?" Evan asked Cass, but his friend did not respond. Evan turned to Melinda and started to answer, but he had to regain his composure before he continued. "He said it was a good one and the next time it was his turn."

Melinda said, "I don't understand. What exactly was his turn?" She righted one of the stools at the bar and sat.

"I figured someone had told him about the Magic Man dare and that he thought it was cool—and maybe he wanted to do one next time."

"Evan," Cass began as an idea formed behind his sad eyes. "What if someone went to Beau with the pretext of him doing a dare?"

"I guess it could've been read like that." Evan rubbed at his eyes. "I thought it was the water dare he was talking about."

Melinda spoke. "In the video, he's doing a dare and it looks..."

"If there's a video, I gotta see it," Evan interrupted her. He pushed up from the floor and stood. He looked from Cass to Mel and then back to his friend. "I need to see it." He went to his bedroom and returned with his laptop. He put it on the bar beside Mel and started powering up the machine.

Cass got up and stood behind his buddy. He put his hand on Evan's bicep as Evan used the keyboard to open Dare Ya's homepage. "Hold on, brother," Cass said. "It's not a pretty sight. Maybe you should hold off and not watch it just yet."

Evan looked down at the hand on his arm. "Cass, I'm watching the damn video. He was my friend." He turned back to the computer and asked, "Where is it, Mel?"

She looked to Cass, who shrugged, and then she answered, "I took it off the main site, but I put a copy on my administration page." Evan proceeded through the site until he came to her work page. He looked to her questioningly. She said, "The password is M Cassidy." Evan's eyebrows shot up, but she merely shrugged. Evan typed in the password and started the video.

****

Beau climbed out of his truck and walked through the gravel parking lot with an enormous grin on his face. He looked to the sky in front of him and then back directly into the camera lens. "This is gonna be kick-ass."

"It sure is," a voice came from under the camera shot. From the angle of the footage, it appeared that a Go-Pro style camera was being used. It was probably being worn on a helmet by the cameraman. His arms could be seen from time to time as the camera filmed wherever he looked. He panned the lens from Beau across the lot to a multicolored hot air balloon tied to stakes and bobbing in the wind. "Masters and Cassidy are going to love it," the faceless voice continued.

Beau walked to the basket and shook hands with the balloon operator who had been waiting on the two approaching men. They spoke for a moment, and then the man busied himself getting everything ready for flight. Beau pulled his cell phone from his pocket and began typing a text. He looked into the camera lens and said, "I'll get them next time." He laughed.

The recording went black, and when it started again, the scene was from the basket of the balloon rising over a stand of pine trees. In the distance, the Mississippi River snaked its way south toward the city of Vicksburg.

The cameraman stood in one corner and filmed as the balloon operator pulled a large bungee cord from a nylon bag on the floor. He said, "I think we'll do it with the Vicksburg Bridge in the background."

Beau replied, "That'll be cool." His phone chirped, and he read the text. As the balloon drifted over a sandbar and the Big Black River, the camera moved from the driver to Beau. Beau looked up after typing a response text, and a metal object appeared at the bottom right of the camera view. The gun erupted and punched a hole in the top of the balloon operator's head.

Beau looked in his direction as the man slumped to the floor of the basket, his arms protruding from under his body at odd angles. "What the..." Beau began, but the cameraman produced a knife with his left hand and plunged the blade to its hilt into Beau's chest.

Beau looked down at the bloody knife handle, dropped his cell phone, and tried to grab at the killing tool. The video operator laughed and said, "No need; you can keep it," and then he shoved Beau over the railing. He tumbled backwards out of the basket, and the scene followed as his body plummeted to the water below. A purple shirt with the Dare Ya logo could be seen as Beau plummeted toward the waterway.

The video went to black.

****

Melinda took Evan's hand into hers and gave it a squeeze. He did not seem to notice as he turned from the computer screen and walked across the carnage of his living room. He plopped into a wingback chair and stared out the glass wall overlooking the city.

No one said anything for a while until Evan finally broke the silence. "Did I ever tell y'all about how Beau and I met?" He spoke with no inflection and continued to gaze out over the metropolis. "If that's what you'd call it, anyway. I'd been born for all of an hour when James Beauchamp III was brought into the nursery. Our dads were both standing at the glass partition, smiling. My old man told me two nurses brought us both over at the same time for our first official viewing. Our parents had grown up together, so it was almost like we were twins." Evan wiped a lone tear from his cheek. "We spent every birthday growing up together: two cakes, always side by side. Every memorable event in my life starts with Beau's laugh, or of that sigh that he gives... gave..., at anything that annoyed him."

Melinda and Cass leaned on the counter in the kitchen, listening to their friend tell his story. They had heard this tale before, but if Evan felt better telling it, they would definitely listen. Evan put his head into his hands and rubbed at his temples before he continued. "Since that damn accident, yeah, we sort of grew apart." He continued to glare at the floor in front of him.

"It's okay," Cass tried to comfort him. "We're here for you."

Evan nodded his head up and down but never looked over to his friend. He went on. "But the drifting apart was more my fault because I felt so damn guilty about what I'd done. Goddamn it, I'm going to miss him." The pain in his voice was overwhelming.

"We all are," Melinda tried. "We had all gotten close over the last few years."

"He sure could make me laugh by giving you pure hell, E." Cass snorted a cheerless laugh.

Evan smiled a little, but it fell away quickly. He ran his hands through the hair on the sides and interlocked his fingers on the back of his head. He leaned back in the chair and said, "The sick bastard used our first dare to lure Beau in. Why, Cass? Why would anybody want to hurt him?"

"I don't know, E, but I promise you we'll find out."

Evan stood, stretched, turned to Cass, and said, "Whoever it is, they thought it was easy to kill my friend, but he'll find it much harder to live with the hell I put him through."

**\*\*\*\***

The Director sat motionless, Indian style, on the floor. His eyes were closed and his hands rested lightly, one on each knee. He took slow, rhythmic inhalations barely perceivable to the burly man who had stepped into the darkened room a few moments before.

The Director's breathing became deeper with each intake, and he held each for exactly seven seconds. The man beside the entranceway stood and watched the boss rouse himself from wherever his meditation had taken him. Then the Director's eyes sprang open, and he went from sitting to standing in one swift motion without the use of his hands.

Still not acknowledging the giant man, the Director leaned forward, bent at the waist, and blew out the lone candle resting on the small shrine before him. Finally, he turned around and asked for an account of the information for which he had been waiting.

"Mr. Shefton reports that all went according to plan in Mississippi," the man told his boss, pronouncing every syllable of the Southern state as only an outsider would. "He has returned to his home and is awaiting further instructions."

"Yes, yes. Excellent news, Max. Have we any word from my dear Constance?" The Director walked by Max, and his huge employee fell into step behind his supervisor.

"She has not checked in," he answered to his superior's back as their footfalls echoed down the corridor. "Should I contact her and tell her you wish an update, sir?"

The Director stopped in front of a door and pivoted to face Max. "That won't be necessary; she knows perfectly well the plan and its importance to me." He turned and opened the door, stepped through to his living quarters, and added back to Max, "Keep me up to date, if you should receive any more information. Things should be accelerating from here on." Then he closed the door without waiting for a response.

The Director had a small smile on his face as he sat at his desk in front of the computer screen. He looked at a silver picture frame on the corner and said to the man staring back at him, "Accelerating, indeed. We should have our recompense very soon."

He moved the mouse on his computer and his screen saver disappeared. After logging onto the internet, he typed the address to a website. His smile slipped from his face and a look of hate took its place as the Dare Ya logo and sign-in page popped onto the screen.

# Chapter 34

## Ten days later

Evan Masters and Matthew Cassidy landed in Dare Ya's G5 at the Vicksburg Airport. They were returning to the city of Evan's youth to attend the memorial service of his cherished friend James Beauchamp. A few hours after Evan had first watched the cold-blooded killing of his friend, he called the Warren County sheriff's office in Mississippi. He told them about the video and then sent one of the detectives a copy.

The sheriff's department instigated a massive search of the river basin for Beau and the surrounding area for the missing balloon. The following night some high school kids happened upon the colorful remains of the balloon almost two hundred miles west of the Mississippi River in a rural wooded part of Louisiana. After five more days of searching the waterway south to the Gulf of Mexico and finding no body, Beau was eventually declared dead based on the video footage.

The two Dare Ya creators climbed into their rental car for the final leg of their long trip east. Earlier in the week, they had gone to Lincoln, Nebraska to attend the on-campus memorial for the murdered students. Yes, that service had been extremely sad; but for Evan, the scene he walked into at Beau's memorial was surreal.

Beau's mother had treated Evan with a cool hostility from the moment of the accident that took her son's arm. She was never overtly mean, but she had a look in her eyes that said she blamed him, and she always found reason to leave a room whenever Evan walked into it. The day of the funeral was different, however. Evan was welcomed like a soldier returning from war. Ms. Pam put her arms around him and hugged him with all her might. She said, "He loved you like a brother, you know?"

"And I him," Evan whispered into her ear. "He was the best friend a man could grow up with. I'm so sorry, Ms. Pam."

She patted him on the back and they broke the embrace. She sniffled and dried her eyes with a Kleenex she clutched in her hand. Ms. Pam ran her arm through his and added, "Help me get through this, Evan."

He rubbed the back of her hand as Cass walked over and joined them. "Ms. Pam, Beau was a great man, and even though I hadn't known him for too long, he was becoming a great friend. I will miss him."

Again Beau's mother dabbed at her eyes, and Evan looked away to let his own eyes reabsorb the tears that wanted to fall. Ms. Pam put her other arm around Cass and they walked to the front of the funeral home. As they went through the crowd, Evan and Ms. Pam talked to people they had known for years. They made introductions until all the faces jumbled together for Cass. The two talked to each of the mourners about more people Cass did not know, so his mind wondered back to the previous week when they had left Las Vegas on their tour of grief.

Melinda had driven them to the airport, and as Evan was stowing their luggage into the plane, she stood on the tarmac with Cass. He asked, "Are you sure you don't want to come with us?"

"Somebody has to run the show out here," she answered, looking up into his eyes. "Besides, you two need a little reconnect time after the other night."

"You're probably right," he said. Planes were taxiing and taking off all around. The noise was loud, but Cass and Melinda seemed to only hear and see each other. "I'll call you every night and let you know if we find anything new."

"Yeah, that's probably a good idea." She slowly stood on her tiptoes, making herself taller as he leaned into her.

"There you go, Trigger," Evan yelled over all the roaring aircraft as he stepped beside the two. He bumped his hip into Cass's and continued, "Kiss her, already." Melinda blushed and stared at a crack in the concrete. Cass shook his head and pushed Evan out of his personal space. Evan chuckled and continued, "I'm not blind or stupid. There's something between y'all that Madam Curry could see."

"Come on, E," Cass said. "Not now, okay?"

Evan put his arm around Melinda and pushed Cass on the shoulder. "All right bro, but when we get back, this is priority numero uno. Life goes on and all that bullshit."

"Not the time, Fly Guy."

"I heard you, but y'all both promise me we'll sit down and talk about my favorite two people hooking up when we get back home."

Cass snapped back to the service as the preacher stepped to the microphone and started the opening prayer. Cass bowed his head, but as the reverend prayed, he saw Melinda's face as she looked up at him with her forehead creased when they'd both agreed with Evan. Every night that he had called her over the past week, he wanted to broach the subject; but each time, he decided to wait. He would tell her and Evan how he felt later. Then he'd let the chips fall where they may, but it would have to wait until they returned to Vegas. If two funeral services in a week had taught him anything, it was that life is too short to hide emotions.

After the memorial service, since there would be no graveside service, everyone went back to Ms. Pam's home. Evan stayed with the woman through every moment of the day. All the people present had some story to reminisce about—usually something crazy Beau and Evan had done in their youth. On that day of remembrance, no one mentioned the crash or the aftermath of that afternoon all those years ago. Evan was thankful. The anecdotes told were of happier times, and that helped Evan as well Ms. Pam get through the day.

After many stories were shared and old times remembered, people began saying their good-byes and going back to their lives. When Ms. Pam and Evan were the only two left in the suddenly-quiet house, she asked, "Where did Matthew get off to?"

"He took the rental car up to his parents' place," Evan answered. Then he smiled into his whiskey glass as he turned away from her and took the last swallow.

He stood from his stool and went to the wet bar across the room to pour two fingers more of Jim Beam over his remaining ice cubes. When he had his drink to go with his somber mood, all he needed was the music. He knelt in front of an old record player, pulled one of Beau's old B.B. King records from its cover, and let the needle scratch out the blues.

His mind flashed still shot photos of all the treks Beau had dragged him on when they were younger. Beau loved the blues, and Mississippi is full of places made famous for their blended tunes. The Howlin' Wolf Festival in West Point, The Blues Fest in the Clarksdale - and they had been staples at the B.B. King Festival in Philadelphia. Evan thought back to the red plastic cups and the mismatched plastic chairs as he let the Blues Boy and his baby Lucille's sweet melody wash over him.

He let the memories of his past fade as he went back to the kitchen bar. He put a hand on Beau's mother's arm and asked, "Is there anything I can do for you, Ms. Pam? Anything at all?"

She looked into his face and pursed her lips, fighting emotions. Evan could see the struggle she fought, trying to contain the tears. She patted his hand, stood up, and went to the record player to give herself time to regain her composure. She skipped the record ahead a few songs, and as the new tune began, she stood tall, closed her eyes, and hugged her arms tightly around herself. Evan never took his eyes from her.

When she finally opened her eyes, the resolve was back once again, and she eventually spoke. "He loved this song. I bet I've heard it a hundred times." She watched a scene only she could see and then turned and looked back at Evan as she continued, "There are a couple of things you can do for me, Evan. First, you call me Mama Pam like you used to when y'all were kids." She took another pause to build her strength, and then, through clenched teeth, she said, "Second, you find the bastards who did this. I want you to take all these emotions," she tapped her chest above her heart, took her time, and slowly pronounced the list. "Love, hate, grief, loneliness, and all the others that I feel at the moment, and let those people feel them, too. Can you do that for me, Evan?"

Evan slammed back his whiskey and felt the burn as it went down his throat. He walked in front of her and met her stare. "Don't you worry, Mama Pam; when I'm done, these assholes'll have reached levels of hurt that the devil himself couldn't have put on 'em. That's a promise."

# Chapter 35

Cass worked out a plan as he drove north on Highway 25 across the state he had grown up in. He would not be in his hometown long, but he and Evan had decided on the plane from Vegas that he should check any and every possibility. As he drove, he thought back to his departure from Ms. Pam's when Evan had walked him out to the rental car and given him the keys. Evan said, "Look, Trigger, I've been giving this some more thought, and I need to spend some time with Ms. Pam while you run this lead."

"This lead? Now who sounds like a full-fledged cop?"

"Yeah, I'm a regular Dick Tracey. Screw you and listen. You keep your head down, and I'm sure it'll be nothing, but we've gotta check this out while we're here. This should be the last time we separate until we get a handle on this thing."

"Agreed," Cass had said as he climbed into the car. Evan leaned with one arm on the open door and one on the roof as Cass kept talking. "I'll meet you back at the hotel tomorrow afternoon sometime."

"Oh, by the way, Trigger." Evan looked around to make sure no one was around. "Remember you owe me one for the Magic Man, right?"

"Whatever." Cass looked up with suspicion. "I guess I owe you one. Why?"

Evan smiled big and laid out his 'Dare' to exact his revenge on his friend. After he had heard it all, Cass said, "You're a sick son of a bitch."

"Ain't I, though?" Evan asked as he slammed the car door, slapped its roof, and turned and walked back to the house.

****

Early the next morning, as the gravel crunched beneath the tires of the rental car and stray rocks pinged off the undercarriage, Cass shook his head. "I can't believe I'm doing this," he said aloud to the interior of the car as he pulled it to a stop.

Cass climbed from the vehicle and looked around the yard as he went up the curved walk to the front entrance. He approached the front of the house, looked at the doorbell, decided against it, and pounded loudly on the door with his fist. A few seconds later, the door swung inward, and the young sheriff's deputy stood with his uniform shirt unbuttoned and untucked. He stared in disbelief at Cass standing on his front stoop.

Finally the cop's demeanor returned, and he hiked his pants up higher on his hips and said, "Boy, this had better be good. You coming to my house like this and all."

"Hello Michael, you piece of shit." Cass stepped closer to the deputy and invaded his personnel space. "Remember me?"

The officer swallowed hard and tried to hold eye contact with Cass. It did not last long before he blinked and took a small step backwards, retreating into his house. At that moment, Cass knew that Deputy Sheriff Michael Passton was not behind any of the murders. He was just a simple man from a simple little town that Matthew Cassidy had left behind long ago. It had been a long shot, but Evan had convinced him to check it out just to be sure, probably more for the dare he had sent Cass on than to actually check on the policeman. Cass was certain that this man did not own a decent computer, let alone be able to start an elaborate plan of multiple murders.

Cass turned and started to walk away, but after only a few steps, he turned back and pulled a pink G-string thong from the front pocket of his jeans. He let them dangle on his finger for a second before he stepped to Michael and shoved them into the deputy's shirt pocket. "Oh yeah, tell Ami she left these in the car, will ya? Wouldn't want somebody to think I was stealing anything."

Cass clapped the man hard on the shoulder, showed him a toothy smile, and left the front porch. He looked back toward the house as he was driving away and saw that Michael had not moved. He still stood with his mouth hanging, following Cass's car with his eyes only.

Evan was sitting in a rocking chair on the front veranda of the small hotel when Cass walked up the steps. Evan lowered his sunglasses on his nose, grinning like a possum. "Well, how'd it go, Big Boy?"

"It wasn't him," Cass answered as he eased into a chair beside his tormentor. "He's probably still standing there trying to catch flies with his mouth open."

"Good man," Evan said, pushing his shades up once more and leaning back rocking the chair. "I take it the dare went without a hitch?"

"Yeah, we skipped piano practice this time," Cass answered, and blushed.

"Did you happen to get a quick pic or video for your old friend?"

"Piss on you." Cass gave him the bird. "And no details for you either, so don't ask."

"Ah well, at least you settled up with ol' Ami. We knew Deputy Dog was a long shot." Evan pushed Cass on the arm as he took the seat beside his friend. "I know what you're thinking, Trigger, and Mel will never know. I swear."

"I sort of feel like I betrayed her or something."

"Damn; you're whipped and y'all ain't even gone on a date yet. Be honest, was Mrs. Ami worth the Farm and the wait?"

"My conscience may haunt me forever, but I have to say she was damn near worth the wait, but not the Farm," Cass said as the edge left his voice. Both men laughed, and it felt good.

After they settled and sat in silence for a few minutes, Evan pushed up from his seat and said, "Let's go see if we can find out who Beau was with on that dare."

Mama Pam had told Evan the previous day that she could not remember anything about the man Beau had been with except of course for the bright-colored Dare Ya T-shirt and cap he had been wearing. "I wasn't paying him much attention. He was just some guy that talked way too much but didn't really say much of anything. One of those types," she had said. She then told Evan that her son had lately been hanging out with a guy named Billy Joe. "You remember him, don't you, Evan?" she had asked. "His dad owns the big furniture store uptown. Billy Joe helps the old man down there while he's learning the business."

Evan did remember Billy Joe, although they had never been much more than acquaintances in high school. BJ had been a second string tight end when Evan was a senior on the football team. While those memories swam around in Evan's head, Cass pushed the door to the furniture store open and a small bell hanging over it rang when they walked in. An old black man approached the pair to see if they needed any assistance. "We're looking for BJ," Evan responded.

"Over here," a voice called from behind a mock bedroom display. Cass watched a giant man come around an armoire carrying a recliner as though it were a child's seat. He sat it down and said, "I saw you at the funeral, Masters. It's been a long time."

With his huge gut hanging low over his belt buckle, BJ waddled over and shook Evan and then Cass's hands. Evan introduced the two, and BJ slumped down into a couch that was part of a living room set on exhibit. He motioned, and Cass sat on a matching love seat while Evan declined and remained standing.

"BJ," Evan started as he looked down at the big man. "We're trying to figure out who Beau was with on the day or so before... well, you know."

"Yeah, sure, I know. It was some Yankee guy." BJ combed through the little bit of hair he had on top of his head with his fingers. "A real cocky SOB. He talked a lot, I do remember that."

BJ told them about the afternoon he, Beau, and the stranger had spent drinking some beers and not doing much. Then he pointed at his right ear and added, "He did have a scar that ran from here down his cheek-bone. Seems like it split, like a fork in a road, right before it went into his shirt collar." He traced the lines with his fingers down his own jawbone.

Evan looked over at Cass and all of the blood had drained from the big man's face as he listened to BJ. Evan asked him, "What is it, Cass?"

By way of a response, Cass motioned toward the front door with his head. Evan did not hesitate for even a second. He thanked BJ for his time and he and Cass left the store. Out on the sidewalk, Cass finally said, "It couldn't be," as he flexed and unflexed his right hand.

"Couldn't be what?"

"Heat," Cass answered, coming as close to a growl as a human being could.

"Heat?" Evan stopped a short way down the street. He turned to Cass and added, "You mean that piece of shit from Bagdad, that Heat? What was his name, Sheppard or something like that?"

"Shefton," Cass said in a murderous voice. "That bastard."

"Easy, Trigger," Evan responded, looking up and down the street. "Let's not jump to any conclusions here. Maybe it's just a coincidence with a scar that's close to his."

"Bullshit, Evan. You don't believe in coincidences any more than I do."

They started toward the rental car once again. As they walked, Evan asked, "Okay, okay why would this Shefton prick go through Beau to get to you?"

"That's just how the sick fuck thinks. He'd hurt you or anyone else to get to me. Trust me." Cass hit the key fob and the doors unlocked. Over the roof he added, "If this was Shefton, I'm going to kill him this time."

"Well, if he's the asshole that killed Beau, you may have to wait in line." Evan climbed into the car. As they slammed the doors, he added, "How are we going to find this dude, Cass? Hold that thought." He pulled his phone from his pocket and dialed. He put it to his ear and after a few seconds, he said, "Melinda." He drawled it out in his sauciest Southern accent. "Whatcha wearing, good looking?"

Cass felt the warmth on his neck, and his face flushed. Evan was laughing at Mel's response. "Don't worry girl, I just wanted to see lover boy's face. You should see him right now; it's one of those 'I don't know if I should be mad or if I should throw up' faces." More laughter followed, and none of it was from Cass.

Cass reached over and took the phone. To Evan he said, "Very funny, hardy har har." To Mel, "Hey, yeah ain't he so damn hilarious? Anyway, look, we're still down here in Vicksburg. Yeah, we're going to the airport right now."

Evan finally got his laughing spell under control, regained his composure, and took the phone back from Cass. After he started the car, Cass backed out as Evan was speaking to Melinda. "It's me again. We'll be out there in a few hours. While we're airborne, find out all you can about a guy named Shefton." He looked to Cass and raised his eyebrows.

"Daniel. Daniel Shefton."

"Right," Evan said into the phone. "Anything you can get. Okay, bye."

After he hung up, Evan scrolled through the contacts in his phone and dialed another number. He told his friend Rob the same thing that he had informed Melinda of and then disconnected. "Rob the dirty cop again?" Cass asked.

"You call him dirty; I call it connected. Whatever." Evan shrugged. They drove through the town, but neither was paying any attention to the scenery.

When they reached the airport, Cass finally said, "I figure Mel can dig up Heat; we don't need some crooked cop."

"Jesus, choir boy, he's just got a thing for strippers. Don't make such a thing out of it. He's not into illegal shit or anything, and he was in Intel with the Army before he was a cop." Evan got out of the car in front of the rental service. When Cass was out as well, he continued, "He's not a bad guy, Trigger. Trust me he can be useful."

"If you say so." The two walked out to the plane and loaded their luggage. They settled into the comfortable cabin seats for the flight back out west. Neither man said a word the entire flight.

# Chapter 36

## A Month Earlier

Daniel Shefton started his day like most others since he was discharged from the Marine Corps, using the same routine and trying not to let the demons in his head show. He returned home several years ago with aspirations to turn his military training into a rewarding civilian career with a police department. Every department he applied to let him know quickly that his services were not needed or, more to the point, were not wanted.

His anger with the system grew. To Shefton, he was a perfect example of an officer of the law—a protector of peace and champion of an orderly society. He was born to do those things. It's not his fault that the people in the Corps always assigned a dumbass to positions above him. They never saw his potential, much less let him take the reins and demonstrate his capability.

Shefton refused to let lesser individuals keep him from defending the American way of life. He was a patriot through and through, but this great nation was not formed by bureaucracy or cowering to Arab nations, terrorists, or even politicians who attained their station by family name or money. It was built on the backs of great men who sometimes did not follow all of the rules but who had freedom as their goal. It boiled up and angered Shefton every time he thought about how the citizens of this great country seemed to forget his kind and pretend they did not need them.

Shefton believed he was one of those great men. His chain of command in the Marines and the stupid police departments simply could not see it. He often thought that if such men were protecting his beloved country, then it was in serious trouble. Some day in the future, a future not too far away, people like him would have to step to the plate and take charge of the situation, but why did the bastards have to make it so hard on him at every turn?

A year following the Marines, he finally found a home with a group of like-minded men who owned over a thousand acres—a place full of compatriots with whom he could at last identify. The first time he stepped foot on the compound, Daniel Shefton knew he was where he belonged. Almost five years after joining the faction, he had worked his way to second in command.

*These guys see it in me,* Shefton thought to himself as he paced behind the firing line. The crack of semiautomatic weapons woke him from his reverie. He kicked a rock with his combat boot, into which his camo fatigues were bloused. His brown, military-issue skivvy shirt was tight on his muscled body and tucked into the trim waistband. With this group, just like in the Corps, every member must be a basic rifleman. That rule applied to cooks, recruiters, wives, and children. Therefore, his assignment as range and armory officer was crucial.

Kneeling down, he was instructing one of the snipers with tidbits of wisdom when the gallery phone buzzed through the speakers set along the line. His assistant answered, gave a loud whistle, and signaled that the call was for Shefton. He stood, angry at the interruption, and strode to the shack.

To his aide he said, "This better be good." The young man stood at attention and handed his boss the receiver without a word. Into the phone Shefton barked, "Yeah, what is it?"

"Mr. Shefton? Or should I call you Heat?" the caller asked.

Shefton's head started spinning. He had not heard that name in years. Only his Marine buddies, and they were few, called him that. He tried to regain composure and asked, "Who the fuck is this?" Then he growled, his anger quick to boil.

"Careful how you talk to strangers, Heat. One never knows when that person can become an ally," the voice responded.

"Look, whoever you are, I'm busy and don't have time for games. Get to what you want or this conversation's over."

"What I want and what you want, I have found to be very similar, Heat." Shefton could hear the man's smile in his voice. "Why don't we have a sit-down and talk about how we can build a wonderful partnership?"

"I'm in the middle of something here," Shefton said. "You've got to do better than that."

"Several people have told me that your organization, and *you* in particular, would be useful to some of my endeavors." Shefton strained to listen as a loud burst of rifle claps came from the range. The caller continued, "I believe you will find that we have some of the same adversaries and, as the proverb says, 'The enemy of mine enemy is my friend.'"

"Okay, buddy," Shefton answered after the volley ended. "You can rattle off Sun Tzu all day long, but it'd be better if you'd simply answered two questions." Shefton's voice betrayed that his patience was wearing thin. "First, what's in this for me? And what the hell is your name? Since you seem to know so much about me."

"Money and revenge for you, Heat; and you may call me the Director."

Shefton blew a snort through his nose that sounded like a chuckle, "Oh brother. Code names? Seriously? I want one." He took a deep breath and blew it out before he continued. "You know what, man? Whatever. I'll listen to what you're talking about because you've piqued my interest. When and where?"

"Dinner in two hours at a pub called O'Shays. You familiar with it?" the Director asked.

"Sure," Shefton answered. Then, after a few seconds of thinking, looking up at some used targets hanging on the wall, he added, "This better not be a waste of my time, Mr. Director," with dripping sarcasm.

"I assure you, Heat," the caller answered, ignoring the disdain. "It will be anything but."

"One more thing—you might not want to call me that again."

"And why would that be?" he asked with a chuckle.

"Because the last prick who did, I put a bullet in," Shefton answered and then hung up the phone.

He went back to the firing line and let his mind wander back to the conversation. In the lifestyle Daniel Shefton lived, he could not entirely trust anyone, but from time to time, crazy people were lucrative. He had already decided he would listen to this Director character—see what he had to say. The group he hoped to lead could always use the money.

**** 

Shefton made his way to the back of O'Shays. It was crowded, but not so much that all the tables were occupied—not many more than half were full. He had taken a quick shower and changed clothes to remove the cordite smell. He wanted to get to the bar early to have a few beers and calm his nerves. A couple of pitchers of MGD Light later, Shefton believed the guy was going to be a no-show. Shefton began to get irritated at himself for letting some yahoo talk him into coming to town for nothing. After he had downed one more drink, he decided to leave and head back to the compound.

As Shefton dropped a few dollars on the table, a pretty young woman stood in front of him without saying a word. She was dressed similar to a waitress, and at first he mistook her for exactly that. He was trying to keep his eyes open for the Director, but he had caught her coolly looking at him and blocking his exit. Shefton lost interest in everything else and took a good look at the woman for the first time. She had an exotic, if not dangerous, look about her. She was not runway-model hot but very curvy and sexy all the same.

"Excuse me but were you about to leave?" she asked.

"Why; is that not a big enough tip?" Shefton blushed. "I'll leave some more money." He was not very good with the ladies, and he usually felt like he was doomed in that department.

"I'm not the waitress, stud."

"Oh, um, yeah, my bad," he stammered. "Well, I was going to leave, but you could convince me to stay," he added trying to recover and giving her a coy smile. At least that is how he intended it.

Shefton nodded to a man at the bar and then returned to his table with the woman. He had agreed to meet with the Director, but he was never told to come alone. Shefton's buddy at the bar kept an eye on the door as Shefton ordered another pitcher.

As the authentic waitress walked away, Shefton noticed his new companion staring a hole in him. "So what's your name? I'm Daniel."

"Constance." She nodded and reached her small hand across the table for a quick shake. "I know who you are, Mr. Shefton. My employer sent me here for this sit-down."

A quick flash of anger crossed Shefton's face. "Ah, the mysterious Director." He tried a smile to hide his frustration. "Not that I'm complaining, but I figured the guy would be here himself."

"That's not how he does things," she said as the waitress returned with the pitcher of beer and two fresh mugs. After the server left, Constance continued, "He sends me, and I make his pitch. It has served us well."

"Hell, look - Constance is it?" He took a long pull from his beer and held her glare. She nodded. "I don't have time for this Agatha Christie bullshit. Make me understand what the fuck's going on, and do it quick, or I'm outta here." Shefton's demons coiled around in his brain, and he was having a tough time containing them.

"First, my employer wishes to eventually employ your group, through you, to move a substantial amount of firearms into the greater Los Angeles area."

For the first time, interest showed on his face. "What sort of firearms are we talking, here?"

"All of that will be explained at the right time. We must - how did the Director put it? test your trustworthiness." She watched him closely for a reaction.

"Before we test anything, I need to know the potential profit for my guys." Shefton looked around the room, pausing briefly on his cohort at the bar. He was thinking if he could bring in a lot of money, pushing the old man out might be easier. Then, he would be the one in charge.

Constance placed her elbows on the table and laced her fingers. She waited for Shefton to look at her again. "The profits have the possibility to be enormous. Believe me when I say it could change the entire fabric of your organization." She sat back in her chair and locked her eyes on Shefton's.

Shefton gave her a demented grin and then scratched the stubble of his beard. He tried desperately to hold eye contact but broke it rather quickly and looked into his beer. "Explain the damn test," was all he said.

"Yes. That is why I am here. I'm supposed to tell you that to get the revenge you want, it would behoove you to work with us."

"Revenge? What the hell are you talking about, lady? You and this 'Director,'" (Shefton made quotation marks with his fingers as a thin line of spittle connected his lips), "have been talking in riddles since his phone call this morning."

"You are not holed up on that compound because you have no enemies, Mr. Shefton."

"That does it," he erupted, and stood to leave. Some of the other patrons turned to see what the commotion was. He reined his voice back down and went on. "I can't take any more crazy talk."

"Sit down, Mr. Shefton," she calmly responded to his outburst. She looked up and again met his eyes. Something in there chilled him to the bone. He stopped and sat down again, watching her intently. "We need you in Nebraska three weeks from today."

She continued laying out the entire plan to Shefton. He listened as the beers between them turned lukewarm. Constance told him his part in the plan and explained exactly what such actions would accomplish. When she finished, Shefton reached out and grabbed his mug. He stared into the golden hops but did not lift it for a drink. He let her plan wash over him. Constance waited.

Shefton clutched the glass so tightly that his knuckles turned a bright white. He looked up and said, "The son of bitch has something exactly like this coming. It's about freaking time he's brought down a notch or two."

****

After Shefton left the pub, Constance sat and thought about the conversation. Her boss would not be happy, that was for sure, but she would help him deal with it any way he saw fit. She pulled her phone out and called the man in charge. He answered on the first ring, and she told him that the conference had concluded.

"And how is Mr. Shefton?" the Director asked.

"He loves the money and weapons part of the deal, as we knew he would: but get this, the prick refuses to go after Cassidy. It's like the bastard was scared of a ghost or something because as soon as I said the name, he went white and almost fell out of his chair. He said he'll do anything except bring Matthew Cassidy back into his world."

"I don't follow."

Constance tried to explain the weird conversation she'd had with Shefton. "He said that it took him years to get all the knots out of the ball of yarn Cassidy put in his head and he wasn't about to let him twist him up again. His words, not mine, boss."

The Director took a long pause before he finally responded. "Well, let him continue to Nebraska, but after that, it'll have to turn very unfortunate for Mr. Shefton." The frustration was evident in his voice.

"I'll be happy to handle the very unfortunate part for him," Constance said, clearly anticipating the act. "He rubbed me the wrong way today."

"My dear Constance, I'm sure he did; he is but a brute," the Director said with a chuckle, finally relaxing and letting the aggravation pass. "But I have a better idea. We have that thing in Mississippi to handle, and a plan is just forming in my mind." He sat silent pondering for a few minutes. Constance knew better than to interrupt his musings. "Yes, yes. It'll work nicely," he said at last. "I'll put it all together and fill you in after the Nebraska job."

# Chapter 37

Walking into the building at Dare Ya, Cass looked around at the walls and floors, and he saw memories everywhere. He saw Tom from accounting, Meg from advertising, and Sally, who had been Al's secretary from the beginning. This place, these people - they were his second family, and his family was under attack. It was time to deal with this threat and deal with it accordingly. People were in danger because of them. Now was the time to set it straight. As Cass and Evan made their way into the elevator, Evan noticed Cass flexing his fist, and that his jaw was taut. Evan put his hand on Cass's shoulder and said, "I know, Bro. I feel the same way."

"We can't let whoever is doing this get away with it, E," Cass said.

"Not gonna happen."

Evan was the first off the lift; he strode into Melinda's office and straight to the bar. Cass was right on his heels but stopped at her desk.

Evan said "Anybody care to join me?" Cass and Mel both declined. "Well, did you turn anything up there, Miss Kitty?" Evan joked.

"Miss Kitty? Very funny," said Cass.

"Yeah, that's real funny, Evan. Anyway, I turned up bunches, as you rednecks say."

Cass laughed at that. Although they were going through hell, it felt great to be back in that building with his friends. Evan took a sip of his drink, grinning, obviously thinking the same thing. Melinda was smiling as well and shaking her head at the same time. They would find a way through this. Cass felt it in his bones.

"Let's hear it," Evan said, bringing Cass back.

Melinda told the tale of Daniel Shefton as Evan and Matthew listened. She followed his life after the Marine Corps, through the rejections by police departments all over his home state. Then he'd headed out west to California, and she explained that she found one year of tax returns as a security guard for some small firm, but no more. "You can get a lot of information from a Google search and a few phone calls," Melinda told them. "But after that, like six years ago, he dropped off the map. I mean, nothing that I can find about his whereabouts, anyway."

"That would be exactly how I saw his life turning out," Cass said.

Melinda stood up and walked to the bar. She poured a whiskey straight over three cubes of ice and took a sip.

Evan responded, "But it doesn't really tie him to us, does it?"

"Yeah," Cass said. "I was definitely hoping for more."

"There *is* more." Melinda took another swallow and proceeded. "But I needed a drink for this part."

Both Evan and Cass simultaneously asked, "What is it?"

Melinda walked back to the desk and gathered her notes. She sat down and began again. "This Shefton character belongs to another Organization. Anybody care to guess?"

"I don't know, Mel, the NRA?" asked Evan.

"Please," said Cass.

"The Dare Ya Organization," she said. "He and his group've been members since the year before last. They've got a charter called "Protectors." After doing some checking, I found they've even been to a couple of the Dare Ya parties that you two hosted. Lately, though, most of their activities have been off the rez—the sub sites that do more of the non-sanctioned dares. People on the site call them sub-cults. Unfortunately, there are more of these sub-cults than we can keep track of."

"Yeah, I've done some looking into those myself," said Cass. "Mostly Goth kids doing crazy dares that we won't let on Dare Ya, and a few hardcore groups doing some dangerous stuff. I never gave it much thought because we can't tell people what to do, and Legal told me not to worry about it because they put links to their sites on their private messages, and it's not tied to us in any way."

Evan joined in with, "A few of these nut cases have approached me with some of their dares; wanted me to help them promote their own websites. One dumbass went so far as to say that they would help us make money." He shook his head and rattled the ice around in his glass. "Like I need that schmuke's money."

Cass turned to Melinda, and steering the conversation back, he said, "Any ideas where we can find Mr. Shefton?"

"The trail goes cold there," she replied.

Evan laughed and said, "Let me go check in with Rob; maybe he'll have something."

"Evan," Cass began.

Evan held up his hand, knowing where his friend was going. "I've got this, Big Guy. Let me handle it."

"If you say so," Cass responded, and turned from his partner.

As Evan was leaving the office, pulling his cell phone from his pocket, he turned back to Cass and Melinda. "Oh, I almost forgot," he said with a huge 'cat in the birdcage' grin smeared across his face. "I made reservations at Alize, in the Palms, for eight o'clock, while we were on the plane. I think it's about time you two had that first date. All this can wait one night."

Neither Melinda nor Cass could find their voice, so Evan continued as he left the office: "Y'all can thank me later. Love you guys!"

# Chapter 38

Melinda woke with the smell of fresh flowers in the air. She rolled over, sticking out her arm, feeling for Cass. What she found instead was a single long stem rose, sans the thorns, of course. She smiled, put the red petals to her nose, and called out for Cass. "Matthew! Where are you? CCAASS! You better not be working out. I still have some work for you to do in here." She giggled.

When she heard no response, she propped up on her pillows and thought of the night before. She and Matthew had walked into the Alize arm in arm; Melinda in her favorite little black dress and Cass wearing the charcoal grey suit that she loved so much. How had he known? The purple and yellow tie, always the Dare Ya colors with Cass, made her worry again about how this would affect the company. Would things change? Was it a bad thing if it did?

They had agreed not to discuss or think about how their first date would impact tomorrow or the days that followed. They would think no further than dinner.

That seemed to be the problem after the maître d' took them to their table. The two of them sat, and when they did talk, it was like two strangers on a blind date. Cass waited for her to order, and then he placed his as well. The couple was silent again as soon as the waiter left.

Melinda took a nervous sip of her wine and glanced around the room at all the smiling faces. When she placed her glass back on the table, Cass took her hand in his. She looked from the crowd into his eyes. He took a few seconds to look up at her, and then he asked, "What are we doing? We're acting like a couple of teenagers on their first date."

She smiled at him and put her other hand on top of his. "Why? I have no idea, because you are the person I feel the most comfortable with in the entire world."

"Except Evan, of course," she said, and winked.

"No, Melinda, not 'Except Evan.'" He took her hand and brushed his lips over her knuckles. "There's only you—especially tonight."

"Oh, Matthew," was all she could say. Then it was as if they had been married for fifty years instead of this being their initial date. They laughed and talked. Dinner went by in a blink. The restaurant and the food were faultless, but neither Melinda nor Cass noticed.

She stood up and wrapped the housecoat around her body. The night before had been more wonderful than she could have ever dreamed. They had left Alize and went dancing. Then the two went back to her house to culminate the perfect evening.

Mel was warm and cozy in her robe as she pushed open the French doors of her bedroom and stepped onto the loft landing overlooking her living room. What she saw made her gasp. "Oh, Cass."

There were dozens of roses everywhere—white roses, red roses, orange roses, yellow roses. All over the room below, vases held the fragrant flowers. Melinda closed her eyes and inhaled deeply. "Oh Cass," she said again as she opened her eyes and took in the scene before her once again.

She walked down the curved staircase along the wall and saw an envelope on the table at the bottom of the steps. She opened it and read the card inside.

*Miss Kitty,*

> *Please forgive me for not waking you. You looked so peaceful. I hope you enjoy what's in the box.*
>
> 

*See You Tonight,*

*Cass*

Where the card had been, she saw a black, velvet box. She was shaking when she opened the top. Two of the biggest, brightest diamond earrings she had ever seen lay in the perfect case. *Priceless*, she thought. *I think I'm falling for him.*

\*\*\*\*

Cass rode the elevator up toward Evan's suite. He could only grin at his thought of the debauchery he would find when he got there. After all, Evan was notoriously famous for his nights out in Vegas—infamous, actually. Well, it would not be the first bimbo Cass had paid off and escorted out of the apartment.

He decided to forgo pounding on the door. He slid the key Evan had given him into the lock. When he did so, the door flung inward, and Evan stood there, looking bright-eyed and bushy-tailed, smiling at Cass.

Evan handed Cass a steaming cup of coffee and asked, "Where you been, Trigger?"

They walked into the living room as Cass answered. "I figured you'd need time to sleep off your homecoming party, so I took my time."

"You're good, my friend, but I can see it all over your face." When Cass would not make eye contact or respond, Evan kept talking. "I was just about to come get you. Lord knows you've interrupted enough of my mornings in bed with a good-looking woman."

"Piss on you, E," Cass said, and then took a sip of his coffee as his face turned a dark shade of red.

Evan laughed as he said, "I take it dinner went well." He went into the kitchen and made some turkey and cheese sandwiches. He put one on a plate and slid it across the bar toward his friend.

Cass took some chips from a bag, put them on the plate, and then smeared a little mayonnaise and mustard on the bread before he answered. "It went great. Thanks, bud, and I mean that."

"Yeah, yeah," Evan said through the first bite of his sandwich, "but please tell me you didn't go all Boy Scout on me and 'fess up' about the deputy's girlfriend."

Cass popped some chips into his mouth. As he walked to the refrigerator and bent down to get a bottle of water, he answered, "Of course not. You think I'm some kind of dumbass?" Then in a mumble he added, "I bought her some earrings instead."

Evan shook his head. "You're a piece of work." He pulled the crust from the side of his sandwich and dropped it on the plate. "But leave it at earrings. Ami was unfinished business. Now it's finished and behind you. Leave it there."

"So far in the rearview that I can't even see it. Whatever. What's the word from Rob?"

Evan put his sandwich back down on the dish and eyed his friend. He decided to let Cass off the hook and move on, so he answered, "We're supposed to meet him in an hour and a half. That's why I was just about to come get you."

Cass shook his head. They continued to eat in silence when the phone on the wall rang. Evan waved his hand

and said he would just let the machine get it. The call was from a breathy- voiced woman who said it was imperative that Evan call her back because she had an emergency only he could help her with after her night at the club.

When she hung up and the answering machine beeped, Cass looked at Evan and rolled his eyes. "You ever gonna settle down, or just keep whoring around for the rest of your days?"

Evan tossed the last bite of a pickle spear in his mouth and replied, "I'll take door number two, thank you very much, Trigger."

# Chapter 39

Evan and Cass took Evan's Chevy Tahoe across the city to meet Rob. They left the hustle and bustle of the Strip and its surrounding area and dropped off into a part of town that tourists rarely saw. Cass looked at their surroundings and then glanced over at Evan's profile in the driver's seat. Cass shrugged it off and figured Evan knew where he was going.

The spotless white SUV pulled to a stop in front of a dilapidated diner. The parking lot was full, but Cass figured some of the vehicles had not been moved in years. Trash blew in the desert wind across the sidewalk in front of the door leading into the restaurant.

"What the hell, man? This is where we're meeting Rob?" Cass asked as he looked up at the rusty sign that showed the place had the extremely unimaginative name of 'The Diner.' The 'r' halfway hung off the sign.

"It's as good a place as anywhere else he'd be. You should see his hacienda. Whew, not good." Evan laughed and climbed from the truck. He raised his hand up and over his shoulder and clicked the alarm. It gave a chirp as it activated.

"I thought this guy had money," Cass said. "Hell, non-corrupt cops aren't this broke."

They made it to the door and Evan grabbed the old handle, but looked back at Cass before he opened it. He answered, "I guess he's a fan of that 'crime noir' shit or just likes slumming. I don't know, Big Guy." He snatched the door open, and it creaked as a chime rang somewhere toward the grill. "Who gives a rat's ass what winds this dude's watch? He is what he is. Now just follow my lead."

They walked to the far corner of the café to where Rob sat in a window booth with his back to the wall. He was cutting a sirloin steak when Cass slid into the compartment on the opposite side and nodded. Evan shook Rob's hand and grabbed a chair from a nearby empty table. He swung it around and sat in it backward.

"You guys hungry?" Rob asked before he stuffed a piece of his steak into his mouth with a fork.

"No," they both replied simultaneously.

Rob laughed and chewed. After he swallowed, he took a drink of a large vanilla milkshake. "It's pretty good food and the shakes kick-ass; probably the best in town."

Cass looked around at the interior of 'The Diner,' and although it was not as awful as the exterior suggested it would be, it was bad enough that he did not want to sample the food. He and Mel would definitely not be rushing down here, best milkshakes in town or not.

Evan did not seem to notice the ambiance or did not care when he said, "We just want to wrap this Shefton thing up, Rob, so pardon my French, but fuck the milkshakes."

Rob turned toward the window to the seat beside him and pulled a manila envelope from a leather satchel. Evan looked at Cass and shrugged. Rob slid the envelope to Evan across the grimy table and said, "There ya go," as he sawed at the steak once again.

"Give me the Cliff's Notes version," Evan said, without reaching for the package.

"Basically it's the address of their compound, which is about forty miles northwest of LA, and a place they got that's closer to the city." Rob put another bite of steak and then a couple of fries into his mouth. He chewed, looking from Cass to Evan.

Cass said, "And?"

Rob took his time and exaggerated swallowing. "I've got some info on nearly all of the commandos in his outfit. Most are 'wanna-be military,' but some are like Mr. Shefton and actually joined up." Another slurp of the shake through the straw. "Shefton's worked his way up to number two, and ole number one's hanging on by a thread. So he'll be the CO before long. Not a lot of records, really. They're not really high on any watch lists."

"I was hoping for more," Evan said.

"There just isn't more. I'll tell you that they are heavily armed, though. Even got a shooting range set up out there. Oh yeah, my guy says that your boy may be planning a move overseas."

"Overseas? Is he going on vacation or something?" Evan asked, not sure how to take the news.

Rob shrugged and sat his fork down on his plate. "Apparently he's scouting a move for the group. They've supposedly hooked up with some foreigner or some shit. He only has bits and pieces." Evan stared at Rob, waiting for more. Rob looked from Evan again back to Cass and then down to his milkshake. Finally, he said, "That's what he told me. So, anyway, what've you guys got planned? Should I be worried, Masters?"

"Nothing to worry about, Rob." Cass put his elbows on the table and answered for his friend. "We just want to have a little chat with Mr. Shefton—no big deal at all."

Rob nodded and dipped a hand-full of fries into his ketchup. Evan stood and put the envelope under his arm as Cass slid out of the booth. He nodded down at Rob and turned to the front door. Rob asked Evan to hold up for a second.

Evan gave Cass a thumbs-up and a grin before he turned back to Rob and said, "What's this going to cost me?"

"Well, I was hoping for a little time off," Rob answered sucking a piece of meat from between his teeth. "Maybe down at Havasu or skiing at Big Bear. Know what I mean?"

"Yeah, I got ya." Evan sighed, but it was how things worked. He pulled several bills from his wallet and laid them on the table. "It won't finance the whole trip, but that's a start."

Rob smiled up at him. Evan turned to leave but then spun slowly back and peeled off some more money. "You worked pretty quickly on this one, Rob. We appreciate it." He placed the extra hundreds beside the others.

Outside the restaurant, Evan climbed behind the wheel of the Tahoe, and Cass asked, "What was that all about?"

"Money, like always," Evan muttered. Then he put the SUV in reverse and looked behind them, adding, "But something's a little off here. Let's just be careful on this, Trigger."

"Aren't we always?" Cass answered sarcastically, and both men roared with laughter.

****

Evan and Cass left the seedier part of Las Vegas and drove back to Dare Ya Headquarters. They went immediately to Mel's office and filled her in on what Rob had told them at The Diner. She called her assistant in, gave her the list of Shefton's known associates, and got her started on a search for more information.

Melinda went to her computer and pulled up Google Earth for a glimpse of Shefton's compound and the other property Rob had included in the packet. The compound was miles from Los Angeles and out in the middle of nowhere, far from its nearest neighbor. The living quarters, she could see from the satellite image, were surrounded by a high fence and had a guard shack at the entrance.

"Damn," Evan said as he looked over her shoulder. "Don't that place look formidable?" Cass rolled his eyes as Evan grinned. "You like that, don't you? I've been watching the History Channel—formidable."

Cass let his hand brush Mel's on the desktop as Evan amused himself with his joke. She looked up and winked as she put her hair behind her ear to show him the earring. Then she mouthed, "Thanks for the flowers—beautiful," as Evan came around in front of her quickly.

"Flowers, huh, Trigger," Evan said, having read her lips.

Ignoring his friend and trying to change the subject, Cass said, "Let's have a look at the other place."

"Okay, Jarhead," Evan said as Melinda typed in the other address, "Y'all just tell me it was a good night. Do we have a new couple here at Dare Ya or what?"

"Come on…"

"Yes, Evan; it was very nice," Melinda interrupted Cass. "Thank you very much. We'll see where it goes." She grinned at Evan as Cass turned red. He found himself doing that often, lately. Then, trying to let Cass off the hook, she said, "All right, this place looks to be a little nearer to civilization. Just a big warehouse in an industrial park. Nothing to it, really."

Each of them sat around the office thinking about what they should do next. Cass said, after a few minutes, "I don't think we can hit that compound. Too many variables we don't know."

"We'll hire a couple of PI's," Evan responded, "and they can watch the place for patterns and see if our boy ever leaves the place. I think I know a guy in LA."

"That could take forever," Cass said, sounding exasperated. He stood and paced in front of the windows just as Melinda's assistant came through the office door.

"Mrs. Brooks, I think I may have found something," the young lady said, a little too bubbly.

"What ya got, Katie?" Evan asked, and smiled at her.

The girl blushed and answered, "Well, Mr. Masters, these guys seem to have an underground bash scheduled for tonight."

"Is that right?" Cass asked, looking over at Evan.

"Yes, sir. I had to use the administrative codes to get to their private pages, but its right there." She handed Cass a printout of the announcement.

"Thank you, Katie," Evan said as she left the office.

When she was gone, Cass said, "Looks like we might not have to wait that long to get ol' Heat after all."

"Where is the bash, Matthew?" Melinda asked.

He read her the address and she looked to her computer screen. It was the warehouse she had found on Google Earth. "Well, how 'bout that, Jarhead?" Evan asked when it hit him that the rave would be in the warehouse. "Looks like my old buddy Rob nailed that one now, don't it?"

"Don't it, though?" Cass asked looking to his friend.

Evan stood and headed for the office door. "I'm going to get us some wheels. You two play kissy face, and I'll pick you up in an hour."

"Piss on you again, E," Cass said, but Melinda stood and came around the desk.

She put her arms around Cass's neck and kissed his lips. Then she turned, looked at Evan, and said, "We have this. Do what you have to do." She winked.

# Chapter 40

## The next day

Sand makes a very distinct sound when a shovel is being pushed through it—very different from the hushed sound that Mississippi dirt makes with the same shovel. Desert sand has an eerie dry sound which is utterly unfamiliar to most people. In the middle of the Mojave Desert, far from the nearest soul, a sand-shovel sound pierced the silence.

When the hole was neck deep, Shefton called out, "Come on guys, don't do this! Cassidy, I'm fucking sorry I shot you. Please don't do this." Shefton had been repeating one form of this or another since Evan handed him the shovel several hours earlier and told him to start digging.

As he dug, Shefton tried to explain about some woman and her boss, but Cass had told him that he would get a chance to explain when the digging was finished. "Just shut the hell up and get the hole done before I change my mind and we don't even need it anymore," Cass said with a calm edge to his voice.

With Shefton neck-deep in a hole in the desert, Evan reached in and snatched the shovel from his hands. Evan handed it to Cass and exchanged it for a pistol. Then Evan stuffed Cass's firearm into the back of his waistband and leaned on the rear fender of the car to let Cass handle the action. He let his own pistol hang down at his side. The car was only ten feet from the hole, so Evan could cover his friend as he went to work.

Cass pushed sand into the hole around Shefton's feet and calves. Shefton yelled for him to stop and tried to lift his legs out of the dirt. Evan raised his weapon and said flatly, "Shut up, and stop moving." Shefton could see no hesitation in Evan's expression. He stopped moving.

Cass pushed sand until it was to Shefton's waist. The sun shone bright and the wind subsided, making sweat run down his face.

When the sand got just below his shoulders, pinning his arms to his sides, Shefton began to whimper. Crazed fear ran behind his eyes as they darted from the shovel to Cass's face, to Evan, and then back to the spade. Cass had not spoken a word since taking the shovel. He worked methodically, letting the day burn down on his shoulders.

Finally, he had Shefton's entire body covered, with only his head sticking up from the ground. Cass walked a slow circle around the head, packing loose sand with his boot. When he made the entire circuit and was back in front of Shefton, he threw the shovel toward the trunk of the car. It rattled loudly on the rocks and then came to rest. The desert was quiet—the only sounds the popping and clicking or the car's motor and Shefton's ragged breathing.

His nervous eyes no longer moving from the big man's face, Shefton watched Cass. Neither man said a word, but every so often Shefton would whine aloud, and a long exhalation would blow the sand in front of his face. Cass stretched and rolled his neck, relaxing from the exertion and anger. They had to have answers, and only because of that, he would not allow himself to snap.

Cass walked to Evan and held out his hand. Evan reached behind his back, pulled out Cass's pistol, and handed it to Cass butt first. Cass walked back, and five feet from the hole he squatted and locked eyes with Shefton, the pistol resting across his knee.

****

The night before, Evan pulled in front of Dare Ya Headquarters and called Cass on his cell phone, letting Cass know he was waiting. When Cass came out the front door, Evan sat on the hood of a canary-yellow Camaro. Cass asked, "What is this, Transformers or something? Don't tell me you bought another freaking car."

"Nah," Evan answered as he slid off the hood and made his way to the driver's side door. "I rented it. Figured we'd better not take one of our own, just in case it gets hairy."

"Gets hairy? Yeah, I could definitely see that happening."

They climbed into the rented muscle car and Evan fired up the engine. The rental place had obviously installed an aftermarket exhaust because Cass could hear the roar and feel the rumble through his feet and up his entire body.

"Maybe I will buy me one of these when we get back," Evan said as he jammed the accelerator, leaving Las Vegas behind.

"Let's worry about that later. You know, focus on the task at hand. You got a plan on how the hell we're going to slip in there and get Heat out?"

Evan did not answer for several miles. Then a smile crept across his face and he said, "You know what, Trigger? Screw a sneak attack. I think it's time we put our fame and celebrity status to good use."

While the stars grew brighter in the desert sky, the two men worked out their plan to get Shefton away from the rave. "I like everything but the ending, E," Cass said. "That could get tricky, and a lot could go wrong."

"Don't worry your pretty little head off; endings are just my thing," Evan said as the Tom-Tom GPS told him their exit was approaching. "All the planning in the world doesn't mean a hill of beans when you put dumbasses like Shefton and his crew in the mix."

They left the interstate and followed the GPS' instructions to a long-forgotten industrial park. The warehouse they were looking for was surrounded by parking lots and was so dilapidated that Cass was certain it would never again pass a fire code inspection.

Evan pulled into a parking space a couple of hundred feet from what he assumed was the entrance and killed the rumbling engine. The vibration they felt during the drive was replaced by music pulsating from inside the building.

"Looks like the speakers may rattle that place down," Evan said as he climbed out of the car.

They walked toward the building, and on the way to the structure, several gothic-looking young people passed them coming and going to the party. Cass stared at a girl who looked to be barely out of high school. With solid black clothes, eight-inch elevator shoes, and enough piercings in her face, it would take her an hour to get past security at the airport. He looked from her to Evan and then down at his own attire. Both he and Evan were dressed casually in blue jeans, a polo shirt, and Sketcher hiking boots.

Cass slowed and then stopped, grabbing Evan by the arm. "Are you sure this is gonna work? I'm thinking we're not going to fit in here. I got a bad feeling, Fly Guy."

Evan shook Cass's hand off and resumed his walk to the warehouse. Cass had to trot to catch up, and when he did, Evan said, "You said the same thing about our first dare and look how that turned out."

"Yeah, my private parts all over the Internet every day," Cass said shaking his head.

"Don't forget about the news and cable shows. My favorite was that, 'Dumb Things Millionaires Do' show." Evan was laughing now.

"What're you laughing at?" Cass asked, smiling. "You were on there too."

"But at least my mother wasn't pissed about seeing my junk when she watched it."

Cass smiled bigger, but he forced it from his face as they got to the door. "Let's put our game faces on." Evan's joke had worked. Cass was calm when they walked into the hoard of youthful bodies cramped into the building's empty work floor.

"Hoorah!" Evan yelled the battle cry over the blare these people called music, which was assaulting their eardrums.

The air smelled of smoke, alcohol, and body sweat. It was so loud that between songs, they could barely hear for the ringing of their ears. As they made their way through the crowd, the D.J. yelled something over the PA system that was incoherent. Amateurs, obviously, had put this together because everything seemed out of place. Cables and wires were thrown everywhere, with mismatched lights pointing in no particular direction. It was a fireman's nightmare.

By the time Evan and Cass had made their way to the bar, a slight murmur had started among the crowd. They could see the whispers even though they could not hear them. Evan ordered a drink and it arrived with a question from the female bartender whose face was covered with white make up, black eye shadow, and multiple piercings. She asked, "Hey, you're that guy?"

"What guy would you be referring to, little Ms. Sunshine?" Evan asked, and nudged Cass. He had to shout to be heard.

"You and him," she yelled back as she leaned over the makeshift bar with her small cleavage in their face. "The guys that started Dare Ya?" she inquired.

"You are correct. Evan Masters and Matthew Cassidy, at your service." Evan smiled and winked at the girl.

"Thought so. A few people asked me if you were them, but I told them no. That way they wouldn't bother you all night. I don't think it worked, though."

"Why's that?" Cass screamed. He could not hear most of what she said, but he pieced it together.

"Looks like some of them are already starting to come this way," she cried as she walked back down the bar.

The girl was right. Three men were making their way to Evan and Cass. All sported cleanly shaven heads and had expressions on their faces that almost said 'mean,' but more closely resembled "constipated." They did not appear to be huge fans. The guys were dressed in dark urban camo, which actually went well with the Goth look, Cass thought as he watched them push their way through the throng.

The clear leader, the largest of the three, stepped forward. He was in his early thirties and in good physical shape. "Hey, you those guys from the website, Eddie and Mark, right?" he asked.

Evan turned to Cass and said, as a lull came in the music, "So much for fame, huh?" Then he looked back to Baldy. "The name's Evan, and this is Matthew."

"Well, what can we do for you, Evan? This here's a private party." The man in command challenged. The music stopped completely and the cavernous room was relatively quiet for the first time since they entered.

"Look, fellas," Evan yelled before he realized there was no need. Then, at a lower tone, he continued. "All we're doing is looking for an old friend. We just need to talk to him, and we'll be on our way. How's about that?" Evan shrugged.

"Depends on who you're looking for, Frat Boy," the guy said, and crossed his arms across his chest.

Cass spoke up. "His name's Shefton. Daniel Shefton. He's got a scar on his face right here." He pointed to his chin. "You know if he's here?"

"I'm not sure if he's here; there are a lot of people upstairs. Like I said, it's a private party."

"Well, tell him an old Marine buddy's here to say hello," Cass replied, looking around the room at the many faces watching him.

Baldy turned on his heels and headed for a set of stairs on the far wall, leaving the other two standing guard. The music resumed its deafening level, causing Evan to lean down to Cass's ear. Evan told him to excuse himself and go to the bathroom, then head outside in case Shefton tried to bolt. "If he tries to run, it'll be out the back. Hit me on the cell if you see him. I'll do the same."

A few minutes later, Baldy came down the stairs and back into Evan's view. On the way across the room, he made a point of viciously shoving the kids out of his way.

"Mr. Shefton's busy right now, but maybe you could come back tomorrow."

"So he's here; thanks." Evan nodded but held eye contact. "When my friend gets back, if ol' Shefton isn't down here to see us, you'll take us up to him." Evan hated all this talking, but he had to buy time for Cass to get into place. Evan was sure Shefton was watching him.

"Is that right?" Baldy asked, flexing his muscles and straining the one-size too small T-shirt he wore.

Evan pushed himself to his full height, inches from Baldy's face. He tingled with excitement at the chance to let some of his anger and frustration out. Before it went further, Evan's phone vibrated in his pocket. He took it out and read the text. Evan pushed past the snarling man. "Maybe another time, then," he said, slamming his forearm into Baldy's chest and pushing past him.

Evan hit Cass's preset number on his phone as he ran through the crowd trying to get to the door.

"He's bailing, E," Evan heard Cass shout.

"I'm on my way," Evan told Cass. "Get the car started."

"Way ahead of you. I'm sitting by the door waiting," Cass replied. Evan crashed through the front entrance, and Cass had the passenger door open. He yelled, "Get in!"

By the time Evan got settled in the seat and the door was closed, Cass was halfway out of the parking lot. "Whoa, Trigger," Evan cried. "Don't kill us before we catch him, you big, dumb Marine. "Where is he?" Evan asked, scanning the traffic ahead and reaching back for his seatbelt.

"He's up there, three cars ahead." Cass removed one of his white-knuckled hands from the steering wheel and pointed. Traffic was still heavy coming to the rave, so Cass had to take his time getting around the other vehicles.

Trying to find a clear path and a way to get some speed, Shefton turned on a side street that paralleled the highway. His '68 Pontiac GTO did accelerate, but the clear road left an unobstructed path for Cass to reach Shefton's bumper. The Camaro easily ate the gap, and within seconds, the two cars were hurtling down the deserted road, nose-to-tail.

Evan shouted, "I bet he's heading to that compound of his. Can't let that happen, Trigger." He held the dash with one hand and the door frame with the other.

Shefton's old GTO screamed through the night, but Cass stayed right with him. Cass pulled into the opposite lane and came along the side of Shefton's car. Shefton looked through the passenger side window and locked eyes with Cass. The fear in Shefton's eyes was evident, and it caused the fleeing man to find more speed in his old car. He actually pulled away once more. Cass swerved back in on his tail. The Camaro slightly fishtailed as it crossed the yellow line. "Chases are a hell of a lot funner when I'm driving," Evan said grabbing tighter to his handhold.

"I got this, Jet Jockey."

They followed right on Shefton's taillights for a mile when Evan pulled his pistol and asked, "You want me to shoot out his tires like in the movies?"

"Put that thing away before you shoot out the airbag or the windshield," Cass answered, never taking his eyes from Shefton's car.

Evan snorted a small laugh and replied, "I bet I can do it." He pushed the window-down button, and the desert air rushed in around them.

"Just watch this," Cass yelled. "They don't teach this in the Air Force!"

Cass crossed the yellow line again and pulled the Camaro's right front fender even with the GTO's left rear-quarter panel. He whipped the steering wheel to the right, and the two muscle cars came together with the squeal of tires and crunch of metal.

At over eighty miles per hour, Shefton's Pontiac spun in front of the Chevy as Cass lightly hit the brakes to avoid further contact. As they slowed, Evan released his grip and watched the other automobile spin. Smoke billowed from the tires, and as one revolution took it sideways, the wheels caught, and Shefton's car went into a roll.

Both doors flew open. The roof collapsed, blowing glass from all the windows, but the flipping continued. Finally, after several revolutions, the destroyed car came to rest, pointing the way it came from and sitting on four flat tires. Steam from the radiator hissed around the edges of the crumpled hood. Cass slid to a stop a few feet in front of the wreck with his headlights illuminating the carnage.

"I think you probably killed the bastard," a big-eyed Evan said in disbelief.

"Nah, he didn't fly out, so he's probably alive; just hurting." Cass opened his door and climbed out.

Evan pointed at a stream of liquid running down the asphalt under the rear of the car. He said, "Let's get him out of there before it blows."

They ran to the wreckage just as Shefton was pushing the driver's door open with his shoulder. He spit blood onto the ground at their feet and then yelled, "What the hell's wrong with you? You could've killed me, you pricks!"

He put his hands on his forehead and slowly shook his skull back and forth.

Cass reached in and dragged Shefton out by his shirt. Cass slammed him into the side of the car, leaned in close to his ear, and whispered, "Not yet, you son of a bitch." Holding him at arm's length with his right hand, Cass swung his left into Shefton's jaw, knocking him into kingdom come. Lights out. The unconscious man slid down to the pavement and did not move.

Evan looked up from Shefton to Cass and made a 'what the hell' gesture with his eyes and shoulders. "You could've waited 'till we got him to the trunk."

Cass shrugged. "Just shut up and help me carry him."

****

They put Shefton in the trunk and sped into the night. Evan and Cass traveled north on Highway 15 when Cass's cell phone vibrated. He answered it, and Melinda told him she had some news. He told her to hold on, pressed the speaker phone button, and placed the phone in the center console between him and Evan. When Melinda spoke again, both men could hear what she had to say.

"First, was Shefton at the bash?" she asked.

"Yep, he was there," Evan answered. Then he looked at Cass to see how he wanted to play it.

She waited for a second to see if Evan would elaborate. When he did not, she asked, "Could you guys get to him with all his people around?"

"The road's gonna split up here; take it to the right," Cass said to Evan as they were passing through Barstow.

"Forty West; gottcha, Trigger."

"Okay," Melinda cut in. "Let's pretend I asked a question and see how that goes."

"Uh, Mel," Cass began tentatively. "It's after three in the morning. What are you still doing at Headquarters?"

"All right, I don't need to know about Shefton; that's what you're trying to say. I got it, but please tell me he didn't somehow die in front of a hundred witnesses."

Evan glided the car to the right lane and took the fork. He merged with the late night, semi-truck traffic. Then he gunned the accelerator and passed everyone he came to. Cass finally answered Melind. "No, doll; he's still alive and well."

"He's alive," Evan added. "Not sure about the well part."

"Touché," Cass said with a chuckle.

"I guess I don't want to know." Melinda exhaled, but then she composed herself and told them the reason she was at the office. After that, she added, "Al and I will probably be here for a couple more hours, seeing if we can find anything else."

"Okay, but don't wait up; we may be a while," Cass told her.

"Stay out of trouble," she said, and hung up.

Evan turned the radio up and asked Cass where they were headed, since 15 would have taken them into Vegas. "Up here to the south is the backside of 29 Palms." Cass explained about the gigantic Marine Corps base that was actually one very large firing range. "I know a very secluded place out there. We can see what this jerk-off has to say." He pointed his thumb toward the trunk.

# Chapter 41

"Okay, Heat, here's how we're gonna play this," Cass said, still squatting in the sand with his pistol, with Shefton still buried to his neck. "I ask, you answer. Understand?"

"Cassidy, look, I knew when that bitch said your name, it was bad. I didn't mean to shoot you way back when, man." Shefton pled with his eyes. "Okay, okay, whatever. I shot you; you buried me in a freaking hole. Surely that makes us even. Come on, bro."

Cass did not respond to the talking head. He half turned to Evan and caught a glimpse in his peripheral vision. Evan yelled, "Strike one!" Cass turned back to Shefton as Evan continued, "I'd stick to answering his questions, Shefibaby."

Cassidy nodded his head. "Let's try this again Heat. An associate of ours found that you recently flew to Nebraska, and then she followed your movements to Jackson, Mississippi. So what's up with all this traveling?"

"Just some jobs for that asshole I've been trying to tell you about. What the hell's it got to do with you, Cassidy?" As Shefton talked, the sweat from his forehead mixed with the blood running from his cuts and down into the sand. He was constantly shaking his head to keep the mixture out of his eyes.

Cass ignored the blood-sweat problem. "You're not making sense, Heat. Why in the fuck did you kill those kids in Nebraska? That's a hell of a thing to call a job!" Cass let his composure slip and screamed. He leaned forward and continued, "They didn't do shit to you!" Spittle flew from his mouth.

"Whoa, Cassidy." Shefton tried to figure a way to proceed. "I didn't kill anybody in Nebraska." He took a breath and scattered more sand as he let it out. "All I did was deliver some cars to a back road in the middle of nowhere."

"Strike two, Shefalopackus," Evan shifted his weight on the fender and said. "Don't strike out now; trust me here."

Shefton's eyes went to Evan's voice but quickly went back to Cass's face. "Honestly Cassidy, I just dropped off some cars."

Evan walked up, put his hand on Cass's shoulder, and patted. "Catch some shade, Trigger. Let me talk to this dumbass for a sec."

Cass stood and walked to the little sliver of shade beside the car. His phone vibrated in his pocket. He pulled it out and read a text from Melinda.

*Something fishy with this video.*

He was too angry to think about it or answer it, so he simply tossed the phone in the front seat. He sat with his back on the rear tire with his stare locked on Shefton and the pistol across his lap.

Evan paced in front of Shefton in a tight circle as he spoke. "Heat, Shefton, whatever your freaking name is, you were in the military, right? Hell, you even shot my buddy here in the ass -which, by the way, I found funny as hell." Evan grinned down at Cass, and Cass gave him the bird without looking from Shefton's face. Evan continued,

"My meaning is: surely you can fully appreciate the situation we have here." He spread his arms and turned in a complete circle. The sand scraped on his boots. "We are completely committed to leaving you out here and letting the buzzards pick your head bare."

"I'll answer. Whatever..."

Evan held up his hand. "Wait, I'm not finished." He walked to the Camaro and reached into the open trunk where the shovel had been and pulled out an amber-colored plastic bottle. He persisted as he held the bottle up and walked back toward Shefton, "I even managed to secure a little honey. I bet there are some hungry little critters hiding out here somewhere who'd love this." Another shake of the bottle.

He opened the snap top and squeezed a short stream of the honey onto the hot desert sand. "So let's cut the innocent-act bullshit."

"We can figure this out, man," Shefton croaked. "We don't need buzzards or honey or anything else." Then, to Cass, he begged, "Please, Cassidy, let's work this crap out." Evan could see tears mixing with the sweat and blood running down Shefton's face.

Evan bent over, picked up a rock, and bounced it in his hand a couple of times. He threw it down and hit Shefton on the top of his head, causing Shefton to flinch as much as the sand around his neck would allow. "Not only did you kill those kids in Lincoln but you murdered my friend in Vicksburg, too. Even had the nerve to video tape it, you sick bastard. Maybe you're dumber than Cass told me you were, but did you really think we wouldn't find you? Come on, man."

Shefton blew at a drop of sweat dripping from his nose. Then he answered, "I don't know what the hell you're talking about. I didn't video-tape anything. I..."

The gunshot roared across the desert and echoed back to Evan several times as he looked around at Cass. The forty-caliber was propped on his knee and Cass was still sighting down the barrel. "Strike three," Cass said.

Evan spun and saw Shefton scrunching his eyes shut and grinding his teeth, obviously in pain. His ear was missing a large chunk from the middle and looked as though it had been cut in two. Blood poured from the wound. "You fucking shot me," he shrieked. "Cassidy, you fucking shot me!"

"Shut up," Cass answered him. "You're lucky it was your ear and I didn't put one between your eyes."

"I never thought I'd say this, Trigger, but chill out and let me handle this."

"Just get on with it, and let's get the hell out of here," Cass responded, still aiming the firearm at Shefton's face.

Evan resumed his pacing and told Shefton to explain about Nebraska and Mississippi. Shefton told them about being contacted by some guy called The Director and his lackey, Constance. He said they had paid him and two of his guys to go Nebraska and deliver the two cars to the remote location. That was it.

As to the Mississippi trip, he was a little more reluctant to give the details, but he finally let it all spill out. He told them that he flew to Jackson and picked up some guy at his hotel. He took the man to dinner and then to a parking garage downtown. Shefton paused for a while, but then he looked from Evan to Cass, and lastly, down to the sand. "I shot the guy and left him there. Made it look like a robbery, but I've never been to Vicksburg, I swear."

The blood was still flowing out of his destroyed ear and the sweat continued to roll down his face. Evan turned to Cass, and they looked at one another, neither one actually believing Shefton's story. At last Cass asked, "Why Heat? What's the point?"

"That Constance bitch said that they were going to hire me and my guys to distribute guns in LA. That these jobs were like a trial to see if they could trust me." He looked to each man in front of him, sensing a little hope. "She tried to get me to kill you guys, but I told her which end of that she could stick up her ass. I told that cunt I didn't want shit to do with you, Cassidy. You have to believe me."

Before he could respond, Cass' phone vibrated and beeped from the front seat of the car. He decided to use it to stall, so he stood, reached through the window, and pulled it out. Melinda had sent a video. He pressed the play button. Melinda appeared on the tiny screen with a swollen eye and busted lip.

Evan was still pacing, explaining the futility of Shefton's lies, when he looked to his friend. Cass's face had drained of blood, and Evan could see the big man's hand shaking. Evan stopped mid-sentence, and in two long strides he was behind Cass, looking over his shoulder at the phone. He started to ask what was wrong, but as soon as he saw Melinda's face, he felt the blood leave his own face as well. She stood in her office with her hands bound behind her back and a large man holding her elbow up at a severe angle.

Melinda spoke. "Matthew, Evan, I..." Abruptly, a small, athletic woman stepped in front of her and slapped

Mel's face, hard. Her head snapped, and the red print of a hand blossomed on her cheek. The other woman motioned with her head, and the man holding Mel dragged her from the camera shot. Constance turned to face the camera lens and started to speak.

From his hole, Shefton shouted, "What! What the hell's going on?"

Evan pointed his finger at him, but did not look his way, as he said, "Shut up, Shefton," and leaned closer to the phone in Cass's hand.

Constance said, "We wanted your undivided attention. I hope Carrot Top accomplished that." The anger hit Cass like a hammer. "My employer finally wants you to know that he's been after the two of you for years—but all of that was on your turf." She paused for a moment as she lit a cigarette and took a deep drag. After she blew out the smoke, Constance continued. "He now wants to see how you guys perform on his territory. We'll hold Red for a few days, and while you wait, get that fancy-ass jet of yours ready. I'll send the destination soon." She took another puff and blew smoke at the camera. "I'm sure I don't need to be so melodramatic as to say 'don't contact the authorities or she dies,' but don't, or she does." She walked closer to the recorder and reached up. The screen in Cass's hand went black.

Cass rewound back to the middle of the video and pressed "pause" with a good picture of the black-haired woman on the screen. He walked quickly to Shefton, squatted, and grabbed him by the hair. Cass jammed the cell phone into Shefton's face and yelled, "Who is this bitch?"

"That's Constance; she's the one I told you worked for that dickhead. He calls himself The Director. It's what I've been saying!"

"Where are they?" Cass twisted his hair harder.

"I don't freaking know, man. I've been trying to tell you that. They wanted me to wax you, Cass, but I told her hell no. That's gotta be what all this Nebraska/Mississippi killing's about. They're setting me up."

Cass stood and kicked sand into Shefton's face. It caked on the sweat, and he spit some of it out of his mouth. "Nice try," Cass said as he walked back to the car.

"That's got to be it, Cassidy!"

"Get in the car, E," Cass said, and patted the top of the Camaro. He looked up into the sun and tried to burn some of the anger out of his mind.

Evan walked around the car, closed the trunk, and then went to the passenger side door. He opened it and called over the roof, "This is for Beau, you fuck!"

"Cassidy! Cassidy!" Shefton shouted, the terror thick in his voice. "You can't leave me here to die! Please!"

Cass left his door open and turned back to Shefton. "You're lucky I can't stay and make it even worse. I was so looking forward to watching the whole show, maybe pissing on your dead skull."

After he climbed into the car, Cass slammed the door. It did nothing to drown out Shefton's screaming as they drove away. Evan looked back between the front seats and then said, "Damn, Trigger, that was some cold-blooded shit."

"Fuck him; that's over. We've got to find Mel."

Evan could see the pain on his friend's face, and he felt the same way, but this was not the time for hurting. They had to focus. He said as much to Cass, and the big man took a couple of miles to let the anger and worry harden into resolve. He said to Evan, "She sent me a text earlier. Read it and see if it makes any sense to you."

Evan read the text.

*Something fishy with this video.*

Then he asked, "What video?"

Cass shook his head, wondering the same thing as he pushed the gas pedal all the way to the floor. "I don't have a clue; we'll have to ask Al when we get back to Vegas."

Evan agreed with Cass and then stared at the desert horizon. After a moment he said, "Did you notice how Shefton reacted when you asked him about moving overseas?" He looked over to Cass but did not wait for an answer. "I think he was really confused, there, like he'd never heard of it."

"I agree, but what the hell's it mean?"

"It means we should pay Rob a visit after we check in with Al. See where the hell he got his info."

They rode the rest of the trip to Vegas lost in thought, but neither gave Daniel Shefton one second of those thoughts. Sometime—very rarely, but sometimes - a person gets exactly what he deserves.

# Chapter 42

As the two cofounders rushed into their building, Dare Ya was abuzz with its normal, daily activity. People spoke to them as Evan and Cass trotted by, but neither man spoke back as they rushed to Al's office to see what he might know about Melinda or the mystery tape.

In front of Al's office, Evan asked his secretary, "Sally, is Al in?"

"No, Mr. Masters," she answered, smiling. "He hasn't been in the office all morning."

"Has he called?" asked Cass as he went around her desk and looked into the office beyond.

Sally watched him until he came back, shaking his head at Evan. She then answered his question. "I assumed that he and Mrs. Brooks worked late last night and they'd be in later, or perhaps tomorrow."

Both men said "Thanks" at the same time as they sped back down the corridor. Reading each other's mind, they decided to forgo the elevator and hit the stairs at a full run.

When they got to Melinda's office, they did not slow as they passed Katie's desk. She started, "She's not..." but neither slowed enough to hear the rest. They pushed into the room, and it was in total disarray. The computer was smashed on the floor; papers were everywhere, and on the floor beside the small settee in the corner, Al lay crumpled in a fetal position. His head sat in a large puddle of partially-dried blood that had turned nearly black.

Katie stepped to the open door and gasped. She put her hand to her mouth and whispered, "My god, I didn't know." Then she sobbed quietly.

Cass rushed to Al and checked for a pulse. He called back to Evan, who was already on the phone, "He's barely alive. He needs an ambulance. ASAP."

"On it," Evan responded with the phone to his ear. As Cass rolled Al onto his back, Evan told the dispatcher what was happening and where they were. After he hung up, he knelt beside Cass and added, "They're on the way."

"I've got him. You go see what Katie knows and what you can find in this mess." Cass took a pillow from the sofa and very gently put it under Al's head. He was checking for other wounds besides the one on his head, when Evan stood and went to Katie.

Evan tenderly took her arm, led her from the doorway, and ushered her into the waiting area. After he helped her into a chair, he squatted in front of her. He took her hands in his and told her it would be okay. The sobs lessened as she explained that when she came in, the door to Melinda's office had been closed. She had buzzed her boss, but Melinda did not answer.

"She told me yesterday that she and Al were gonna be working late." Katie sniffled and dabbed at her eyes with her sleeve. "I just assumed she'd taken the day off. We didn't really have anything pressing. I only had to cancel one appointment. Where is she, Mr. Masters?" Evan could tell she was scared to hear the answer.

"That's what we're going to find out. You go downstairs and wait for the paramedics, and when they get on the property, bring them back up here." He patted her knee and stood. "I'm going to go check on Al again."

She did as she was instructed, feeling better having something to do. Evan went into the office to search, but without any luck. The medical crew showed up later, secured Al to a stretcher, and rushed him away. Two police officers came soon after Al was gone, and Cass and Evan did their best to answer the questions without giving away the whole story. Neither man trusted the authorities very much. The cops would not let Evan or Cass continue to search the office, as it had turned into the crime scene for an assault investigation.

Evan had looked through most of the mess while he was waiting on the ambulance and knew that nothing there would be helpful in their hunt for Melinda. They asked the detective who had finally shown up on the crime scene if they were still needed. The small man in a rumpled suit told them no, but if they were needed later, he would call their cell phones. He had the numbers.

The Headquarters had grown quiet since they had arrived earlier in the evening. Most of the employees had gone home, and night had fallen hours ago while they waited and were questioned. Cass and Evan pushed through the front doors into the cool desert air, and Evan said, "It's getting late. I bet ol' Rob's home by now. Let's go see what the prick knows."

They ran to the Camaro and raced across town.

*****

Evan slid sideways to a stop in front of Rob's rundown apartment building. He killed the engine, and both men hesitated with their hands on the door handles. Cass asked, "What the hell's going on, E?"

"I don't have a clue, but I hope this shithead can give us some answers."

"What if he can't?" asked Cass, looking up at the dilapidated building, thinking of Melinda. "Then what?"

Evan took a deep breath and exhaled loudly. The weight of the day was beginning to drag on him. He looked around the neighborhood. All around them were signs of construction; but from jobs that had gone unfinished for years. Evan's eyes followed the alley, and he saw an old construction dumpster that was overflowing with household refuse. A trash chute was still attached to the side of the building.

At last, Evan spoke. "If he doesn't know anything, Al'll at least know what video Mel was talking about. It'll be a start, and we'll run with that if we have to. Or that bitch Constance, we'll track her down somehow." Evan looked at Cass, trying to convey some strength. "This isn't our only hope, Trigger. We'll get her back."

"All that'll take too damn long. We've got to get her back fast." The broken windows, the rusty fire escape, the horns blaring—even the stench of sour garbage had faded, to Cass. All he could see, hear, or smell was that night at the Alize with Melinda.

Evan touched Cass' elbow, snapping his friend back to the present; then he said, "Put that crap in a box, bro." Evan took his pistol and ensured it was loaded. "Right now, all we can focus on is the turd in front of us."

Cass gave a dry, humorless chuckle and got his mind back to the task. He checked his own weapon and shoved it back into the rear of his waistband. They opened the doors and climbed from the car. Both men pulled their polo shirts over the handles of their guns. "We'll get her back," Evan told Cass again over the top of the car.

Cass reached across the roof and they tapped knuckles. "Or die trying," Cass said as they took off into the shabby lobby.

They found the stairwell and slowed, deciding to go for stealth over speed. Cass took point, and Evan whispered, "Fifth floor, apartment 531."

Cass gave the thumbs up as he pulled his weapon. Evan did the same, and on the fifth floor landing, Cass asked, "Plan?" as he crouched and looked through a crack in the door.

"We'll go knock on the door. Duh," Evan said as he stepped into the fifth floor hallway. He walked toward Rob's apartment with his gun pointing down behind his back. Evan rapidly passed the entrance to the dwelling and leaned with his back against the wall on the far side. He motioned for Cass to put his back to the wall on his side. Evan took a stick of gum from his pocket, popped it into his mouth, and let the wrapper fall to the floor. He shrugged at it and then knocked on the door.

After a few seconds, Evan pointed to himself, then his ear, and then to the door, meaning 'I heard something inside.' Cass nodded as the first of three deadbolts turned with a loud clack. "I'm coming." Rob's voice sounded through the door.

When Rob had unlocked the door and was pulling it open, Evan stepped in, pushed it wide open, and grabbed Rob by the front of his shirt. He put the pistol in Rob's face, and the cop's eyes grew as big as saucers. Rob stumbled backwards as Evan pushed him deeper into the living room. Cass closed the door behind them.

Rob at last found his voice. "What the hell, Masters? What's going on?"

Cass walked around the room, kicking old pizza boxes out of his way as he went. The coffee table was covered with empty beer bottles and overflowing ashtrays. The couch had a blanket crumpled on it, half hanging to the filthy floor, and it looked as though Rob had been sleeping there when they knocked on the door. The television was on some late night talk show when Cass reached down and clicked it off.

After the chatter of the television personality was gone, Cass went to the kitchen. He grabbed an old chair from under a cracked glass-top table. In the center of the table, Rob had rolled his shoulder holster around his service revolver and put it there with his badge and wallet. Cass noted the gun, took the chair, and dragged it behind Rob. Evan pushed him in the chest and said, "Sit."

Rob sat and looked from one man to the other—or more accurately, he looked from Evan's pistol to Cass's gun. He tried to sound brave and unfazed. "Well, is one of you cocksuckers going to explain this shit or what?"

Evan popped gum between his teeth, looking down at Rob. After a few seconds, he said, "You lied to us about Shefton and God knows what else."

"I didn't lie about a motherfucking thing," Rob said still trying for bravado.

Cass said behind him, "You gave us that info pretty damn quick." He kicked the edge of the coffee table just enough to knock over most of the bottles. As they clanged down onto the dingy carpet, he continued. "Almost like you wanted us to make sure we were there for that bash."

"I don't know shit about a bash. You wanted the info, I got it." He looked up at Evan and added, "Evan, tell this jackass I work fast, man."

Evan loudly chewed with his mouth open. "Yeah, you have, but never that fast." *Smack-Smack-Smack.* "Who's the Director?"

At the mention of the name, Rob's eyes fell to his lap. Evan pushed, "Who's Constance?" *Smack-Smack-Smack.* "What the hell do they have to do with me or Cass?" *Smack-Smack-Smack.*

"Damn it, E! Who the hell gave you a piece of gum?" Cass yelled. "Jesus."

Evan held the gun on Rob but looked at Cass, grinning. "It's called an interrogation technique, Smart Guy." Evan turned to the back wall of the living room, furled his tongue into a tube, and blew the gum across the room. To Cass, he added, "That's my one and only flaw. Do I point out all of your..."

"Not the time, E."

"Yeah, right, whatever." Then he turned back to Rob and said, "You were saying."

Without looking up from his lap, Rob answered, "I don't know those people," but there was not much conviction in his tone.

Cass slapped him on the side of his head, just hard enough to get his attention. Then he said calmly, "The bitch and her goon kidnapped our office manager and put our lead tech guy in a freaking coma. If that ties to you, you'll never get the stink off."

"You're a cop, Rob," Evan added, "so you know what an accessory to a felony is. It's a fucking felony, too, dumbass. That's what it is."

Cass clicked the safety off and put his pistol barrel flat on Rob's thigh. Evan sucked air through his teeth, making a wincing sound. "I bet that's gonna hurt."

"Wait, wait, wait." Rob raised his hands. "I had nothing to do with a kidnapping or an assault. They just told me that they wanted you two in LA. I swear."

To Evan, "These guys sure do swear a lot." Then to Rob, who was looking at the pistol against his leg, he asked, "Who's 'they'?" Then he ground the barrel deeper into the thigh muscle.

"I figured if anybody could handle themselves, it would be you guys. I'd make a little money, you'd kick some ass, and they'd get egg on their faces like they deserve."

"Last chance: who's 'they'?" Evan asked.

"I don't know shit about a Connie or a Director, but my uncle Donavan McNewman gave me the envelope with Shefton's info in it."

"The Senator?" Evan's eyes grew, and he looked at Cass.

"Yeah, well, it was his aide, Bradley Bishop, actually. Ol' Uncle Don wouldn't get his hands dirty. They've been paying me to keep tabs on you two."

Cass removed the gun and started pacing. "A United States Senator?"

"Yep, said to give it to you as soon as you asked for it and make sure I said that part about him leaving the country." Rob looked hopefully into Evan's stare. "See, I didn't have anything to do with that other crap. I just fed you some information."

"I'm going to burn you down, Rob." Evan squatted and came face to face with the man. "Prison sucks; believe me, but I'll send some money to your commissary account. You're going down for clearing us out for this kidnapping. You're going down."

"You already said that part," Cass told Evan.

"Just wanted to make sure he knows it was us that brings him down." Evan walked toward the television.

Cass looked at Evan, then back to Rob, and said, "Where did they take..."

Rob burst from the chair and ran for the door. He ripped it open, bounced off the jamb, and sprinted down the hall. Cass took off, right on his heels. Evan, who was on the other side of the room, tripped on the overturned chair but righted quickly and followed the two out of the apartment.

As Rob reached the stairs, Cass caught him and tackled him through the doorway. The cop weaseled his way out of Cass's grasp and pushed away from the bigger man. Cass had fallen to the floor and was blocking the stairs leading down, so Rob turned and ran up the steps, two at a time.

Evan barreled into the stairwell, almost taking Cass's head off as he was getting to his feet. Evan grabbed him under the arm and snatched him the rest of the way off the ground. "Up!"

Evan turned and raced in Rob's footsteps, with Cass behind him. Soon they came to the door leading to the roof. With their weapons at the ready, they exploded through, with Cass going left and Evan going right.

Rob was across the rooftop directly in front of them, looking like a wild animal. His knees were slightly bent, his arms out to his sides, and his eyes darted in every direction, searching for any escape. Cass called out, trying to get Rob's attention. "Where is she?" He and Evan eased closer to their prey.

"I don't know, Cassidy." Rob was not able to keep the whine out of his voice. "I told you everything."

"Rob, come with us," Evan said. "Come with us and in the morning, we'll all go see Uncle Don and see exactly what that son of a bitch has to say. Maybe..."

"Fuck you, Masters," Rob shouted. "I'm not going anywhere. You don't know these people!" With that, Rob made a sudden step to his right, and Cass moved to cut him off. Rob planted his right foot in the gravel-covered tar, turned hard to his left, and ran full speed toward the edge of the building. Evan was only five feet behind him and gaining.

Rob reached the fire escape ladder, grabbed the handles on top of the partition wall, and leapt it in one fluid motion. When he hit the fire escape platform, his momentum took him hard into its rail. With a squeal and loud pop, the metal bar broke away and Rob Moffat continued going forward with it.

Evan made it to the edge of the roof in time to see Rob fall the last three stories to the alley below. He never released his grip on the handrail. Cass ran up beside Evan in time to hear the wet thump splatter as Rob slammed into the asphalt. They both peered over the edge at the broken body six stories below.

"Just for the record," Cass said as he stood up, "I never liked that puke."

"Hell of a time for an 'I told you so,' wouldn't you say?" Evan asked, walking back to the door, shaking his head.

"Okay," Cass told Evan, looking at his watch as they trotted down the stairs. "First thing in the morning, I'll try to get us an appointment with the good Senator."

"The earlier the better," Evan responded, peering into the lobby to see if anyone was in there. "We should probably get to him before he finds out about Nephew Ronnie, wouldn't you think?"

"My place is closer; you can crash for a few hours on the couch. Hell, it's already three."

"I've got some things to handle before I call it a night," Evan told Cass as they darted to the Camaro. "I'll drop you off and you call in the morning."

"It'll be early; be ready," Cass said on the way to the house he kept in the city. Then his thoughts turned to Rob, but only for a split second. To Cass, Rob's fall from his roof was just another perfect example of someone getting precisely what they deserved. That was all the time he had for Rob and his memory. After that, all his feelings turned to Melinda. Through his quick shower, making a snack, and lying in bed unable to sleep, she was all he thought about. At five-thirty, his alarm went off. He could only hope politicians were early risers.

# Chapter 43

Just before lunch, Evan and Cass drove into the parking area of Senator Donavon McNewman's Las Vegas office. Cass had arranged an appointment, finally getting in touch with the governor, who was a huge fan of Dare Ya. He and Cass had been friends almost from the time Dare Ya moved to Nevada. The governor pulled every string he could and got Cass and Evan twenty minutes with McNewman.

Evan had returned the Camaro as soon as the rental place opened. He told Cass it was time to dump the one Chevrolet for another because he missed his pride and joy. They pulled into a parking space in Evan's electric blue Corvette, about fifteen minutes early for the engagement. Cass looked over at Evan and said, "You look rough, like you've been up all night, Fly Guy."

"Trust me; you won't be winning 'America's Next Top Model' with the way you look either. I had some people to see last night," Evan answered without so much as a glance at Cass.

It was obvious Evan did not want to continue the conversation, but Cass asked, "Care to fill me in?"

Evan let out a loud sigh, and the exhaustion of the night before washed over him. "In due time, Trigger." As tired as he was, a hint of a smile crossed the edge of Evan's mouth. They sat and discussed what the Senator might or might not be able to tell them. They needed him to have something because their options were dwindling.

Then, out of habit, Cass said, "I'll send Mel..." but he trailed off and sat quietly for a few seconds after reality hit him. Cass said, "We gotta get her back,"

Evan said, "We're gonna get her back."

After that, they climbed from the car, both men stretching their arms over their heads. They decided to wait inside the building. Maybe McNewman would see them early. No such luck—the Senator's secretary told them he was running behind and they would have to wait. As they did so, Evan fidgeted in the seat next to Cass. Both men were amped up on coffee but knew they had to find a way to focus.

At last the secretary told them they could go back for their meeting. As they stood, Evan leaned in and whispered, "Let's put this guy on his heels from the start." He bounced on the balls of his feet and shook his arms like a cage fighter going into the ring. Cass shook his head.

Cass knocked on the door and then heard, "Come." Cass thought the Senator must be a pompous ass for answering his door like that. They entered an office that seemed bigger than the entire rest of the building. Dark paneling covered the walls, and each was laden with pictures of the Senator and other politicians, the Senator and movie stars, and the Senator and professional athletes. The only common factor in all of the photos seemed to Donavon McNewman's dazzling white teeth.

The huge desk had more pictures in frames spread over it. These must have been the A-team, Cass decided, because they depicted the more famous people around the world. The Senator was with the President, The Dali Lama, and many more. All frames turned to face the senator's guests. 'See how important I am,' it said of the man in the office. *Yep*, Cass decided, *definitely a conceited prick.*

The Senator did not offer a handshake or waste time standing as they entered. He simply glared at the men and pointed at the two chairs across the desk from him. Cass tried to get the ball rolling before Evan could 'put the guy on his heels,' by saying, "Sir, my name is Matthew Cassidy and this is..."

"I know who you are, dipshit," the Senator interrupted. "Do you think you could just walk into an office such as this unannounced? What do you want?" He looked at his watch before he added, "I don't have a lot of time. I have a lunch I must get to." While the Senator spoke, Evan plopped into the left chair and Cass sat in the right.

Evan ignored the rebuff. He said, "You got your camera close by? Maybe you could buzz old brown eyes out there and she'll snap it for ya."

"Mr. Masters, what in the hell are you talking about?" McNewman gave him a perplexed look.

"Just figured you'd want our photograph on the wall up there," Evan answered, waving at all the shots. He gave the Senator a fake, toothy grin and continued, "While you can still smile, that is."

"Stop right there, you little bastard. I do not have to listen to this. Leave my office this minute."

"Hold your horses, slick," Evan said, leaning forward in his seat. "I could come around this table you call a desk, and break your ocular . . . something or other, but that would just slow us down." He stood and leaned down on the desk with one hand pushing some papers aside and the other knocking over a picture of the Senator posing with the Pope.

McNewman simply stared at Evan. Cass finally said, "We want to know about the Director and why the hell Rob's been keeping tabs on us."

"I don't know what that dumbass nephew of my wife has been telling you," McNewman said as he looked from Evan and to Cass, "but I haven't a clue what you're talking about; and just so we're clear, nor do I care."

"Look, sir," Cass tried again. "This Director guy has kidnapped my girlfriend and is taking her God knows where. Help us catch this man and get her back."

The Senator looked unfazed about Melinda's kidnapping. He simply glanced at his watch again and began to speak, but Evan cut him off. "Okay, Donny, my friend tried to be civil and reason with you. I won't." There was ice in his voice. "I've been up all freaking night talking to people down on the strip—a fairly seedy bunch, but they're all associated with the lovely Tessa McNewman." Again, he gave the phony smile. "I'd hate for something to happen to that 'innocent' young lady—or her reputation."

"Are you threatening my family, you son of a bitch?" The Senator leapt from his chair and pointed his finger in Evan's face. "You don't have an ounce of brains up there, do you, country boy? I'm going to crush you both like the two insignificant bugs you are! I'll call every friend I have..." He began counting them off on his hand. "The FBI, the IRS, the NSA, maybe even the CIA, and when I'm finished, your life won't be worth living, and that silly little company of yours will be Dare Who to everyone."

When the Senator finished his rant and was thoroughly red-faced, Evan gave him a half yawn. Evan pulled out his cell phone, pushed some buttons, and slid it across the desk. The Senator did not even look down. "That's a bunch of letters you rattled off there, Big Boy." Evan reached over and tapped at the screen to get the Senator to look down. Then he stood upright and counted off on one finger at a time. "How about JPEG, BMP, or GIF?"

McNewman at last looked down, and as he scrolled through a collection of pictures, his mouth fell open. He closed his mouth and then opened it again like a fish. A second later he found his voice and said, "Where did you get these? Is that Tess?"

Evan took the phone back and closed the folder with the photos. The once-through of the slideshow had allowed the Senator to observe his daughter in kinky sexual acts and various forms of drug use. One showed her snorting cocaine, another with a needle in her arm and a slack expression on her face. Evan said, as the Senator fell back into his chair, "Since you seem to be such a fan of lists, you don't have to worry about me uploading any of these to Dare Ya, Facebook, Instagram, or any other site, so long as you give us the Director."

"Son, I can't do that," McNewman said with a look of utter shock on his face. "That man is very dangerous."

"We want Melinda back; that's it," Cass said, "but we're gonna put this bastard in the ground getting her. There'll be no blow back on you with this, sir."

"How can I be sure you can do that, Mr. Cassidy? At least with him, I make money. This one here," he gestured at Evan with his head, "is threatening to ruin the rest of my little girl's life and possibly my career. Where's my incentive?" McNewman asked trying to regain a foothold on the situation.

Cass began, "Sir, we will..."

Evan cut him off. "Fuck the 'sir' shit, Trigger." He stared hard at McNewman for a few seconds. Then he said to the Senator, "I will destroy you and your whole damn family if I have to. If you don't help us, I'll assume you're choosing to side with the Director. Our enemy. Should be an easy choice."

After opening another folder on the phone, Evan pulled up a different series of still shots. He sat the cell phone in front of McNewman once more and scrolled through these photos. "Oh my god," McNewman said, and leaned back in his chair.

"Look at them," Evan roared, holding the screen up to the Senator's face.

"What the hell? What has that got to do with me?"

Evan did not respond; he simply flipped from picture to picture. The Senator recognized the images. They had been all over the news, and no one could forget the scene of the Lincoln Water Tower shootings. After the last picture passed by on the screen, Evan said, "The Director did this."

"No, no, he couldn't have." But the argument from McNewman was a weak whisper. He promptly decided that he could not let himself be connected to such an atrocity.

Cass said, "Yes, he did, and when we take him down, we'll put you down too, if you're on that team." He pointed at the phone in Evan's hand. "Screw Tessa's indiscretions. I'll tie you to those kids' deaths, and you'll fry."

"But I—I had nothing to do..."

"In for a penny," Cass cut him short, "in for a pound. You're not near as stupid as you've been acting, Don."

Evan took up the persuasion, "Give it up. We want Mel back, like I said, and we're going to turn the guy's lights out once and for all. Either you're with us or with him." After a few seconds he continued, tapping on his watch. "Might want to figure this out. I wouldn't want you to miss that lunch date."

Senator McNewman stared at the ceiling for almost a full minute. Cass could see the fear on his face, but that did not concern Cass one bit. All he wanted was Melinda back. If he had to threaten and take down a hundred men and their pathetic daughters, line 'em up. He'd do it in a heartbeat.

After a while, McNewman made his decision. He leaned forward and pressed a button on his phone. Then to Evan and Cass, he said, "Here's the deal. My aide, Bradley Bishop, is my go-between with the Director. He knows things that I do not wish to know. He'll tell you everything you need to know."

"Don't try to be tricky, Donny," Evan said. "If this is some kind of bullshit, I'll not stop until you're in a cage or a grave."

The Senator held up his hands in surrender. "I'm trusting you two. All I ask is that you don't let this come back on me or Tessa. She's been through enough." Cass simply looked at him, not able to believe that McNewman could put his career over his daughter's wellbeing. A knock sounded on the door, and a small nerdy man poked his head in. "Ah, Bradley, come in; come in." The Senator stood.

Bradley Bishop stepped all the way into the office. He looked from Evan to Cass and lastly at the haggard look on his boss's face. "Yes sir, what can I do for you?"

"Bradley, these gentlemen, Mr. Masters and Mr. Cassidy," McNewman introduced the men in front of his desk, "need some assistance from us, and we're going to provide it completely."

The aide looked quizzically at the Senator. McNewman continued, ever the politician. "It's time to burn some bridges and perhaps build some new ones. We are changing course because our former associate, the Director, has gotten out of hand."

Clarity came to Bradley's face. "I see. If you say so, sir."

"These two men are going to take care of the situation. Right, fellows?"

"With extreme prejudice," Cass answered coldly.

"Very well." McNewman looked from Cass to his aide and swallowed hard. "Bradley, go fill them in on Mr. Keegan Cole. I still need to be ignorant of certain aspects of this situation—plausible deniability and all."

At the mention of the name, Evan's eyes snapped back up to McNewman. Cass saw the look of recognition, but let it pass for the time being.

On the way out of the office, Cass said, "We'll try to send your boy back in one piece. You just better hope what he has to say helps Melinda." He held the Senator's stare until McNewman looked down. "Because whatever happens to her, I'll bring down on your head tenfold."

After closing the door, Evan told Bradley that the three of them were going to lunch and he could fill them in on Mr. Cole there. Bradley told him that he needed his coat from his office, but before he went up the hall, he asked,

"You said you'd try to bring me back in one piece. What did you mean by that, 'one piece'?"

"He said we'd try, didn't he?" Evan pushed him down the hall.

When he was gone, Evan did a sad impression of Cass saying "Bring it down on your head tenfold." He laughed. "A little biblical, wouldn't you say?"

"How 'bout you saying 'break your ocular...something or other'?" Cass looked around. "What the hell was that?"

Evan laughed. "I saw it on the Science Channel, but I forgot the whole name of the bone. I think he got the point, though."

"Yeah, I'm sure he did. You know, for Mr. Night Life, you sure watch a hell of a lot of TV." Cass chuckled as Evan gave him the bird. Then, more seriously, Cass added, "You recognized that name, Keegan Cole, didn't you?"

"I did. Seems like we've been chasing Heat, but it was actually a ghost from my past all along."

Cass wanted more, but Bradley came back up the hall, so Evan gave him a look, saying he would explain later. They left Senator Donavon McNewman's offices.

The three of them, Matthew, Evan and Bradley Bishop, went to a crowded barbecue place a couple of blocks down the street. "It's a perfect spot to talk," Bradley told them. "So much laughing and chatter, nobody will pay us any attention."

After they took a table in the back part of the restaurant, Cass looked around. It was a good place for a meeting. He watched some of the smiling faces, and a pain shot through his guts. Evan saw it on him and gave his friend a small nod of encouragement. His eyes told Cass they would get her back.

"All right, BB," Evan started as the waitress left with their orders. "What's this have to do with Keegan Cole?"

"It started in '08 for Senator McNewman and me," he said, took a sip of tea. "All I can tell you is what happened back then in D.C."

****

A little over four years after the worst day of his entire forty-two years, Keegan Cole landed in the U. S. Capitol for the first time in his life. He was finally able to reconnect with some of his family's old contacts. Yes, in hindsight, Cole could see how it had been a mistake to provide weapons to Saddam, but his father had said it was very profitable, and since the family had fallen on a stretch of hard times, lucrative jobs were necessary, no matter how foolhardy.

Old Man Cole had assumed that his contracts in the United States would protect him if the shit ever hit the fan in the Middle East. That was before Colin Powell's ignorant promises about the presence of weapons of mass destruction in Iraq and the fact that none were found. Those things, combined with other bad luck, brought much more heat on the small-time arms dealers such as William Cole, Keegan's father.

Why could Powell not have told the truth and said that George W. had a vendetta in Iraq? Why could Keegan's father not stick with the strategy that had always worked before he got too greedy—building the business back up on small skirmishes? Never go against a super-power. That had been William Cole's rule for years. Why change it in Iraq? Why had Keegan distanced himself from the family? Why did Keagan not go with the family to Syria? Keegan, even after all these years, felt he could have been the difference, and changed the outcome.

All these questions swirled inside Keegan Cole's head more days than not. For the four years since, those and hundreds of other 'what if's' plagued his waking and sleeping hours. All he could think of was a way to put out the fire that was his desire for vengeance. It burned bright because his father would never be able to see how he came back to the fold and rebuilt everything the old man held dear.

In the beginning, Keegan pulled back all traces of the ancestral trade and did nothing for six months. The fact that the family had been whipped out in the arms trade kept him from trying to get into that. He tried his hand in everything from the drug trade to sex trafficking, as he had done in his youth, but to no avail.

In his failed attempts to become a criminal, Keegan had not submerged his everything into those activities. Therefore, his insolvency in those prior effects eventually gave way to desperation. This forced Cole to push past his apprehension and slowly venture out to remote conflicts all over the world—using his father's old connections to start selling weapons once more. Any other arms supplier foolish enough to oppose him met with extreme violence. Keegan decided he would bulldoze his way back into the business again, if he must.

The only rule he made was to stay under the radar of America. After the first year and a half back in business, Keegan moved almost as much weaponry as William moved in the last year of his life. He did not have to fool with extremist countries or their overzealous leaders. He found more than enough drug producers in South

America, small misunderstandings in Balkans, and other aggressors who needed his product.

People in Washington D.C. eventually did take notice of Keegan Cole, but for good reasons. They wanted him to do their bidding on jobs with which they did not want to be associated. Powerful politicians reached out to him and explained that his father had been a maverick who had gone against the grain, in the end. If he could be a team player and only supply to strategically sound groups, then he could make a ton of money. Why not be backed by the strongest government in the world? they asked him. Keegan wanted to scream, 'Because you killed my father!' Instead, he smiled and went along. *Keep your enemies close,* he told himself.

Keegan had agreed to work with them, but not for the money. He realized, on the day his father and brothers died, that money meant nothing. How much was too much? He calculated and decided he had surpassed that number a long time back. Therefore, he had other motives for regaining connections with the United States.

All of these things swirled through his mind one November day, four years after Turkey. The time had finally come to set his plan into motion. Information on the man who killed his family and ruined a huge part of his life was the reason for his trip to Washington. A chauffeur for the family that had survived the attack later told Keegan that his father would have more than likely survived had it not been for one, crazy cowboy bastard. One man had shattered Keegan Cole's world—the least he could do was return the favor.

Cole stood at the window in his suite with the Washington Monument sticking through the trees in the distance. The Junior Senator from Nevada had reluctantly agreed to provide the cowboy's name and his current whereabouts. The money Keegan had offered Mr. Donavon McNewman had not worked in itself, but with the threat of tying him to William Cole, provider of weapons to Saddam Hussein, McNewman conceded.

He sent his man, Bradley Bishop, to meet with Keegan and provide him with the knowledge Mr. Cole was seeking. Bradley had used a few discreet associates on the Senate Arms Committee and even a few contacts at the Central Intelligence Agency to discover the name of Keegan's adversary. Bradley had to use some of the best politics of his career, but at last Evan Masters' name drifted up out of the ether.

****

"I told the fool bastard," Bishop said to Evan and Cass in the barbecue restaurant, "if that information ever came back on Senator McNewman, the world wouldn't be big enough to hide him."

"Real tough, BB," Evan said, rolled his eyes. "You're real freaking tough."

Cass looked at the small senatorial aide with a burning glare. "But not tough enough to tell this Keegan-fuck to go to hell, huh?" He pushed his drink away. "Or have him taken out some time along the way—to protect one of our own."

Bradley looked at Cass with the briefest of glances and then stared down into his plate of half-eaten appetizers. His mouth opened to reply, but nothing came out.

"Where is Cole now, BB?" Evan asked.

"He's got a place just outside of San Diego." Bishop again spoke to his plate. He reached inside his coat pocket and removed a slip of paper. "Here's the address."

"So he's set up here. What are you guys doing?" Cass' voice raised, and he slammed his fist on the table. "Providing him with guns in America, now?"

Bishop shook his head and looked up at Cass. "No, he's distributing small arms to several major cities: LA, Dallas, Chicago. Maybe a few others."

"Christ, I can't look at this douche bag anymore." Cass stood up and threw his napkin at Bishop's face. To Bishop, he added, "You better pray this turns out right."

"Yeah, BB, I appreciate the sell-out, too," Evan said, and pushed his chair back. "And turn out right or not, you and Donny Boy had better watch your six. There's no telling when I might return the favor."

Both men looked down angrily at the small aide. Evan turned and grabbed Cass's elbow as he said, "Come on, bud; let's go get Mel. Screw this shitbag for now."

After leaving Bishop, they returned to the Camero and headed back to Evan's apartment to plan their trip to San Diego. Cass turned to Evan, as much as the tiny seat would allow, and asked, "So you know this Keegan Cole guy, right? I saw it on your face when McNewman first said the name."

"Yep," Evan said sounding tired. "I know the bastard, and if he's anything like his old man, we're in for a hell of a ride."

"I knew you'd say that. Tell me about him."

When they got back to the suite, he did.

# Chapter 44

## Spring 2004

Evan Masters and his Combat Control squad had been conducting some serious cross training exercises with the Syrian Special Forces along the southwestern boarder of Turkey. The region was not as unstable as it would eventually become, but it was well on its way. The two weeks of war games had been grueling, but for Evan, that was exactly what it always should be. He always told his men, "Perfect practice prevents piss-poor performances."

Before training with the Syrians, the band of brothers was temporarily based at Incirlik Air Force Base, deep in the heart of Turkey. Now that the action concluded, they were in their tent city outside of Aleppo, Syria, gearing down for a week of rest and relaxation in the Grecian islands. Another motto Evan lived by was 'Work hard, play harder!' He was in the team's tent, cleaning his equipment and getting it ready for the transport group that would be taking his stuff home.

Evan was bobbing his head to a Nickelback song on the radio. He actually hated the song, but who could listen to a Nickelback song and not move to the beat? As he sang with the lead singer, another captain came half through the tent flap and said, "Masters, they need you in the command hooch. Like yesterday!"

Evan did not bother to continue what he was doing or to ask the captain why. No need, anyway—the captain was gone when he looked up. *Something must be up; that guy's a talker,* Evan thought.

He double-timed down to the CO's tent and knocked on one of the poles holding it up. He heard a voice inside that told him to enter. Evan snapped to attention in front of the Lieutenant Colonial's desk. "At ease, Masters," the older man said, and Evan slightly relaxed, putting his hands from his sides to behind his back. "Fine work on those missions the last few weeks; real progress with the towel-heads."

"Thank you, sir," Evan said looking over the man's head at a spot on the wall.

The Lt. Colonel shuffled some papers on his desk and continued. "Looks like you've got some leave coming." He looked down. "Ah, Greece. Damn good place to unwind."

"Yes sir, it is."

"Postpone it."

"Not a problem, sir," Evan said with his Spidey senses going off so loud he had to suppress a smile. Since he had known and worked the Lt. Colonel for a long time, he asked, "What's up?"

He took a thick folder from the corner of his desk and passed it to Evan. "William Cole," he said as Evan looked down at a picture which was paper clipped to the outside of the file.

A distinguished, silver-haired man looked back at him. The gray eyes were piercing with hints of small crow's feet on either side. Evan's commanding officer told him that Mr. Cole and his three sons were re-growing a family business out of Johannesburg, South Africa. "They aren't the biggest arms suppliers in the world, Masters, but they're definitely growing. Let's just say they've gotten a little too big for their pen. Somebody's taken notice and says it's time to shut down the enterprise."

"Isn't that what the CIA's for, sir?"

The CO looked up at Evan and cocked his head to the side. "Don't be a smartass, Masters. When the Air Force General on the Joint Chiefs sends an order, I don't question it. Are we clear?"

"Gottcha, sir." Evan slightly shuffled his feet at the dressing down.

"But just so you know, I hear the operatives for the CIA in the area are currently spread thin." He had asked the same question himself. "We seem to be the next best thing in the area."

"I'd say we're the best thing period, but I wouldn't want to sound like a smartass, sir." Evan gave his CO a small, sheepish grin.

The old man gave a half smile back but continued. "Now, assemble your team in the mess tent. We'll have a briefing on the mission in twenty minutes."

Evan popped to attention and said, "Roger that, sir," and left the CO's tent.

****

Evan spent the twenty-minute-wait studying the file on William Cole and his three sons. The oldest child, Blake, seemed most likely to take over the family business, according to all reports. Keegan, the middle son, was exactly what many middle children were: rebellious. Being neither the heir to the throne nor the baby in an affluent family tends to do that. Scottser Cole was the youngest and, from everything Evan read, he had become a shadow of his oldest brother, Blake.

Blake and Scottser followed strictly in the arms trade business their father had built. Not Keegan, however—he liked to use the family wealth to rub elbows with the South African upper class, but he also dabbled in anything that could bring spice to his life. He experimented with various criminal activities of his own, giving himself excitement that he obviously did not find in weapons. Evan decided that Keegan more than likely enjoyed throwing all of his carousing into his father's face.

Keegan felt like he was not included in the family trade any more than one of his father's employees. He seemed to have wanted Blake's responsibilities, but the father felt he was too unruly or maybe out of touch with what was required in trading weapons.

From the file he read, Evan could clearly see that Keegan was probably a disappointment to William. "Well," Evan said aloud, closing the folder to go to the briefing. "Neither one of 'em will have to worry about that much longer." He chuckled.

When Evan walked into the meeting, fashionably late as always, the Commanding Officer said to him, "Nice of you to join us, Captain Masters. Take a seat."

Evan looked around and sat. He nodded to some of his six-man team. Then he caught the eye of another group of Syrian Special Forces sitting in a tight wad closer to the podium, looking back at the latecomer. Evan looked from them to a giant map of Syria which had been taped to an old blackboard and wheeled into the mess tent. He easily found Aleppo. Then his eyes moved over the map. A couple of hundred miles east of Damascus, the small town of Ad Dumayr had been circled several times in red. Ad Dumayr was approximately halfway between the Syrian capital and the Iraqi border.

Evan smiled to himself because even he could put this together. *Let's see, what could it be?* Evan thought, laughing on the inside.

The CO passed the stage off to a man Evan had never seen before. The guy was not in uniform but wore a dark rumpled suit, like he had been traveling and sleeping in the outfit for a couple of days. Evan figured him for CIA, but the man made no effort to introduce himself. Rumpled Suit went directly into the mission plan. Evan, his team, and the Syrians listened intently.

Evan had already deduced that William Cole and his three sons were meeting three high-ranking members of Saddam's Republican Guard in Ad Dumayr. "The Iraqis are shopping for some powerful weaponry, and Intel says that the Cole clan has recently been seen in Damascus, six days ago," Rumpled Suit told the group. "They have taken possession of eight cases of some very powerful armaments and brought those along to Syria." He looked around the room and waited for a small whisper to die down. Then he added, "Mission one, retrieve the eight crates. Mission two," Rumpled Suit paused for effect. "Capture or take out the seven primary targets."

Evan raised his hand, and Rumpled Suit acknowledged him with a slight nod of his head. Evan asked, "What exactly are in those cases?"

"It's not precisely certain, Captain." The disheveled man responded, looking back at the CO sitting behind him. "But if William Cole is meeting members of the Republican Guard, you can bet your ass it's big time."

"Well sir, let me get this straight," Evan said, as he was never afraid to speak his mind for the betterment of his team. "You're telling us that your Intel nerds know where these bad guys're going to be and who they're meeting, but not what's in those crates? Really, can we trust their conclusions?"

Several of Evan's team members nodded agreement. The CO stood and answered for Rumpled Suit. "Captain Masters, this information is coming from some of our best sources. Just complete your mission and it won't matter what's in those damn crates."

"Roger that, Skipper. Kick-ass and ask no questions," Evan said with just enough sarcasm to avoid insubordination. "Gottcha, loud and clear."

Rumpled Suit thanked the CO and then flipped the old blackboard over. On the reverse side, a there was a blown-up map of Ad Dumayr. It was a small community on the main road, west out of Damascus. The town was situated on the northern side of the highway, but a small part spilled over the road in the southwest quadrant. Two small roads left the main highway south and formed a U shape around this neighborhood. At the bottom of that U, a structure had been circled in the same red as Ad Dumayr on the other map.

"This is the rendezvous," Rumpled Suit said, pointing at the circled building. He then tapped a close-up picture of the front of the structure taped on the very edge of the blackboard. "We don't want them to get here. As you can see, it's pretty well fortified."

"Combat Control, the plan has you guys hitting the Iraqis coming down the western road." He traced the right side of the U, looking at Evan. Then, to the Syrian Special Forces commander, he said, "And our friends here will hit the Coles on the eastern road."

He showed everyone the designated ambush points that had been reconnected the day before. Rumpled Suit told them that their insertion would be at zero-three-hundred, and they should expect the targets around noon the next day. "Any questions?" Before anyone could ask anything, he continued, "We'll meet back at Incirlik tomorrow night with any captives. Good luck, gentlemen." With that, he gathered up his paperwork, shook hands with the CO, and left the mess tent.

After he had gone, Evan went to the Lieutenant Colonel and asked, "If the cases are the primary, why are the Syrians on them?" Then, as an afterthought, he added, "Sir."

"Captain, that's what the big-headed politicians call 'good public relations.' Like the Syrian's are in charge of this goat rope. Boost the morale of those boys, blah-blah-blah." He shook his head and held up his hand to stop Evan from talking. "It's higher than me. Probably some supply jerk-off who just got his star. Just do your part, and it'll work out. I'll have a spotter from B-team on the Syrians' position."

"They should leave the planning to us, sir," Evan said as another crack in his faith in the United States Military formed. "Damn politicians."

The CO left, and Evan stayed behind with his teammates. They all went over to the maps and formed their own plan and positioning. After everyone had it down perfectly, they left to catch some sleep before the zero-three-hundred rally time.

****

The next morning, just before noon, Evan and his team were in position on the western road. He had told the spotter from B-team, who was watching the Syrian team, that he wanted a play-by-play of the action of the other assault.

Right on time, the Iraqis rolled down the small street in three Mercedes luxury cars. When they reached the predetermined spot, Evan's explosives guy blew a charge that had been placed in the road. It went off under the engine compartment of the lead car, stopping it immediately. Several regular Iraqi army soldiers jumped out and attempted to fire at their aggressors. They were dead as soon as their fingers touched the triggers of their weapons.

The senior Republican Guardsman instantly realized they were against U.S. Forces, so they exited the second and third cars with their hands raised in surrender. "Saddam's in trouble," Evan yelled as he zip-tied one of the men, "if this is the best he's got." His men restrained the other captives and congratulated each other in a way only military bothers can do.

As he drug his man to his feet, Evan listened to the assault by the Syrians which was still going on. It seemed that the South Africans were a great deal more aggressive and a lot less likely to surrender than the Iraqis had been. Over his headset, Evan heard, "The middle car is ramming the rear vehicle. Syrian Special Forces are hunkered down, receiving heavy fire from lead and rear cars."

"Shit," Evan said. The other attack was about eight hundred yards to his east. He could clearly hear the pops of rifle fire over the city sounds.

"Damn it, Captain," the B-team spotter said, full of exasperation. "Second car hit an alley, headed north into the neighborhood. No pursuit by the Syrians!"

"Of course not," Evan spoke aloud to himself. He looked around the cramped street for a vehicle to pursue the Cole targets. Nothing. Then he noticed a local man leading a huge camel down a side street. The beast had a bright red saddle on its back, and without thinking, Evan threw his MP5 sling over his head and shoulder, across his back, and took off at a run. He clambered up onto the camel's saddle and kicked the beast with his heels. In his mind, riding a camel could not be much different from the horses he had ridden back in Mississippi, and after a minute, he got the hang of the mount.

He headed northeast with one goal—to cut that car off before it reached the main road to Damascus. He galloped the camel down streets with the locals going about their normal lives, forcing them to dodge, dive out of the way, or be knocked over as he pressed on in his pursuit.

He caught a glimpse of Cole's Mercedes one street over. It was slowly trying to navigate the narrow thoroughfares and was being blocked by a cart loaded with local wares. Evan pushed the animal harder and came out of an alley immediately ahead of the car. He leapt from the camel, swinging his MP5 around in mid-jump. Evan sent two three-round bursts from his rifle into the luxury car's engine block and the passenger's side front tire.

Smoke billowed from under the hood. Before Evan could reach the cart for cover, the driver was out of the car and returning fire. The chauffer rounded the hood, pinning Evan in a doorway, but shooting wildly. Huge mistake. Evan aimed and took the man off his feet with perfect round placement in the center of his chest.

Evan took refuge behind the cart that a local had abandoned. He yelled to the disabled automobile. "It's over! Give it up and come on out!" He popped his head up for a quick glance.

William Cole had been the only passenger in the car. He was standing behind the rear driver's side door, and as Evan looked, Cole fired several rounds from an automatic rifle, causing Evan to duck down again. With a heavy English accent, Cole answered, "It's over, my ass!" He fired several more rounds.

Evan knew he did not have time for a long, drawn-out firefight. In that part of the world, few people were sympathetic to Americans. He looked under the cart at the underside of the Benz. In an instant, his mind calculated. The vehicle was riding too high to be armored. So Evan rolled into the street and fired into the door that Cole was standing behind. Four of the six shots found their mark, and the look on Cole's face, as he went down, told Evan that the old man had believed he was in a bulletproof car.

Evan trotted to the fallen man and kicked the weapon away from his outstretched hand. It would not have mattered; William Cole's shooting days were over. He was breathing raggedly as blood ran from the corner of his mouth. Speaking barely over a whisper, he said to Evan, "Please get me some help, mate." Evan knelt down beside Cole so he could hear him better. "Not...ready...to...die."

"You better get ready pretty quick, partner." Evan opened Cole's suit coat, and the dress shirt underneath was covered in foamy, dark blood. Lung shots; probably hit the liver as well. Evan nodded to the dying man's chest and said, "Not much helping that—sorry."

William Cole's eyes glazed over as death took the place of his life, but they did not close. Evan stood and looked around. His team had commandeered an old Toyota pick-up truck. They barreled around a car in the middle of the road and braked beside Evan. They jumped out and loaded Cole's body with the Iraqi prisoners. The explosives guy sat behind the wheel. As Evan jumped in the bed, he slapped the roof of the cab, and they turned around, taking the pick-up truck back to the Syrians and the remaining Coles.

When they returned to the scene of the other assault, Evan looked at the carnage. Not a single enemy combatant remained alive. Evan said to his counterpart, "Guess there was no surrender in these boys," as he hit the man's shoulder in congratulations.

"One Cole was missing. Keegan, I believe, but we captured the weapons," the man told Evan.

"Not our problem. We got the bad guys that were here. That's all we could do. Let's get the hell out of here." They took another vehicle from the street, loaded the cases and the other bodies, and headed to the extraction point.

****

After Evan told Cass the story, they sat in silence for a few minutes.

Finally, Cass said, "A freaking camel. Really?"

"Yep, a camel, Trigger." Evan nodded and then shrugged. "It's all I had."

"When all this is done and over with," Cass looked over at Evan and smirked, "I dare you to recreate the crazy camel chase on the Strip."

"If we get Mel back safe and sound," Evan smiled sadly at his best friend, "you're on."

They tapped knuckles and prepared to leave for the end game. Cass said over his shoulder, going through the foyer, "Remember you said that, Fly Boy. Now let's go kick some ass and get Mel back."

# Chapter 45

Keegan Cole, the Director, was sitting at his desk when Constance walked into the office. "How are the preparations coming along, my dear?" Keegan asked.

"Right on schedule," she answered as she sat in front of him. "The plane's loaded, and we'll be good to go for the 2:15 flight from LAX."

Years ago, Keegan had set up an elaborate scheme to smuggle guns, money, or anything else out of the United States using the small airstrip he owned. The airfield was just over the mountains from Los Angeles and was perfectly in line with one of Los Angeles International's main runways.

As a late night flight would leave from LAX, Keegan's blacked-out cargo plane would sit on his runway and wait. His pilots timed their own takeoff perfectly and then lifted into the dark night with no lights or transponders signaling their flight. The darkened aircraft would climb quickly until it was tucked underneath the much larger 787 international flight leaving LAX.

The control tower only saw one blip on their radar. That way, the unscheduled trip could leave without a flight plan. Keegan's pilots listened to the 787's communications, calling their turns and headings— mirroring them perfectly. Out over the Pacific Ocean, the crazy airmen in the stealth plane would drop low and turn south, leaving the larger plane to its own travels while Keegan's plane then flew to Costa Rica to another airstrip he owned. From there, they could go anywhere in the world, unmolested.

This plan had served Keegan well over the years, and he had no doubt it would do so again. He nodded slowly, happy to hear all was going smoothly. At least on one front, he thought, before he asked, "Any word on Rob? What the hell are Masters and Cassidy up to?"

"I've told you we can't trust sleazy cops. Rob's off the map, and I have no clue where he is," Constance answered, shaking her head. She never liked working with Rob, but McNewman had said he would be reliable if the money was right. "Last we have on the Dynamic Duo is that they smashed and grabbed our boy Heat." They both laughed.

"They probably have him holed up somewhere," Keegan said, not knowing how right he actually was, "trying to figure out what's going on."

Constance stood and paced the room. Keegan watched for a minute and then continued, "Shefton will be exactly the distraction we needed. The winds are finally perfect for takeoff at LAX tonight. Calm yourself." He glanced to his wrist and then back up at her.

The petite vixen stopped walking and put her hands on the back of the seat, watching her boss. Constance could tell by his mannerisms that he was also nervous about getting out of the country as soon as possible.

"I'm going to call Masters soon," Constance decided. "I'll tell them to prepare to fly out to Johannesburg tomorrow night."

"Yes, we'll be ready for them when they arrive." Keegan steepled his hands on the desk. "This has been consuming me for entirely too long. Time to end it."

"True," Constance replied. "It'll be behind us soon enough; then we can get on with our lives."

"Go make the call, and let me know if anything is out of the ordinary." Keegan turned and stared at the picture of his father and brothers on the corner of his desk.

Constance left the office to find a secluded place from which to make her call.

**\*\*\*\***

Cass and Evan were heading back to LA for the final showdown. Starting years ago on the Farm at Parchman, their friendship had been built on trust and the determination to survive. Men do not know much about themselves or their 'friends' until faced with hardship. Neither doubted the other in the least; therefore, going into the fight with Cole would simply be one more fire to harden the resolve of their friendship.

As they circled the City of Angels toward the address the Senator's aide had given them, Evan's cell phone rang. He did not recognize the number, but quickly answered. Evan listened to the woman on the other end of the line.

Evan quietly listened and looked over at Cass, who was driving. Cass raised his eyebrows as to ask, 'Who is it?' Evan held up a finger, telling him to wait. After a few minutes, Evan hung up and put the phone back in his pocket.

"Was that them?" Cass asked.

"Yeah," Evan answered, staring straight ahead at the dark highway. "They want us to fly to South Africa tomorrow night."

"So they're probably leaving tonight. That way they can get there and be set up in time for our arrival."

"Exactly what I was thinking," Evan said, and looked over at Cass.

The pain was evident on Cass's face as he spoke. "We can't let them get her over there."

"It ends tonight, Trigger," Evan encouraged. "I think that group of buildings up ahead is what we're looking for." He nodded to the right side of the road. Then he continued, "We'll get her, bro. We'll get her."

They drove past the fenced-in airfield. Six buildings surrounded one hanger, with a large, black cargo plane sitting in front of it. Two sentries at the front gate looked bored as Evan and Cass passed.

Cass drove a half mile on down the road, pulled off to the shoulder, and killed the lights and engine. They checked their pistols, and Cass took a sawed-off shotgun from behind the seat. They nodded to each other and took off at a trot back toward the guard shack. Cass had the shotgun in both hands in front of his chest, and Evan carried his pistol in his hand, ready for action.

As they neared the small front gate at the entrance of the airfield, both Evan and Cass slowed and then crouched beside the road, out of sight. They watched the uninterested guards; one playing with his cell phone, the other reading the local sports page.

The building's door was on the other side of the fence a few feet away, and the guards were behind their desks inside the small structure. The front three walls each had a large window so the men could see in all three directions. "No way can we get in there before they sound an alarm of some kind."

Evan agreed, so he stood, tucked his pistol in the waistband of his jeans, and pulled his shirttail over its butt. He tapped Cass on the shoulder as he stood, and said, "Let's just go talk to them."

They slowly walked to the entrance gate, and Cass leaned his shotgun against the fence, out of sight. He and Evan went to the gate and called out to the guards. Evan told the one that stuck his head out of the door that their car had broken down and that they needed to call someone.

The security man who had been playing on his phone said, "Sure, man, come on in." When the three of them went inside, the security officer looked at his partner bug-eyed and motioned his head toward Evan and Cass.

Evan saw the gesture and reached behind his back for his weapon. Just as he wrapped his hand around the pistol, the guy that had led them in said, "You're Evan Masters and Matt Cassidy, the Dare Ya founders, aren't you?" A huge grin broke across his face.

Cass elbowed Evan, and they returned the man's smile. "That's us," Cass replied. Evan let his hand drop back to his side.

"Hot damn, Joe," the first guard said. "I love that site. Hell, I just checked in with my charter fifteen minutes ago."

The man called Joe grabbed a pen and some paper from the nearest desk, and asked for their autographs. The two guards talked fast and asked many questions about all the stuff they had seen on Dare Ya. Finally, Cass glanced at his watch and held up his hand. "Whoa, fellas, we're kind of in a rush." He reached behind his back and pulled out his pistol. Evan did the same.

Evan handed Joe their signatures and said, "We hate to do this to loyal members, but you guys've gotten mixed up with some really bad dudes."

Cass asked them about other people on the facility and had them describe its layout. Then he said, "E, give Joe, there, your phone." Evan did so without question. "Joe, put your number in there, and after this is over, we'll come to one of y'all's charter meetings and hang out. I give you my word on that."

Both men smiled, even though they were being held at gunpoint. "Cool," Joe said as he put his number into Evan's phone and handed it back to its owner. They told Evan and Cass exactly how many people were on the grounds and where everyone should be. "The plane leaves a little after two. Then we were told to lock the gate and call it a night."

Evan looked around the room as he listened. He found a bag of zip-tie type handcuffs and took some over to the two guards. "Sorry about this, guys." He zipped Joe's wrists. "I'm sure you understand. We'll be back later to let y'all go. Then tomorrow, you might want to look for some new jobs." He secured the other man's wrists and then eased both of them to the floor and tied their ankles. Cass exited the hut, retrieved his shotgun, and stepped back into the shack.

Evan went to the back wall and opened a large metal cabinet hanging there. Inside was an assortment of weapons. He pulled out two silenced Wather PPKs. "Look here, Trigger; these are just like on '007.'" a video game they played often. "This South African dude has some kick-ass toys." He clicked the safety off the pistol in his right hand. "You ever shot a silenced pistol before?" Evan aimed at the desk and squeezed the trigger twice. Two wisps were the only sound made before the bullets tore through the wood.

Cass ducked and brought his arms up reflexively. "Damn it, E, stop that shit."

"That's cool as hell," Evan said as he went back to the cabinet and gathered more clips of ammo. He tried to hand the weapon to Cass as he said, "Here, shoot something."

Cass ignored him and headed for the door. They left the guard shack and each man ran from shadow to shadow until they came to the side of the nearest building. Their plan was to find Melinda and get the hell out of dodge before the scheduled two o'clock takeoff. That only left them a little less than an hour for their hunt.

They searched the first four buildings but found nothing. The last two structures were on either side of the hanger, so they decided to split up and check them at the same time. It was getting close to one-thirty. Evan took the closest building and snuck inside as Cass took off into the dark for the other structure. Evan's exploration was simple because the entire building was completely empty. He quickly went from room to room to make sure Mel was not there, but she was nowhere to be found.

Evan ran back in the dark to meet up with Cass. As he hid behind a parked car, he watched his friend exit the building and go around the corner away from the hanger. Just after Cass rounded the corner, a man dressed like a pilot came out of a door to the hanger in front of Evan and lit a cigarette. This forced Evan to stay in his hiding place and wait. He wondered what the hell Cass was up to.

Finally, the pilot turned, and Evan walked at a crouch, as fast as he could, to the corner that Cass had gone around. He put his back to the wall and looked around. Cass was squatting behind a dumpster, and a guard walked by him. Cass jumped up and smashed the shotgun stock into the man's head, causing him to go down in a heap.

Cass propped his weapon on the wall and dragged the unconscious man behind the dumpster. As he did, Evan watched a giant of a man step behind his friend. The giant punched Cass hard in his kidney. Cass winced in pain, but swung his elbow back and jumped laterally to avoid further punches.

Cass was big, but he had to look up at the much larger man in front of him. Regretting laying his shotgun down, Cass bounced on his toes, preparing for a hell of a fight. Evan stepped out of the shadows and leveled his new pistol on the monster. "Hold up there, Big Show." The huge man looked over in Evan's direction. "You're the bastard that took Mel. I've gotta say, you look a little taller in person. Where is she?"

"Fuck you," the leviathan said. "I'm going to save Mr. Cole the trouble and kill you both right now. Then he won't even have to put her on the plane."

"We'll see about that," Cass said. "I owe you for that kidney shot." Cass turned to Evan and added, "No wonder Al's still in a coma. This prick hits like a sledgehammer."

Evan never took his eyes from the man's face. As Evan stared at his opponent's caveman forehead, he said to Cass, "You think you can take him, Trigger?"

"No doubt about it." Cass said, and then to the giant: "Come on, big boy."

Evan glanced swiftly at his watch, looked back up, and squeezed the trigger. He shot the behemoth with three quick rounds to the chest. Not a sound was made until the guy crumbled to the ground like a puppet whose strings had been cut.

Cass turned to Evan and asked, "What the hell?"

"You said you could take him; that was enough for me. You believed you could whoop his ass, so I believed it." Evan shrugged and grinned. "You don't have to run around proving your manhood like we're back in junior high. Besides, we've got shit to do. Come on."

Cass shook his head and chuckled. "Yeah, time's running out; let's go check out this hanger."

They went to the corner of the hanger and crouched down beside the big doors leading to the tarmac and runway. Cass was closest, and peeked around through the hanger door as Evan whispered from behind him, "Damn, Trigger. I didn't even hear anything 'till The Jolly Green Giant's ass hit the deck."

Evan turned the silenced PPK over in his hand, admiring it. Cass shook his head as he peered into the cavernous room. Evan continued, "I gotta get me a couple of these."

"You've got a couple," Cass said, looking back and rolling his eyes. He looked out to the runway and added, "Now shut up and follow me."

Cass had seen that the hanger was full of people and activity. There would be no way they could get in there, find Melinda, and get away undetected. Not only that, but the space inside the hanger seemed to be the only brightly lit place in the area. The flight line and even the runway were pitch-dark. Cass and Evan found that peculiar, but they did not know that the darkness was necessary to Keegan's method of smuggling.

Cass used the night to their advantage and led Evan away from the hanger to the old cargo plane, away from the building. The plane was an older model of something resembling a C-130, but slightly smaller. Evan did not recognize the type of aircraft, but he quickly put that thought aside. *Who gives a damn what kind it is?* he thought. *It's got wings, engines, and a drop-down cargo door. That's all that matters.*

The two partners rushed up the loading ramp, keeping an eye out for any flight crew, but there was no one onboard, yet. This allowed Evan and Cass to get a look at the interior of the airplane and find a good place to hide for an ambush.

The plane was lit by red overhead lights, which it gave the feel of a tactical operation. In the center of the cargo hold, a twenty-foot shipping container was strapped to the floor, with two doors facing backwards. They ran past the container and saw rows of seats along the walls. In front of the shipping container, several more crates were secured to the deck. Past that, the door led to the cockpit.

Cass figured they used the shipping container to offload fast, and since there were no other places to hide, they went to see what was inside. They eased open the doors and saw two Harley Davidson motorcycles and several large cartons. They did not have time to check the cartons or admire the motorcycles.

Evan looked at his watch; it was nearing two. Time was running out. He closed the doors on the container, closing himself and Cass within. Then Cass whispered to him, "This's the best we've got. Be ready if they try to open this thing."

"Where's your cape, Captain Obvious?" Evan gave him a nudge and smiled in the dark. "Like I was going to stretch out for a nap."

# Chapter 46

Evan and Cass didn't wait long before the sound of people boarding the aircraft came through the walls of the container. Then the engines turned over and started, followed by a whine from the cargo door.

Cass visualized the seats in front of the container and whispered, "Let's do this before they take off." Evan eased the shipping container door open, hoping the engine noise would cover any sound the creaking exit would make. After a few seconds, they were out and had the container door secure. The loading ramp was closed in front of them as they faced the rear of the plane. Their backs were to the large metal box and each man tried to hear over the taxiing aircraft.

Cass looked around the corner on the left side and saw people sitting on the seats toward the forward section. Melinda's bright red hair caught his eye, so he ducked back and signaled to Evan that she was there. Evan did the same corner quick look, and when he didn't see people on his side, he whispered, "My side's clear; let's rock and roll."

They moved slowly along the right side of the cabin, Cass with his shotgun and Evan with one PPK at the ready. They neared the forward edge of the container as the airplane continued to rumble across the tarmac toward the runway.

Evan held up his closed fist to stop Cass. "Hold up; see if we can tell how many there are, first." They could barely make out the voices over the engine roar. Listening intently, they could discern one individual from the other.

Finally, after their ears adjusted, they were able to follow the conversation.

"Listen," Cass said. "I hear Cole, with his accent, and that bitch that was on the kidnap video's out there. That's two."

"Mel's arguing; that's my girl." Evan half grinned. "We know there's gotta be two pilots."

From the other side of the container, they heard Keegan say, "That damn Max, he was supposed to check in before we left."

Constance replied, "He's probably asleep somewhere. He loves his beauty rest." She paused a moment and then added, "His big ass knows what he's got to do tomorrow...following Masters and Cassidy."

"You're right," the Director replied. "He's never let us down before."

Evan said to nobody, "Well, there's a first time for everything." He shrugged.

The plane turned onto the airstrip and stopped at the end. The pilots listened to their radios and waited for the LAX flight to take off. Cass leaned forward and said, "Two unfriendlies back here to worry about; let's hit 'em."

Evan took his pistol off "safe" and nodded. About that time, they heard Melinda. She shouted, "You're such a bastard!" Anguish consumed her speech. "How the hell could you do that to him? Bastard!"

The voice that answered froze Evan and Cass and sent a chill down their spines. "You don't know what it was like." The blood left Evan's face, and tears swelled in his eyes as his childhood friend, Beau, spoke to Melinda. "To be a damn freak! All these years, and all Evan did was pull further and further away."

The plane's engines spun up as the pilots increased power and the plane started moving down the runway. Evan strained to hear Beau as he held onto the wall. Beau continued, "He sent me money like I was some kind of charity case. Like that could bring back my fucking arm! Then the son of a bitch became famous and he couldn't stand to come home and see the monster he created!"

"They sent him to prison for the *accident*!" Melinda roared. "And he loved you!"

"Yeah, he loved me so much he went into business with that prick bastard Cass and left me behind."

Behind the crate, Cass raised his eyebrows and mouthed, "Me?"

"James," Keegan said over the noise. "Like us, she doesn't understand what it's like to have your entire world flipped upside down because of Evan Masters."

Melinda looked from the Director to Beau and asked, "How the hell did you end up with this monster?"

"You'd be surprised at all the like-minded people on the internet," Beau said as he shot her an evil grin.

The plane hit takeoff speed and climbed into the night air. It made a slow left turn, mirroring the plane above it. Evan looked back at Cass, the blood still gone from his face. He thought, *how could this be?*

"I knew that damn video was a fake," Melinda told Beau accusingly.

"No shit, it was fake," Beau answered. He went on to explain how he and some of Keegan's experts had put his murder scene together on a computer. They filmed different parts of the stunt and then overlapped all of them. The computer specialists spliced it perfectly. They had to kill the balloon operator in one part and have a man 'stab' Beau with a fake knife in another. Beau told her how Shefton came to Mississippi to take out the *stabber,* getting rid of that loose end. "He *stabbed* me and I jumped, but we weren't near as high as it appeared."

"My god," Melinda said. "Your mother. She thinks you're dead, too."

"Yep," Beau said. "It's better this way, anyway. All she did was pity me. Now she can get on with her life."

Then she turned to Keegan and asked, "Why in the hell did you kill all those college kids?"

"Wasn't me." Keegan smiled and raised his hands in mock surrender. He pointed one finger to Constance and the other at Beau.

Evan glanced around the corner of the storage container again, and Cass watched him actually get paler. Evan slowly shook his head 'no.' This was beginning to be too much. Cass tapped Evan on the shoulder and mouthed "Let's go," gesturing his head toward the front of the plane.

"Wait," Evan said, and listened some more.

Beau was talking again. "Mr. Cole wanted Cass to go back to Vegas—seems he hates Cassidy as much as I do, for all the help he's given Evan." The plane leveled off and Beau undid his seatbelt, stood, stretched, and laughed.

Constance unbuckled her belt as well and stood on the other side of Melinda. She walked over to one of the crates secured to the floor, leaned on it, and said, "Will you two shut the hell up?" Melinda and Beau looked over at her. The Director smiled. "Here it is, Red," Constance added. "These two hate Evan Masters; no surprise. Your little lover boy, Cassidy – well, he's just been with the other one so long, the hate rubbed off." She shrugged.

The aircraft hit a rough pocket of air. Beau grabbed one of the straps holding the shipping container down. Melinda held tightly to her armrests. After the plane returned to a smooth flight, Constance continued, "After we get to South Africa, your two heroes will be a day or so behind. Then..." She gave Melinda another shrug and a bigger smile as she put a cigarette between her teeth. "Then we'll probably kill you, just to show them we're serious."

"That'll be followed closely by Mr. Cassidy's demise." Keegan finished her thought, stood, and walked toward Constance. "I want Masters to watch everyone he loves breathe their last breath in front of him."

Constance locked eyes with Melinda. "So, shut up. We've got a stop in Costa Rica, and then we'll be in Johannesburg later tonight."

"I don't think you're going to make it," Cass shouted as he slipped around Evan and stepped around the corner into sight. He had heard enough. He pointed the shotgun at Constance's face, but she was fast, and she almost had her pistol up as he spoke again. "Please do, you crazy bitch!" He motioned with the barrel and she dropped the weapon.

Evan took a second before he shook it off, followed Cass, and moved his new silenced PPK between Keegan and Beau. Neither one moved, as hate spread across their faces. Melinda unbuckled her lap belt and ran to Cass. He held the shotgun in one hand and hugged Melinda with the other. For a while everyone stayed frozen, taking in the change of events.

Evan broke the silence. "How could you do this?" he asked as he implored Beau with his eyes.

"How could I?" Beau yelled. Then he loosened the straps on his prosthetic and pulled it off. He raised the stump of his arm into the air and boomed, "This is how!"

Cass broke his embrace and handed Melinda his forty-caliber pistol. "Cover the devil bitch." Melinda took the gun and nodded.

Still holding the shotgun, Cass looked around for something to bind Keegan. As he searched, he listened to Beau berate Evan. Then, from the corner of his eye, he saw Beau step in and slap his best friend. Cass half turned, and that was all the opening Keegan needed.

He lunged for the shotgun and snatched it from Cass's grip. Without hesitation, Cass unloaded a hard right punch into Keegan's face, and he stumbled backwards. Melinda pivoted her weapon and told Keegan not to move. This gave her captive a chance, and Constance pounced like a cat. She had her hands on Melinda's pistol and tried to tear it from her grip.

Beau closed his fist and hit Evan powerfully on the side of his head. Evan turned with the punch and took it as he glared at his friend. "How could you do this to Mama Pam?" A single tear ran down Evan's cheek.

Like a man possessed, Beau stepped back and charged Evan, wrapping his good arm and his stump around Evan's waist, tackling him into the wall. Evan fell back, not putting up a fight. His shoulder hit a switch, and the rear loading ramp began to descend. The noise grew louder and the wind swirled around the six people in the cabin.

Keegan rebounded from Cass's blow and squared off with the bigger man. The two foes traded blows like gladiators, circling and punching each other. Cass also tried to pay attention to the struggle between Melinda and Constance.

Constance could not believe Melinda's strength. Melinda swept Constance's legs from under her, and the two women went to the floor, still wrestling for control of the pistol. As Cass watched the women, Keegan landed another shot to his face.

Evan rolled Beau over and pinned him to the deck at the edge of the ramp as it locked in the open position. Three or four binding straps connected to floor mounts on one end flapped noisily from the back of the airplane. Evan held fast and told Beau, "Stop it, damn it. I'm not going to hurt you!"

As Evan looked down at Beau, Cass stepped in and shoved Keegan into the bulkhead separating the cockpit and the cabin. He went down, so Cass turned and went to help Melinda. Just as he was about to grab Constance by her hair, a shot rang out behind him. Keegan had found the weapon that Constance had dropped, and fired at Evan.

The bullet tore through Evan's bicep and his arm felt as though it were on fire from the inside out. Evan lost his balance on the cusp of the loading ramp and tumbled down its angled surface. Beau rolled with him and grabbed Evan by the shirt-tail, arresting his fall long enough to allow Evan to grab one of the flopping straps.

Cass left Melinda and grabbed Keegan by the back of the neck with his right hand and the wrist with his left. He slammed a knee into Keegan's stomach and the pistol clamored to the floor. All the air rushed from his lungs and

Cass went for a knockout uppercut, when another shot echoed through the cabin. Terror gripped Cass's insides, as he clutched the back of Keegan's neck. Cass looked back, and Constance lay on top of Melinda. Neither female was moving.

Keegan recovered and took a long, deep breath to refill his lungs. He hit Cass with all the strength he had left. Cass tripped, causing both men to go down. Melinda finally shook off the shock of the gun firing and pushed Constance's body away from her. Melinda stood, looking down at the dead woman at her feet. Cass saw that she was okay, then instantly remembered seeing Evan rolling over the edge of the ramp. He knew he had to end this struggle with Keegan.

Evan was hanging onto the loading strap as the blood ran down his arm. The wind tore at him, but he still stretched back, trying desperately to reach his friend. Beau, after grabbing Evan, had slid over the cusp himself. The momentum had carried him down the ramp and almost out of the plane completely. With his one arm holding the edge, Beau had his leg looped into one of the straps that flopped violently in the fierce wash from the airplane.

Evan reached and grabbed another strap attempting to slide down further toward Beau. "Hold on, I'm coming," Evan screamed desperately over the rush of air. Beau did not say a word; he simply stared into Evan's eyes. Evan yelled again, "I'm coming!" With the wound in his arm and the wind in his eyes, Evan inched closer to the open sky, the hole in his upper arm burning fiercely and the wind stinging tears from his eyes.

Cass grabbed a wrench that was lying in a seat and smashed it into Keegan's skull with everything he had. The South African went completely limp, and Cass pushed him aside. Melinda ran to him and wrapped her arms around Cass's waist. He held her for a second, and then he saw Evan sliding down the ramp. "Watch Keegan," he told Melinda. Then he turned and ran to the rear of the aircraft as he shouted to his friend, "I'm coming, E! Hold on!"

Evan stretched for Beau with all he had. Beau's eyes never left Evan. Beau mouthed, "I'm so sorry." This made Evan frantic, and he loosened his grip on the strap, trying to get to Beau. That was when he heard Cass shout. Evan turned and saw the big man coming at full speed towards the back of the plane.

Evan hollered, "I'm fine!" He pointed over his shoulder and begged, "Grab Beau! He can't hold on!"

The words barely registered to Cass as he got to the edge of the open door. In an instant, he surveyed the situation. Cass took hold of a flapping strap and thought, *Fuck Beau,* as he dove down the ramp.

# Epilogue

Three weeks after the dust had settled, Cass stood in his office, and Melinda came in. She leaned her head into his chest and he kissed the top of her head. She asked, "You okay?"

"Not really," Cass softly replied, the familiar sting coming back. "I did every damn thing I could to save him." He stepped back from her embrace and drank a long swallow of bourbon.

"I know you did," Mel said, touching his arm. "We all know you did."

"It wasn't enough. I keep seeing his face looking up at me as he fell." A shiver went up his neck, into his hairline, and he sat the empty glass on the corner of his desk.

Melinda crossed her arms over her chest, and several tears ran down her cheeks. She pushed them away as she said, "Evan wouldn't want you to keep beating yourself up over it. Like you said, you did all you could."

Looking at the hurt on her face, Cass knew it was his turn to comfort Melinda. They had been taking turns since the ordeal on Keegan's plane. He put his big arms around her shoulders and squeezed. "I'm sure he wouldn't, but I can't help it."

"Wherever Evan is," she said as she turned her face up and kissed him, "I'm sure he knows that you gave it everything."

"I'll always have to live with it not being enough," Cass said as they hugged.

"What wasn't enough?" Evan asked from the doorway.

Cass looked toward the door and grinned as tears gleamed in his eyes. Evan flashed a tired smile back at him. His arm was out of the sling, but his bicep was still heavily bandaged. Cass answered, "I can't stop seeing Beau fall."

The smile left Evan's face. "Me, neither."

On the ramp, out over the Pacific, Cass had done exactly what Evan had asked. He dove for Beau, but Beau did not want to be saved. As Cass got close to him, he let go and fell from the plane.

Cass screamed and watched him plummet to the ocean below. When he had fallen from Cass's sight, Cass climbed over and drug Evan up the ramp, laid him on the floor, and wrapped his shirt around his wound. Melinda had entered the cockpit, pointed the pistol at the pilots, and told them to return the airplane to Los Angeles.

Evan walked into Cass's office at the Dare Ya Headquarters and sat in a chair by the window. He finally added, "He made his choices," as he remembered Beau clutching his shirttail and stopping his fall. "We can't keep suffering because of his actions."

Melinda walked to Evan, leaned down, hugged his neck, and kissed his cheek. She grinned and said, "You're smarter than you look."

Evan gave her a perplexed look and replied, "Thanks, I think." They all gave a chuckle, though it was half-hearted.

Cass and Melinda joined Evan around a small coffee table. Evan filled them in on the previous several weeks. Keegan Cole was in the custody of Homeland Security and singing like a canary, mainly about the Former Senator of Nevada, Donavon McNewman. The ex-Senator had stepped down, and he was under investigation on a number of charges. Of course, he blamed everything on his aide, Bradley Bishop, and Bishop was also in a six-by-eight cell making deals to testify against his old boss. The authorities assumed that McNewman's nephew, Rob Moffett, had jumped to his death to avoid associations with the trouble in which his uncle found himself.

Evan had called in every single favor he'd ever had and, for the most part, he had kept his and Cass's names out of the investigations. Everyone was so pleased to have major players like McNewman and Cole off the board, they had no problem taking the two friends' credit for themselves.

Evan told them all this then added, "On the way back, I went by 29 Palms, but our hole was empty."

"The hell you say," Cass said, raising his eyebrows, causing a line to run across his forehead. "Coyotes?" Melinda looked from Evan to Cass with questioning eyes. They did not fill her in about Shefton. Cass simply shook his head as to say 'don't ask.'

"Let's hope so," Evan replied.

A knock came on the open office door, and Al stepped inside. His head was heavily bandaged, but the double vision and haloes around lights had finally left him. "Al, my man," Cass said, standing and shaking his hand. "Good to see you up and around."

"It's good to be up and around," Al responded, and rubbed the back of his neck. "I keep having that dream about me and Mel at the computer, but I still can't figure out what we're looking at."

Evan, Cass, and Melinda had all decided not to tell Al about the fake video Beau had made—no need in forcing him to deal with Beau's deception. Evan said, "It's just a dream. I wouldn't worry about it. We met the Goliath that clubbed you, and as big as his hands were, you're lucky you're even able to dream."

"Yeah," Al retorted. "I'm kind of glad I don't remember all that."

Cass chuckled as he poured himself another drink. "As ugly as that dude was, you should be. He could definitely give you some hellish nightmares." They all laughed.

Al thanked them for letting him have time off, but said he needed to get back to work. He left the office, and when he was gone, Cass asked Evan, "So what did you tell Mama Pam?"

Evan had flown down to Mississippi to be with Beau's mother. "I told her that we had avenged Beau and that the people responsible for his death were suffering badly—and that a few weren't suffering at all anymore." He looked at the floor and ran his hand through his hair. "She seemed okay with that."

Cass stepped to him, put his hand on Evan's shoulder, and gripped his trapezius muscle. Melinda took Evan's hand in hers. Evan looked into Cass' eyes and added, "I just couldn't make myself tell her the truth."

"You did right," Cass said. He shook his head and added, "We'll live with it, but she won't have to."

Melinda continued to hold Evan's hand and snuggled into Cass's hip. She asked, "Now what?"

Evan told her that he had decided to take some time off from Dare Ya and perhaps focus on those underground websites doing unsanctioned dares. "Maybe go around and shut 'em down, you know?"

"I put my apartment in New York up for sale," Cass told him. "Figure I'll move back out here."

Melinda raised her head and kissed Cass on the chin. Then she said, "Stick around, E; we can all go after those guys as a team." She winked at Evan.

"Now, who could pass up such an offer?" Evan asked, and smiled at his two best friends. He turned to Cass and added, "Plus, you owe me a kick-ass dare."

"I'll give you that; but if I remember correctly," Cass slapped Evan's shoulder, his smile turning to a loud laugh, "first, you've got a date with a camel!"